Love
Me or Leave Me

Essence Bestselling Author
GWYNNE FORSTER

ARABESQUE®

Recycling programs
for this product may
not exist in your area.

LOVE ME OR LEAVE ME

ISBN-13: 978-0-373-53450-0

www.kimanipress.com

Printed in U.S.A.

Dear Reader,

I hope you enjoy reading *Love Me or Leave Me,* the story of Drake Harrington, the third and youngest of the three Harrington brothers, and the people who make up this delightful family. Many of you have written to me asking about this series, and I am so pleased that Harlequin is reprinting this and previous Harringtons books. I hope that you like the story of the most handsome, and yet disarming, of the Harrington men, and the woman who captured his heart.

If you enjoyed reading about strong, dependable and loving Telford (*Once in a Lifetime*), the handsome and fiery Russ (*After the Loving*) and their cousin—tender, powerful and tenacious Judson Philips-Sparkman (*Love Me Tonight*)—you will fall for Judson's best friend, Ambassador Scott Galloway, a man who takes his own sweet time to find romance. You'll read Scott's story in *A Compromising Affair,* which Kimani Arabesque will release later this year.

I enjoy hearing from my readers, so please email me at GwynneF@aol.com or leave a message at my website at www.gwynneforster.com. If you want to write by postal mail, you can reach me at P.O. Box 45, New York, NY 10044, and if you would like a reply, please enclose a self-addressed stamped envelope. For more information, please contact my agent, Pattie Steel-Perkins, Steel-Perkins Literary Agency, at myagentspla@aol.com.

Warmest regards,

Gwynne Forster

ACKNOWLEDGMENTS

I am indebted to Mrs. Linda Biney,
wife of the Ghanaian diplomat to the United Nations
and member of the distinguished Fanti tribe, who
discussed with me Ghanaian culture and loaned me
video tapes that depicted the slave castles, other
notable landmarks and a re-enactment of the ways
in which people were sold into slavery. My thanks,
also, to all of the Ghanaians in New York and in Ghana
who I have been privileged to know and associate with.

A special thanks to my husband who creates most of
the promotional materials designed to support this book,
and to my loyal readers who urged me to write.

Chapter 1

Drake Harrington loped down the broad and winding stairs of Harrington House, his ancestral home, and made his way to the back garden, his favorite place to sit and think or to swim on early summer mornings. He stopped and glanced around him, the familiarity of all he saw striking him forcibly. He surmised that he'd looked at that same evergreen shrub every day—when he was at home—for as long as he'd known himself. He sat down on the stone bench beside the swimming pool, spread his long legs and rested his elbows on his thighs. He had slept in the same room for thirty-one years, from his days in a bassinet to the king-size sleigh bed he now used. Wasn't it time for a change?

His long, tapered fingers brushed across his forehead, their tips tangling themselves in the silky wisps of hair that fell near his long-lashed eyes, giving him a devil-may-care look. He liked to measure carefully the effcct of a move before he made it, but he wasn't certain as to the source of his sudden discontent, so he was at a loss as to what to do about it. He loved his brothers and enjoyed their company, and he liked the women they had chosen for their mates, but he recognized a need to make headway in his own life, and that might mean leaving his family. A smile drifted across his features, features that even his brothers conceded were exceptionally handsome. He couldn't imagine living away from Tara, his stepniece, or Henry, the family cook who—with the help of his oldest brother, Telford—had raised him after the death of his father when he was twelve years old.

As he mused about his life as he saw it and as he wanted it to be, he began to realize that because his older brothers had found happiness with the women of their choice, he was pressuring himself to decide what to do about Pamela Langford. He dated several women casually, including Pamela, but she was the one he cared for, though he hadn't broadcast that fact, not even to her—and he often sensed in her nearly as much reluctance as he recognized in himself. He had been careful not to mislead her, for although he more than liked her, he was thirty-one years old and a long way from realizing his goal of becoming a nationally recognized and respected architectural engineer, and he was not ready to settle down. When he did, it would be with a woman who—unlike his late mother—he could count on, and he had reservations that a television personality such as Pamela fit that mold. He'd better break it off.

Hunger pangs reminded Drake that he hadn't eaten breakfast. As he entered the breakfast room, the loving voices of Telford and his wife, Alexis; Tara, their daughter; his older brother, Russ; and Henry welcomed him. He took his plate, went into the kitchen, helped himself to grapefruit juice, grits, scrambled eggs, sausage and buttermilk biscuits, and went back to join his family.

"I said grace for you, Uncle Drake," Tara said, "and that's four times, so you'll have to take me to see *Harry Potter.*"

He turned to Russ, who had spent the weekend with them at the family home in Eagle Park, Maryland. "We're looking at a six-year-old con artist, brother. *She* decides who's to say grace, and *she* decides there should be a penalty if that person doesn't say it. *She* also metes out the punishment."

"Yeah," Russ said. "That's why I get down here before she does."

"You notice she never dumps it on the cook?" Henry said, obviously enjoying his health-conscious breakfast of fruit, cereal, whole-wheat toast and coffee.

"That's 'cause I don't want to eat cabbage stew," Tara replied. "I'm ready, Dad," she said to Telford. "Can I call Grant and tell him to meet us, or are we going to his house to get him?"

Telford drank the last of his coffee, wiped his mouth, kissed his wife and took Tara's hand. "We're going to Grant's house. His dad can take you and Grant fishing. I have some urgent work to do."

Drake relished every moment he spent with his family, but was a stickler for punctuality, hated to wait on others and rarely caused anyone to wait for him. He excused himself, dashed up the stairs and phoned Pamela. He didn't believe in procrastinating. He wouldn't enjoy what he had to do, but he couldn't see the sense in postponing it and stressing over it.

"Hello." Her refined, airy voice always jump-started his libido, but that was too bad.

"Hi. This is Drake. Any chance we can meet for dinner this evening? I'll be working in Frederick today, and I can be at The Watershed at six-thirty. You know where it is—right off Reistertown Road at the Milford exit."

"Dinner sounds wonderful. See you at six-thirty."

Pamela finished her third cup of green tea for that morning—she had substituted green tea for the five or more cups of black coffee she used to drink every day, thankful that she'd never taken up smoking. Being the only newswoman at a television station that had eight male reporters—half of whom considered themselves studs—was more pressure than she could enjoy, but she held her own as a newscaster, and her boss's mail verified that. She didn't prefer dates so soon after work—especially not with Drake, and not when she couldn't go home and dress for the occasion.

If Drake Harrington knew how she felt about him, he would probably head for the North Pole, as skittish as he was about committing himself. After a calamitous affair when she was a college sophomore—the boy seduced her not because he cared, but for bragging rights among his buddies—she had sworn never again to get involved with a man who had a pretty face. And Drake wasn't only as handsome as a man could get—all six feet and four inches of him—he was also very wealthy.

"He came up on my blind side" was how she explained to herself the way Drake mesmerized her when she met him. Fortunately, she'd had the presence of mind not to show it.

"How's about a hug for the nicest guy at WRLR?"

At the sound of Lawrence Parker's voice, Pamela spun around in her swivel chair. "Would you please knock before you open my door, and would you try being more professional? Your kid stuff gets on my nerves."

"Aw, come on, babe. Give a guy a break. I know a real sexy movie, and then we can go to my place and—"

She glared at him. "Lawrence, you're making me ill. I'm not going out with you, now or ever. Besides, I have a dinner date. Beat it so I can finish the copy for my five-o'clock newscast."

"What's he got that I don't have?" He raised his hands, palms out, and rolled his eyes toward the ceiling. "All right. All right. Don't tell me. I know."

She heard her office door close and hoped he'd left, but she didn't risk looking up for fear that he might be leaning over her, as he'd done a few times.

Pamela was much like Drake in that she believed in making the best of every opportunity. She decided that before she slept that night, she and Drake would have achieved a level of intimacy they hadn't previously shared. Oh, he'd kissed her a few times, though he hadn't put his soul into it, but this time she was going for the jugular. If she had to seduce him she knew how, and she would. She had coasted along in the relationship doing things his way, but beginning tonight, they would be using her road map.

She raced home on her lunch hour and changed into a red sleeveless silk dress that had a flouncy skirt and a matching long-sleeved jacket, and put her pearl jewelry in her pocketbook and her makeup and perfume in her briefcase. Within an hour and fifteen minutes, she was back at the station.

Her news report that evening included an account of one homicide, an attempted rape, Southwest crops ravaged by drought and a local practicing physician who was exposed as an eighth-grade dropout and possessed no formal medical knowledge. She exhaled a deep and happy breath when she got to her last story, which described the return of a missing baby to its parents. At the end, she folded her papers, shoved them into her drawer, locked it, grabbed her briefcase and pocketbook, and started for the elevator.

"Where're you rushing off to, babe? It's early yet. What about a drink next door at Mitch's Place?" The elevator arrived, saving her the necessity of answering Lawrence.

She stopped at the service station about a mile before the Milford exit, bought gas and got an oil change. She liked that station because the attendants still serviced cars, and she didn't care to pump gas or measure the air in her tires while wearing her best cocktail suit. The attendant came back into the station, made out her bill and handed it to her.

"She'll run like new, Miss Langford. In the future, don't let your oil get so dirty. It's not good for your car. I checked your tires. You're good to go."

She paid the bill and added a tip. "Thanks. I'll bring it in for a thorough checkup one day next week." She looked at her watch. Five after six. She had plenty of time and didn't have to speed, for which she had reason to be grateful five minutes later when her car swerved dangerously as she was crossing an old bridge that had only wooden railings. She eased the car to the elbow of the little two-lane highway, stopped and got out. With the sun still high, she had no difficulty finding the problem. Both of her front tires were flat.

Hadn't that service-station attendant just told her that he'd checked her tires and they were fine? She searched her pocketbook for her cell phone, but couldn't find it. She dumped everything in her purse and in her briefcase on the front passenger's seat. Then she remembered having taken the phone out and placed it on her desk to charge it.

"Now what?" she said aloud. She opened the trunk of her car, got the sneakers she kept there for the times she played tennis, locked her car and started walking. Several cars slowed down and two drivers stopped to offer her a ride, but she wouldn't risk it. She walked the two miles back to the service station, all the time wishing she wasn't wearing that brilliant-red outfit.

"You told me my tires were fine," she said to the attendant, "but as soon as I turned into the ramp going to Milford Road, both of my front tires blew."

He stared at her. "That's impossible, Miss Langford. Those are new tires in perfect condition. Did you drive over glass, or maybe some pieces of metal?"

She shook her head. "Neither one, and this is messing up what may be the most important day of my life."

"I'm sorry, ma'am. I'm truly sorry. I'll call a patrolman and alert him to the location of your car. Then I guess you need a tow truck, 'cause you only have one spare, and there's nobody on duty tonight but me, so I can't leave here."

She waited for what seemed like hours until she could get in her car and drive on to the restaurant. She prayed that Drake would still be there, but she wouldn't blame him if he left. She rushed into the restaurant so eager to know if she would see Drake that she walked past the maître d'.

"I beg your pardon, madam," he said with his nose just a little higher than she imagined it usually was.

"A gentleman was waiting here for me. I suppose he left."

The man gave her a dismissive look. "He did, indeed, and I can imagine that he was greatly embarrassed to wait an hour and a half with an untouched glass of wine in front of him."

She spun around and went to the pay phone near the women's room. "Oh, my Lord. I could have called him when I was in the service station, but all I thought about was that I didn't have my cell phone." When he didn't answer his cell phone, she called Harrington House.

"He ain't here." It was Henry, the cook, who answered. "He said he was having dinner out. Who should I tell him called?"

"His... Tell him that Pamela called. Thank you." She hung up and began the long drive home. No one had to tell her that wherever Drake was, he was furious, for he hated to wait for anyone and didn't make anyone wait for him. She trudged into her house, locked the door and checked her answering service. He had not called. A ham sandwich and a glass of milk sufficed for dinner, which she ate pacing her kitchen floor. What had caused those tires to blow out?

She phoned the station attendant. "Did you check those old tires to find out what caused them to blow?"

"Yes, ma'am, I did. Somebody slashed them."

"What? When could anybody have done that?"

"Beats me. The slashes were so long and so deep that you couldn't have driven out here from East Baltimore on those tires. It— Say, a big yellow Caddy drove in here right behind you. It was here while you were inside the station paying the bill, and it took off without getting anything. I wonder... Well, anything can happen these days."

She thanked him, finished her sandwich and went to bed. She'd left a message telling Drake that she called. Now it was up to him.

Drake let himself into Russ's apartment, dropped his suitcase on the floor and went to the kitchen to find something to eat. He knew that Russ wouldn't be home until much later, and he hoped that by that time, he would have rid himself of his anger and frustration. He wouldn't have expected Pamela to leave him sitting in a restaurant without phoning him to say she couldn't make it. It was out of character. Bowing to his protective instincts, he phoned a policeman, a long-standing friend, to know whether an accident had been reported on Reisterstown Road or Milford after five o'clock that afternoon. There hadn't been. He wanted to telephone her, but she had his cell-phone number and hadn't used it. He took the phone from his briefcase, saw that he'd forgotten to turn it on and checked the voice mail for messages. There were none. His emotions warred with each other, anger battling frustration, hurt struggling with anger.

He defrosted some frozen shrimp, sliced some stale bread and toasted it, found some mayonnaise and bottled lemonade, and ingested it. However, the ache inside of him didn't respond to food. Russ got home around ten-thirty and found Drake sitting in the living room in the dark with his shoes off and his feet on the coffee table.

"What's going on?" Russ asked.

"Sorting out my thoughts."

"Yeah? Can't you sort 'em out with the lights on?"

"Very funny. Will you have time to drive me to the airport tomorrow morning? If not, I can call a cab."

"Of course I'll take you. Leave your flight schedule, and I'll meet you when you come back. Say, man, what happened to you tonight? You're in the dumps. Wouldn't be that you're strung out because you'll soon be the only single man you know, would it?"

"You're the one to talk. You practically barricaded yourself against the idea of marriage, when all of us knew you loved that woman so much that you didn't have a hope in hell of staying single."

"Let that be a lesson to you. When it grabs you, don't waste energy trying to resist. Who's Sackefyio marrying?"

"Ladd? He's marrying Doris Adenola. He went with Hannah Lamont the whole time he was at Howard, and a couple of days before graduation, he told her he had to marry someone of his tribe. Hannah was so far down, I thought she'd commit suicide. A lot of African guys do that. When it comes to marriage, they do as their elders tell them. Hannah was a good-looking gal. I can't wait to see what Miss Adenola looks like."

"It must work for them, but it certainly wouldn't work for me," Russ said.

"Me neither. When are you going back to Barbados? Splitting myself between there, Frederick and Baltimore is tiring. I think we ought to consider getting another engineer."

Russ sat down in his favorite chair—a big, overstuffed leather one—stretched out his long legs and relaxed his feet on the footrest that matched the chair. "Hiring an engineer would relieve you, but Telford wants this to remain a family business. It would help if we chose jobs more carefully. When do you expect to finish in Barbados?"

"A couple of months more, if all goes well."

Russ sat forward. "What could go wrong? We've got a great gang of workers. Drake, it isn't like you to be negative. If you can't talk to *me* about whatever it is, talk to Telford, or Henry, or Alexis."

"Thanks. I'm all right. It's just… You know I never go into anything without nursing the idea before—"

"Yeah, I know, but you're nursing it to death. Is it Pamela? I sure as hell hope you're not considering anything serious with Louise."

His head shot up. "That butterbrain? What do you take me for? I dated her twice as a favor to her brother. He had some fish to fry and wanted his sister out of the way."

"You sure must think a lot of her brother. The angel Gabriel couldn't have gotten me to go out with that dame a second time."

"Tell me about it. I think I'll turn in, Russ. I have to

catch a nine-o'clock flight, and that means leaving here at six-thirty. Sure you want to take me to the airport?"

"No problem. You make the coffee."

Drake hung up his tuxedo, took a shower and crawled into bed. He didn't remember ever having thrashed in the bedcovers trying to sleep. But he couldn't get Pamela out of his thoughts. He reached over to his night table and turned on the light. Twice he dialed most of her number and hung up before completing the call. After an hour of turning and twisting, he sat up. Why should he care that she hadn't kept their dinner date? Hadn't he planned to tell her it was best they not see each other? He slapped his palms on his knees and let out an expletive. Did he want to stop seeing her, or didn't he?

At the airport the next morning, he checked in, passed security, bought a sandwich for later and went to the seating area at the departure gate. *How would you feel if she left the country without saying a word to you?* his conscience demanded. At five minutes before boarding time, he capitulated to his conscience and his feelings and telephoned her, and a hole opened up inside of him when she didn't answer at home, at her office or on her cell phone. He took his seat in first class, thanked God that his seatmate was a woman with good hygiene habits, fastened his seat belt and closed his eyes. He didn't want to talk with anybody except Pamela Langford. *Please, God, I hope she's not in any trouble. When did I get to the place where I don't know my own mind?*

Pamela was no less disturbed than Drake about the course of their relationship. Surely Henry gave Drake her message, but Drake hadn't paid her the courtesy of an answer. She dragged herself out of bed, went through the motions of her morning ablutions, made a pot of coffee and decided she had no appetite for breakfast. After moseying around her apartment for nearly an hour, she threw up her hands in disgust. She couldn't call Henry and ask him whether he gave Drake her message.

"Guess I'm the one eating dirt this time," she said to herself, put on a yellow linen suit with a white-bordered yellow tank, got into her car and headed for work. "The sun will revolve around the earth before I cry over a man," she said to herself, sniffing to hold it back. "Not even if the man is Drake Harrington, I won't."

At the station, she breezed past the newsroom, went into her office and closed the door, wishing, not for the first time, that their offices had locks. If Lawrence Parker walked into her office, she wouldn't be responsible for the words that passed through her lips. As if he had extrasensory perception, he knocked once and walked in.

"How's my little yellow bird today?"

She turned and faced him. "Lawrence, do you know the definition of the word *nuisance?* If not, look in a mirror. I am not interested in your company. I've got a man in my life, and I don't need another one."

"Be careful, babe," he said in what amounted to a snarl. "I may get a promotion, and then you'll wish you'd been nice to me."

She rolled her eyes toward the ceiling. "Your getting a promotion in this place is the least of my worries. Please close the door when you leave." She turned her back to him and began going through her in basket. After some time, she heard the door close. She figured that he'd find a way to get revenge, because he was a man whose ego needed constant stroking, and she'd just knocked him down a peg.

"I didn't have breakfast, so I'm taking an early lunch," she said to Rhoda, her assistant. "Want to join me?"

"Sure thing, Pamela, as long as you don't want fast food."

Fast food wouldn't nurse her wounds. "Not a chance. I want some good catfish."

They walked to Frank's, an eatery frequented by politicians, as well as newspaper, radio and television people, but she went there for the soul food.

"I'm having fried catfish," Pamela told the waitress.

"With or without?"

"Definitely with. I haven't had anything to eat today," she said, savoring the thought of catfish with corn bread and stewed collards.

"I'll have the same," Rhoda said, "but hold those hot peppers."

"Not to worry. We only give you those if you ask for 'em."

"What's Lawrence up to these days, Pam? If I turn my back, he's in your office. Is there… I mean…do you want to see him?"

"Me? Want to see Lawrence? That man affects me exactly the way a swarm of mosquitoes would, and he's got the hide of a rhinoceros."

"I wouldn't like to be the object of his affection. He's too devious. I'd better tell you he's boasting that you and he are an item."

She nearly spilled her ice water. "*In his dreams.* Put a note on every bulletin board in this building to the effect that Lawrence Parker is lying, that he's never been anywhere with me outside of the building and that I want him to stay out of my office."

Rhoda struggled without success to keep the grin off her round brown face. "That will give me more pleasure than this catfish. And girl, I do love me some catfish."

"Sure would quicken my steps, but I guess we'd better not do that. I'll find another way to make him grow up."

She had treated the matter lightly, but the man worried her. A normal man over thirty-five years of age—she was certain of that much—didn't behave as Lawrence Parker did.

"I sure hope I'm around when you blow him over. Say, how was your date Friday night?"

"My date? Oh, you mean... Disaster, girl. I had not one flat tire, but two, and by the time I got to the restaurant, almost two hours late, he'd left."

"You didn't call him? I mean, doesn't he have a cell phone?"

"He does, but mine was at the station on my desk." She stopped eating, lost in thoughts of what might have been.

Rhoda rested her knife and fork and leaned back in the chair. "But you patched it up later, right?"

Pamela lifted her right shoulder in a quick shrug. "I phoned his house and left a message. But if he got it, he didn't return my call."

"I see. You sound crestfallen. What's this guy like?"

"A tan-colored Adonis. Mesmerizing good looks. A grin that will make you cross your knees, and sweet as sugar. He's too good to be true."

"If what you say is right, he sure is. I'd be scared as hell of him."

Pamela ate the remainder of the catfish and pushed her plate aside. "He knows he's great-looking, but when women fawn over him, it gets on his nerves."

"You're kidding. You mean, he's not a stud?"

"Good Lord, no. If he was, I wouldn't have gone out the door to meet him."

Rhoda looked into the distance, her expression suggesting

a sense of wonder. "I wish you luck, but I'd stay away from that brother."

It was much too late for that advice, but she didn't tell Rhoda that. Lecturing herself about Drake Harrington had gotten her nowhere. She knew him well enough to be certain that he was far more than what he looked like— six feet and four inches of male perfection—that he was a serious-minded, hardworking and caring person who loved his family and was generous with his friends.

"I'm no slouch," she said to herself, "but what makes me think Drake Harrington is going to settle for me when he can have just about any woman he wants?"

"I don't give advice," Rhoda said, "and especially not to you, since you've done far more with your life than I have with mine. Still—"

"Out with it," Pamela said. "Who knows? It might be just what I need to hear."

Rhoda savored the last morsel of catfish, placed her knife and fork across her clean plate, and leaned back in her chair. "I was going to retract what I said a minute ago. If he's all that nice, and he's interested, go for it and enjoy it for as long as it lasts, but don't fall too deeply in love."

Pamela leaned forward as if to be certain Rhoda heard her. "I'd like to see the woman who could bask in that man's attention and, when his interest cooled, walk away unscathed as if she'd merely said 'hi' to him."

Rhoda's eyebrows shot up. "That bad, huh?"

They barely spoke as they walked down Linden Avenue to Monument Street, each in her own mental realm. "I'll tell you one thing," Rhoda said as they entered the building that housed the TV station, "I'd watch my back. Half the women you know will be trying to get close to you, hoping to catch his eye."

"Not me. My dad says that if a man wants to go, buy

him a ticket. The sooner he's gone, the better, because eventually, he will leave. You won't catch me clinging to anyone, male or female. My friends have the freedom to do as they please." She waved at the desk officer, who checked entrance badges.

"You two are looking great there," he said. "Nothing like a couple of fine-looking sisters to brighten a man's day." They smiled and kept walking. Ben enjoyed complimenting them.

Back in her office, Pamela checked her desk phone and her cell phone, saw that she didn't have any messages, pulled off her jacket and went to work. Twice that morning, she'd changed her lead story for the local evening news, and now this. A woman was shopping in the supermarket, turned her back to select a head of lettuce, and when she looked around her three-year-old daughter had disappeared and had not been seen since. She got busy trying to piece together the bits of information floating in and, once more, rearranged the order of her news item. By five o'clock, she had what she considered a first-class report, but Lawrence cracked the door and handed her a sheet of paper.

"Sorry, pal. Your producer gave me this a little while ago, but I swear I forgot it. No hard feelings?" She didn't answer him. His smile, brilliant and false, nearly sickened her. He had deliberately withheld one of the most important items of the day: Station WRLR had just joined the NBC family of stations. She pushed the button on her intercom and got the producer.

"Jack, when did you tell Lawrence to give me this merger notice?"

"Around eleven this morning. Why?"

"Because he gave it to me less than a minute before I paged you, and he knows I'm going on the air in ten minutes."

"Okay. Read it straight. I'll take care of Parker."

On her way home, she stopped at a garden center and bought a rubber garden snake. The next morning, she got to work early and glued the serpent to Lawrence's door. Even if he took it off, the perfect outline of a snake would be there until the door was painted. She dusted her hand as if she were getting rid of something unwanted, went to her office and left it to Lawrence to discover the identity of the donor. She understood now that Lawrence would be even more of a problem as she continued to reject him.

"I've fought worse battles," she said aloud. She gathered her notebook and headed for the station's library, wondering why Drake didn't call her.

As the big British Airways plane neared Kotoka International Airport in Accra, Ghana, Drake began to wonder what he would find. He disliked such tropical pests as mosquitoes, flies, sandflies and especially snakes. And he didn't know whether he was going to a thatched roof in a rural area or a skyscraper in Accra. He knew that Ladd belonged to the Fanti tribe—historically the elite of Ghana, not that it mattered what status his friend had—and that meant he'd be somewhere near the coast. The plane landed, and in his befuddled state of mind, he thought that his trip would have been more enjoyable if Pamela had been with him. Try as he may, he could not remember why he wanted to end their relationship. He hadn't ventured too far with her, not even when he kissed her. More than once, she'd indicated a desire for a little more passion. He dragged his fingers through his hair. He'd known other girls, so why was he focusing on Pamela?

He disembarked, walked into the terminal and saw Ladd waiting, his face shining with a brilliant smile.

"Welcome. Man, am I glad to see you! I need a calming

influence. Never get married. Women think the purpose of marriage is to spend money and reinvent the world in the process. Man, I'm worn out just watching them."

Had he forgotten Ladd's ability to talk nonstop for hours? He could almost feel the man's happiness. "Don't watch them," Drake said. "Besides, I didn't know Ghanaian women did that. I thought that was peculiarly American."

"Oh, no. Something tells me it's worldwide. How was your flight?" He motioned to the man standing beside him to take Drake's bags.

"Smooth as silk. I slept most of the way between London and Accra." They stepped out into the heat. "Whew! I'd better remove my coat. Say, I'm anxious to meet your bride."

"She's nice, man. Really nice."

"Way to go, buddy." A question had plagued him ever since he got the invitation and the note saying Ladd wanted him to be his best man. Well, he was paying his own fare, so he could ask if he wanted to know. "What kind of service are you having? Are there a lot of things I have to learn?"

Ladd stared at him. "What kind of— Oh, we're Protestants. Everything will be familiar. All you have to do is stand there and keep me from passing out. How long can you stay?"

"Keep you from passing out?" Laughter rippled out of him, partly at the idea of Ladd fainting, but mainly because he knew what was expected of him. "Sorry. I didn't think I'd need smelling salts. I'm leaving day after tomorrow. We've got buildings going up in two different states and in Barbados, and I'm strapped for time."

"Too bad you won't get to see much of the country. I told our interior minister that you might give him some ideas about the new shopping mall he wants built. Think you can spend about an hour with him?"

"No problem. Remember that I'm an architectural engineer, not an architect."

"Yeah. I told him that. He wants to meet you. I had white trousers, an agbada, a dashiki and a kufi made for you. I'm sure they'll fit, except maybe the kufi, but you'd better try them on."

Drake paused momentarily when he remembered that a few steps away stood an air-conditioned car in which he would get relief from what seemed like taking a sauna while wearing a woolen sweater and an overcoat.

"I know the agbada is a long gown and the dashiki is a shirt, but what the devil is a kufi?"

"It's a matching…you know…cap. We're having a modern Christian wedding, but to satisfy my grandfather, you and I are wearing traditional dress."

"What about the bride?"

He shrugged. "I'm not supposed to know, but she told me it's a white dress."

The following afternoon, around three o'clock, Drake dressed in the traditional clothing worn by a groom and his party and looked at himself in the mirror. "Hmm." Adjusting the kufi, he wondered if any of his ancestors had worn one, shrugged and rang for the car that would take him to Ladd's home. As he stepped out of the M Plaza Hotel—palatial by any measure—and into the Ghanaian heat, he wished he'd been going for a swim, but the air-conditioning in the Mercedes limousine immediately arrested his wayward thoughts. Ladd was ready when he arrived, and Drake had only a few minutes in which to observe his friend's elegant living style.

At five o'clock, still struggling with the effects of jet lag, Drake stood with Ladd Sackefyio and his bride—who was dressed in a white, short-sleeved wedding gown decorated with white embroidery that was inset with brilliant crystals, and wearing a matching white crown—took their vows before an Anglican minister at the foot of the altar. Deeply touched by the simplicity of the ceremony and the smiles that never moved from the couple's faces, he wondered if Russ had been right, that he'd begun to feel the loneliness of bachelorhood. He shrugged it off and went through the rituals of his duties at the reception, which included a toast and standing with the couple in case it seemed that they would topple the five-tier cake while trying to cut it.

Now, what am I supposed to do with this dame? he thought as he looked at the bridesmaid who made it clear to him and everyone at the reception that she wanted more from him than a smile. He had to be gracious. But he'd have preferred to paddle her for her lack of discretion. To worsen matters, she was an American, and the locals probably thought her behavior de rigueur for African-American women.

"Look," he said to her when her cloying behavior annoyed him to the point of exasperation. "Cut me some slack here. I'd like to get to know some of the Ghanaian people."

When she put her hands on her hips in a feigned pout, he walked away and a Ghanaian man immediately detained him. "I'm John Euwusi. We want to build a modern shopping mall here, and Ladd tells me you're the man to talk to."

Drake extended his hand. "He told me about you. I have to leave tomorrow afternoon, but we could speak in the morning, if you like."

"Good. I'll send my driver for you."

At the end of their conversation the following morning, Drake agreed to discuss the matter with his brothers, for he didn't work alone, but as a part of the Harrington, Inc. team. He hoped they could make a deal, because he wanted to get back to Ghana and see the country, including the old forts and castles associated with the slave trade.

As the Boeing 737 roared away from Kotoka International Airport, Drake glanced at the aisle seat across from his and nearly spilled the rum punch on his trousers. There sat Selicia Dennis, the bridesmaid who had attempted to hook her long pink-and-green talons into him. He liked assertive women, but the kind of aggression she displayed irritated him. He decided to behave as if he didn't know she was there. And she wasn't there by accident, he knew. In that circle, getting information about his departure and seat number was a simple matter. With the right influence, you got whatever you wanted.

He decided to focus on his seatmate, a man who bore the trappings of a gentleman, and introduced himself. "I'm Drake Harrington. Are you traveling all the way to the States?"

The man extended his hand. "Straight from London to San Antonio. I'm Magnus Cooper."

They spoke at length, and Drake learned that the man was a Texas rancher, as well as a builder.

"How's that?" he asked, when Magnus told him that he'd be in Baltimore at an undecided date to tape a program for his cousin's TV news show. "People don't seem to know that ranchers come in colors," he added. "In Texas, you'll find a number of hyphenated American ranchers—Spanish, Italian, black, Scottish, you name it."

Drake mulled that over for a second before laughter rippled out of him. "I'm in Baltimore frequently. Who's your cousin?"

"Pamela Langford. Her mother and my father are sister and brother. You know her?"

"I sure do." He let it go at that and didn't budge, not

even when both of Magnus's eyebrows went up and stayed there.

They spoke amiably until the plane landed at London's Heathrow Airport. They exchanged contact information and agreed to talk soon. Drake was transferring to Delta and headed for his flight's gate, but to his chagrin, when he arrived, Selicia Dennis stood to greet him. Having no acceptable choice, he took a seat and wished for something to read other than the *International Herald Tribune* that he carried in his briefcase.

"I live in Washington, D.C.," she began. "How far are you from there?"

He told her he didn't know, and she asked what state he lived in.

He folded the paper, put it back in his briefcase and faced her. "Miss Dennis, I don't see the point in this. I don't want to be rude, but you and I have absolutely no basis for a friendship of any kind, so let's stop with the small talk. It's a waste of breath." He folded his arms, closed his eyes and managed to give the impression of someone asleep. He heard the call of a flight to Washington, and immediately she gathered her things and left. He walked a few paces down the corridor, bought a bag of fish-and-chips and a bottle of lemonade, went back to his seat and relaxed. Beautiful, sure of it and shallow. The kind of woman he avoided.

Maybe he didn't sufficiently appreciate Pamela. Not once had he been bored in her company. He could talk with her for hours and not know how much time had passed. If she would only accept his need to grow a little more. If she'd wait until he reached his goals... He stared at the bag of soggy chips for a second before throwing them into the refuse bin. And what if she wouldn't wait, but found another guy? A woman who looked like her could have just about any man she wanted, and with her charm, gentle manners and…well, intelligence and competence, she was choice. And sexy. He'd never known another woman who got next to him as she did.

He ran his fingers through his silky hair. *So where the hell was she when she was supposed to be having dinner with me?*

"Flight 803 to Baltimore now boarding first-class passengers and passengers with small children or who need assistance." He heard the announcement, got up, went through security a third time and took his seat in the first-class section. He had six hours to think about what he wanted for himself and Pamela…provided she wanted anything from him at all.

Six hours and twelve minutes later, he walked into the Baltimore/Washington International Airport terminal, looked around and saw Russ walking toward him. As usual, after any of the brothers returned from a trip, they embraced each other. "That sun must really be something," Russ said. "You were there less than three days, and you look as if you stuck your face in an inkwell. I saw Pamela in the market this morning."

Drake stopped walking, a habit that annoyed Russ, but so what. "Did you speak with her?"

"Yeah. She asked me about Velma, but that's all. She was as beautiful as ever, but downcast. I didn't see any of that easy charm that I associate with her."

He tried to hide his response to that kick in his gut, but he wasn't sure he managed it, for Russ asked in his usually candid manner, "Something gone wrong with you two?"

"Let's just say we're not in touch right now."

"Her choice or yours?"

"I'm not sure."

Russ raised an eyebrow. "If it was her choice, she made

it because you weren't behaving the way she wanted you to. She was not a happy woman this morning."

His heartbeat accelerated, and he had to breathe through his mouth. He didn't want her to be unhappy; at least, he didn't think so. But for what other reason was he experiencing such relief, almost a sense of glee? He threw his bag into the trunk of Russ's Mercedes and got into the car beside his brother.

"When did you realize you loved Velma enough to marry her?"

Russ was in the process of starting the car and suddenly stripped the gears. "What? Oh. A long time before I admitted it to anybody, including Velma. Something happens, and suddenly you know. You just know it's right." He moved the car into the traffic. "Is that what you're going through?"

"I don't know. I was planning to tell her we shouldn't see each other for a while, but while I was in Accra, I couldn't for the life of me remember why I felt that way."

Laughter rumbled in Russ's throat. "Seems to me I've heard that song before. Don't do anything you'll be sorry for. Women hurt easily."

"Yeah, and they're not the only ones."

Chapter 2

Pamela finished whipping a hem in her evening dress, slipped it on and examined herself in the mirror that covered the inside of a closet door. Burnt orange was her best color, and she wore it often. "I look great," she said, and pulled air through her front teeth. "But what for? I don't give a hoot about anybody who's going to be at that reception." Given the choice, she would have stayed at home. However, she didn't have that option where a reception given by her boss was concerned, so she put on her mink coat, got the black satin evening bag that matched her shoes and went down to the apartment-building lobby.

"Could you call a taxi for me, please, Mike?"

"My pleasure, Miss Langford. I hope you're meeting a fine young man. In my day, a lady such as yourself wouldn't be alone for long." He switched on the call light. "If you don't mind my saying so, Miss Langford, I was hoping to see more of that gentleman—Harrington is his name, I believe he said. I've lived a long time, and I know a man when I see one. He's just what I'd want for my daughter if I had been fortunate enough to have one."

The taxi arrived, and she thanked Mike, her favorite among the doormen who worked at her building. The short, fifteen-minute ride took her to the Sheraton and as she paid the driver, he turned, looked at her and said, "Some guy sure is lucky."

"If you only knew," she said as she stepped out, careful not to get her shoe heel caught in the hem of her dress.

"What? What did you say?"

She walked on without answering, and to her disgust, Lawrence met her at the door of the reception room. She knew at once that he'd waited there to give the impression that she was his date. Without a word, she swung around and went to the other entrance, which meant she would skip the receiving line, but she didn't care. Immediately, she spotted Jack Hanson, her boss, and his wife and walked over to where they stood. Within less than a minute, Lawrence was at her side.

Seething, she knocked his hand away from her elbow. "Lawrence, I skipped the receiving line in order to avoid you, and I would appreciate it if you would stay away from me. If you don't, I'll make a scene."

"Lovers' spat," he said to the couple.

"How dare you! You have never had your hands on me, and you know it. Furthermore, you never will. Not even if you were the only man on this earth." She looked at her boss. "I'm sorry if this has spoiled your evening, but it's what I have to tolerate in the office every day. Please excuse me." She went to speak to her host, left the reception and went home.

As she entered her apartment, the telephone rang. "Hello."

"Hi, this is Rhoda. I saw you leaving the reception as I was arriving. Are you all right?"

"My health is fine, but Lawrence tried to give the impression that we're an item—even told Hanson and his wife that we were having a lovers' spat. I've been in a rage ever since."

"The pig! You didn't let him get away with it, did you?"

"Of course not, but I was too mad to be sociable, so I left. You have a good time."

"Thanks. So far, I'm bored to death."

She undressed, crawled into bed and attempted to banish the images that frolicked around in her head. Images of her with Drake on a small, fast boat in the Monocacy River near Frederick, the way he loved the speed, his face alive with childlike joy. Images of Drake with her on the previous Christmas morning in Eagle Park as they stood just outside the front door of Harrington House looking at six feet of pristine snow. He had squeezed her hand, kissed the tip of her nose and told her how much he loved snow.

"Surely the Lord wouldn't dangle that man in front of me just to tease me," she said aloud. When sleep finally came, she had been exhausted for a long time.

The following evening, Wednesday, the day after his return from Ghana, Drake met Lawrence—a former schoolmate—at an alumni meeting in Baltimore. As usual, Drake greeted him cordially.

"How's it going, man?" Drake asked.

"Couldn't be better. I'm seeing Pamela Langford these days. Man, she stood up a dinner date in order to see a movie with me. We're getting pretty tight."

He hoped the sharp pain in his chest didn't signal the onset of a heart attack. However, he put a half smile of casual interest on his face and said, "Really. When was that?"

"Last Friday night. We're together, man."

He let the smile freeze on his face, patted Lawrence on the back and said, "Way to go, man."

He had no reason to disbelieve him. After all, she hadn't bothered to tell him that she couldn't make their date or to use her cell phone to let him know she had a last-minute emergency. He shook his head from side to side, acknowledging that it strained his credulity to believe she would callously leave him sitting in a restaurant waiting for her for almost two hours. It was unlike her. He left the meeting, went to Russ's apartment—where he would spend the night—and turned on the local evening news.

"Good evening. I'm Pamela Langford, and this is WRLR Evening News."

That bottom lip of hers always tantalized him, and on that night, it seemed more luscious than ever. He caught himself as his tongue rimmed his lips, and he slid farther down in the big, overstuffed chair in Russ's living room. *Lord, but this woman is beautiful.* He wondered if she'd be stupid enough to develop an affair with a coworker, and when Russ came home, he told him what Lawrence said.

"I guess I don't know her," he said. "I wouldn't have thought she'd do a thing like that."

Russ dropped himself on the sofa. "Maybe she didn't. Why would he tell you that? Sounds suspicious to me, and if you weren't annoyed with her, you'd find that story suspect. Anyhow, every suspect deserves a hearing before he's sentenced. You ought to ask her what happened that evening. As unhappy as she was when I saw her, I wouldn't think she'd just begun a relationship with a man. That would make a person sparkle, wouldn't it?"

"Yeah. I should think it would. If I find out that Lawrence lied about Pamela, I'll— Oh, hell! I'll call her."

Pamela packed her briefcase, knowing that she wasn't in a mood to work after she got home; but what else was there to do? With her three-quarter-length leather coat on her arm, she headed for the elevator, and as she reached it, saw Lawrence approaching her.

"Lawrence, if you say one word to me or touch me, I will get an order of restraint against you for harassment. What you did last night was unconscionable. No decent man would have done what you did. Now, please move aside."

"Look, I was just—"

"You are harassing me."

She stepped into the elevator, pushed the button and prayed that he wouldn't trail her to the basement garage where she'd left her car. Relieved that he didn't follow her, she put on an Aretha Franklin CD and sang along with the diva as she drove, her spirits livelier than at any time since she'd missed her date with Drake.

At home, she warmed up the remainder of the previous evening's lasagna, made a salad and sat down to eat her supper. The telephone rang as she chewed the last morsel of it, and she debated whether to answer it, thinking that Lawrence might call her at home. However, the identity of the caller aroused her curiosity and she answered.

"Hello?"

"Hello, Pamela. This is Drake."

At the sound of his deep, mellifluous voice, her left hand slammed against her chest as if to decelerate the beating of her heart, and she let the wall take her weight.

"Hello, Drake," she said, as coolly as if her head wasn't spinning and her heart was beating normally. It was his call, and she wasn't going to make small talk. She waited for him to tell her why he'd called.

"I'm not satisfied with the way things are right now," he said. "I'm in Baltimore, and I'd like us to have lunch tomorrow, if you can make the time. I'm going home to Eagle Park later in the afternoon."

Hmm. Cut-and-dried, as usual. She didn't believe in being coy, and besides, she wanted to know why he hadn't returned her calls to his home and to his cellular phone.

"All right. Can we lunch at about twelve-thirty, and would you come by my office for me?"

"Uh… Sure. Be glad to. I'll see you at twelve-thirty." She wondered at his seeming hesitation.

"I'll be ready. My office is on the ninth floor. See you then."

Again, he seemed to hesitate. "Right. Till tomorrow."

For a while, she stared at the receiver that she still gripped tightly. Then, like a robot performing a programmed task, she hung up in slow motion. If she had ever had a more unsatisfying conversation with a man, she didn't remember it. *Oh, well. By this time tomorrow, I will know where I stand with Drake Harrington.*

She dressed carefully that morning, choosing a burnt-orange woolen suit with a beige blouse and brown accessories. She rarely wore makeup at work, but she did so that morning, settling for lipstick the color of her suit, and though she longed to wear her hair down, she put it into the French twist that she wore at work and on the air. Along with her makeup-repair bag, she put a vial of Poem, her daytime perfume, in her briefcase, said a prayer for the day and headed for work.

She tried to prepare herself for the moment when she would see him. *He's not the be-all and end-all, and if he fades out of my life, someone else will move in,* she told herself. However, when her secretary announced him and she heard his light tap on her door, she swung around, hitting her knee on the edge of her desk and sending pain shooting through it.

"Come in," she managed to say.

"Hi."

"Hi."

They stared at each other until he laughed—whether from nervousness or embarrassment, she couldn't tell. He had always been most handsome when he laughed, and she sat there, mesmerized and as still as a catatonic.

"We're behaving like strangers," he said, walked over to her, bent down and brushed his lips across hers. Her lips parted involuntarily, and he straightened up and stared down at her, his face devoid of expression.

"I guess we'd better go," he said at last. "Where's your coat?"

"I'll get it. Are we driving or walking?"

"I thought we'd walk to Lou's Ristorante. The weather's reasonably mild. Okay with you?"

"Fine. I like Lou's."

Her door swung open. "Don't get uptight. This is about… Oh!"

"What is it, Lawrence?"

"Uh…nothing. I can…er…come back later."

"Excuse me, man," Drake said. "I don't want to interfere with your romance. I can come back later."

She whirled around and glared at Drake. "You don't want to what? Where the devil did you get that idea? There's not a damned thing between this man and me, and if he doesn't stop harassing me and lying about me, I am going to have him arrested."

Lawrence backed toward the door. "I'll...uh, see you later."

"Not so fast, buddy," Drake said in a tone that would have halted the toughest street habitué. "Did you lie to me? You told me that you have a relationship going with Pamela, and that she stood up her dinner date in order to go to a movie with you. How did you know she was meeting me for dinner?"

Her lower lip dropped, but she quickly restored her aplomb. "Give me one reason, Lawrence, why I shouldn't indict you for lying about me. This isn't the only time you've done it."

"Look," he said, hands up and palms out, "you can't blame a guy for trying."

"No," Drake said, his facial expression stern and harsh, "but you can blame him for not having any integrity." He turned to Pamela. "We'd better be going. If you have any more difficulties with this fellow, report him to the police. After you," he said to Lawrence, effectively ordering him out of the office.

"When did Lawrence tell you that?" she asked Drake after they seated themselves in the restaurant and gave the waiter their orders.

"When I saw him last evening at an alumni meeting. Both of us attended graduate school at the University of Maryland. He worked on the campus paper. How did he know you were having dinner with me?"

"He asked me for a date, as he frequently does though I've yet to say yes, and I said I had a dinner engagement. I suppose he's seen us together and assumed I was meeting you."

He leaned back. "Right. What happened to you, and why didn't you call me?"

"I stopped at that filling station just before you turn into

Milford, got an oil change, my front and rearview windows washed, and my tires checked. A few minutes after I turned off the highway, both of my front tires blew out. Fortunately, I was on that ramp, so I wasn't driving fast. I walked the two miles back to the station, and—"

"Why didn't you use your cell phone and call me? I would have gone there and helped you."

Her right shoulder flexed in an automatic shrug. "I forgot it and left it on the desk in my office. When I got to the restaurant, you'd left, and the maître d' implied that I had bad manners for having stood you up. I called your home from a pay phone in the restaurant, but you weren't there. Henry took the message."

"I haven't been home since then, so he hasn't seen me."

When both of her eyebrows shot up, he explained. "I stayed in Baltimore that night with Russ and left for Ghana the next morning. I got back Tuesday night. Incidentally, did you ask the station attendant to check your tires to see what happened?"

She nodded. "He said someone slashed them, probably while he and I were inside the station straightening out my bill. He said a yellow Cadillac drove up, but when he went back outside, it had left, and the driver didn't make a purchase."

His fingers moved back and forth across his chin in the manner of one deep in thought. "Sooner or later, you'll know who did it. A yellow Caddy is hard to hide."

She fidgeted beneath his direct gaze, uncomfortable because of her reaction to him, but also because she couldn't fathom his demeanor.

"What is it, Drake?"

"You're so beautiful. I watched you on television last

night and, well…all that polish and intelligence in such a beautiful package."

She could say the same about him, but she didn't because she knew he wouldn't like it. He had made it clear on a number of occasions and in several situations that he wanted to be accepted for himself. "I can't take credit for the way I look. That's a genetic accident," he once told a matronly hostess, "but I gladly take responsibility for the man I am."

"Last night, you said you weren't satisfied with the way things are. I want you to clarify that."

"We were estranged, out of touch." He leaned forward, reached across the table and took her hand, sending shivers of apprehension through her system. "Last Friday night, I had planned to ask you to allow us to step back from where we seemed to be headed." She lowered her gaze so that he wouldn't be able to discern her feelings. "I dream of becoming nationally recognized in my profession, and I'm so far from that goal. Oh, I know Harrington, Inc. is well thought of in this part of the country, but I want more than that. I want to take chances, do original work, set the pace the way the engineers who worked with Frank Lloyd Wright did, and I can't do that unless I'm traveling alone. When I was away from here, in Ghana, I couldn't remember why I wanted some breathing space between us. I'm not even sure now if that's what I want.

"When I was watching you on TV last night, it certainly wasn't what I wanted, and it isn't what I want right now. But I'm thirty-one years old, and I'm not ready to settle down."

"I don't remember having asked you to settle down with me."

"This is true, but I've thought about it. A lot, in fact. I

don't mislead women, and I don't play relationship games with them."

"Is there another woman you'd like to get to know or that you prefer?"

"Of course not. If there was, I would have told you. I am also not having this conversation with any other woman."

She looked at him, wondering if he knew he'd just told her that of all the women he knew and associated with, she was the one to whom he was closest. He may want breathing space, but she didn't. Still, a relationship with a man who didn't want to settle down was not in her best interest. "Drake, I'm thirty years old, and if I'm ever going to have any children I have to get started soon. Thirty is already old to have a first child."

"I'm aware of that, and it may account for my need to be direct with you." His fingers plowed through his hair. "But I'm not saying I'll be happy to break this off. I definitely won't, but I have to be straight with you."

She patted his hand and forced a smile. "Come on. I have to get back to work. If I need an escort that will knock 'em dead, I'll phone you."

With cobralike swiftness, he grabbed her left wrist. "That wasn't called for. I don't squire women around. If you needed to strike out at me, that was as good a way as any." He stood and walked around to her side of the table to move her chair. She took her time getting up because he was standing there and she'd be inches from him. As she expected, he didn't move when she stood, but stared down into her face, his own ablaze with passion. Lost in the moment, she rimmed her lips with her tongue, knowing that she'd fastened her gaze on his mouth, on that firm masculine mouth that with the barest touch could singe her with desire. She closed her eyes, but quickly opened them when his fingers encircled her arm.

"Come on," he whispered. "Let's get out of here."

They walked back to the TV station without speaking, each deep in thought. Half a block from the building, his hand captured hers and squeezed her fingers.

"A man doesn't ask if he can have his cake and eat it, too. He makes a choice, and I thought I'd done that." At the entrance to the building, he leaned forward, kissed her briefly on the mouth and gazed down at her for a full minute before saying, "I'll be in touch."

She tripped to the elevator with a spring in her steps. Oh, she wanted to fly through the air like a prima ballerina, free and unfettered. He could say what he liked and tell himself all the tales he wanted to, but he wasn't ready to break off their relationship, and she wasn't going to do anything that would encourage him to. She meant a lot more to him than he was willing to admit. *But he'd better hurry up. I want him, but not badly enough to sacrifice motherhood.*

Before she could sit down and begin work, Rhoda knocked and walked into her office. "I know you're busy, but I'm not leaving here till you tell me who that hunk was who kissed you right in front of the door here. Talk about moving from the ridiculous to the sublime. Whew!"

Rhoda's raving over Drake annoyed her, and she wasn't sure why. She liked Rhoda and found her work more than satisfactory, but the remark and the question were out of place. Better not leave any doubt in the woman's mind. She leaned back in the swivel desk chair and looked Rhoda in the eye. "Since you're aware that he kissed me on the mouth, you don't need to know who he is."

"Whoa. Like that, is it? Well 'scuse me. Girl, you know how to pick 'em."

"If I recall correctly," she said, intent on imprinting in the woman's mind the fact that Drake sought her and not vice versa, "I was working a building industry conference at the convention center on Camden Street, and he walked up to me, introduced himself and asked if I'd have lunch with him. Looks like he picked me, doesn't it."

"Oops! Touchy subject. I'd better get back to work. See you later."

Pamela got busy writing her evening report. She had fought hard and long for the privilege of writing her own copy, and she spared no effort to make it complete, informative and interesting. The messenger knocked, walked in and handed her a press release entitled "Breaking News." She thanked him, looked it over and wrote a quick summary that she would read at the beginning of her report, provided she didn't get any more breaking-news releases.

"May I see you a minute, Langford?"

"Be right there," she said to Raynor, her managing editor, and made a note of what she'd been thinking when the intercom barked at her. She headed down the hall to what she assumed was a conference call. Instead, she learned that Lawrence Parker had been transferred to the seven-to-nine morning news show.

"There'll be no reason for him to contact you in the line of work. I apologize for his crude behavior, and I hope he's learned a lesson."

She thanked the man, but didn't expect that Lawrence Parker had undergone a metamorphosis; he was lacking in too many important respects. By five o'clock, she had her report in order.

"No calls, please," she said to her secretary. "I'm testing my copy, and I don't want to be disturbed."

"All right, Ms. Langford. I'll take your messages."

After her newscast, she headed for her office and looked through her messages. *Well, what can I expect?* she thought, crestfallen when she didn't find one from Drake. She packed the briefcase, made a note as to what she had to do when she arrived at work Monday morning and headed home. Her cell phone rang as she drove out of the garage. She turned the corner, stopped and answered it. She didn't talk on the phone while driving.

"Hello."

"Hello, Pamela, this is Drake. Feel like a movie tomorrow evening? Or if not that, dinner?"

Oh, my Lord, she said to herself. *Am I going to fold up every time I hear his voice unexpectedly?*

"I'd love dinner, but I haven't seen a movie in ages. What do you want to see?"

"You may think this is foolish, but there's an old movie that I'm nuts about, 'cause it's funny. It's *The Russians Are Coming, The Russians Are Coming.* It was made during the Cold War, and it's hilarious. We could have dinner and make the nine-o'clock show. Interested?"

"Yes, indeed. Where's the movie?"

"In Baltimore. I'll pick you up around five-thirty. All right?"

"I'll look forward to it."

"So will I. Bye."

She hung up, put the car in Drive and went home. For a man who needed breathing space, he seemed bent on suffocating himself.

Pamela couldn't have been further from the truth. Drake accorded himself the right to be certain of his moves, and if that meant exposing himself to his mounting passion, so be it. If he could have his dreams and her as well, he wanted to know it. But if he had to choose, not only did he need to know that, but he also had to be certain of his choice.

"How about a game of darts?" his brother Telford asked, joining him in the den. "I could use some activity that will take my mind off those Florence Griffith Joyner Houses."

"Yeah. One of these days, we ought to work at getting a mobile crew. As long as we have to hire construction crews in whatever city or country we're building in, we'll have problems. Speaking of problems, how'd you like to take on a real one?"

He knew Telford, the builder for Harrington, Inc., loved a challenge, but he wasn't certain that even Telford could overcome the problems he envisaged in building a shopping mall in Accra. He told his brother about the project he discussed while in Accra attending his friend's wedding.

"But if you think Barbados posed a problem, you ought to see what you'd be up against in Ghana. The weather saps all of your energy. I don't see how a man can work day after day in that heat and humidity."

"What about a split shift…early mornings and late evenings?" Telford asked him.

"Yeah. Right. Just in time for sandflies and mosquitoes. Besides, you have the heat till the sun goes down, and then it's immediately dark."

"Let's see what Russ has to say about it. He might enjoy designing a shopping mall for a tropical country."

Drake heaved himself from the comfort of the deep, overstuffed leather chair and allowed himself a restorative yawn. "Maybe, but I'm not sure I'd enjoy engineering it. See you later."

"Wait a minute," Telford said, rising to face his youngest brother. "Russ said something had gone awry with you and Pamela. This probably won't impress you one bit, but I like her a lot—all of us do. Not even Henry has anything negative to say about her."

"'Course not. She sang his favorite song to him. Look, brother, I'm feeling my way, here. She wants a family and she's already thirty. I'm thirty-one, and I haven't proved anything to myself. I'm not sure I'd be happy giving her up, but what about my goals?"

"You'll reach those. No doubt about it in my mind. But if you get to the top, and you're there all alone, who will you enjoy it with? Who will you share it with? Alexander the Great conquered the world and wept because there was nothing left to conquer."

"Point taken. But you waited until you were thirty-six, and Russ is getting married at thirty-four. What does anybody want from me? I'm behaving in true Harrington fashion." Laughter bubbled up in his throat. "It may not be up to me. Every man can see what I can see."

Telford's right eyebrow shot up. "If you thought she'd drop you, you wouldn't be so sanguine about it."

"Well, I'm not that sure of her either, which is why I'm seeing her tomorrow night."

"Yeah? Way to go. See you later. Say, what about the darts?" Telford called after him.

"Give me a few minutes. I'll meet you in the game room."

Telford and Russ had found women who were perfect for them and who loved them. Would he be as fortunate? He met Alexis, his sister-in-law, on the stairs, and her hand on his arm detained him.

"What's the matter? You seem perplexed. What can I do to help?"

"I don't know if you can. I don't like being caught up in the tide and being swept along as if I have no control over my life."

Her smile, at once motherly and wistful, reassured him, as it always did. "You only have to do what you want to do. Other people's dreams for you are their dreams and plans, not yours. You can love the adviser and still ignore the advice. Get the message?"

"You bet I do. Will Russ be here for dinner?"

"No. He and Velma are coming in tomorrow afternoon."

"Too bad. I wanted the three of us to discuss that Ghana project. Maybe we can do that Sunday morning."

"Good idea. Bring Pamela with you."

He continued up the stairs. "I can ask her."

"Eoow! Uncle Drake!" Tara ran to him with open arms. "I missed you, and when my dad said you'd be back today, I was so happy."

He picked her up and swung her around while she giggled in delight. "How's my best girl?"

"I have a lot to tell you. My dad said it's time for me to get another music teacher, and Mr. Henry wants to buy me a grand piano. The trouble is we would have to put it in the living room, and I would get on everybody's nerves practicing."

"We could put it downstairs in the game room."

"I dunno. Maybe you can tell my mommy you want to play darts in the game room, you and Uncle Russ, and she won't put it there."

"Well, sometimes it's damp downstairs, and I imagine that's bad for a piano."

She clapped her hands. "Really? Think up some more bad things about downstairs. I want to put the piano in my room."

He put her down. A six-year-old con artist, and as frank about it as a fashion model on a runway.

He went to his room, closed the door and walked over to the window. "I've been looking at this scene for all of my life. Maybe if I did as Russ did, if I left and went on my own, I'd see my life more clearly. I don't think I'm reaching too high by wanting career recognition, but when I get it, I want to share it with someone extra special." He thrust his hands in his trouser pockets and slouched against the window frame. As he watched, birds flittered among the several feeders Alexis kept laden with bird food, took their fill and then flew away.

He planned to learn to fly, and he didn't like keeping secrets from his family. But he knew that, out of concern for his safety, they would discourage him, so he decided to tell them when it was a fait accompli. He stretched out on the bed and let his mind travel over his life since Alexis and Tara entered it, recalling the many ways in which the little girl brightened his life, and accepting that having Alexis among them enriched their lives. He got up, put on a pair of sneakers and went down to the game room where Telford and Tara awaited him.

"Dad, Uncle Drake said it's damp down here and that's not good for a piano."

Telford hunkered in front of the child. "Getting your troops together, eh? Well, your mother and I have decided that it's going into the den, and Henry said that's fine. I want you to stop trying to snow people to get your way. Use your charm sparingly."

Tara looked up at Drake. "Do you know what that means, Uncle Drake?"

"Yeah, but don't worry. Just be yourself."

Having gotten assurance that the piano would not be in the basement, Tara raced up the stairs to tell Henry. Telford looked at Drake with a narrowed right eye. "The chance that she'll have your personality is nearly one hundred percent. Let's hope she's lucky enough to have your common sense to go along with her alluring ways."

He could feel the grin forming around his lips and

spreading all over his face. "Thanks for the compliment. It may surprise you to know that it came at a good time."

Telford selected a dart, aimed it and missed the bull's-eye. "Why did you need your ego massaged?"

"I didn't, but you wouldn't tell me I have common sense if you didn't mean it, and I'm questioning that these days."

Telford walked over to the long brown leather sofa, sat down and patted the place beside him. "Pamela?"

"Right."

"You don't have to make up your mind about anything today, do you? It isn't as if she's pregnant."

Drake's eyes widened. "Heavens, no. We've never been intimate. I've avoided that, because I know she thinks a lot of me. And since I don't know where I'm headed with her, I try not to do anything that she'd be sorry for."

A half laugh that sounded like a hiccup eased out of Telford's throat. "She may be sorry if you break up and nothing's happened. Better to love and lose than never to love at all, or something like that."

"She's a very special person, Telford, and—"

Telford interrupted him. "And she's beautiful, soft, intelligent and fun. Need I say more?"

Drake sat forward, rested his elbows on his thighs and supported his chin with both hands. "When did you know you loved Alexis so much that you wanted to marry her?"

"I knew I wanted her the minute I saw her. In fact, I think I fell for her on sight, and I knew it was mutual. At first, I fought it, but every day that hook sank deeper. The first time I had her in my arms, I knew I'd never get her out of my system. She's the one who slowed the relationship. Not me. When we were in Cape May, she, Tara and I had adjoining rooms, and we did everything as a family. It was the happiest time of my life up to then. I knew then that I would marry her if she'd let me. Tara wanted us to continue to live that way here at Harrington House, but of course it wasn't possible until we married."

"I knew the two of you hit it off immediately and that she was right for you. How do you feel about impending fatherhood?"

"I'm already a father, and I have been ever since I met Tara. Alexis wants a boy, and I hope we get what she wants, but I don't care as long as we have another healthy, happy child. If you're lucky enough and smart enough to choose the right woman, you'll be a changed man and happier for it."

Drake patted Telford on the shoulder and got up. "I think I'll go see what Henry's doing."

"Henry and Tara were supposed to go to Frederick to look at grand pianos. Alexis is cooking dinner."

"How's Tara's piano playing?"

"Fantastic. That's why I'm sending her to a professional teacher."

"See you later." He dashed up the stairs, didn't see Henry in the kitchen and went on up to his room. If only he could be as sure as his brothers. He dialed Kendra's number and hung up before the second ring. That wasn't the way to go. She wasn't for him, and he shouldn't mislead her. He opened his briefcase and gazed unseeing at Russ's drawings for extensions to the Florence Griffith Joyner Houses. What kind of evening did he want with Pamela? At times, thinking about her softness aggravated his libido until it made him uncomfortable. At other times, he could see her and think of her dispassionately.

"No point in stewing over it," he said to himself. "We'll see what happens tomorrow."

Pamela, too, had concerns about the course of their relationship. Now that she knew he cared but was uncertain as to what he wanted for them, she meant to teach him to love her. If that didn't work and soon, she meant to invite him to take a walk. She put on a red woolen suit and silver hoop earrings, let her hair hang on her shoulders, added Calèche perfume and black accessories, and looked at her watch. He'd be there in five minutes. Almost immediately the doorman buzzed her.

"Good evening, Miss Langford. Mr. Harrington to see you."

"Thanks, Mike. Ask him to come up."

"Yes, ma'am." He sang the words, because he liked Drake and encouraged her to be with him.

She walked around the living room rubbing her hands together, fingering the art objects that she had collected in her travels, lecturing herself that she shouldn't seem eager. And then the doorbell rang and she sprang toward it, calmed herself and walked the remainder of the way.

"Hi," he said, handed her a bouquet of tea roses and grinned. "You look better every time I see you."

"Stop fibbing and come in while I put these in water. They're beautiful. Thank you." She went to the kitchen, got a vase, put water in it and arranged the flowers, taking her time in order to retrieve her aplomb. She brought them back, said, "I'm putting these on my night table." and brushed past him on her way to her bedroom, the fabric of her suit gently caressing his.

"I'm ready," she said when she came back to the living room.

"I'm not."

Before the words registered, she was in his arms and his mouth was on her. His lips parted over hers; she inhaled his breath and the tip of his warm tongue probed for entrance into her mouth. Stunned by the swiftness of it, she hadn't time to summon control and submitted to the passion that swirled within her. She sucked his tongue into her mouth, and he demanded that she take more. Her nipples hardened and she heard her moans as he gripped her hips to his body with one hand and, with the other, tightened around her shoulder until she could almost count his heartbeats. His hand roamed over her back as if he sought the answer to what touched her, to what would make her his alone. Her hand went to his nape, caressing, asking for more, and he gave it, darting here and there to every crevice in her mouth, squeezing her to him until she had a raw, aching need to have all of him.

Shamelessly she rubbed the painful nipple, and he moved her hand, pinched and caressed it until she cried out, "Drake, I can't stand this."

He stopped the torture at once, and with both arms around her he enveloped her in a gentle embrace. "I don't suppose you intended for it to go that far. I know I didn't, but I'm pretty sure I'll do it again, unless you make it impossible."

When she didn't respond, he tipped up her chin and gazed into her eyes. Knowing what he saw, she quickly closed them. The feel of his lips on her forehead, her cheeks and the tip of her nose told her that he cherished her. *At least for now, he does,* she thought.

"I think it would be a good thing if we headed for the restaurant."

The expression on his face and the tone of his voice made it clear that if they didn't leave, they might be there till morning. "I'll get my coat."

"You know," he said near the end of their dinner, "I like the fact that you're comfortable enough with me that you don't feel a need to chat. Self-possession is a good trait."

She nearly laughed. "Drake, I'm not one bit comfortable with you right now. I am overwhelmed by what you did to me in my apartment. It's the first time in my life that a man destroyed my will. I am self-possessed most of the time, or so people tell me, but not right now. I'm quiet because if I talk, I'll probably say something I'll regret…like what I just said."

His stare seemed to penetrate her. Then, he laughed. "If I was sitting beside you, I'd hug you. I wondered if I was out of line back there. You're not alone, Pamela. I also got a surprise. A big one. As long as you're not sorry—"

"I'm not."

"Neither am I."

He held her hand as they walked to his Jaguar, which he'd parked three blocks from the restaurant. "I'll be terribly disappointed if you don't like this movie," he said.

"Not to worry. I need a good laugh."

"I'm going to assume that that remark had no negative implications."

"I don't believe in indirect insults. A stab ought to be clean and lethal."

He opened the passenger door for her, fastened her seat belt and closed the door. "Something tells me I'd better get a breastplate," he said after settling into the car and closing the door.

"Why? I wouldn't harm a strand of your hair. Besides, do I look like I'd hurt a flea?"

He turned fully to face her. "If my hair is so safe with you, move over here and let me get my arms around you."

She did as he'd asked and was rewarded with a tenderness that was new to her, with him or with anyone. "I could get used to this with you," he whispered, "but I'd better move slowly, because I don't know what the end will be."

She didn't release him, because she didn't want to, because she needed to prolong and savor that moment when she first knew she loved him. She reached up, ran her hands over his hair and then let her fingers trail down the side of his face and her thumb caress his bottom lip. It was an intimate gesture, she knew, but she felt like being honest with him. And it was the one way she could tell him he was precious to her without saying the words.

As if he understood the meaning of her gesture, he whispered, "Yeah. Me, too," turned the key in the ignition, put the car in Drive and headed for the movie.

Chapter 3

This must be my day, Drake thought as Pamela's head lolled on his shoulder while she laughed hysterically. "Everybody must to get off from street," the on-screen Russian sailor said to the old woman in his broken English as he pretended to be a representative of the local authorities. His submarine had accidentally surfaced off Nantucket, and he and his fellow sailors were trying to get back to it without causing an international incident.

"Did you really enjoy it so much?" he asked her as they left the theater. "I confess I've seen it a dozen times, beginning when I was a teenager, and I've laughed as hard each time I've seen it as I did the first time."

They walked out swinging their locked hands, and throughout the drive to the apartment building in which she lived, they reminisced about the movie, laughing at the funny parts. He walked with her to her apartment door, uncertain as to how he wanted to end the evening, though he knew lovemaking or the suggestion of it would be a mistake.

She proved the wisdom of his intuition when she said, "This evening was very special. Do you still need breathing space?"

Unprepared for the question, but aware that she had a penchant for candidness, he took his time answering. "I don't remember having equivocated about anything of importance to me, but how I answer your question could have a powerful effect on my life. I like being with you, and I want to see you, but right now, that's as far as I can go."

She laid her head to one side and looked hard at him, so much so that she nearly unnerved him. "That isn't far enough for me, Drake. Limbo isn't a place where I would knowingly go. I realize that you need to assure yourself that you have a firm grip on your future, that you're managing your life's course, and I respect that, but I also have to manage mine. You can start a family when you're sixty, but I don't have that option."

Standing on tiptoe, she kissed his cheek and dazzled him with the smile that showed a half dimple in her right cheek. "If the tide was moving in the right direction, you could mean everything to me. But it isn't, and I'm not going to wait for you to make up your mind. Good night."

He told her good-night, and as he walked down the hall to the elevator, it was as if the weight of his feet dragged him along. He heard the lock turn on her door and swung around, wanting with all his heart to turn back and find solace in her arms. But he comforted himself with the thought that what he needed was a good rest, a chance to empty his head of work and of the minutiae cluttering his life, a chance to focus on what was important to him personally.

He had planned to spend the night with Russ, but changed his mind and headed for Eagle Park. He got home after midnight, and it surprised him to find Telford and Alexis sitting in the den watching a movie. He was tempted to slip by and go to his room. He had never been less willing to share himself with another person. But that was not the way of the Harrington brothers, so he went into the den, mixed a Scotch whiskey and soda, and joined Telford and Alexis.

"I hardly expected you back tonight," Telford said. "I hope all's well."

He pulled out the hassock from beneath his chair and propped his feet on it. "Let's put it this way. For now, at least, everything depends on me. But she's not waiting while I figure out where I'm going."

"I always thought you were the most resolute person imaginable," Alexis said. "Do you have misgivings about her?"

"That's one of the things about this that perplexes me," he said. "She's the kind of woman I want. Nothing's wrong with her, and she suits me, but still I seem willing to risk losing her. I don't think that any woman I want will be available to me, nor do I believe I'll meet another one like Pamela, at least not soon. I guess the problem is that there is unspoken pressure on me to fall in love and get married. Nobody's said it, but all this marital and soon-to-be marital bliss is making me feel that I'm missing a lot. I can see the difference in you and in Russ, and I also want to feel equally secure with the woman who's special to me." He threw up his hands. "Oh, what the hell. I guess I'm just not ready to settle down."

"So she told you she won't wait while you shilly-shally?" Telford asked, pushing the needle where he knew it would hurt, for Drake prided himself in his ability to think through a problem, come to a decision and act on it without equivocating.

Drake spread his legs, leaned forward and rested his forearms on his thighs. "You could say that."

"Man, I hope she doesn't settle on someone else."

"I hope for her sake that she does," Alexis said, causing both men to sit upright and stare at her. "If she wants children, she'd better do something about it, or she will forever regret it. A man can't possibly understand the instinct that makes women want to be mothers."

"I know it's powerful," Drake said. He wished he'd gone directly to his room. Alexis was right, but knowing that caused a cloud of weariness to settle over him. "I think I'll be getting to bed," he said. "Thanks for the company." He plodded up the wide, winding stairs, his mind on Pamela and how he'd felt earlier that evening at the door of her apartment. And he thought back to the times she had caressed him so sweetly and so lovingly—asking nothing and demanding nothing—and he'd felt as if he could move mountains.

He reached the landing and banged his fist on the railing. "What the hell's wrong with me? I know damned well I don't want any other man to have that woman." But did he love her? "Hell, I'm not going there," he said to himself. "If I do love her, I'll probably act like it."

After a shower, he dried his body and slid between the leopard-print sheets that he preferred. "The day will come, I hope, when I look back at this time and laugh at myself." He turned out the light and went to sleep.

At that moment, Pamela worried less about Drake's decision than he did. She had made up her mind to relegate him to her past and look for a man with whom she could build a life. She loved him, and she believed in his integrity, but he'd already killed enough time. Long after telling him good-night and, in effect, goodbye, she sat on the edge of her bed trying to deal with her inner conflict and her sense that their song hadn't played out.

But I can't go on like this. I need someone I can count on, a man who will give me the family I long for.

"Oh, Lord," she moaned. "Why did I have to fall in love with him?"

Refusing to succumb to the moroseness that threatened her, she went into the living room and put on *Jump for Joy,* a compact disc that she bought in Paris two years earlier. Where but in Paris would one find the music of Josephine Baker, who died decades earlier? Pamela never failed to dance to that music, and she danced then. Danced until she fell across her living-room sofa exhausted. Danced until the tears cascaded down her cheeks like water from a broken dam. She lay there for a few minutes, getting used to the pain, then got up from the sofa, splashed cold water on her face and laughed.

"Drake Harrington, you're the only man who can lay claim to making me cry, and, honey, you're the last one."

Awaking the next morning to the ringing of the telephone, she slammed the pillow over her head, dragged the blanket up to her neck and got more comfortable. The ringing persisted, and she reached from beneath the covers to knock the phone from its cradle, but missed and bruised her hand against the lamp.

"All right," she grumbled and sat up. "Hello."

"You still in bed? Sorry to wake you up. I know it's Saturday, but I thought you'd be up and around. I called to remind you that Tuesday is your mother's birthday," her father said, "so don't forget. You know how she loves her birthdays. We don't expect you to come down here during the week. Just call."

"I'd be there if I could get off, Daddy. How are you and Mama?"

"We're good." His deep and musical voice had always given her a feeling of security, as did the strength he projected with every word he spoke, even when he was being amusing. "We watched you on the national news the other night. First time we saw you on camera. I can't tell you how proud we were. I opened a bottle of champagne, and we congratulated ourselves on what we'd created." Laughter rumbled out of him, the self-deprecating and mischievous laughter that she loved so much.

"Bob Kramer had an emergency, and the producer grabbed me the last minute and said, 'You're on.' How did I do?"

"Great. You don't think I'd open my best champagne to commemorate a flop, do you? We're proud of you. It was first-class."

"Thanks, Daddy."

"And you looked great in that red suit. Where's that engineer you were talking about? Isn't it about time he spoke to me?"

"That may never happen, Daddy. There's something real good between us, but… Well, he isn't ready."

"From all you said about him, he's probably a good man, but if he isn't ready, move on. A lot of first-class white guys would flip backward over you. I keep telling you that."

"I know, Daddy. I know. Where's Mama? Let me speak with her, please."

"She's at the hairdresser's."

"Well, give her a hug for me. I'll be sure to call her Tuesday."

She hung up and got out of bed. Her father wanted her

to marry a man who, like himself, was white, but the last thing she wanted was a marriage complicated by the social problems that her parents faced. Besides, she was attracted to black men. Her father could hardly be called prejudiced considering that he'd married an African-American woman and embraced her entire family. Pamela tossed her head as if in defiance and headed to the kitchen to make coffee. *He married the person he wanted—and against his family's wishes, I might add—and, if I get the chance, I'll do the same.* As soon as she got to her office, she phoned a florist and ordered flowers for her mother, specifying that they arrive Tuesday morning.

Shortly before noon on Saturday, Russ arrived at Harrington House—the place where his room always awaited him—with Velma Brighton, his bride-to-be and Alexis's older sister. Weeks had passed since Drake and his two older brothers had been together, and it seemed to him almost like Christmas as they greeted each other with the customary embrace. He loved his brothers and welcomed the women of their choice as he would have blood sisters.

"Only three more months," Drake said to Velma. "How do you keep Russ's feet on the ground?"

Velma winked, displaying the wickedness that he associated with her dry humor. "With patience."

"Not so," Russ said. "I'm a changed man. I wait till the light turns completely green before I enter the intersection."

"I never knew you to do otherwise," Telford said.

"Was he always like this?" Velma asked, standing against Russ with his arms snug around her.

"Always," Henry put in. "Ain't a one of these boys changed one bit since they were little. Instead of being an impatient kid, Russ is an impatient man." He rubbed his chin as if savoring a pleasant thought. "But I'll say it right in front of him. He's as solid as they come."

Although Henry had worked as the family's cook since Drake was five years old, Drake and his brothers regarded him as a member of the family who did most of the cooking. Long before their father's death, it was Henry to whom they looked for guidance and nurturing, for Josh Harrington worked long hours to build a life for his children and to ensure their status in Midwestern Maryland. They couldn't count on their mother—a woman who didn't want to be tied down and who left home for lengthy periods of time whenever it suited her—to be there when they needed her. So they turned to Henry, who treated them as if they were his own children.

Henry's pride in the three men was obvious to anyone who knew the family. Indeed, acknowledging his role as a father figure to the Harrington men, Alexis had asked Henry to escort her down the aisle at her wedding to Telford, for which she earned his gratitude and deepening love.

"You got all your wedding plans straight?" Henry asked Velma. "Let me know if you need me for anything."

"I wish I had me to do the catering," she said, and not in jest, for she had achieved wide fame as a caterer of grand affairs. "And I just found out that one of my bridesmaids is almost four months pregnant and showing. Since I have a *matron* of honor, I don't know what to do with her. In three months, she'll be over six months and even bigger than she is now. Other than that, everything's fine."

"Aren't you going to replace her?" Alexis asked. "She's got a lot of chutzpah to spring a late pregnancy on a bride."

"Not to worry," Velma said, "I'll think of something. For

the last three days, I've been lecturing to myself that she doesn't deserve any more consideration than she's giving me, but…she's a friend."

Drake listened for Russ to tell Velma that what that bridesmaid was proposing to do was unacceptable, but Russ said nothing, and he wondered at the change in his brother. Time was when Russ would have pronounced that the woman be excluded, and in a tone so final that his bride-to-be wouldn't dare object.

Later, as the three men sat together in the den discussing the advisability of entering into a contract with the Ghana interior minister to build a shopping mall, Drake observed the calm and assurance with which Russ accepted Telford's rejection of one of his ideas, where months earlier, he would have complained that his two brothers always got their wishes because they voted together. On this occasion, Russ merely said, "What's your reason?" then listened and nodded his approval.

She's all the balm Russ's ego needs, Drake thought. *She's good for him.* Again, the memory returned of those moments with Pamela's arms around him, teasing him, and how like a king he felt when she unashamedly adored him.

Henry looked into the den. "Drake, did you see the mail I put on yer desk?"

"I haven't looked at that desk since I've been back here. Thanks."

"I'd like to know who scrambled yer brain," Henry said. "If it's who I think it was, you shoulda been home Friday night before last when she called ya."

"I'll be back in a few minutes," he said to his brothers, bounded up the stairs and went to his room. He dug through a week of mail and found the one thing he didn't care to see:

the tiny, stingy handwriting of Selicia Dennis. Although tempted to throw it away without opening it, he decided to read it.

Dear Drake,
I'm sorry that we haven't hit it off. I fear I've mis-represented myself to you. Doris Sackefyio was kind enough to give me your address, and I'm apologizing if I made a nuisance of myself. I'm enclosing two tickets to the memorial jazz concert at the Kennedy Center next month. I hope you'll use the second ticket to take me with you.
Warmly, Selicia

He noted that she included her phone number, but not her email address. He put the tickets in an envelope, debated whether to enclose a note, decided not to and sealed it. To be sure that she got it, he would send the letter by certified mail, return-receipt requested. Feeling the need to be out-side and alone, he put on a storm jacket, stopped by the den to tell his brothers he'd see them later and walked out toward the Monocacy River. If he encountered a living being, at least it wouldn't be able to talk.

On Monday, having convinced herself that she should attend a luncheon of industry professionals, Pamela found herself seated beside a likable man who obviously had the respect and—she thought—the envy of his peers. Oscar Rankin—tall, handsome, fortysomething, white—had the veneer of success wrapped securely around him. He set his cap for Pamela and made no effort to hide his interest. She'd heard of Oscar Rankin—who hadn't?

"Would you like more wine?" he asked her. When she rejected the wine and his other offer to be of service to her, he changed tactics. "I saw you on the national evening broadcast a few nights ago," he said, "and you brought that show to life. Of course, looking as you did—stunningly beautiful with a no-nonsense attitude—would captivate any sensible man." In a subtle and innocuous way, he managed to claim her attention throughout the luncheon.

"Let me help you with that." She looked up and saw him beside her at the cloakroom window, and before she could discourage him, he was holding her coat for her. Mildly irritated, she asked him, "What do you want, Mr. Rankin?"

With a diffidence that she didn't believe was real, he shrugged slightly and let a smile flash across his face. "You shouldn't ask a man that question unless you want the answer. I want to get to know you, because you've got me damned near besotted, and I've only known you an hour and a half."

She stared at him for a full minute in disbelief, but his facial expression didn't waver. For reasons she didn't fathom and didn't try, laughter floated out of her. "Are you serious?"

"As serious as I've ever been in my life. Have dinner with me this evening."

She released a long breath. He didn't look one bit like the father of her children, because they would have dark brown, sleepy and long-lashed eyes. Harrington eyes. "Not this evening. I'm busy."

"Tomorrow evening. Before you give me the brush-off, get to know me. If I come up short, I'll take my medicine and graciously step aside."

Talk about self-confidence! "Where do you want us to meet?"

"At your front door. Where do you live?"

His directness reminded her of boardroom tactics. He'd

have to learn that she wouldn't roll over for him. "We'll do it my way this time. Where may I meet you?"

He looked at her with narrowed eyes. "Are you married?"

"No, I am not. Are you?"

"Definitely not." With that remark, she heard the implication that he wasn't planning to marry anytime soon.

"Well?" she asked, letting him know that she'd stated her position and that the next move was his.

"I acquiesce to your wishes." However, both his faint smile and his demeanor told her that acquiescing was not a thing with which he'd had much familiarity. "Meet me at Le Cheval Blanc. Seven o'clock. I do hope you will extend me the courtesy of seeing you safely home."

She let a quick grin suffice for an answer. "See you tomorrow evening at seven."

He was punctual, as she knew he would be, and he rose and went to greet her as she followed the maître d' to his table. He thanked the maître d' and tipped him, then leaned down and brushed her cheek with his lips. "I was afraid you wouldn't come."

"I try to keep my word. I've always liked this restaurant. It's one of the most elegant in town. Thanks for choosing it." She wondered why he seemed crestfallen and asked him, "Did I say something wrong?"

"No. I suppose I'm disappointed that you know the place well. I had hoped to give you a unique experience, but I imagine a woman like you has been treated to everything special that Baltimore has to offer."

She chose not to answer. She hadn't seen it all, but that wasn't his business. She soon decided that he was most comfortable talking about himself, his ideas and his accomplishments, and she let him do that. She didn't find him offensive, but he didn't appeal to her, so she decided to settle for a pleasant evening with him, and whenever he made a joke, she laughed.

The evening passed pleasantly enough, and when they stood in front of her apartment door, her one thought was of gratitude that Mike, her favorite doorman, was not on duty. "You're pleasant to be with, and I would like to spend a lot of time with you. Did I make any headway with you?" Oscar asked her. "I have a sense that, while I didn't strike out, I haven't gotten to first base. I won't ask if there's someone else. Just tell me if he's special to you."

How was she to answer that? "There is someone, and he is very special."

He grasped her hand, looked at her ring finger and shook his head as if perplexed. "I hope he knows what a lucky man he is. If I were special to you, I'd do something about it."

"Thank you, and thank you for a very lovely evening."

He gazed down at her until she had to struggle not to fidget. "Forgive me. That was rude, but you're so beautiful. Goodbye."

She went inside and closed her apartment door. Had she gone out with Oscar Rankin because of her father's nagging? If so, her libido, or whatever caused her to be attracted to men, proved more reliable than filial regard for her father's wishes. But why couldn't she like him? It wasn't as if he were like Lawrence Parker. She checked her phone messages, didn't have one from Drake, flipped off the machine and got ready for bed.

"There're other men, and I am going to be attracted to at least one of them," she said aloud. "Drake Harrington is not the only man I can like." Then, in her mind's eye, she could see him leaning against the doorjamb of her front door, his height of six feet, four inches nearly reaching the top of the door frame. She pictured him relaxed and lithe, his long-lashed dark brown eyes glittering with some pleasant thought and a smile on his incredibly handsome face. And every time he laughed, really laughed, the look of him reduced her to putty. Mesmerized.

Maybe it wasn't intended that such a man should give himself to one woman. "He's trouble," Rhoda had said to her the last time they lunched together. "Every woman who sees him will be after him." However, Drake seemed to have no grandiose notions about himself. And although Rhoda swore that Drake was a stud, that he'd go after any woman who showed an interest in him, she knew better.

"I'm going to join the Urban League, the NAACP, and I'm going on the next Million Man March," she said aloud, and then laughed at herself, for she knew she wouldn't do any of that. She crawled into bed and fought for sleep.

Several mornings after that, Drake entered the construction site of the Josh Harrington–Fentress Sparkman Memorial Houses in Frederick, Maryland, that honored his late father and uncle. As the project's engineer, he planned to check the pipes that had been installed up to the first floor, and arrived early so as to complete the inspection before noon that day. A series of strange noises got his attention, and he followed the sounds to an area where boards were measured and cut.

"What the devil are you doing in here?" he asked a small boy who held pieces of wood that should have been too heavy for him to carry.

The child stood before him clutching the boards, his body shaking. "I…uh. You're not going to put me in jail, are you?"

"This is a hard-hat area. Something could fall on you and kill you. What's your name?"

"Pete. Pete Jergens. Are you going to call the police?"

"No. How old are you?" He noticed that the boy still held the pieces of wood close to his body. "Well?"

"I'm nine, sir."

Hmm. Good manners. Drake took the boy by the arm and walked with him out to the van that bore the legend Harrington, Inc.: Builders, Architects and Engineers. "Get in here. You and I are going to talk."

"But can I go home first, sir? My mom will be worried about me, and I have to be at school by eight-thirty."

"What are you going to do with that wood?"

The boy held his head down as if ashamed. "Cook breakfast, sir."

He stared at the child. "With wood? You have a kitchen stove that burns wood?"

"No, sir. We have a gas stove, but the gas was turned off, so we have to cook in the fireplace."

His whistle split the air. "Where's your father?"

"My dad's in jail. A man called him the n-word, and he beat him up so bad the man had to go to the hospital."

"How many sisters and brothers do you have?"

"Four. I'm the oldest. Can I go now, sir? Please. I'll be late for school."

"I'll drive you home. Where do you live?"

Drake drove the three and a half blocks thanking God that he didn't grow up in an environment where broken glass littered the streets, cars had to skirt automobile tires, boarded-up houses lined every block and the stench of refuse offended one's nose. He parked the truck, locked it and walked with Pete to the house.

"What are you going to do?" the boy asked him.

"I'm going to get that gas stove turned on." He imagined that the children were nearly frozen. "Call your mother to the door."

"Mom. Mom, can you come here? My new friend wants to see you." He realized the boy referred to him as a friend so as not to alarm his mother.

Stella Jergens, a tiny woman little more than five feet and one inch tall, appeared at the door and gazed up at him. "Please don't punish him for stealing the boards. If we didn't have them, we would freeze, and I couldn't cook."

"Don't worry about that. I don't countenance stealing. But he was trying to help you." He looked at the boy. "Next time you have a problem like this one, go to the social-service center on Franklin Street."

After getting information on the name and location of the utilities company, he gave the woman three twenty-dollar bills and drove Pete to school. "Get some milk and a sandwich," he said, offering the boy a five-dollar bill, "because you didn't have any breakfast."

"Thanks," the boy said, "but I can get something to eat at school. What's your name, sir?"

"Harrington. Drake Harrington. Those are my buildings you've been stealing from. Tell your mother I'll be by your house around five."

"Thank you, sir. I think my mom is happy now. See you later."

He drove directly to the utilities company, ordered the gas restored and paid the gas and electric bills for the next six months. Then he went to a local market and purchased coal and firewood for the fireplace, since he didn't know whether the Jergens family had another source of heat. On his way home, he stopped by their house to find out whether the gas had been turned on, discovered that it had been and asked Stella Jergens if she needed anything for her children.

"Thank you, Mr. Harrington, but we're warm now. I can cook, and the money you gave me will last awhile." She blinked back a tear. "I can't work because I can't leave the little ones alone. I've been praying so hard. God will bless you."

"Thank you, ma'am, but I'm already blessed." And he knew he was, because he'd never been hungry in his life.

Pete ran to him. "Thanks, Mr. Harrington. I'm real glad you caught me this morning. I don't like to steal, but—"

He patted the boy's shoulder. "But never do it. There's always a better way."

"Yes, sir. Can I come by the place and see you sometime? I bet you can help me with my arithmetic. I like it, but I don't have time to study. I have to help my mom."

"I'm not always there, but if it gets rough, you may call me." He gave the boy his cell-phone number. "Never mind the money. You may call collect. Be a good boy."

"Yes, sir. Absolutely, sir."

He drove home glad that it was he and not his foreman who caught the boy. Jack would have called the police immediately. The man had no compassion for those less fortunate. And he wondered what miracles Stella Jergens would work in order to make sixty dollars feed six people "awhile."

"It's just you and me tonight," Henry said to Drake when he got home. "Tara's in the school play, so Tel took them out for dinner before the performance."

"Yeah? In that case, don't cook. Let's you and me drive into Frederick and eat at Mealey's or some place like that. No dishes to put in the dishwasher and no pots and pans to scrub. What do you say?"

Henry removed his apron and threw it across a kitchen chair. "I never knock me self out doing nothing I don't have to do. Be ready in half an hour."

As a child, Drake had followed Henry from room to room in that big house, occasionally panicking when he couldn't find him, and after his father's death, Henry became even more precious to him. As the Jaguar sped along Route 15 in the direction of Frederick, he imagined that he would never be the same if the time came when Henry wasn't there for him to understand him, jostle and needle him, and to offer his quaint form of love...

"Have you decided you're not having anything else to do with Pamela?"

"No. Why do you ask?"

"The way Alexis was talking, I figured you was planning to self-destruct. I don't waste me breath giving a man advice about a woman, 'cause he ain't gonna take it no way. But whatever it is you're after, you're gonna get it, 'cause you don't mind hard work and you treat people right. Just be sure to get your taste of heaven while you're conquering the world. Otherwise, heaven ain't gonna be there. Or if it is, you'll either be too old, too worldly, too set in your ways, or all of those to appreciate it when you get it—that is, if you can let yourself accept it.

"And mark my word, caring for babies and toddlers when you're fifty years old can't be no fun. Tell me something, son. Did she say she'd wait while you discover yerself?"

"Stop being facetious, Henry. She didn't promise to wait. And before you ask, I don't like it, but she's a grown woman and she doesn't need my permission to date other men."

"And if she got any sense, that's just what she'll do."

"Alexis said something like that, but I have to act on the basis of my feelings and my judgment. All of you wish me well, but I'm the one who has to live this life."

"I just hope when you come to yer senses, you won't find out that someone else is sleeping in that bed. Mr. Josh used to say Russ was hardheaded, and that you were the easiest of his boys to raise. He didn't seem to know that Russ only insisted on getting and doing what he knew he was entitled to. You were just as determined—only you smiled, conned, cajoled and charmed him for whatever you wanted, and yer daddy never realized it. But I was on to you."

He felt a grin spreading over his face. "I know. You wouldn't let me get away with a thing, and I am grateful to you for that. Fortunately or not, I've become as cut-and-dried as Russ is."

"No-nonsense is what you mean," Henry said. "Look. There's the old church where me and me Sarah took our vows, God rest her soul. The Quinn Chapel A. M. E. Church dates back to the late 1700s. It's a landmark, and the local African-Americans are real proud of it. Every time I pass her, I think about that day way back then. You never saw the sun shine like that, and me Sarah looked so nice in her white lace dress and hat. Gives me the shivers thinking about it."

"I can imagine. She was one sweet woman, the only person who ever sang me a lullaby. My mother didn't have the maternal instinct of a flea."

"Don't bother to think about that. Does Pamela want children?"

"She does, and that's the problem. She wants to start on that now."

"Yeah, and she'd better. Me and me Sarah waited too long. She was five years older than me, and she just couldn't go full-term. If we stay on this topic, we'll be drinking our dinner 'stead of eating it though. Fortunately, neither of us drinks enough for the alcohol to make a difference."

"One thing," Drake said, "and then I want to drop this. Why does everybody want me to marry Pamela?"

"I don't know about the rest, but when I've seen you with her, you behaved like a satisfied man. Besides, if I was yer age right now, I'd give you a run for yer money with that girl. You'd think I was Seabiscuit coming down the homestretch. She's beautiful, kind, soft and got a real good head on her shoulders. And she can sing!"

They spent an amiable evening together, dining gourmet-style and reminiscing about their lives together, causing Drake to reflect more than once that Henry had been a lifesaver to him when his father died. Going over the joys and tragedies that they had experienced together reinforced his love for home and family.

"Henry has a subtle way of twisting my arm," Drake said to himself after telling Henry good-night and heading to his room. He kicked off his shoes, stretched out on his bed and did the only thing he wanted to do. He telephoned Pamela, and it seemed as if the phone rang a thousand times before she answered, though he heard only four rings.

"Hello?"

"Hello. This is Drake. I was beginning to think I'd primed myself to hear your voice to no avail. How are you?"

"I'm all right. I was considering washing my hair. Then I thought I'd better start the research for a program I'm doing mid-July. Then I thought, 'I'm going to play my record and read. I don't feel like working.'"

"Telford and his family were out this evening, so Henry and I had a really nice dinner in Frederick. We're just getting back."

"Why did you call, Drake?"

He hadn't expected the question, but somehow it didn't surprise him. "I miss you, and I needed some contact with you. That's why."

"All right. Let's talk awhile. I'm going to California on Monday for an industry conference, and I'm nervous about it because my producer is sending me in his stead. He said I don't need a briefing."

"Are you going to let him get away with that?"

"I don't know. Men are always getting away with things."

He sat up on the bed and rested his back against the headboard. "What men are you talking about? I don't remember your letting me get away with anything...well, not much, anyway."

"No? What do you call kissing the sense out of me and three hours later as much as saying that if you didn't see me again, too bad?"

"I didn't say that. Woman, I will not allow you to misrepresent me. Anyhow, you're not bad at that kissing business yourself."

"What you did was foul play," she told him.

"No such thing, lady. I was not playing. I was never more serious in my life. You're the criminal. I still have that gaping hole you left in me."

"Really? Well, for heaven's sake, come here, and I'll do my best to plug it up."

"Are you a gambler? Don't you know I can get to Baltimore in forty minutes?"

"Normally I don't gamble, but when I do, it's for high stakes. If you feel like taking a forty-minute ride, it'll take me about that long to make cookies and coffee."

He looked at his watch. Nine thirty-five. "See you at ten-fifteen."

He hung up, slipped on his shoes and walked over to Henry's cottage. "I'm going to Baltimore, but I'll be back tonight."

Henry put his hands on his hips and stared at Drake as if he didn't believe what he heard. "Humph. Seems to me if you're smart enough to go, you ought to have sense enough to stay all night."

He winked at Henry, knelt down and patted Henry's puppy, a golden retriever, on the head. "When I do that, you'll know something serious is going on."

"Looks to me like it's serious now, 'cause when you left

me, you weren't going anyplace but upstairs to bed. Don't drive too fast."

"'Course not. See you."

He went inside, brushed his teeth, checked his face for evidence of a beard, got into his Jaguar and headed for Baltimore.

She met him at the door in an orange-colored silk jumpsuit that fit her body as if it had been made on her.

Okay, he said to himself. *She's declared war, but I'm a pretty good shot myself.*

"Hi," he said to her. "You look like moonlight shining over a peaceful lake. You take my breath away."

A wide smile welcomed him. "Come on in, and be careful what you say, because I intend to hold everything you say and do tonight against you."

He pushed back the strand of hair that fell over his left eye, giving him what Henry called the look of a rascal. "In that case, I can't win. But I can't lose what I don't have, either. Hell, Pamela, I really have missed you."

"Me, too. And if you're the gentleman you claim to be, you'll make amends."

"I'm here, aren't I? If you don't call that making amends, I needn't even start trying." She looked so warm and sexy in that getup that he… "I… Pamela, put your arms around me. I need to hold you."

"If you do what you did to me the last time, I'll throw that pot of coffee at you."

"Would you hurt me?" He didn't know how much he meant that question until he heard himself whisper it. "Would you?"

"No. Oh, no." Her arms opened and he walked into them. The feel of her soft, warm body and the scent of her faint perfume teased him, stirring his libido and awakening something in him that he wanted to remain dormant. She was on tiptoes now, and her hand at his nape guided his mouth to her waiting lips. His senses seemed to reel, and he plowed into her, demanding, asking and then—with his lips, arms, hands and his whole body—begging her to possess him, to love him. His hands roamed her back, arms and hips, and she held him, giving all he asked for, heating him until he thought the inferno inside of him would explode like a volcano.

"Pamela," he moaned. "What have you done to me?" He crushed her to him, kissing her hair, face, ears and neck. "I want to make love with you, but if I do, that will be the end of it."

She stepped back from him. "Why?"

"I can have protected sex with a woman I barely know, and it won't mean anything beyond physical relief, but with you it would be life changing."

"And you don't want your life changed."

He followed her into the kitchen, took the tray and carried it into the living room.

"A few weeks ago, I was certain I didn't. Now, I'm less sure. I do know that I'm here right now because I needed what you just gave me, and I needed it with you."

She poured the coffee. "You have needs. Right? So do I. The problem is that I can't conceive of being intimate with a man I don't care deeply for. But I think I should set that old-fashioned attitude aside. Who says a single woman can't have a baby?"

He nearly choked on the cookie. "A child has a right to have the love and guidance of its father, as well as its mother."

"Agreed. In the best of all possible worlds, it would be that way every time, but honey, this world doesn't come anywhere near that. We get what we're lucky enough to find. I've been considering adopting a child."

"Tell me you're not serious."

"I wouldn't lie, Drake. Tell me that you are not going to disappear from my life for another three weeks, because if you do that I won't welcome you again." She laughed. "Can you imagine my father asking me when you were planning to speak with him? I told him it was unlikely that you ever would." She stood. "When you kiss me good-night, do a good job of it, because it will probably be our last time."

He put the cup on the coffee table and stood. "I care far too much for you to trivialize it in any way. I can't say I won't see you again, unless you forbid it. Each time I'm with you, I know you better, what I see pleases me and I need you more. Will you wait for six months?"

"And then you decide you were right all along? As much as you mean to me, I won't promise you that."

Like a nail moving toward a magnet, he reached for her, folded her body to his and kissed her until he nearly lost his breath. "Good night."

"Goodbye," she said.

He turned around and looked at her. "Not this time, sweetheart, and maybe never."

Chapter 4

"Well, I asked for it," Pamela said to herself as she headed for work that Monday morning. "I as much as told him that whatever he wanted was here for him, if he'd come and get it." She parked in the WRLR basement garage and took the elevator to the ninth floor.

"Did you have a good weekend?" she asked Rhoda as she passed her assistant's desk.

"Not particularly. I'm thirty-five, you know, and believe me, the pickings are slim and getting slimmer every year."

She didn't respond. It amazed her that an educated, intelligent and competent woman's social conversation always centered on men or—as in this case—the lack of a man in her life. She wanted to tell Rhoda to make both her despair and her search less obvious.

"I'm not going to allow myself to become a desperate man-hunter," Pamela said aloud. She opened her office door and looked around. "No siree. I'm somebody even when

I'm lonely." Remembering Drake's advice, she phoned Jack Hanson, her producer.

"I see my travel orders and ticket authorization, but I don't see any instructions as to what I'm to do at this meeting. I can't go all the way to Oakland, California, just to listen to some guys sit around a long table and talk. What's my role?"

"WRLR has produced two special programs for the network, programs that made money for the network. A lot of money. We want to produce more of them, especially human-interest and historical subjects. We don't want to do sitcoms, and none of that reality stuff. I'm thoroughly sick of both. Got it?"

"Okay, but weren't you planning to tell me this? Do I need to divulge the content of the special I'm doing?"

"Hell, no, and don't let any of those guys force you to do it. They'll try to trick you into spilling your guts. Tell 'em I forbade you to mention it."

The door opened and Rhoda walked in. "Here're those two reports you wanted. I don't mind telling you I spent the weekend on it. By the way, is that hunk going with you? I sin just thinking about that guy."

Pamela stopped writing and looked up at her assistant, not a little annoyed that the woman confessed to having the hots for Drake. "Rhoda, if WRLR sent you on a business trip, would you use the occasion to have a romantic tryst, or would you behave professionally and keep your romance separate from your work?"

Rhoda didn't appear the least embarrassed. "You sure do know how to draw blood. If you need anything else before you leave, just buzz me."

Pamela thanked Rhoda, but the woman's fixation—as it were—on Drake, and her eagerness to let her know it didn't sit well with Pamela. She had a feeling of apprehension about it. *To be forewarned is to be forearmed, and this one definitely bears watching.*

She reached Oakland at three o'clock in the afternoon, thanks to the three-hour time difference, checked in, stepped into her room and dropped her hand luggage on the floor, barely missing her toes. She stood just inside the door gaping at the huge red balloon on which was painted, "You light up my life," and at the vase of red rosebuds beside it. She wanted to scream, thinking that Lawrence sent them and that he'd begun harassing her again.

Yet the strong handwriting on the card beside the vase was unlike Lawrence's tiny scribbling. She tore open the card and sat down on the bed, unable to believe her eyes.

Have a wonderful time. Wish I was there with you.
Kisses, Drake

More annoyed than pleased, she took her cell phone out of her briefcase and called Drake on his cell number.

"When did you get in?" he asked by way of a greeting, having recognized her number on his cell phone's caller ID.

"This minute. You called my office to—"

He interrupted. "Yeah. When I identified myself, your secretary seemed reluctant to tell me where you went, but another woman took the phone, and not only did she give me your hotel and the phone number there, but hoped I'd have a good time. I told her I only wanted to send you some flowers, but she preferred not to believe me."

"That was Rhoda, my assistant. Apart from her work, her mind doesn't entertain anything that isn't related to sex."

"I'm not going to touch that one. Do you like the balloon?"

The mellifluous beauty of his voice made her heart do flip-flops, and she closed her eyes, imagining that he was there beside her. "I admit it was a pleasant surprise... that is, after I realized it wasn't Lawrence Parker who sent them. The flowers are beautiful, and the note... Well, it's interesting to say the least."

"What do you mean by that?" he asked in a voice that came across as a growl.

"You don't have to be a brain surgeon to figure it out. You said you wished you were here, but if you were, you'd probably register at a different hotel on the chance that if you stayed in this one, you might find my room while sleepwalking."

"I think I've just been insulted," he said, and in her mind's eye, she could see a boyish expression on his suddenly innocent-looking face.

"Didn't mean to," she said airily, because she hated to lie. "You're as perplexing to me as I am to myself. From the inscriptions on this balloon, one would think I'm important to you."

"If one had any sense at all," he shot back, "one would know it." He didn't soften his words with a humorous tone.

"Actions speak louder than words," she countered.

"I rest my case. When are you coming back?"

"I get in at ten-twenty on Wednesday night."

"Can we have lunch Thursday?"

She wanted to see him as much as he wanted to see her. But as long as she didn't know where she stood with him, she wasn't going to make it easy for him. "My boss might want to have a working lunch." That was true, but she didn't have to acquiesce.

"Your lunchtime is your own," he said, his voice laced with impatience. "Tell him you have an engagement that you can't break. I'll be at your office at twelve-thirty sharp."

She stared at the phone. This man could be bossy, and there was nothing uncertain about his tone of voice. "Why do you want to see me, Drake?"

"You want the unvarnished truth?"

She sat forward, wondering at the question. Uncertain. *If I say yes, he'll tell it just like it is.* And she didn't think she could bear it if he said his interest in her was only concupiscent. But if it was only sexual, wouldn't he have spent the night with her the last time they were together?

"What's the matter, Pamela? Scared of the truth?"

"Just because I don't welcome it with open arms doesn't mean I'm scared of it."

"What, then?"

"Drake, among the men I've known, you are an enigma. You want me, but you make no attempt to get what you want. I know several women who'd tell me I'm lying if I told them that."

"Not because they would know what they're talking about. I've told you that I do not play with women. I've been misunderstood at times when I haven't done a thing, so I'm careful. What about the unvarnished truth? You don't want to hear it?"

What she didn't want was the experience of having her emotions shattered. "I…uh… Tell me another time. Okay?" The silence seemed interminable. "Are you still there?" she asked him.

"Of course I'm here. Do we have a date for lunch Thursday?"

"I'd rather call you around nine Thursday morning and let you know."

"All right, but I'm not going to Baltimore except to see you. How about a kiss?"

She made the sound of a kiss and nearly dropped the phone when he did the same.

"See you," he said, and hung up before she could respond.

"Keep it up," she said, still staring at the phone, "and you'll help me make up your mind for you."

If he would talk with her about his dreams, his goals, he would understand that she wouldn't do anything to hinder him.

She opened her briefcase and looked for her notes on their program plans. *I can't deal with my relationship with Drake now. I have to take a victory for WRLR with me when I leave here. A child could figure out why Jack sent me in his stead. He was afraid of failing.*

During the conference, she spent almost as much time negotiating the placement of Mark Scott's hands as she did securing a coup for WRLR. And each time she moved her seat, Scott maneuvered to a seat beside her.

"If you don't keep your hands off me," she told the WLTN anchorman, "I'll demand that you do so loud enough for every person in this room to hear me. Or maybe you'd like this coffee in your face."

His face took on a sultry expression. "A pretty girl like you wouldn't do a thing like that," he said as he eased his hand toward her knee.

For an answer, she picked up the cup of hot coffee and glared at him. "Just try me. I'm not a girl—I'm a woman. If you fool with me, Mr. Scott, I'll make you case-study number one in our national report on sexual harassment of women."

His face became ashen, and he put both hands on the table and busied himself taking notes. Laughter spilled out of her, and when he flinched, she laughed harder. Her gaze took in the gold band on the third finger of his left hand, and she stopped laughing.

"I'd hate to work with a married man who found pleasure in groping strange women. You need help," she said, looking directly into his eyes and assuring herself that he wouldn't bother her anymore.

She didn't telephone Drake on Thursday morning as he'd asked, because Jack Hanson, her producer, pounced on her for a report as soon as she entered the office and spent the entire morning with her discussing the programs they would create for the network.

"You did a fine job, Langford. That gang would never have agreed to let WRLR do this if I'd gone, but they didn't know how to get around you. Well done. I'll see that you get a bonus."

She stared at him. "I wouldn't turn down a raise, Jack."

He inclined his head to one side and stared back at her. "I imagine you wouldn't, but you just got a raise last month. If I recommend another one now, my boss will think I've got something going with you. You know how tightfisted he is. Six months from now would be a better time."

"And you'll recommend it then?"

"You have my word on it."

Pamela hadn't promised to have lunch with Drake, but it distressed her that she hadn't been free to telephone him as she'd promised. She had not dared tell Jack to excuse her while she made a personal phone call, because he considered attention to any personal matter while at work unprofessional behavior. She called Drake's cell-phone number as soon as she was alone in her office.

"I'm sure you're going to tell me why you didn't call me

this morning," he said, having recognized her number on his caller ID. "What happened?"

She told him and added, "As a professional yourself, you'll appreciate my position."

"I also appreciate it as a person of normal intelligence. You're getting a bonus? You should have asked for a raise. That kind of success is supposed to send you up the corporate ladder."

"I asked for one, but he reminded me that I just got a raise last month. He said I'll get another one in six months."

"And hold him to it."

"Trust me. I will. I'm sorry I couldn't make our lunch."

"So am I. It was my only chance to be free this week. I promised my brothers we'd work out a tentative schedule for building that shopping mall in Accra. It means we have to coordinate our work on the three projects in Maryland and the one in Barbados with work in Ghana, and it won't be easy. Also, we have to factor in Russ's marriage and his honeymoon time, so it will take us a few days to work this out. I'll have to go to Frederick from time to time because I'm not satisfied with my foreman and the project has advanced so far that I'd rather not change."

"Okay. Keep your cell phone charged."

"I will, and you do the same. I'll be in touch."

She did her best to hide the disappointment that she felt. "Me, too." She needed to feel close to him, to know that he cared and cared deeply for her. She had no doubt that he wanted her, but that didn't impress her; so did other men. Until he opened his mouth and told her he cared for her, she intended to keep on looking. She packed her briefcase, cleared her desk, locked it and headed for the elevator.

"Haven't seen you around much lately."

She knew before she spun around that the words came from Lawrence Parker's mouth. No other man at WRLR talked to her while walking behind her, and she wished he'd stop it.

"Hello, Lawrence." She didn't ask how he was, because she didn't care to know.

"I just heard that you're bucking for Jack's job."

The elevator door opened, and she stepped inside. "You're making that up on the spot. Remember, I'm on to you, and if you spread that rumor, I will report you. Lawrence, it would be a good and useful thing if you would grow up."

She stepped off the elevator on the first floor to make sure Lawrence didn't follow her to the basement, walked down the stairs to the garage, stopped and listened for footsteps. Hearing none, she started for her car.

"Ooh!" she yelled, and swung around when she heard someone running toward her.

"Why didn't you take the elevator all the way down here? Did you think I didn't know why you got off at the first floor?" He towered over her, his dark face blotched with the anger that made him shake. "You're at my mercy, so you'd better be nice to me."

She hadn't thought she would need the whistle she always carried, and neither her nail file nor her manicure scissors was handy. She decided to find out how much trouble she faced and asked him to release her arm.

"When and if I get ready," he said, and she wondered if he had considered that his actions would cause him to be fired from WRLR.

"You had Raynor switch me to morning news, that reporters' graveyard, didn't you?" She gaped at him, unsure of his move or what hers should be. "Didn't you?" he repeated, his face a mass of hatred. "You think you're better than everybody else, don't you? I wonder if Mr. Got-It-All will want you after I—"

She turned to her side, reared back as far as his grip on

her wrist would allow and aimed her right foot for his groin, a perfect blow from her size-ten pointed-toe shoe. Thank God she'd worn a pantsuit that morning.

His exclamation was loud and fierce as he bent forward in pain, and she raced for the stairs, deeming a wait at the elevator too risky. At the first floor, she ran to the guard, told him what happened and demanded that he call the police. They arrived immediately and found Lawrence writhing in pain on the concrete floor.

"What's this all about?" Raynor asked, having responded to the guard's call.

No longer in danger, her teeth chattered and both of her hands shook as she tried without success to articulate to her boss Lawrence's transgression. The two policemen brought him upstairs handcuffed and on a stretcher.

"He can't walk," one officer said, "and from the looks of things, it may be a while before he does. If you want to press charges, you'll have to come down to the precinct. We're taking him to Maryland General Hospital, and he'll be under guard."

"You're out of danger now, so take a deep breath and tell me exactly what happened. Everything," Raynor said.

She told him and added, "I've never seen such hatred on a person's face. He really intended to hurt me."

"I've suspected for some time that Lawrence was psychotic. In any case, his tenure at WRLR is over."

She stared at him. Aghast. "You're going to *fire* him?"

"I'd prefer that, but if I let him go, he'll be more of a menace to you than ever. So I'm transferring him to our local station in Honolulu, and I intend to let him know that he can be grateful."

"Thanks. I'm stunned."

"You shouldn't be. A man who pretends to be conservative yet buys himself a yellow Cadillac bears watching."

"I suppose you're ri…" Something clicked in her head. "What did you say? Lawrence drives a yellow Cadillac?"

"Why, yes. Why?"

She shook her head from side to side. "Well, I'll be doggoned."

She didn't tell Raynor that Lawrence had slashed her front tires to prevent her from keeping a dinner date. Why hadn't she guessed the identity of the culprit? Men in Lawrence's position didn't tag along hangdog fashion behind a woman, pestering her with unwanted attention.

However, as much as Lawrence annoyed her, she didn't wish him harm, and she hoped he would receive the treatment that he needed. Still, she couldn't help being grateful to Raynor for sending Lawrence as far away from her as his resources would allow. She went back to the garage for her car, and as she passed the yellow Cadillac, she battled a sense of unease. *What if Lawrence refused the transfer and resigned?*

At home that evening, she dallied around her apartment, unable to focus on any one thing. Finally, at about nine o'clock, she capitulated to her feelings and her need and telephoned Drake.

"Excuse me," Drake said to his brothers, interrupting their conference on the feasibility of undertaking a project in Ghana thousands of miles away on the west coast of Africa. He left the den and went into the hallway to answer his cell phone, aware that Pamela was the caller.

"How are you, Pamela?" he said, battling the something inside of him that wanted to address her differently. More intimately.

"I'm here," she said, "and grateful for it."

He bounded up the stairs. "Wait a minute until I get into

my room." Inside, he closed the door and settled himself in his desk chair. "Is everything all right with you now?"

"Mostly."

He jerked forward. "Where are you, and what's the matter?"

"I'm home."

He listened to her incredible story about a man he had known since his college days whom he had regarded as a normal person. "How badly did you hurt him?"

"I don't know, but when I called the hospital a while ago, a policeman said he was in shock, still unable to walk and under police guard."

Drake felt no sympathy for the man and didn't try to muster any. Psychotic or not, he was a criminal and could have ruined Pamela's life if, indeed, he hadn't taken it. "So he's the person who slashed your tires. The man *must* be sick. I imagine you're feeling pretty shaky."

"I am, but it will pass. Well. I just wanted to touch base."

He listened for what she didn't say and heard her doing what they so often did when talking with each other, shadowboxing around the truth, afraid to reveal their feelings. She, waiting for him to lead the way and he, equivocating about the course he would take. She had called him because she hurt, although she wasn't going to admit it. And he had to let her know that he was there for her.

"When you called, I was in the den with Telford and Russ and we were deciding on our work program for the next three years, and that's important for our company's growth. But if you need me, I'll be there in an hour."

"Thank you." He thought he heard relief in her voice. "Of course, I want to be with you, but I guess what I really needed was to know that you're there for me. You haven't said or done anything to suggest to me that you ought to be, but I needed it all the same. Go back to work. I'll be fine."

"Are you sure?"

"Yes. I'm positive. Good night."

He told her good-night, covered his face with his hands and lowered his head. *We're a pair of the worst hypocrites,* he thought. *I wonder what would happen if we leveled with each other.* He treaded down the stairs, moving slowly, his mind filled with images of Pamela writhing beneath him in ecstasy.

"You boys going to be in there all night?" Henry asked Drake as he approached the den. "Once a year, I want to watch television, and you pick that time to sit around talking."

He laid a hand on Henry's shoulder, frail and bony to the touch, though he was only fifty-eight years old. "Henry, each one of us has tried to buy you a television set, and to each one of us you said you didn't like watching TV. Now you're complaining."

"I don't like sitting alone staring at a bunch of nuts jumping around in front of a camera doing foolish things, but Willie Nelson's gonna be on in a few minutes, and Buddy Guy is his guest. My two favorites."

"All right. We can talk someplace else." He walked into the den. "Henry wants to watch Buddy Guy and Willie Nelson. Let's go into the living room."

"Better still," Telford said, "let's quit for the night." He looked at Henry. "Make yourself comfortable."

Henry sat down, as comfortable in Harrington House as in his own cottage that Telford and his brothers built for him about fifty yards beyond the south side of their own home, a modern home that they deeded to him so that he could call it his own.

"Be comfortable," Henry repeated after Telford. "That's just what I was planning to do. Any cold tonic water in that little refrigerator over there?" He pointed to the bar.

A grin spread over Russ's face as he sauntered over to the bar for a glass, poured Henry a drink of cold tonic water and took it to him. "You're a piece of work, Henry, but I wouldn't exchange you for your weight in gold bullion."

"Glad to know that," Henry retorted, took a sip of tonic water and added, "I'd ask even more than that for you."

The four men laughed in a moment of shared love and camaraderie.

This is almost the best of all possible worlds, Drake thought. *Almost.*

The next morning, he left early for Frederick, changed clothes in the trailer at the Harrington-Sparkman Memorial Houses site and called the plasterers together for instructions. That done, he began checking the first-floor window sashes.

"A little boy out there to see you, Drake," one of the workers told him.

He left the construction area and glanced up and down the street until he saw Pete standing beside a car almost in front of him.

"Hello, Pete. Why aren't you in school?" He didn't much like to greet people with "hi" unless he was on intimate terms with them, and rarely used it even with the members of his family.

Pete seemed unsure of himself, so Drake hunkered in front of him in an effort to ease the boy's discomfort. "My mom had to take my baby brother to the clinic this morning, so I had to stay with my sisters. I'm going to school as soon as she gets back. She'll write me an excuse."

It hadn't occurred to him that children as young as

Pete had to assume adult roles, though he supposed he'd seen evidence of it many times and the fact simply hadn't registered.

"How's your math? Did you complete those tests in your exercise book?"

"Yes, sir, and I got an A. Mr. Harrington, do you think I could work for you sometime? Maybe after school today? I won't charge much."

Drake stood and looked down at the child, whose face bore an expression that was at once plaintive and hopeful. "You and I are going to talk. What did you eat for dinner last night?"

The boy hung his head. "I'm not hungry, sir."

He placed his right hand gently on Pete's thin shoulder. "Do you think anybody else in your family might be hungry?"

Pete didn't look at him, so he had his answer. He had learned that the boy preferred not to lie. "Maybe, sir."

Just as he had thought. "You run along home, because you're supposed to be looking after your sisters. I'll be around there in half an hour." He called Jack, his foreman, on his cell phone. "I'll be off the site for about an hour."

He felt in his back pocket for his billfold, counted the bills he found there, got into the Harrington van and drove to the supermarket. On an impulse, he paid for his purchases with a credit card, for he suspected he'd need the cash, and arrived at the Jergenses' home simultaneously with Stella Jergens. Ignoring both her surprise and her expression of indebtedness, he followed her to the kitchen where they unpacked his purchases. He gave her all the money he had except forty dollars. He would have given her that, but he was a good distance from home and needed a cushion in case of an emergency.

"If you need money for medicine, send Pete over to get

me or tell him to call me on my cell phone. He has the number," he told Stella.

Her eyes clouded, and he tried not to see her tears, for it was not his place to comfort her. "I didn't have a dime. I walked to the clinic and back. We had insurance, but it lapsed, because I couldn't keep it up. I don't question your kindness, Mr. Harrington, because I prayed hard, and I know God sent you to us. Social Services is still working on our case…" Her voice drifted off. Then she looked directly at him and said, "*Thanks* is a piddling word, but it's the only one I have. God bless you."

He put his hands into his trouser pockets because they seemed as useless as he was helpless. "I've been blessed all my life, Mrs. Jergens, but until now, I had no idea how much." His glance caught Pete gazing up at him, and he patted the boy's shoulder.

"You promised to call me, Pete, and I'm counting on you to do that if you have a problem again."

"I went to see you this morning, sir."

He nodded, understanding that the child didn't want to appear to beg. "Yes, and I'm glad you did."

He told them goodbye and went back to work, but his thoughts remained with the family. He suspected that Stella Jergens's husband was a good man—though perhaps with a short temper—because his children were well-mannered and respectful.

"I hope I'm fortunate enough to have a son like Pete."

At the end of his workday, after washing up and changing his clothes, he hesitated as to his next move. He had promised his brothers that the three of them could continue discussing their work program that evening, but his mind directed him to Baltimore and Pamela.

He telephoned her. "I need to head home, because I promised Telford and Russ that I would, but I also need to

see you for at least a few minutes. I don't think I should go
to your place."

Her voice—so soft, so warm and so feminine—never
failed to fan the fires of his desire, and he waited impatiently
to hear it.

"I can wait for you here at the office, and we can go down
the street to Jugs and Jars and have tea or something."

Tea. Imagine a thirty-one-year-old man steps out of a
hard-hat construction area and rushes to meet a woman in
order to sit somewhere and sip tea. *I hope I'm dreaming.*
To her he said, "Great. I'll see you in thirty-five or forty
minutes."

He liked seeing her when they hadn't planned it in
advance, when she was her everyday normal self, without
props. Makeup imperfect, if not faded away, and hair
looking as if her fingers had plowed through it all day. To
him, she was most beautiful at those times. Natural and
sweetly feminine.

As he neared WRLR, his heartbeat accelerated as he
anticipated the moment when she would see him and a
smile would light up her face, reminding him of the night
sky when the moon suddenly appears from behind the
clouds.

"Come in." Her voice, low, soft and sultry, made him
immediately aware of his masculinity, and he realized that
her voice always affected him that way. To his surprise, she
stood, embraced him and kissed his cheek. "I know you
can't stay with me long, but I'm so glad you came."

"So am I," he said and knew that he meant it. Her lips
on his cheek drove home to him his reason for being there.
He had needed to hold her, to know that she had overcome
her angst from her encounter with Lawrence Parker. *Admit
it, man. You needed to protect her.*

"What is it?" she asked, making him aware that his face mirrored his perplexity at himself.

His right shoulder flexed in a shrug. He knew better than to say "nothing," so he decided that the best answer was an innocuous one and said, "Self-knowledge is a priceless thing. I'm giving you mixed signals."

A grin displayed her even white teeth. "No, you're not."

He stared at her. "I'm not?"

She locked her desk drawer, put her briefcase in her left hand and grasped his left hand with her right one. "No, you're not. Come on. Let's go."

His behavior was inconsistent, and he knew it, his honorable intentions and his seeming inability to behave differently notwithstanding. If she acted as wishy-washy as he did, he'd be furious. In that bona fide tearoom, where floor-to-ceiling drapes and matching damask chairs at small marble-top tables adorned with flowers attested to its authenticity, he sat among about two dozen well-dressed women and couldn't help feeling foolish. He'd bet that every other Maryland man of his age and station who was in the company of a woman like Pamela was probably sipping a cocktail. He shared the thought with her.

"This is true," she replied, "and quite a few of those men will have an accident as they drive home."

No arguing with that. He pushed the tea aside, leaned back and enjoyed looking at her. "Any more news about Parker?"

"I called the precinct just before you got to my office, and an officer there told me that whatever I did to him won't permanently maim him, though he'll be walking with a cane when he leaves the hospital. Raynor, my managing editor, filed harassment charges against him with the station. When he recovers, he'll be transferred to Honolulu."

Drake knew that the frown he'd worn for the past few minutes deepened. "He's pressing charges. What about you? Aren't you—"

She held up her hand, interrupting him. "I did that this morning before I went to work."

"Good." He looked at his watch. If he speeded, he'd be home at seven, in time for dinner. "I'd better phone Alexis. She likes to have dinner promptly at seven."

After talking with his sister-in-law, he paid the bill, took Pamela's hand and walked with her to the corner where they had parked their cars. "This wasn't a good idea, Pamela. Leaving you here on the street...I can't even..." He let the thought go.

"Then follow me home. I don't like leaving you here like this, either."

Her voice, so soft and sweet, held a longing that touched him, and as he gazed down at her, something jumped to life in him. He wanted to hold her then and there, and for once he found no pride in his mastery of himself and in his ability to deny himself.

"All right," he told her. "Lead the way." At her apartment, he didn't wonder at the trembling of her fingers as she fumbled with the key in the lock. He covered her hand with his, turned the key, opened the door and walked into the foyer with her tight in his arms.

The feel of her soft breasts against his chest and her body locked to his, warm and willing, rocked his senses. "You're a drug, a fire I can't put out. Kiss me. Kiss me and mean it."

Her fingers gripped the lapels of his jacket, then she seemed to move up his body like a vine climbing a stake. Her lips parted, and he joined them with one deep thrust of his tongue into the sweet haven of her mouth. Heat roared through his body, searing his limbs and settling in his loins.

He had to move. He couldn't let her… He attempted to move her away from him. But she pressed her hips to his body as she captured his tongue, feasting on it, pulling and sucking, showing him what it would be like if she exploded all around him while he was buried deep within her. Tremors shook him as the scent of her hot desire drugged him, and then she undulated against him, demanding what he wanted and needed so badly.

Shackled by the force of his desire, he grabbed her buttocks to lift her to fit him, and his own moans startled him, bringing him back to near sanity. He unlocked her hands from the back of his neck and pushed her away from him, although in spite of his strength, he couldn't separate them with ease, so tenacious was her hold.

She stared up at him, her breathing almost a pant and her eyes nearly black with desire. "Don't tell me you're sorry," she said. "I don't want to hear it. You wanted that, and you needed it just as badly as I did."

If only he could… He couldn't tell her how he felt, for it would be tantamount to declaring his love. All that he'd bottled up inside would spill out of him like a river emptying itself into the sea. As he looked at her, her face became a mass of tears that she made no effort to hide, and it shook him to the core of his being.

Without thinking of what he did, he pulled her closer and his lips roamed her face, kissing as he moved, symbolically drinking her tears. Then, with his hands, he wiped them away.

"No, I'm not sorry. How could I be? Nonetheless, until I can back up what I'm feeling, I'm not going to seek you out again." He clasped both of her hands in his. "But if you need me, call me. Promise me that. Will you promise?"

As he gazed down at her, he could see that her confusion was, if anything, greater than his. "I…I don't know. Right now, I feel as if I've been hit by a speeding locomotive. You're right in saying we should stop seeing each other. I can't endure more of these electric storms you and I create. Wasted energy."

She turned to the door, holding his hand. "Don't speed. The risk isn't worth it, not even to get home by dinnertime."

He resisted kissing her goodbye, but she reached up, eased her hand behind his head, and he bent down to receive her closed-mouth kiss.

"See you," he said. Words that to his own ears carried a ring of dishonesty, for they were not what he needed to say. She didn't reply, but stood at the door. When he glanced back before getting into the elevator, she still stood at the open door.

Pamela closed the door, locked it, leaned against the doorjamb and stared at her elongated shadow against the opposite wall. She didn't like shadows, especially not an eerie likeness of herself. Feeling as if she'd been blown around by a cyclone, she made her way to a chair in the living room and dropped down into it.

That man loved her. Why couldn't he admit it to himself, if not to her? Didn't he know that a man didn't behave as he did with a woman unless she was precious to him? He couldn't be so tender and gentle with her, so caring and loving if it didn't come from his heart.

One day, he would realize what she meant to him, and it would be too late. Too late for him and too late for her. She was entitled to exercise her right to bear and nurture children, just as she had a right to realize her potential as an intelligent and creative human being. With her career ascending, the latter was within her grasp. Even if she had to have the help of a total stranger, one day she would hold in her arms a child who would call her *Mother.*

She ignored the ringing telephone, for she didn't want to speak with Drake or anyone else. On impulse, she walked over and looked at the caller ID screen. Why would Rhoda call her at home? Hadn't they spent an hour and a half that afternoon discussing Rhoda's work?

"Hello, Rhoda. What's up?"

"Hi, Pamela. This has nothing to do with work, which is why I'm calling you at home. I'm having a garden party at my parents' house, and I want you to come and bring your significant other if you like."

She didn't have a significant other. "When's the party?"

"Saturday, July twenty-first, and it is not an office party. A real garden party where women will wear wide skirts, frilly hats and white gloves. Old-fashioned and very feminine."

She figured she could use a change, and the more drastic, the better. "Count me in." Old-fashioned, eh? Trust Rhoda to mandate a dress code that would allow her to hide the rolls of fat around her waist and to expose her ample bosom. Those garden-party dresses might have modest, flared skirts, but the deep cleavage compensated for it.

"At least Rhoda's call changed my mood," Pamela said to herself. She wanted to telephone the precinct for news of Lawrence's condition, but refrained, reminding herself that she injured him in self-defense. Still out of sorts from her encounter with Drake, afraid that fate would consign her to a barren life, empty of reciprocated love and of children she could call her own, she ate a sausage-and-biscuit sandwich and went to bed.

Drake fared no better than Pamela. His somber mood at dinner—rare for him—cast a pall over the meal, robbing it of the joshing, teasing and wordless gestures of love and affection that characterized mealtime in the Harrington household.

"I'm going to turn in early tonight," he announced, avoiding their after-dinner session in the den. "See you all tomorrow morning."

Tara left the table and caught him as he reached the stairs. "Don't you feel good, Uncle Drake? Maybe my mommy has an aspirin."

He hunkered before the little girl. "I'm fine. Life can get a little rough sometimes, and you don't feel like smiling, but I'm all right. I promise."

Her little arms went around his neck, and he hugged her warm little body, enjoying the unconditional love that she always gave him. "Tomorrow morning at breakfast, you'll be fine, won't you?" she asked him.

"I'm fine now. You're the best medicine a person could have."

She kissed his cheek and ran back to the dining room. Her words reached him as he climbed the stairs.

"Uncle Drake is fine. He said I'm the best medicine a person could have. Am I, Mommy?"

He didn't hear Alexis's answer before he ducked into his room and closed the door.

After sleeping fitfully, he awoke more tired than if he hadn't gone to bed. He showered, dressed and went downstairs where he knew he could expect Henry's meddling.

"What ailed you last night? I know you ain't gonna tell, but it's time you stopped locking yer problems inside of you and talked to somebody."

"I'm not hobbling under any great burden, Henry. I deal with my problems as they come."

"You ain't dealing with whatever it is that ails you now. Never seen you so lifeless."

Drake had asked both Telford and Russ the question, but their answers hadn't satisfied him. He walked over to the stove and began frying the pancakes—something he had done regularly before he left for college—relieving Henry to tend the sausage and bacon. His action wasn't lost on Henry, who remembered that, in Drake's youth, he'd chosen the times when Henry was cooking breakfast to seek advice and share his thoughts. Henry lowered the flame beneath the meat.

"What's wrong, son? You know it'll stop right here."

"How did you know you loved Miss Sarah so much that you wanted to marry her?"

"When it got to the place that I couldn't stay away from her, when I was with her and didn't want to leave her, and when I left her and wanted to turn around and go right back to her. I fought it just like you're fighting this, and the day came when she lost patience with me and told me to forget it. I thought I would die. She was everything to me."

"I know that," Drake said. "As young as I was, I knew that. And it was mutual. I used to say I wanted a wife like her, not like my own mother. I still remember her singing me to sleep."

"She was a loving woman. Don't play yer cards too close to yer chest. When you do that, not even you can see 'em."

Drake finished making the pancakes, put some on a plate for Tara along with butter and bacon, set her place at the table and then set his own and waited until he heard her steps as she raced to the breakfast room.

"Do you want milk this morning, or cocoa?" he asked her.

"Both. My mommy says I'm eating for two."

The coffee sloshed into the saucer and onto the tablecloth. *"What?"*

"She said 'cause I eat so much. Want me to say grace?"

He definitely did not, because he didn't have an hour to spend while she blessed everybody she ever knew. "Thanks, but I'll say it." And he did.

She walked with him to the front door, kissed him good-bye and went back to the kitchen to be with Henry until her parents came downstairs for their breakfast.

When he reached the building site in Frederick, Pete was waiting for him. "Hi, Mr. Harrington. I wanted you to know that my dad is coming home today. It's earlier than we thought. Can you come by after work to meet him?"

"Sure. It will be my pleasure."

He finished work at four-thirty and, after showering and changing his clothes in the company trailer, he drove to the Jergenses' house. And knocked on the door. He hadn't stopped to consider what he looked like in a light gray business suit, pale gray shirt and yellow tie. Bond Jergens opened the door with Pete holding on to his hand.

"Dad, this is Mr. Harrington we told you about. Mr. Harrington, this is my dad, Bond Jergens."

Drake gazed into the eyes of an unfriendly man, a proud man about an inch shorter than himself. He extended his hand. "I'm glad to meet you, Mr. Jergens. I'm sure you're happy to be at home with your family."

Bond Jergens did not accept the offer to shake hands. "And it looks as if I got back just in time."

Tension swirled around Drake, but he was used to tough men because he worked with them every day, and he had never seen a man he feared. "Am I missing something?" he said. "I didn't understand your remark."

"And I don't understand your interest in my family."

Drake stepped back. "Ask your son."

"And not my wife?"

"Wait a minute. If you think—"

"Daddy," Pete said, "Mr. Harrington is my friend. He caught me stealing wood from his building. That's how I met him."

Bond stared down at Pete. "You were *stealing?*"

The boy hung his head. "Yes, sir, but we were freezing and the gas was turned off, so—"

"Mr. Jergens, if I had a son like Pete, I would consider myself blessed. He was only taking care of the family until you got back."

"But to steal…" He stepped back and offered his hand to Drake. "I owe you both an apology and my eternal thanks. Come in."

He walked into the house where Stella Jergens stood wringing her hands. "I'm sorry, Mr. Harrington, but Bond just got home and I hadn't had time to explain how things were with us. He got the story from Pete, and since you're Pete's idol, you may imagine how he related things."

Drake forced a smile. "I can, indeed. What kind of work do you do, Mr. Jergens?"

"Ground-up plumbing, cement laying, and for years I drove a crane. I can still do that. Call me Bond."

"My name is Drake. Can you return to your old job?"

"No, indeed. The foreman called me that n-word, and I spent ten months in jail for beating him almost lifeless. No man, white nor black, is going to lay that on me."

"The basic plumbing at my site is finished, but none of the fixtures have been installed in the bathrooms and kitchens. Are you interested?"

"And here I was prepared to spend weeks, maybe months, looking for a job. Yes, indeed. I'm interested. I can give you good references."

Drake waved his hand to indicate that that was not important. "After meeting the members of your family, I figured out the kind of man you are." He looked at Pete.

"Bring your father over to the site tomorrow morning on your way to school."

He had a feeling that his relationship with the Jergens family would mean more to him than it did to them. He couldn't put a finger on it, but something, maybe a sixth sense, told him this was his lucky day.

Chapter 5

Sunday morning, several weeks after her last encounter with Drake, Pamela drove out to Druid Hill Park and sat on a bench beside the lake. The strong breeze rippled the quiet water, and she closed her eyes, held her face up to the sun and breathed deeply of the clean fresh air. She had a decision to make and had sought the peaceful surroundings to help her clear her head and focus on the pros and cons of the most important step she was likely to take. In the past two months, three seemingly eligible men—excluding Drake—had waltzed through her life. Among them she could have chosen looks, charm, status, prestige or sex appeal, but none offered tenderness and caring, stability and the prospect of abiding love. She'd turned her back on them all.

She had been writing in the notebook she brought along, and suddenly, she scratched out those thoughts and told herself the truth. She wasn't physically attracted to any of them, couldn't imagine herself in bed with any one of them, and compared them unfavorably and unfairly to Drake. Tom was attentive and strongly attracted to her, she recalled, but when she danced with him, she could have been holding a broom. And after her second date with Jeff, she refused to answer the phone when she saw his number on her caller ID screen. What woman wants a man who starts talking about sex before she even kisses him? Oscar Rankin held no appeal for her.

She folded her notebook and put it in the carryall bag she'd brought along. "I'm not going to barter myself for a baby, as badly as I want one. There are plenty of little babies who need a mother, and I'm going to adopt one," she told herself. The weight of her anxiety over childbearing at a late age slid away from her and with it the stress of constantly looking for a prospective father for the child she wanted. As she drove home singing "Oh, Happy Day," the gospel song her maternal grandmother loved so much, a feeling of freedom pervaded her.

Later, relaxed and more content in spite of her longing for Drake, she phoned her parents. "Hi, Mom. I'll be home next weekend. I'll email you my itinerary tomorrow."

"We were expecting you, darling. To miss this occasion would almost be like missing Christmas. There's a big party Friday night, so be sure and bring along a formal. Everybody will be dressed to the nines."

"Thanks for reminding me. Where's Daddy?"

Her mother's warm chuckle—a sound that had the ring of love to it and which she had adored from the time she knew herself—was audible through the wire. "He's still at church. For years he wouldn't go near one, but I dragged him there Easter Sunday, and he's been going ever since. I'm so happy he goes that I do not ask why."

Next, somebody was going to tell her she owned the

British crown jewels. "Just proves anything can happen, Mom."

"Or maybe if you pray as hard and as long about something as I have about your father and his attitude toward organized religion, your prayers get answered."

"Give him a hug for me. I'll see you in a few days."

"Take care of yourself, dear. Bye."

She hung up and went to the closet in which she kept her dressier clothes. Her gaze fell on the burnt-orange chiffon. "Nope," she said aloud. "My man-hunting days are over." Looking farther, an off-shoulder sleek gown the color of tea roses and with a slit to just above the left knee caught her attention. "You're it," she said. "Man or no man, at least I'll feel good about myself if I wear this one."

Drake stepped off American Airlines Flight 1739 to San Antonio and strode through the terminal, enjoying a chance to stretch his legs after nearly a five-hour flight. At the baggage-claim area, he saw a large sign that bore his name and a smile bloomed on his face as he walked toward it.

"I brought the sign in case you didn't remember what I looked like," Magnus Cooper said. "Drake Harrington, this is my wife, Selena Sutton-Cooper." Drake shook hands with the tall, elegant and beautiful woman—precisely the type of woman he would expect Magnus Cooper to have.

"Welcome, Drake," she said in a voice that set him back with its low tone, soft timbre and slight hesitation between syllables. It reminded him of Pamela's sexy way of speaking. "We've been looking forward to this. The fatted calf is on a spit and the pigs have been roasting slowly all day. I hope you're not on a diet."

Drake looked hard at her, aware that he was frowning. "Did you say *pigs?*"

She turned to her husband. "Didn't you tell him? Drake,

our relatives and friends come from all over the country for this occasion. Tomorrow night, we sponsor a grand ball at the Hyatt, so…" She looked at Magnus. "You *did* tell him to bring a tux, didn't you?"

"Yes, he did. In fact he underlined it," Drake said. He liked Selena Cooper at once and set his heart on enjoying a rare vacation.

Relaxing during the forty-minute drive to Waverly, where the Cooper ranch was located, Drake found himself enjoying the great expanse of the Texas landscape, the rolling hills and the rich greenery. When at last they reached the wrought-iron gate with a big bronze letter *C* at its top, he sat forward and pinned his gaze to the window beside him. He got an idea of the wealth and size of the estate as the town car eased along the road leading to the big white house, a field of bluebonnets on either side of the road and more butterflies flitting among the flowers than he'd ever seen. As they reached the house, he glanced at his watch. A seven-minute drive on the man's property from the public road to the house. He didn't know why, but the scene gave him a joyous feeling. He was going to have a weekend free of worries about himself and Pamela, and of concerns about overstretching Harrington, Inc.

A man took his bags from the trunk of the Lincoln and stopped to speak with Magnus. "Drake Harrington, this is Jackson. He's my foreman and my friend, and he and his wife, Tess, look after Selena and me."

He shook hands with the man. "Delighted to meet you, Jackson. Maybe you can tell me why you've got a calf and pigs roasting. Seems to me that would feed an army."

Jackson grinned. "I see you don't know Texans. This is meat-eating country, and meat means beef. The non-Texans will want barbecued pork, and if I'd left it to my wife, we'd be cooking not three pigs but four, plus all those chickens we're frying up. You all have a good time while you're here, Mr. Harrington." He left them to take the luggage to the guest room, Drake surmised. "I imagine you're tired after the trip," Magnus said. "But if you aren't, I'd like to show you around. Do you ride?"

"I do, indeed, and I'll change with that in mind. I'm not one bit tired."

As they rode around the ranch, he listened to Magnus's plans to build a home on the property for Jackson and his wife. "I figured a two-bedroom ranch style would be best. As they get older, they won't want to climb stairs. They've been good to us, and I want them to retire in comfort."

He met Tess later when she and Jackson joined them for dinner. "Get a good night's sleep," Tess told him, "'cause you won't see a bed again till two or three o'clock Saturday morning. When we party, we don't fool around. The people start arriving around ten or ten-thirty in the morning."

He thanked his hosts and went to his room, a masculine chamber with a big walnut sleigh bed—much like his own—and other appointments suitable for a man. "Hmm. A guest room for men and one for women. I'll have to remember that."

The next morning, after a swim and a light breakfast, he read the local paper in his room and, around eleven o'clock, walked outside to see what a Cooper barbecue was like. His bottom lip dropped at the sight of over a hundred people milling around, children in swings and on slides, adults playing softball, tennis, badminton and croquet. *What a sight,* he thought. It was almost like being in a huge public park.

He strolled through the crowd and stumbled, banging his foot against a stake that supported the food tent. It couldn't be, but it was. He stared at Pamela Langford approaching him arm in arm with a tall man of around forty. He didn't move because he couldn't get his breath. What was she doing there and *who was that man?* He recovered from the shock and remained in her path, bold and assertive. If the man wasn't her husband, and that didn't seem possible, he could get lost. First anger and then the pain of rejection sliced through him. The man, as tall as he, bent slightly to hear her words, his manner solicitous and intimate. As they neared him, Drake stepped in front of them, effectively blocking their path.

"Hello, Pamela. I didn't dream I'd see you here."

Her eyes widened and she gaped as if she was swallowing air. "Drake! What are you doing here? I had no idea that you knew Magnus and Selena."

He gazed down at her, beautiful in a yellow shirt, white pants and white sneakers. "Magnus once told me that he had a cousin in Baltimore and that you were that person, but I'd forgotten it." He waited for her to introduce the man, and when she didn't—obviously because his presence there stunned her—he introduced himself. "I'm Drake Harrington."

"John Langford." The man extended his hand. "Glad to meet you."

Excitement streaked through his body, and he thought the bottom dropped out of his belly. "Any relation?" he asked in a voice so calm that it nearly startled him, as he prayed silently that he wouldn't hear the word *husband*.

"Third cousins," John replied. "Pamela is my favorite relative."

He let out a long breath of relief. "She's a favorite of mine, too," he said without a trace of friendliness. "How about showing me how to handle this barbecue, Pamela. I don't know the pork from the beef."

"It's labeled," she said, glaring at him.

Let her glare. He had no intention of giving her over to

that cousin. "How do you like Baltimore?" he asked John, fishing for information as to how close he was to Pamela.

"I haven't seen that town since I was twenty-two."

So far, so good. "I take it you attended a university in Baltimore."

"Johns Hopkins. And you?"

Hmm. So the man was taking his measure, too. "Howard University and the University of Maryland. Architectural engineering is my field." He knew that Pamela was mad enough to spit, but he didn't care. He wanted Cousin Langford to get out of his way, and the sooner the better. "Why don't you Texans show me how to maneuver around that table over there?"

He ignored Pamela's glare. Third cousin John was going to move over whether he liked it or not. They strolled over to the picnic tent that housed a thirty-five-foot-long and seven-foot-wide table laden with food. He put himself between Pamela and her cousin, and slipped his left arm around her waist, a little reminder to her of the way his hands felt on her body.

"What should I start with? I get hungry just looking at all this food."

She explained that the food was presented in sections: with separate areas for fruits, bread, meats, seafood, rice and other starches, drinks and sweets. He wondered at her graciousness, angry as he knew she was, until she deliberately stepped on his foot.

"Oh. Please excuse me," she said, showing her teeth in a brilliant smile.

Drake looked down at her and let a grin take over his face. "I can prove that you know your foot is a lethal weapon," he said, referring to the injury she inflicted on Lawrence, "so you be careful." Let Cousin John frown with displeasure; he couldn't have cared less.

Her sheepish facial expression, much like that of a small child caught with her hand in the cookie jar, told him that she was softening. He pressed his luck.

"Is there a reason why you wouldn't want me to be here today?" He asked her purposefully loud enough for John Langford to hear him.

"Why wouldn't I want you to be here? You could get lost in this crowd. I'm just surprised that you know Magnus and Selena."

Making it clear that he'd had more than enough, John put his hands on his hips, looked Drake in the eye and spoke in a voice that was anything but friendly. "What's going on between you two?"

"Nothing," Pamela said.

Simultaneously, Drake replied, "No point in getting testy, buddy. We're not lovers yet, but we're headed that way."

At her gasp, he slipped an arm around her waist again and caressed her side and back. "You know it's true, Pamela. We have our highs and lows, but eventually, and soon, we'll settle it the way in which God provided for men and women to settle things."

When she neither agreed nor denied it, but continued to gape at Drake, eventually speechless, John put his plate on the table, looked hard at her and said, "See you around."

The man walked away, and Drake couldn't keep the grin off his face. "Did I mess up something?"

She poked him in the chest with her right index finger. "How did you dare to do that, Drake? You were out of order. You don't want a relationship with me, but you don't want me to have one with anybody else."

"It didn't occur to me that you had something going with your cousin. If he'd muscled in on me, I'd have taught him a lesson. Anyway, you didn't object."

She examined something over his left shoulder, avoiding eye contact. "I didn't want to create a scene."

"Really? But you *are* glad to see me, aren't you? I was stunned when I saw you arm in arm with that self-conscious turkey and annoyed as hell."

"What right did you have to be annoyed?"

"Plenty. I remembered how you heated me up, and I didn't like the idea of his having the same pleasure. Look, he's gone now, so let's enjoy ourselves. What's that over there?" He pointed to a pile of avocados-in-shell, stuffed with crab meat and sitting on a tub of cracked ice.

"It's a Cooper special, and it's fantastic," she said.

His arm tightened around her. "Forgive me for banishing John?" he whispered, then leaned over and kissed her cheek.

"Are you trying to con me?"

"I'm trying to make certain that you don't want any of these Joes strutting around here." He didn't smile when he said it. "I didn't like seeing you with that guy."

She didn't smile, either. "You know what to do if you want to claim turf."

He swung around when a hand lay on his arm and stayed there. "Did we meet in Atlanta this past March at a dental convention?" She was a tall, willowy woman with large, wide eyes, wearing more lipstick than he would have thought any one pair of lips capable of accommodating. She didn't remove her hand from his arm, but let it remain like a caress. "I'm Charlotte Bryant," she said in a voice wispy and sultry.

No point in showing his annoyance. "Sorry," he said. "I stay away from anything and anybody having to do with teeth unless I have a toothache. Must have been some other guy." He forced a half smile and turned back to Pamela, who eyed the intruder with all the friendliness of a hungry lioness going for a kill.

"That's a cheap way to get an introduction to a man," Pamela fumed as the woman walked away. He wondered if she noticed that he didn't acknowledge the attempted introduction but instead made light of it.

"Let them know I'm yours," he said, realizing that he'd just taken a giant step, "and they won't do that."

She looked at him with serious eyes, eyes that showed pain, yes, and hope. Her lips trembled when she said, "Are you?"

Only the crowd around them and his intense dislike for public displays of affection prevented him from taking her into his arms, loving her and telling her what was in his heart. He gazed down at her, hoping to communicate with his eyes even a modicum of what he felt right then. Someway, somehow, he had to have his dreams and her along with them. She sucked in her breath, reached for his hand and squeezed it.

"Selena promised me she'd have some eligible men here," a woman said. "And you're the most eligible one I've seen." He didn't turn around.

"This one is eligible, but he's with me."

If his life had depended on it, he couldn't have prevented the smile that floated over his face. Nothing Pamela could have said would have made him as happy. He *was* hers, and he wanted her to take pride in that fact. With his hand gripping Pamela's waist, he turned, faced the woman and lifted his left shoulder in a careless shrug.

"Excuse us, please, miss. I want to try out that pork barbecue down there."

As they walked to the meat, poultry and seafood section, he wondered what he could do right then, short of a public declaration, to let her know that from the moment he saw her arm in arm with her cousin John, he stopped resisting the inevitable: that he didn't want another man to touch her. Not then. Not ever.

He sampled the barbecued pork and enjoyed it, but he noticed that she barely tasted hers. "You don't like it?" he asked her. "I think it's the best I've ever eaten. Try the shrimp or maybe the beef."

"I couldn't eat…anything right now."

He bent closer. "Don't you feel well? I'll take you to the house if you want me to."

She gazed up at him with a slightly baffled expression, so unlike her useful self. "I'm… Drake, I'm overwhelmed."

"I am, too," he said and it was true. He glanced around him and saw that the sun shone brighter, the children— black, white, Latin, Native American and Asian—made a ring around the swings, singing and dancing, and the sky was a vivid blue without a single cloud. Beauty in front of him and all around him. It was as if he saw the world for the first time.

He took her hand. "Let's walk over by that brook. I imagine it's quiet over there."

If she was dreaming, she didn't want to awaken. Surely, this change in Drake did not occur suddenly, for she had learned that he deliberated over his every move. She didn't believe that he would toy with her. Throughout their relationship, he had taken great pains to let her know where he stood. Today, however, he was taking them in a new and different direction, and she couldn't stand a disappointment. She should demand to know precisely where she stood with him, but her instinct told her that she would gain more by trusting him. At the bank of the river—known locally as Rolling Brook after an old man named Rolling, who lost touch with reality panning for gold there—he took off his beige linen jacket and spread it on the grass beneath a grove of blooming crepe-myrtle trees.

"Let's sit here," he said, motioning for her to sit on his jacket.

"I wouldn't want to wrinkle it."

"I'm going to sit on it right beside you. Have a seat."

She did, and he sat beside her, put and arm around her and rested her head against his chest. She didn't speak. She couldn't. What had caused the change in him? She needed to know. But she told herself to be patient, a trait that she had never mastered. She willed her heart to slow down to its normal beat, draped her right arm across his chest and relaxed. The brook, which was high from the recent rains, rushed along, headed for its rendezvous with the Cayman Lake. Fascinated by the moving water, she stared at it until he asked her whether she was asleep.

"I'm not sure. If I am, I'd rather not wake up."

His arm drew her closer. "Why? Are you happy?"

She sat up in order to see his eyes while they talked. "I am, but I'm afraid to be happy. I feel the way I do when I have a glass of fresh cold coconut milk. I enjoy it so much that I begin to dread the moment when I've drunk the last drop."

He didn't respond for a long while, and she knew he was measuring his words. At last he said, "Considering how things have gone with us, I'm not surprised that you feel this way. I'm happier right now, Pamela, than I remember ever being. Trust me and let yourself be happy with me."

She kissed his neck and laid her head against his chest. "I do trust you. I'm…I'm just scared. I welcome daily challenges at work and in life in general, and I don't fear the new. I welcome change when it is good. But…but Drake, I've been hurting. Come here, stay away. Possessive kisses followed by goodbye. I don't want that anymore. It...it pains me."

He shifted her so that she sat facing him, and she caught her breath at what she saw in his eyes. "What is John Langford to you?"

"He's a third cousin on my father's side. That's all."

"You're more than a cousin to him. I'm certain of that."

She didn't want to talk about John. "Maybe, but that's all he is, ever was or ever will be to me."

"I want more than anything to kiss you," he said, "but I can't risk it here." His lips brushed her cheek. "I knew you were Texan, but I hadn't realized you were from this part of the state."

She didn't want to talk about Texas. She wanted evidence that she meant something special to him, that she was the woman he cared for above all others. Saying he was hers was as easy as pouring water from a glass. She needed more.

"You've given me a lot today, far more than ever," she whispered. "But Drake, I need more, and I need you to kiss me. Right now, I need it."

His arm tightened around her, and with his lips inches from her own, he gazed into her face with eyes that had become stormy with desire and stared until she sucked in her breath, wilting as it were from the heat of her libido. With a groan, his tongue plunged into her mouth; the fingers of his left hand gripped her thigh, and he supported her back with his right one. The air around them snapped and sizzled, crepe myrtles swayed in the hot breeze and her blouse clung to her skin, dampened with the effects of her repressed desire. Nearly out of her mind with need of him and not caring that he knew it, she grabbed the hand that gripped her thigh and placed it inside her blouse.

He broke the kiss. "Pamela. Sweetheart, please don't tempt me. I—"

She interrupted him, pressing his hand to her breast as she did so. "Kiss me. Darling, I need it."

His big hand, warm and strong, lifted her breast from the confines of her bra, and his hot breath anointed it seconds before his warm mouth closed over her nipple, and he began to suck it.

"Oh, my Lord," she moaned. He nipped the tiny bud and closed her blouse.

"I didn't want this to happen now," he said, "because I knew I'd be half-mad with desire for you. I want to make love with you right now, more that I want to breathe."

She traced the side of his face with her fingers. "If we were alone, totally alone, would you?"

His gaze, intense and electrifying, like the sun going down, held her captive. Then he said, "If we were totally alone in a private place, I'd be inside of you right now."

It was what she needed to hear. She knew that if he felt that way, his attitude toward their relationship had truly changed. She sat up to adjust her bra and button her blouse, and saw a squirrel gazing at them.

"I feel as if I could eat an entire pig. Let's go back to the picnic area."

His wholehearted laughter surprised her, and she turned to face him fully, for he was most handsome when he laughed that way. "I wonder how hungry you'd be if we'd gone all the way," he said and pulled her to her feet. "I just realized I'm starved."

"Should I ask you the question that you just asked me?"

He took her hand and headed them toward the picnic area. "I don't mind telling you I'd be starved to death and greatly in need of energy replenishment."

* * *

"I know you were born in Texas, but where?" he asked her later as they sat on the bench in the shade of the tent eating barbecued shrimp, biscuits and coleslaw.

"I was born about five miles from here on the outskirts of Waverly, and my parents still live in the house in which I was born."

Both of his eyebrows shot up. "Really? Then you're staying with your parents while you're here?"

She nodded. "My father would explode if I stayed anywhere else. I don't get home often. When I do, I humor my parents and spend all of my time with them."

She wondered at the frown on his face until he asked, "Are they here at the picnic?"

"They always come, but my mother had stomach cramps this morning from the cucumbers she ate last night and which she knows she's allergic to. My father wouldn't consider leaving her for a second, not even if all that ailed her was a splinter in her finger."

He sipped the lemonade as he seemed to ponder her words, but she'd grown used to his way of thinking through a situation or idea before commenting on it. "I gather they're very close. How long have they been married?"

"Thirty-three years, and they're still lovers. Sometimes the fire between them is so intense that I have to look the other way. Drake, they've had a difficult time with friends, neighbors and especially with my father's family. They are white and they have never accepted my mother." She continued in spite of his gasp. "My maternal grandparents objected to my mother seeing my father. But when Daddy went to my grandfather and told him he wanted to marry my mother and that he'd take care of her for as long as he lived, my mother's parents accepted him. Now they love him as if he were their own son."

"Your father's family hasn't relented at all?"

Her right shoulder lifted carelessly in an easy shrug. "I'm an only child, as is my father, so I'm their only grandchild. My father always took me to see them, and they care about me, but they don't accept my mother. Maybe it's because she's so dark, or maybe they're just stubborn. I was around twelve years old when I heard my grandfather Karl tell my father that he would have been rich by then if he hadn't married a black woman. Daddy says their attitude doesn't hurt him any longer because they're old now, alone and suffering from their own bitterness, when they could have had a loving, attentive daughter-in-law."

"So they accept you, but not your mother. That's weird."

"Not really. I'm part of them."

"I want to escort you to the ball tonight. May I call for you at your parents' home?"

"Of course. Do you have anything I can write on?" He gave her one of his business cards, and she wrote her parents' address and phone number on it.

"Thanks. What kind of work does your father do?"

"He's a computer scientist, and he designs specially coded programs. He's well-known in his professional circles. My mother teaches math at the community college."

He sucked in his breath as he remembered the black hole in his life. "My mother was a gadabout, and I could wake up any morning and she wouldn't be there. She'd be gone for weeks, and we wouldn't know where she was. Henry's wife was the only person who ever sang me a lullaby when I was little. When my mother finally came home to stay after my father died, it was too late as far as I was concerned. I didn't give a damn what she did."

Shocked at what he'd revealed, she put her plate on the table, swallowed her food and cleared her throat. Then, she put an arm around his waist, leaned close and sang

Brahms's "Lullaby" in soft gentle tones. He turned so that he could see her face as she sang, but she couldn't read his facial expression and didn't try.

She finished singing, and with his hands gripping hers and in a voice that shook, he told her, "That's the most precious gift I've ever received. I won't try to thank you. Just know I won't forget it."

They finished eating and walked through the crowd holding hands and greeting the people that she knew, some relatives and some who were old friends.

"Where'd you find him?" asked Bridget, a woman about Pamela's age whose facial expression read like a sign that said Man Hungry.

"I don't quite remember your name," she said to the woman, knowing that it was a put-down. But she had become sick of women gushing over Drake, and the fact that he disliked it didn't make her feel better.

To her amazement, Drake's face lit up with an engaging smile and lights danced in his dark, sleepy eyes. "She didn't find me," he said. "I found her, and I consider that day a blessed one."

Crestfallen, the woman looked first at Drake and then at Pamela. "You get outta here, girl." She left without saying goodbye.

"Can't much blame her," Pamela said. "When women around here see an unmarried man who's eligible, he's usually on his way someplace. There isn't much for a man to do if he doesn't want to farm or work on a ranch. There are several large ranches in this area that are owned by African-Americans, but if a black man isn't skilled with horses and cattle, can't teach and isn't in the medical field, he's likely to be limited to whatever unskilled work he can find. Jobs are just as scarce for African-American woman. I left because I didn't see a future for me here."

She looked at her watch. "It's four o'clock. I'd like to leave now. It's getting hotter, but you stay, because the entertainment starts around five. The ball begins at ten, and if you get to my place at a quarter of ten, we'd be here in good time. If I leave now, I can get a shower and a good nap."

"Don't you want to see the entertainment?"

"It hasn't changed since Magnus bought this ranch fifteen years ago." She reached up and brushed her lips across his cheek. "What are you wearing tonight?"

"White tux, black tie. Does that suit you? How're you getting home?"

She couldn't help grinning. "I drove my father's car. A tux suits me perfectly." And to think that she had almost forgotten to bring a formal.

He walked with her to her car. "Hand me your car key," he said, and when she gave it to him, he opened the door, ignited the engine and turned on the air conditioner. "Wait out there for a couple of minutes. It's a furnace in this car."

When the car had cooled, he got out and kissed her lips quickly. "See you at a quarter of ten."

Drake left the parking area and walked around the picnic grounds looking for Magnus. He found him at the far end of the tent passing out glasses of lemonade. "I've been enjoying myself," Drake told his host. "This environment makes me wonder whether some of my plans are what I really want."

Magnus dried his hands on a towel tucked into his belt, put the towel aside and walked away from the tent with Drake. "Let's go this way," he said and began walking toward the stables. "This is not an idyllic life, Drake, though it certainly could be if a person wasn't sensitive. When I walk through that gate, I'm on my ranch, my own property, and I'm sheltered from the injustice that's all around me. In less than a mile, you can see abject poverty and hopelessness that seems to worsen with the years.

"I've instituted programs for children and for seniors, but that's minuscule compared to what's needed. Sometimes, when I look around, I feel helpless."

He saw in the man a kindred soul, and said as much. "I don't see it that way, Magnus. I've found that each time I help someone, that person is likely to help someone else. But most of all, it seems to come back to me." He told Magnus the story of his relationship with the Jergens family. "I hired that man on faith. I've had only one day in which to observe his work and his attitude toward it, and I have concluded that when I hired him, an angel must have been sitting on my shoulder. He is precisely what I needed. He seems to energize my crew, to put grit in their craw. An unexpected blessing."

"I don't look for payback," Magnus said. "But if that happens, I'll be grateful. I saw that you spent a lot of time with my cousin Pamela Langford, and I remembered your cryptic response when I asked if you knew her. I haven't seen much of her in recent years, but she and Selena have formed a pretty good friendship. They'd be much closer if they saw each other more often." He leaned against a hitching post. "Is there something serious between you two? Looked that way to me."

The question called for a straight answer, an honest one. With his hands in his trouser pockets, he propped his right foot on the bottom board of the white fence beside him. "When we were on that plane, I wasn't sure where I was headed with Pamela. She's practically told me to take a hike. Each time we separated, we thought it was over, but soon, we'd be back together. The problem was my unwillingness to settle down and start a family when I hadn't reached my goals, hadn't realized my dreams.

"Seeing her here this morning was a shock, and as the day progressed, it became increasingly clearer to me that I'd have to find a way to reach my goals without losing Pamela. It's something I'm going to work toward with full fervor."

Magnus slouched against the post and kicked at a pinecone that rolled near him with the help of a rustling breeze. "I know from experience that fervor is what it takes with a strong-minded, independent woman. They give you a hard time, man, but any other type will bore you to death."

"Tell me about it."

"I wish you luck."

"Thanks. What do you think of a ranch with horses and no cows? I'm from Maryland, horse country, and I'd like to have a few horses, but I don't really want to breed them as an investment."

"Keeping horses is expensive. When you raise cattle, as I do, you have to have them. Pamela loves to ride, if I remember properly, so if she's in your life, you'd need a mare. From the way you rode Bingston yesterday, I figure you'd want a stallion." A grin formed around his lips and spread to his eyes. "You know the rest. In no time, you'd be breeding horses."

"I'll deal with that if and when I have to. I'm bringing Pamela to the ball tonight, and I'll—"

Magnus interrupted. "You'll find the keys to my town car on a marble-top table in the foyer. Turn left from the gate, drive until you see a white brick church on the left side of the road, about four and a half miles. Turn left at the next exit and drive straight for about half a mile. You'll see a big brown-brick Tudor house on the right side of the road.

There are no houses close to it. That's the Langford place. I assume you brought your driver's license."

"You bet I did. And thanks for the loan of your car. I'll take good care of it."

They walked back to the house, and he saw that the crowd had begun to thin. "Seems a good time to get a swim," he said to Magnus. "I'll see you later."

"We have dinner at seven."

"Thanks."

"And if you'd like a drink, we'll be in the den around six. See you later."

Drake went inside and caught himself whistling as he dashed up the stairs. He slipped into his bathing trunks and then remembered that he ought to call home.

"Hello. Harrington House."

"This is Drake, Alexis. How's everything? I'm calling to let you know the plane landed safely."

Her chuckle always had a ring of home and family. "Somehow, we didn't think that plane was still in the air. How's the picnic?"

"Out of sight! This man does everything with style and class. What's Tara doing?"

"Practicing. She's let me know that when she's studying the piano, as she puts it, she does not want to be disturbed."

"Do you think all children develop as she does? She's six, and a few days ago, she told me I should run for president and she and Grant would vote for me."

"She has learned so much growing up in this house with adults who love her and take time to talk with her and explain things to her. She's had wonderful nurturing here, and I'm so grateful for it."

"Oh, come on, Alexis. You've nurtured all of us. Ask Henry what he wants me to bring him from Texas."

"I'll ask him, but you may be sorry."

"No, I won't. I'd do anything for Henry. Call me on my cell before eight o'clock your time. I have to leave about forty-five minutes after that for the ball Cooper's giving tonight."

"A ball? Who are you escorting?"

He was going to get a real bang out of this, so much so that he could hardly keep the laughter out of his voice when he answered. "Pamela."

"*What?* You took her with you?"

"No. I didn't. This is her home. Either you or Henry call me."

"But you can't drop a bomb like that one and hang up."

"Sorry, sis, but I've got to get to the pool. Bye."

He hung up and enjoyed the best laugh he'd had all day. Running down the stairs to the back of the house where the swimming pool was located, he was glad he'd brought a decent swimsuit and not the scanty thing he usually wore on the beach. Even so, he didn't feel overdressed. He walked out to the edge of the pool, decided not to dive, but walked down the winding steps until the water reached his waist and kicked off. Winded after three laps in the Olympic-size pool, he swam to the edge, pulled himself up and sat down.

Almost at once, he was joined by a woman in the skimpiest of bikinis. A red one. "You're a very graceful swimmer," she began. "I was fascinated."

He didn't like aggressive strangers—male or female— and he was of a mind to tell her so when she said, "And those biceps aren't bad, either. In fact…" She reached out to test the muscle with her hand.

For a minute he battled with his upbringing, wanting to insult her, but was disciplined never to do that. However, he couldn't resist an unfriendly glare and a parting shot. "I'm a man, not a toy," he said, rose and walked back to the house with her loud gasp ringing in his ears. "You're lucky that I'm a guest here," he said aloud to himself. With time to spare, he showered and telephoned Selena, using his cell phone.

"I'm wearing a tuxedo to the ball," he said when she answered, "and I'd rather not eat dinner in it. How may I dress for dinner?"

"We won't dress for the ball until after dinner, so come as casual as you like. By the way, one of my friends, Deana Smith, wants to meet you. She's coming to the ball alone. Interested?"

"Thanks for not springing that on me at the ball. I'm escorting Pamela Langford, and she's all the company I want."

"Really? Pamela didn't tell me that. That's wonderful. We're close friends. Did you meet her today, or did you know her before you came?"

If she wanted the details, she could get them from her husband. "I've known her for a while, and she's…she's very special to me." Her deep velvet-toned laugh raised his antenna. "What's amusing, if you don't mind me asking?"

"Plenty. I hope Pamela wears her boxing gloves. Half the single women there will be ready to pounce. I've lost track of the ones who badgered me today for an introduction to you."

Hmm. "I must say these women are more aggressive than I'm used to. They don't waste time making their wishes known."

This time she laughed outright. "Some of the men are even more adept at that. They'll crowd you until you tell them to back off. I'll keep an eye out tonight to make sure you two have fun. The women will be after you, and the men will be after Pamela, so when the orchestra announces a tag dance, don't give her up. You can bet Pamela isn't going to give you up when the women tag."

"Thanks for the warning. It ought to be fun. I'm looking forward to it." He was also looking forward to meeting Pamela's parents.

However, when he knocked on her door, it was Pamela who opened it, a vision in a rose-colored off-the-shoulder sheath with a matching silk-and-lace stole. "You're beautiful, and you look so lovely in this dress," he told her, and waited for her to ask him to come in.

"I'm ready," she said, and then as if she were seeing him for the first time, her eyes widened. "Drake, my goodness! You ought to see yourself in that tux. I feel like a princess going out with you tonight."

A smile lit up his face, and he leaned over and kissed her quickly on her mouth. "You are a princess, and you know how to make a guy feel great. Thanks for the compliment."

He didn't pray often, but he said a silent prayer then that nothing would happen to blight the beauty of the day. For the first time in a long while, he felt at peace with himself about his life and every important person or thing in it.

"My coach awaits us, Cinderella," he said. "Let's go to the ball."

Chapter 6

Almost as soon as the orchestra leader's downbeat was heard, Drake had reason to appreciate Selena's earlier explanation of protocol for tag dancing. Without waiting for the signal that tag was appropriate—and it never is for the first dance—John Langford strode directly to Pamela and, as if Drake weren't standing there, asked her for the dance.

"I deferred to him yesterday," John said to Pamela, "but not tonight."

"You will either defer now," Drake said, "or we'll step outside and settle it."

"That won't be necessary," Pamela said. "I won't dance with you, John. Drake is my man, and that's why I'm with him."

"Do you know what you said?" John asked her, his face dark with a thunderous expression.

"Of course I know what I said. Do you want me to make it plainer?"

The man seemed to lose an inch of the height that brought him to within a fraction of Drake's six foot four, and his obvious pain revealed itself in his ashen face. He turned and walked away minus the vigor and purpose with which he had joined them.

Drake studied the sag of the man's shoulders, his entire demeanor broadcasting defeat. But he had no sympathy for John Langford; a man was foolish to make demands of a woman unless he was entitled to do so.

"Selena told me that cutting in is allowed when the orchestra leader announces a tag dance. Why would he do that if there's nothing between you?"

"Whenever I come to visit my parents, he drives me around, takes me wherever I want to go and is…well, a good friend. But I think I've misunderstood his motives."

"You certainly have, and he intended for you to mis-understand, hoping to present you with a fait accompli. You'll have to figure out a way to handle him."

"I think it's dishonest for a man to camouflage his inten-tions." Suddenly, as if all thoughts of John had vanished, her face lit up with a smile. "You…uh… Did you mind when I said you were my man? It wasn't my intention to obligate you. I just wanted to avoid further unpleasantness."

"You just wanted to… Why would I mind? I thought you meant it."

Her right eyebrow rose slowly. "You think I'd announce a thing like that to anybody? I mean anybody? It implied something that isn't true. And even if it didn't, it's too much like street talk for my taste. But he was acting out, and I knew that would put a stop to it. For Pete's sake, what are you laughing at?" she asked, glaring at him and no longer on the defensive.

He took her arm and walked away from the two women who approached them. "I was laughing because you're uptight about what Cousin John will think. You told the truth. I am your man, and what that implies will come, and very soon."

Her hands went toward her hips, and he smothered a laugh. "Now, I know we don't put our hands on our hips in public."

"You're going to get yourself into trouble, Drake Harrington."

The first strains of "Sophisticated Lady" wailed from an alto saxophone, and he opened his arms to her for their very first dance. "If it's the kind of trouble you've been giving me all day, I'll welcome it."

She didn't speak, for the feeling of his hand on the bare flesh of her back sent shivers throughout her body, and something like pinpricks danced up and down her spine. He held her a little closer, and she missed a step. As if he knew how his nearness made her feel, he stepped back a bit while continuing the dance, moving his hips in a dazzling rhythm.

She looked at him and nearly lost her balance, jolted by the naked need in his eyes. He pulled her back into him, wrapped both arms around her and danced a slow one-step. "People are looking at us," she whispered, mostly out of nervousness.

"Let them. I'm claiming every one of your dances right now, tag or no tag. Do you understand?"

What could she say? His famous charm and charisma were not on display, and his face—indeed, his entire manner—bore all the seriousness of a judge sentencing a convicted criminal.

"Do you understand me?" he repeated.

She stepped back and looked him in the eye. "I don't want to dance with anyone else. If this is the way you want it, remember that you don't dance tag with the women, either."

He grinned, then winked at her. "I hadn't planned to."

She was going to let him know that he couldn't snow her, that even if he'd mesmerized her, she still had a sound mind. "You've got a lot to live up to. All day, you've been making promises and demands, and I'm keeping score."

His hand rubbed her back, and she gave him a censoring look. His response was a show of his glistening white teeth. "I couldn't rub anything else and I had to rub *something,* so I did the decent thing and rubbed your back."

She didn't risk looking at him, because she suspected that he had wrapped a halo of innocence about himself. *I don't know this man,* she thought. *I see so much in him and about him that I love, and I'm just learning that he can be devilish.*

"Are you priming me for something?"

That time, *he* missed a step. "You bet your life I am."

"That's not what I meant."

The saxophonist wailed the last notes of the scintillating song, and Drake walked with her over to the door and looked at his invitation. "We're at table seven."

After they'd seated themselves, a waiter arrived with a tray of assorted drinks. Pamela accepted a gin and tonic, and Drake took a glass of lemonade. "I have to get you safely home," he explained. "Besides, if I'm going to dance, alcohol is a no-no. It guarantees that I'll be drenched with perspiration."

He took a few sips of lemonade. "If you didn't mean what I meant, what *did* you mean?"

"I meant… You don't have to know everything," she said, seeing the twinkle in his eyes and knowing that he was laughing at her.

"At least you had the grace not to fabricate something,"

he said. "How about going riding with me tomorrow morning? I'm sure Cooper won't object. He told me you love to ride."

"I do. I learned to ride a pony when I was eight, and I've been riding ever since."

From her eager expression, he knew she would be a wonderful riding companion. "I love horses," he told her, "and I have a stallion that I board at a commercial stable. I'd like to know all the things we have in common so I can exploit that information."

She reached out and touched his arm. "Drake, don't move so fast. Give yourself space to back up. When I woke up this morning, I was trying to clear you out of my mind. I had decided to forget about men, and to find a child that needed me and adopt. Now, you—"

"You decided to do *what?*"

"Forget about men and marriage and adopt a child. That's what I said. I could have my own, but I don't think it's appropriate for a woman in my position, a public figure, to give birth unless she's married."

She could see that she'd stunned him. Maybe now he'd realize the depth of her need to experience motherhood.

The waiter brought a tray of broiled chicken livers wrapped in bacon, and he waved it away almost as if he hadn't seen it. "You can't do that. Why on earth would you do a thing like that? Children need both parents."

"If they have both, they're lucky. If they don't, they manage," she said. "I've made up my mind. I've met several men recently who I thought would make good fathers, but I couldn't stand the thought of being intimate with them. So I've given up the idea of having my own child, and I'm going to adopt one who needs me." To let him know she meant what she said, she gave him a level look and didn't waver her gaze.

He leaned forward with both palms pressed against the tabletop and glared at her. "Are you telling me that you've been going out with guys, looking for one you could sleep with?"

"Can you think of another way for a woman to get pregnant, except for artificial insemination, which wouldn't be any fun?"

He continued to stare at her as if he'd been struck dumb. Then he said, "Hell! If you want a baby, dammit, I'll give you one."

She began to enjoy his rising furor, the set of his jaw as he ground his teeth and the flair of his nostrils giving evidence that his mind had begun to play tricks on him. "Thanks, but no thanks. I'm sure you'd fill the requirements of both lover and father very nicely, but as long as I'm single, any weight I gain will come from the calories I ingest."

"You may think this is amusing," he growled, "but I definitely do not."

She lifted her right shoulder in quick, dismissive shrug. "Amusing? Please tell me how giving up a cherished idea, a lifelong dream, could be amusing. If anything, it makes me want to bawl."

It was as if his countenance darkened when a frown creased his face and he reached toward her, then let his hand fall to the table. "Let's… Let's dance." He got up from his chair. "Dance with me."

She rose slowly, knowing what would happen when he opened his arms and she walked into them. She didn't know what step the other dancers were doing, for her gaze was locked with his. Her body swung to his rhythm, slowly, without regard to the dance style of the time. She caught her breath when his hand moved up to her bare back, and knew he saw her reaction. His aura captivated her as a hook snares a fish, and she submitted to his will and his moves until they danced as one. After a time, she stood on the dance floor locked to him, unaware that the music had stopped, for the tune that she heard in her heart played on.

"Want to wait for the next one?" he whispered. "Or would you rather go back to our table?"

She looked around. "People are staring at us. I...uh, guess we should go back to our table. Oops! Did you hear that?"

"Yeah. I heard it, but I'm not playing tag tonight."

A man approached their table. "May I have this dance, miss?"

"I'm from Maryland," Drake said, "and up there we don't do this." As the words left his mouth, a hand tapped his shoulder.

"Tag," the woman said.

"He and I have an agreement," Pamela said. "He doesn't want me to leave him, so I demand that he not leave me. Sorry."

The woman's eyes bulged, and she glared at Pamela. "That's not the way it goes. This is a tag dance."

"If we argue about it long enough," Drake said with a note of optimism in his voice, "the dance will be over. I'm sorry, ma'am. This gentleman is looking for a partner, too, so I suggest the two of you dance."

"I...I've never heard of such a thing," the woman sputtered.

With his apologetic expression, he begged the woman's forgiveness. "I'm a man of my word, and I promised her that I wouldn't ask of her any more than I was prepared to give."

"Now, we can't dance except with each other, Drake, and these people are going to give us a hard time. Before the evening is over, we'll have to explain at least fifty times why we aren't playing tag."

He winked at her and a grin formed around his mouth. "Fine with me. I can be very creative. For example, your foot just came out of a cast yesterday morning, or I could say I've been after you for so long that I'm not about to yield you to another man, tag or no tag. I'd prefer the latter."

"Well, I don't."

"I have a better idea. Let's say our goodbyes to our hosts and get out of here. If they have any sort of imagination, they'll understand. If they don't, we'll give 'em the story about your foot and the cast that came off it."

He said it without any semblance of a smile. The longer she looked at him—wearing a look of expectancy as he waited for her response—the closer she came to expelling the laughter that she could barely control.

"You are not serious," she said.

"No? Then I'm not Drake Harrington, either. What do you say?"

"I'm all dressed up, and you're going to take me home and leave me there?"

He looked toward the ceiling as if begging for patience. "If we were in Baltimore, you wouldn't dare ask me that."

The orchestra leader said, "Tag," and hit the downbeat for the first reggae number of the evening. She nearly laughed at the terror on Drake's face when a buxom woman with all but her aureoles revealed by her deep décolletage knocked over her chair as she rushed to Drake.

"Tag," the woman said, tapping his shoulder.

He looked at Pamela for help, and she wanted to remind him of his creativity, but the look of desperation on his face told her she had better not do it. "We were just leaving," she said. "He's not quite himself."

The woman glared at Pamela. "I guess you'd know. He looked like himself when the two of you all but went at it during that last dance." Then she shrugged. "I can't say I blame you, sis. If he was mine, I wouldn't let him out of the house." She sashayed off and successfully tagged another man.

"Whew." He made a ceremony of wiping his brow. "I really do want to leave, but I think we should thank Magnus and Selena before we go."

She agreed. "Something tells me these women frighten you."

"I wouldn't take it that far, but I hate being treated like a thing."

"Now you know how a lot of men treat us women, and why we're always fighting their overfamiliarity."

It occurred to her as they walked along the sidelines looking for either Magnus or Selena that most men—regardless of age or skin color—would give up a lot to look like Drake. But none of them would believe that such good looks had a downside.

Like a schoolboy showing off his first girl, Drake held her hand as they walked, glancing down at her from time to time with a grin that seemed so intimate. "If you grew up under Henry's tutelage, the chance of becoming a chauvinist would be practically nil. Henry adored his wife and treated her as his equal. I didn't observe that in my parents, because my father worked all the time—or so it seemed to me. And, as I've told you, my mother's heart was not in the home."

"Would you vote for a woman for president?" she asked him.

"Why not, if she's competent? She couldn't be worse than some of the men who've had the job, and she might bring some humanitarianism to it." He nodded in the direction to her left. "They're over there," he said of Magnus and his wife, and they walked over.

"It's a great party, Magnus, and we're enjoying it. But I'm going to leave now and take Pamela home," Drake said. "I'll be back early enough so that I won't have to wake you up in order to get in."

"Not to worry," Selena said. "There'll be someone to let you in."

A grin brightened Magnus's face, and a twinkle danced in his eyes, alerting Pamela to the sally that would come. "These gals can wear you down, man."

Drake ran his fingers through his hair, his face the picture of confusion. "I don't understand it, man. Are these ladies always so...so—"

"So aggressive?" Selena finished the sentence for him. "A man's engagement doesn't stop them. They're in for the chase until they see a band on the third finger of your left hand. These are upper-class women, Drake, and in the twenty-first century, they are still taught that every girl should be married. The competition among them for eligible men makes basketball players seem sluggish."

Magnus winked at Pamela. "If you had any friends here tonight, you've lost them. Indeed, I ought to give you both a bodyguard—quite a few men here would like to take a swing at Drake. You two have fun."

"By the way, Magnus, I'd like to go riding with Pamela in the morning. Is it all right with you?"

"What time?"

Drake looked at Pamela. "It's best to ride early, when the air is fresh. I'd say around seven," she said.

"One of the guys will saddle Bingston and a mare, probably Lady Love. Breakfast will be ready at six-thirty."

Drake thanked their hosts and walked with Pamela to

the town car. "Now that we have the time to ourselves, how far is San Antonio?"

"Ten miles on a modern highway. Why?"

"I'd like to see the River Walk along the San Antonio River at night when it's lit up. How about it?"

"In these clothes?"

"Of course. I like the way you look."

He drove through the big iron gate, followed the sign pointing in the direction of San Antonio and headed for Route 35. At the Hyatt, he gave the doorman his car key, got a receipt and walked with her through the hotel to the back that faced the River Walk.

"I'd been wondering where you'd park."

"I've learned that a couple of bucks will save a lot of time. These men depend on tips, and I use their services as often as I can."

"I've heard you say some things today that tell me you have strong social consciousness, that you're a humanitarian."

"No such thing. I try to do what's right and to treat other people the way I'd like them to treat me. Sainthood is something I've never expected to achieve." Suddenly a grin began to form around his lips and spread over his face, causing her to stare at him, mesmerized. "You could inspire me to achieve it, though."

He had to be joking. She hadn't even been able to inspire him to head toward the altar.

Drake liked his hosts and he liked the family party, including the ball, but he'd begun to feel suffocated with the unwanted attention. In his experience, women didn't hit on a man unless he was alone, and the same especially went for the behavior of men toward women. Men were turf conscious, guarding theirs the way a lion protects his pride. Only a reckless man, such as John Langford, risked invading that territory. Women did, too, he knew. But in his circles, they were more subtle about it.

"Why is it," he asked Pamela as they strolled hand in hand along River Walk, "that you're different from so many of the women I've seen here?"

"Possibly because they don't have Phelps Langford for a father. He still takes every opportunity to impress upon me my worth as a human being, that I don't need to be anything or anybody but who I am in order to have worth and importance."

"It's a healthy lesson, provided he thinks one ought to prepare oneself to be of benefit to oneself and to society."

"He does."

"Want a ride on the Yanaguana?" he asked her of the flat-bottomed boat that cruised the river. He glanced over at the ladies' specialty shop they were about to pass, led her to the door and said, "Wait right here."

Inside, he found what he wanted at once. "Who's the lucky woman?" the sales woman asked him as she wrapped the black stole.

He paid with his credit card and smiled with the pleasure of anticipating Pamela's reaction. "I hope she thinks she's lucky. Thank you." He stepped outside and handed the package to Pamela.

"What's this?"

His heart fluttered wildly. Suppose she didn't like it. "Open it and look."

She did, held up the stole, black lace lined with black silk, and hugged it to her body. "Drake. Thanks so much. How did you know I was cold?"

"I know it's July," he said, "but it's usually cool this time of night if you're near water. Oh, heck. I noticed that several women put a sweater or a jacket around their shoulders, and they weren't wearing a strapless dress, so—"

She reached up and kissed his cheek. "If I had my way…" She let her voice trail off.

He suddenly had a sense of urgency, a desperate need to know the end of her thought. Facing her, he grasped both of her shoulders and stared down into her face. "If you had your way, what would you do?"

Her eyes clouded with unshed tears, and he wished he hadn't pushed her. "I'd…I'd… Just say, I'd be so much happier."

"This is not the time to pursue this, but we'll get back to it before I next sleep in my own bed." He also surmised what she hadn't said; not exactly, perhaps, but he understood the sentiment of it.

As they stepped into the Yanaguana, he had only one thought: *It's time I put my house in order.*

She wrapped the stole to her body, happy that she no longer felt the chill, but happier still that he cared and that he'd shown it. He helped her into the flat boat that floated along the picturesque River Walk, past people from all over the world—if their manner of dress could be taken as evidence—and past scores of lovers, holding hands, stealing a kiss, expressing their intimacy. He tucked her closer to him and eased an arm around her waist. They passed the Fiesta Noche del Rio and all of a sudden trumpets blared, a spotlight beamed and dancers in colorful costumes began to exhibit their talents.

"It's idyllic," she whispered.

"Yes. It makes me realize how much like my father I've become. Don't misunderstand me. I loved him, and I miss him to this day, but he passed his days and many of his nights working, building a life for his family. I'm sure he never saw anything like this and never spent an evening like this with someone he…" He swallowed the words and, knowing that she had to be aware of his hesitancy, squeezed her into him and said, "Someone he cared for."

She pretended not to notice, wondering at what he'd almost said. "Don't you find time for yourself?" she asked him.

"I've spent more leisure time this weekend than I remember ever having spent before. When I'm at Eagle Park, I'm either at a site working or in my room working. After dinner, I spend maybe an hour with our family. Or if it's hot, I'll go for a swim. On Sunday morning, or an occasional evening when there's good weather, I'll take my horse out and ride for a while so he can get some exercise. But that's about it."

"What about your fraternity? You have dates, don't you?"

"I don't enjoy spending time with the good old boys drinking, talking about women and exaggerating one's achievements. As for dates, of course I have them, but an evening here or there. I've avoided having a steady, because I haven't been willing to involve myself in a serious relationship. I understand women and respect their need for security in relationships—something I haven't been willing to offer."

Now was the time to ask, and she wasn't going to pass it up. "Is that why you've had this seesaw thing with me?"

"Especially so. From the start, I couldn't be casual about us, and I knew it was the same with you. I kept as much distance as possible between us, because the more I saw you the more I wanted to be with you. You're a spark I haven't been able to put out."

A whiff of cool breeze brushed across her face. An omen,

perhaps, but she was going to ask him anyway. "Do you still want to?"

Shivers raced throughout her body, and when he said, "Doesn't look like it, does it?" her heart began to race like a runaway train, and she clutched at her chest as if to control its beat.

She turned her body to his so that her breast caressed his side and rested her head against his shoulder. "I hope not. Oh, Lord, I hope not."

His left index finger at her chin urged her to look at him. She did and felt the sweetness of his mouth on her lips. Both of her arms encircled him then, and she squeezed him to her as best she could before easing herself back to her seat. She glanced back to see who had observed her in that moment of weakness.

"It's a good thing there's no one seated behind us."

"Why? This place is for lovers. I'm over twenty-one and I pay my taxes, so what if I do kiss my woman?"

She wondered why he laughed, until he said, "I've always disdained public expressions of affection, and that comment rather amazed me."

After the Yanaguana docked at the Hyatt, they strolled along the banks of the river eating cones of soft caramel ice cream. "I won't soon forget this evening," she said later, getting into the car for the ride back to Waverly.

"You'd better not. I certainly won't."

She sensed a change in him, had sensed it throughout the day, beginning with his possessiveness that morning at the barbecue. And when, at the ball, he had invited John Langford to back off or go outside and settle it, her heart had taken wing. And now, her nerves were on edge as she wondered if he'd back it all up when they reached her parents' home. They rode in silence, for which she gave thanks. She didn't want to hear a single word that didn't give a name to the way he had behaved with her throughout the day. He parked in front of the gracious brown Tudor house and walked around to open her door, but she was already opening it when he reached for it. With her hand in his he walked with her to the door.

"It's dark inside. I'd think they would leave a light on for you."

She looked at her watch. "It's eleven-thirty, so I suppose we got home before they did."

The clear moonlight cast an ethereal glow over him and over their surroundings. The breeze rustled the pines, and the swinging willows had the sound of a straw broom brushing concrete to a simple rhythmic beat. She had never felt so close to him as she did then, not even at those times when he stirred her libido almost to the point of explosion.

"Why didn't they go to the ball again?" he asked, stepping into the foyer with her.

"Because my father is overprotective. Mama wasn't feeling up to eating barbecue, so he pampered her all day as if she were an invalid and took her somewhere this evening for dinner so she wouldn't have to cook."

"It sounds as if he's a loving, caring man."

"Oh, he is that. Definitely. And I want the same."

"You deserve the same." The huskiness of his voice alerted her to what would come. "All day I've waited for this moment when I'd have you to myself with no prying eyes, no need to deny myself a taste of your mouth. Kiss me."

It didn't matter that she hardly recognized his voice, that he hadn't prefaced it with a lot of sweet words. He wanted what she wanted, their arms tight around each other, bodies locked together and his tongue warm and deep inside of her. His hold on her tightened, and she raised her parted lips for the thrust of his tongue. He pushed it into her, gripped her hips with his right hand and locked her to him. Frissons of heat plowed through her and he tested every centimeter of her mouth, darting around, dancing in and out in a demonstration of what he wanted for them, showing her how he'd love her. She heard her groans and could not control them, for her nipples had begun to ache and the fire of desire had found its way to the muscles of her vagina. Of its own volition, her body began to simulate the dance of love and she moved against him, silently asking for what she needed. She placed his left hand on her right breast and rubbed her nipple with it.

"Sweetheart," he said. "Baby, I…I'm human, and—"

"I need it. I need it."

Letting her know that he would deny her nothing, he slipped his hand into the bodice of her strapless gown, released her breast and sucked her nipple into his mouth.

"Oooh," she cried out. "Honey, I can't stand this."

He straightened her dress, and held her away from him, but not before she felt at last the bulge of his sex against her belly. "I'm sorry about that," he said.

With both arms around him, she brought their bodies together. "I'm not sorry. I'm happy that you want me, that it's mutual."

His hips caressed hers again, and then he moved from her and looked into her eyes. "Do you love me?"

"Oh, yes," she said, her voice clear and strong. "I've loved you for a long time, and it's the reason I had decided I'd better not see you again. Do you love me?"

His laugh electrified the silence, and he picked her up, swung her around, hugged her fiercely and swung her around again.

"Oh, yes," he said. "Yes. I have no doubt about it, and you're the only woman I've loved." A half laugh circled his mouth. "Scared the bejeebers out of me when I first realized it."

"And now?"

His smile emitted rays of happiness that enveloped her and warmed her soul. "I have Magnus Cooper to thank for the chance to come to terms with my feelings," he said. "As today wore on, this feeling of contentment settled in me. I got used to it. The restlessness was gone. I didn't want to go anywhere else, do anything else or be with anyone else. Do you understand what I'm saying? It…it feels so right, and I wouldn't exchange this feeling for anything. It's as if I've discovered who I am."

She didn't trust herself to respond to his words, words that, to her, were a more profound declaration of love than, "I love you," which he spoke earlier. She kissed his nose and, in as steady a voice as she could muster, she said, "You're precious to me, so drive safely. Better leave now—if you're here when my father gets home, you may be talking for the remainder of the night. You'll meet my parents tomorrow."

"I'm looking forward to it. I'll be here for you at six. We can eat breakfast with the Coopers and then go riding. Okay?"

"I'll be ready." She kissed him and watched him walk down the path to the car. He loved her, but was he willing to take it to its natural conclusion?

As he drove to the Cooper Ranch, he tried to understand the change in himself, the sense of freedom, the strange emotion that had welled up in him and made him think he could conquer the world if he wanted to.

"Good grief. I'm driving eighty miles an hour." He slowed down to the requisite forty. Maybe they should get married, so he could get himself under control. "Am

I crazy? How do I know that's a good thing? We haven't even made love." *And whose fault is that?* his conscience nagged. He'd played it safe because that had always been his style: if he thought a woman cared, that she was serious, sex was out of the question because he hadn't been serious, and he didn't lead women on to expect what he wouldn't give. He was serious now, and he intended to see that Pamela Langford didn't look at another man.

The sensors on the gate to Cooper Ranch responded to a signal in the town car and opened automatically when he approached. "Oh, well, if she doesn't know, I'll teach her. She's the woman I want."

The next morning, Drake knocked on the front door of the big brown Tudor house precisely at six o'clock. Pamela opened the door immediately and stepped outside.

"Hi. Thanks for not ringing the bell. Daddy's a light sleeper, and they didn't get in until around one. Can I have a kiss?"

"I was so busy admiring your riding habit… Woman, you do everything with style." He lifted her to his body and pressed his lips to hers.

"That's enough. If you turn it on, I'll be mush all day. You look great in that outfit," she said of his beige pants, shirt, jacket, Stetson and brown alligator boots.

He took her hand and headed for the car. "The Coopers will think we planned this. We're wearing the same colors right down to our riding boots. Maybe that's a good sign. Not that I believe in omens."

"I won't go that far," she said. "I've witnessed strange things. I had a cat who would warn me when a big storm, a heavy rain or severe cold weather was approaching. He would rub against my legs until he got my attention. Then, with no evident provocation, he would gaze up at me, and his tail and all of his hair would stand straight up. When he was sure I noticed, he'd lie down under the sofa."

"You're not serious," he said as he turned the key in the ignition. "That's weird."

"I am serious. I gave him to a little boy who was sick and needed a pet. And, strangely, the cat didn't come back to me, but stayed with that child."

"That's way past me. How do you feel this morning?"

"I don't think I can describe it. I walked out on our back deck a few minutes ago, and everything looked new. I've never much liked the daisies that my mother loves so much, but in the reflection of this morning's sunshine against the dew, I couldn't help staring at their beauty. Everything, even the grass, looked different." She glanced at him, warily, as if confused, and he could see that she wasn't sure that she saw what she thought she saw.

"Drake," she said. "I'm different. Honest."

"So am I. It's as if I'm a brand-new man."

Tess, the Cooper family cook, greeted them at the door. "Come in. You're right on time. We're just about ready to start. Bathroom's over there if you need it. If you don't, follow me."

They followed her to the breakfast room where Magnus sat with Selena. Sixteen-month-old Sutton Cooper bounced in his mother's lap, trying to get his fingers into the bowl of raspberry jam. After greeting them, Magnus explained that the Coopers said grace at the table.

"So do the Harringtons," Drake said.

Selena lifted her son from her lap and put him in his high chair. "We'll begin as soon as Tess and Jackson sit down. Tess says grace." Tess joined them, indicated that all should clasp hands, said a prayer and added, "Now, let's get to it, before it gets cold."

The more Drake saw of Magnus and his wife, the more

he liked them. He could see that Tess and Jackson had a place in the Cooper home similar to Henry's status in his home, though perhaps less intimate.

"The horses are ready for you," Jackson said, "and this is the time of day that they most love to trot."

"I thought we'd ride along the Cayman Lake," Drake said, helping himself to blueberry pancakes and bacon. "I saw a bit of it yesterday, and I'd like to explore it some more."

"Good choice," Jackson assured them. "You can just head that way and leave it to Bingston. He loves cantering along there. But he'll walk it if that's what you want."

Drake glanced at Pamela. He wanted to know her preference as to where they should ride, but she seemed unaware of the conversation. Thinking that she might still be under the influence of their intimacy the previous night, he resumed talking about riding and its pleasures. Then he followed Pamela's gaze and nearly gasped aloud. Selena leaned over her son, smiling adoringly as she fed him with a spoon, and the child beamed with happiness, his eyes sparkling and his face bright with smiles.

His heart seemed to plummet to his belly when he identified the apparent sadness on Pamela's face as raw envy. A feeling of helplessness pervaded him. He no longer cared about the food, although he forced himself to eat it with seeming relish. He wanted to be alone with her, to love her and comfort her. Yes, and to assure her that she would one day have her own child, hers and his.

"Do you mind if I hold him?" Pamela asked Selena after the child finished eating.

"I don't mind if he doesn't. Let's see if he's willing to cooperate."

She passed the boy to Pamela, who cradled him as if she'd always done it. The boy found that her nose and her cheeks made perfect toys, and laughed and played with her. So captivated was she by the child's antics and his total acceptance of her that Drake hated to remind her of their plans to ride along the lake.

"You're a natural," Tess said. "Sutton doesn't take to people readily. Usually if a stranger picks him up, he yells at the top of his lungs. Yes, indeed, you have a way with little ones."

Pamela looked up then, and as her gaze caught Drake's eye, he detected a flicker of embarrassment that he knew was meant for only him: he had seen her at her most vulnerable, and she knew it. He smiled to reassure her and hoped that it worked.

Jackson rose from the table, leaned over and kissed his wife. "Up to your usual high standards." Then he said to Drake, "I think we'd better get started."

With obvious reluctance, Pamela returned Sutton to his mother. "He's so sweet," she said in that low, sultry voice that made him imagine all kinds of intimate scenes with her. "Thanks for the breakfast…and for the baby," she added, with a twinkle in her eyes.

"You're welcome. I'll expect you both for lunch at twelve-thirty, and if you want to swim, you'll find bathing suits, swim caps and towels in the cabana by the pool."

They thanked her and, along with Jackson, headed for the stables. Drake watched somewhat anxiously as Jackson led Lady Love out to Pamela. She greeted the horse with a smile, patted her nose and hugged her neck. Then, assured of the horse's cooperation, she put her left foot in the stirrup and swung herself into the saddle with the grace and expertise of a seasoned cowboy.

Not bad. He mounted Bingston, rode up beside her and said, "That was as graceful a mount as I've ever witnessed. Let's go." He patted the stallion on his rump and, as Jackson predicted, the big bay headed toward the lake. He ran his hands over the saddlebag to feel what it might contain. Jackson or Tess had provided them with something to drink, and he was sure that by the time the sun was high, drinks would be a blessed relief.

Branches of the cypress trees and lost maples bent low over the bridal path beside the lake, creating a lovers' tunnel that obscured from their eyes all but what was beautiful. Occasionally, a fish jumped from the water, and the symphonic voices of birds greeting the morning was as pleasant a sound as he'd ever heard. He pulled the reins slightly, and Bingston stopped and looked back at him as if to ask, "What's the matter? Aren't you satisfied with me?"

He patted the horse's rump and dismounted. "Let's walk," he said to Pamela, and they walked along leading the horses and holding hands. Seeing a wrought-iron bench beside the lake, he tethered their horses and sat on the bench.

"If city folk had this quiet, this peace, if they could hear birds sing and water lap, maybe they wouldn't be so stressed," he said. "I've been thinking that when I build my own house, I'm going to have a stable near enough that I can ride frequently."

"I love riding," she said, "but I don't do it unless I'm down here. Selena and I ride together. Where will you build your house?"

"On the Harrington estate. It's much bigger than you imagine. But I want to be near the family. Russ is building up the hill from Harrington House. I want to build closer to the Monocacy River, which would put me a fair distance back of Henry's house. Of course, I'll have to have my brothers' agreement. Russ and I want Telford to keep the family home, and Alexis is happy there. We're building

Russ's house the way he wants it, and when I'm ready, we'll build mine."

He threw a small stone into the lake and watched the water ripple outward. "Pamela, I want to impress upon you how much I love my family and what it means to me to be around them. I'm not a child—I could handle separation, but I wouldn't be happy doing it."

"I understand that, Drake. I've seen the love among all of you, and I think it was expressed best in the way a little five-year-old girl related to all of you. She belonged to all of you, and all of you belonged to her. The love in that house was so strong that it was palpable. I wouldn't want to leave it, either. Will all of you accept Russ's wife? I like Velma a lot, and I thought she suited him. But when I saw her Christmas morning, she said she didn't think she'd made any headway with Russ."

"Doesn't surprise me. Russ is a closed book. He shows what he wants you to see, and nothing else. I hope for Velma's sake that she's penetrated that wall." His laughter seemed to crash the peaceful environment. "But he's marrying her, and he's very happy about it, so I guess she can handle him."

She seemed pensive and then, in a complete change of demeanor, smiled and asked him, "Why do women have to *handle* men? Why can't we just be ourselves?"

Laughter poured out of him until he shook. "Sweetheart, you're not serious. Velma can thank Alexis for partially taming Russ. Al least, by the time she met him, he'd stopped leaving his boots under a chair in the living room, walking around the house in his birthday suit, leaving his socks wherever he pulled them off and dragging himself to dinner anytime it suited him. Russ is like a puppy—he'll do tricks for you, but you have to reward him. He stopped resisting Alexis's orderliness when he learned that she's a great cook, and Russ loves fine, gourmet food. Fortunately for him, Velma is just as good a cook."

By the time he finished that explanation, she had turned fully to face him. "Please tell me that you're not sloppy."

That statement pleased him as much as anything she'd said to him that day. "I definitely am not. I like the finer things in life gracefully laid out, and I was Alexis's ally when she began changing Harrington House from a mausoleum for men to a home." He put his right arm around her shoulder, wanting her to be at ease with him while he asked her some important questions.

"You like horseback riding, and you're good at it. What do you do in Baltimore that lifts you out of your daily grind? Tell me."

"I don't do anything glamorous. You already know I love to sing. I sing even when I'm alone and, of course, in the choir of my church."

"Which is?"

"Presbyterian. I love music and I go to concerts regularly." She rested her head on his shoulder and began toying with the buttons on his shirt. "You probably won't believe this, but my favorite thing to do is fish. I love that more than I love horseback riding or tennis. But there's nowhere in Baltimore to fish, so I drive over to the Chesapeake Bay some Saturday mornings early and go crabbing. But that's not nearly as satisfying as fishing with a fishing pole and going to sleep till you feel a tug at the line."

"You fish in order to get a nap?" He hugged her. "Next time you're at Eagle Park, we'll fish."

She snuggled closer. "The other things I love doing, though not alone, are walking in the woods and, especially, watching the sunset. I'd love to be in a place where I could see the sunset every day."

We'd get on well together, he thought, recalling his

passion for walking in the woods and the serenity he felt watching a sunset.

"I'd better warn you, though," she said. "Dark clouds spook me."

"I'm not crazy about them, but they don't spook me."

Bingston neighed, the horse's way of telling Drake that he wanted exercise. He stood, but with reluctance, feeling closer to Pamela and wanting the feeling to last. She reached for his hand, but instead, he opened his arms, brought her to his body and pressed his lips quickly to hers.

"That'll have to do for now. It wouldn't be wise to start a fire out here. When are you returning to Baltimore?" She told him that she had planned to leave later that day, but was considering postponing the trip until Sunday.

"I have a ten-o'clock flight tomorrow morning, and I'd like us to travel together, unless that would inconvenience you."

"It won't inconvenience me. I'd like it."

"If you'll give me your ticket, I'll change it." She hesitated as if to refuse, appeared to change her mind and told him she'd give him the ticket when he took her home after lunch. "I have to spend a little time with my folks, so I hope you won't mind if we don't see each other tonight."

He did mind, but he understood that she should spend some time with her parents. They mounted their horses and continued the trek around the lake in the idyllic setting of wild blooming dandelions, bluebonnets, black-eyed Susans, flowering grasses and other vegetation native to the region.

"I'm never going to forget this," Pamela said.

"I hope you don't, but I've learned never to say never."

She patted his knee, a familiarity that, only two days earlier, she would not have assumed. "Don't you think your allure has power?" she asked him, thinking he would take it as the joke she intended.

Drake looked straight ahead. Did she assume, as other people often did, that his face guaranteed him anything he wanted? He fought back a sinking feeling. Lord, he hoped not.

"I'm flesh and blood, Pamela, and I ache and sweat exactly like any other man. Don't get it into your head that I don't. I work like hell for everything I get, and it doesn't come any easier to me than it does to Joe Blow. You didn't fall over when you knew I wanted you, did you?"

"Naah," she said, her voice colored with amusement, "but have you ever braced yourself against a hurricane-force wind? I can tell you exactly what it's like."

In spite of his effort to be serious with her, he had to laugh. "You're a nut. I was serious."

"I was, too, but I know why that topic rings your bell. You don't want to be seen as shallow. Have no fear—if I thought that, we might be on speaking terms, but that's all."

"Glad to hear it. When we get off these horses, you'll owe me a kiss, a solid one then and there."

"Be glad to oblige," she said. He liked her comfortable manner with him, the ease with which she bantered and the fact that she didn't try to impress him.

"May it always be this way," he added, and he meant it.

Chapter 7

After lunch with the Cooper family, Drake and Pamela began the drive back to her parents' home with Drake at the wheel of Magnus Cooper's town car. A few miles before reaching their destination, he stopped the car at a deer crossing in order to get a better look at the flowering crepe myrtle that was bunched in a grove beyond the little brook that flowed beside the road.

"I don't know what it is about settings like this one," he said, "but they make me want to slow down and take stock of my life."

They had so much in common. She understood what it meant to be close to nature. "I can appreciate that. When I lived at home, my mother and I would walk along that path on the other side of the brook on summer evenings when the air had cooled. I loved it, and I would daydream of someday walking along there in the moonlight with a man I loved and who loved me."

Her eyes widened when he said, "It's too early for

moonlight—I'll take a rain check on that one." Was he telling her that he intended to nurture their love?

As if he knew what was going through her mind, he explained, "You and I have a long way to go, Pamela. A very long way. Last night, I slept as peacefully as a man can sleep and woke up this morning anxious to get on with the day. What do you think explains the fact that after years of light sleeping and of wrestling with the sheets, I woke up this morning in a bed that looks as if no one slept in it?"

She wanted to hear it in plain English, not in allegories. "I'd rather you told me. I don't want to jump to false conclusions."

He continued as if he hadn't heard her. "You know what impressed me most about this weekend? The biggest and most pleasant surprise, besides the unlikelihood of finding you here, is finally knowing that it's *you* that I treasure. It's realizing that you and I are soul mates, and that has really rocked me."

"I know. When we were sitting on that bench by the lake, I had that same feeling, a sense that we were knit of the same fabric. Still, I'm almost ashamed to say that, in spite of that feeling, I kept thinking of that old adage, 'There's many a slip between the cup and the lip.' I'm not a pessimist, but we moved so far so fast yesterday and today that…well, we need to be careful."

"Some guy made you wary of men, and I definitely do not want to meet him."

"Not of men, but of exceptionally handsome men."

He switched from Park to Drive, started to move and slammed his foot on the brake when a fawn jumped out of the bushes. For as long as it cared to, the animal stood in the middle of the road observing the car and then continued its journey.

"See that?" Drake said. "That fawn trusted me not to

harm him. Since you know me, you should be able to do the same."

"I do trust you."

"Time will tell."

They rode in silence until they reached her parents' home. "Are they expecting you to bring me with you?"

"I told them you would bring me home, and that I would ask you to come in and meet them, but I didn't say what time we'd get here, because I didn't know."

She inserted the key into the front-door lock, and as if by the power of an inanimate sensor, simultaneously the doorknob turned. As the door opened, he prepared himself to smile, but the face that met his eyes bore what he could only describe as a frown of displeasure. Pamela gave the door a little push, and the man stepped back to let them enter.

"Daddy, this is Drake Harrington, of whom you've heard me speak," she said, and he didn't miss the note of determination—or was it defiance?—in her voice. "Drake, this is Phelps Langford, my father."

"I'm glad to meet you, sir."

"Likewise."

"How about some lemonade?" she asked, looking at Drake, and he thought her fingers tightened around his in a plea for understanding. He came prepared to like Pamela's parents and to extend himself so they would be comfortable with the knowledge that their daughter was in his company. But the man didn't receive him with anything approximating hospitality, so he'd let the chips fall where they may.

"I'd love some lemonade," he said, for she and not her father was his focus. Moreover, if the situation was less than comfortable, she would hurt for his sake, and he did not intend to cause her any distress, not even if he had to deal with her father another time. "Where's your mother? I'd like to meet her."

"She's in there primping for your benefit," Phelps said. "She thinks she has to make a good impression on you." He might as well have added, "For what purpose, I don't know," because his tone suggested as much.

Pamela led the way to the living room, holding his hand, and he wondered at the display of possessiveness and whether it was only for her father's benefit. "I'll be back in a few minutes. Have a seat."

Drake chose a big wing chair, one that would complement rather than diminish his stature, for he realized that Phelps Langford did not welcome him and that the man would attempt to put him on the defensive. He hoped Pamela would hurry with the lemonade or that her mother would finish primping and come in, because the idea of a battle with Pamela's father didn't sit well with him, though he wouldn't back away if Phelps initiated it.

As if, by extrasensory perception, she knew his thoughts, Pamela returned quickly with a pitcher of lemonade, glasses, cookies and dessert plates that had a dancing reindeer painted on them. She poured three glasses of lemonade and sat on the end of the sofa that was closest to Drake.

"Pretty hot out there today," Phelps said, serving notice that he would guide the conversation to suit himself.

Drake didn't answer. He disdained banalities and didn't engage in small talk if he could avoid it. At the moment, he simply didn't care to oblige, so he let Pamela agree with her father about the weather and decided that if the man mentioned the recent dearth of local rainfall, he'd leave.

However, he discovered that Phelps Langford was too sophisticated a man for that level of nonsense when he said to his daughter, "See what's keeping your mother," a ruse that guaranteed him at least a few minutes of privacy with his guest.

Pamela got up with obvious reluctance. "Daddy, you know Mama won't come in here till she looks perfect." She threw Drake an apologetic glance and walked toward the foyer where he had observed a wide staircase leading upstairs.

He could see that Phelps was not going to allow him and Pamela any privacy. Whether it was with malicious intent he wasn't certain, but he was getting negative vibes, and he didn't like them.

"I take it you've been seeing a lot of Pamela," Phelps began.

"Less than I'd like." He waited for the man's reaction to that, leaning forward, his sensors whirling, focused like a hound before it snares its prey.

"I see. And you think you deserve a woman like Pamela?"

Hmm. So here comes the nasty. Drake sat back in the chair and draped his left knee over his right one, the epitome of suaveness—cool outside and seething within. He looked Phelps straight in the eye. "I deserve any woman I decide I want." With both his words and his icy tone, he meant to force Phelps Langford to stop fencing and put his cards on the table.

"Pamela's used to comfort." He waved his hand around to indicate the comfort of his home. "When this moon-eyed phase is over, what do you have left?"

"I suppose you'd know the answer to that. I've never married," he said, responding to the man's attempted put-down.

Phelps's eyes narrowed to slits. "You've got a smooth, sharp tongue, but that won't carry you far in this world."

Drake stared at the man, eyeball to eyeball, fighting

back his rising anger. Like so many other people, Phelps Langford had looked at him and classed him as a shallow womanizer.

"Today, the smart men are computer wizards," Phelps said. "They're the ones making the money. If you're computer-savvy, I can get you a job tomorrow easy as that." He snapped his fingers. "It'll pay eighty to a hundred thousand dollars a year, and my word is all that's needed."

"I didn't know you owned a computer business," Drake said, making sure of his ground before he aimed at the jugular.

"I don't, but I'm well-placed in one."

"I'm computer-savvy, as you put it," Drake said. "I *have* to be, in my line of work."

Phelps waved a hand as if to suggest the insignificance of what he'd just heard. "And what kind of work would that be, I'd like to know?"

Heated nearly to the point of boiling, Drake took a deep breath and told himself to calm down. "I'm the architectural engineer for Harrington, Inc., Builders, Architects and Engineers, a company that my two brothers and I own. We have designed and built houses, schools, malls, municipal buildings and hotels here and abroad. In fact, we've decided that we need a resident computer analyst. Would you be interested in the job?"

"Daddy, how could you?" Pamela nearly shrieked, and his head snapped around toward the door, for he hadn't been aware of her presence. "I'm surprised at you, Daddy, and I'm hurt. After what you've gone through with your parents, how could you… Oh, forget it." She walked over to Drake and, in a gesture of support, leaned over and kissed his cheek. "If I had thought anything like this would happen, I wouldn't have asked you to come in."

"There's no need for you to apologize," he told her. "I can hold my own." He raised his voice to make certain that Phelps heard him. "Your father is protecting your interests, although as far as I'm concerned, he could have chosen a better way in which to do it." He tasted a cookie. "Hmm, these are good. I wanted to meet your mother, but I'm leaving now. Please give her my good wishes."

"Sorry to be so long," a soft voice purred, "but when you arrived, I wasn't dressed."

Drake stood and walked to greet the tall, darker version of Pamela. A beautiful woman, whose smile seemed to warm the air-conditioned room.

"Pamela told me about you, but she didn't mention how tall you were, and she knows my taste in that respect."

"Welcome, Drake. I'm so happy to meet you."

He took her hand and held it. "You can't know how pleased I am to meet you. It is stunning how much alike you and Pamela are."

Her smile radiated kindness and warmth. "Yes. Everyone says that. She's truly a love child. Pamela said you're leaving tomorrow, and that the two of you don't have plans for this evening. I don't want to seem to meddle, but—"

He had to interrupt her before she asked him to have dinner with Phelps Langford. He'd had enough of that man for one day.

"That's because she wants to spend the evening visiting with you and her father. We can all get together the next time Pamela and I are here, and that may not be too far off." He glanced toward Pamela to get a sense of her reaction to what he'd said, and let himself relax when she smiled.

"I must be going now, Mrs. Langford. I have to get to San Antonio before the airline office closes. I'm glad to have met you. Goodbye." He looked in the direction of Pamela's father. "Goodbye, sir."

He didn't offer to shake the man's hand, not because Phelps Langford hadn't extended a hand to him when he arrived, but because to do so would have branded him a hypocrite and a liar. As of that minute, he did not like Phelps Langford.

"Will you call me this evening?" Pamela asked him as they walked to the door.

"Of course I will."

"I'm sorry Daddy acted out. His behavior was unacceptable and not a bit like him. I'm going to have a good talk with him."

As far as he was concerned, "acting out" hardly described it, but he didn't want to be an issue between Pamela and her father. "You're his daughter and his only child, and I suspect he dotes on you. Fathers don't believe any man is good enough for their daughters. Don't be too hard on him."

Her failure to promise wasn't lost on him. He urged her into the warmth of his embrace. When she lifted her lips to his, his blood raced to his loins and he braced himself against the force of his libido. Her kiss, warm and welcoming, set his heart to racing, and he hugged her to his body.

"Lay off, sweetheart," he said. "I have to face the public when I leave here."

Her laughter, low and sensuous, like the first bubble when a pot of water begins to boil, curled around him, and he wanted to hold her forever. "That's nothing," she said. "I have to deal with Daddy, and he can read me like a scanner."

Quickly, he brushed her lips with his own. "Call you tonight."

He strode down the steps and when he reached the car, he looked back and waved, for he knew she'd still be standing there. *Phelps Langford may be important, but now he knows he isn't the only man of stature and value. He'll try to keep his daughter away from me, but as long as she loves me, she's mine.*

Pamela waved at Drake, went inside and stood before her father. She knew he anticipated her ire, and she didn't plan to disappoint him. "You didn't greet Drake, and you gave him the impression that you thought him worthless, that he didn't have a decent enough job to support himself and a family. I was speechless. I couldn't believe my ears. Why did you do that, Daddy? Anybody, including you, can look at that man and see that he stands for something worthwhile. If you hurt his feelings, you hurt me."

Phelps flexed both of his shoulders in a shrug. "You needn't defend him—he's got a mouth and he used it."

She didn't want to plead with her father, because the more she begged, the more stubborn he became. "He's a man, Daddy, and a strong one. Would you expect him to hang his head like a whipped puppy when you insulted him? And another thing—your marriage to a black woman isn't proof that you aren't prejudiced against black men. I'm reminded of your advice that I should marry a white one."

He jerked forward. "What you're suggesting is ridiculous."

She'd known since childhood that a wise person didn't put Phelps Langford on the defensive, that he fought hardest and most ruthlessly when he was down. An inner voice told her to let it be, that she may one day want her father and the man she loved to join hands. But she also knew that she was enough like him to ignore her own warning.

"You may know it's ridiculous," she said, "but does Drake? He came to your home with your daughter, the first man who's walked into this house with me since I was eighteen years old, and you didn't shake his hand or welcome him in any way."

He pulled air through his front teeth, a gesture that was rare for him. "If he can't decide whether to ask you to marry him, why should I genuflect when he shows up here?" The comment didn't surprise her. Her father wasn't given to wasting time fencing, but went straight for the jugular.

She told herself to be calm and to use more tact. "Daddy, yesterday for the first time, Drake Harrington told me that he loves me. I understand him well enough to know that he didn't say it until he was sure he meant it and was willing to back it up. For a while now, he has behaved as if he cares deeply for me. He's not a frivolous man." She could see that she was getting to him. "I love him. I tried to forget him, but it was like trying to store water in a sieve. Useless."

He held his hands up, palms out. "If he loves you, you don't have a problem. I tell you, a man who looks like that one invites mistrust. He's an awfully good-looking man."

"Yes," Delta Langford said, having avoided entering into a conflict between her husband and her daughter as she usually did when they disagreed. "He is definitely that, charming, good manners, and he's got success written all over him." She walked over to where her husband sat and soothed his hair. "Why didn't you see that, honey?"

"Oh, I saw it. I wanted to test his mettle, but he tested mine."

Pamela blew out a deep breath and went upstairs to her room. Phelps Langford didn't know it, but he would discover that making peace with Drake might not be as simple as saying, "I'm sorry."

By the time Drake left the airline ticket office in San Antonio, where he exchanged Pamela's ticket for a first-class one and got them seats together, his temper had begun to cool. Controlling it while in the Langford home cost him a great deal emotionally, and it didn't satisfy him merely to return Phelps Langford's insult. But he had to call Pamela, and he needed a change of mood before he did it.

After a pleasant dinner of roast lamb with Magnus, Selena, Jackson and Tess, he sat with them and watched *The Maltese Falcon,* an old Humphrey Bogart movie, on a wide flat-screen television. The experience was similar to seeing a movie in a movie theater. Thinking how much Tara would enjoy watching *Sesame Street* on such a screen, he decided to buy one for the den in Harrington House. Around eight-thirty, he excused himself, went to his room and telephoned Pamela on his cell phone.

"Hi. Did your father ever cool off?" he asked her.

"I have no idea. He's in the doghouse. Mama and I really stuck it to him. He said he just wanted to test your mettle."

Drake sucked in his breath, his furor rising anew. "He could have found a more gracious way to do it." For the time being, that was his last word on the subject. He would take up the matter with Phelps again when he next saw him, and he *would* see him again.

"I changed your ticket. We're leaving San Antonio on American Airlines Flight 1776 tomorrow afternoon at two, so I'll be by for you at eleven. I hope that suits you."

"It does, and thanks. It's a pity we didn't plan to be together this evening. I fulfilled my filial obligations this afternoon. Besides, I got used to being with you."

He definitely liked the sound of that. "You miss me, huh? Keep it up, and I'll be putty in your hands. Does that mean I'll have things going my way the next time we're together?" He meant it as a tease and a test of her sense of humor.

"You serious? On a plane? What can you do on a plane?"

Thank goodness she couldn't see him, for he was sure he gasped and that his face mirrored his incredulity. "I'm not going to comment on that. You've had a long, emotionally draining day, and you're tired."

"What did I say to draw that comment?"

Laughter rolled out of him. "It isn't what you said. It's what your words implied. If you think I'd let an airplane cramp my style, think again."

"If you think... Oh, for goodness' sake. You're making something out of nothing."

"Whatever you say! Do you have plans for tomorrow night?"

"I had plans to do my laundry, if you can call that plans, but that was before I ran into you down here and got my life turned around. A real twister couldn't have shaken me up more thoroughly."

He hoped she proved to be as honest about everything else. "And you didn't do anything. Right? You didn't help stir up that storm, did you? Kiss me." She made the sound of a kiss. "I was going to send one back to you, but hell, I don't feel like pretending. 'Night, love."

He listened for her reply, wondering if one of her parents had entered the room and she no longer had privacy. Finally, her voice came to him clear and sweet. "Good night, darling." She hung up.

"We're making progress," he said to himself. "If we ever open up to each other fully and completely, what a time we'll have!"

"You got me a first-class seat?" she asked as they took their places on the flight to Baltimore.

He put her carry-on bag in the overhead bin and sat down

beside her. "You don't think I'd fly first class while you sat in an economy seat on the same plane, did you?"

"You could have changed yours to economy."

He extended his left leg and eased the pant leg up. "Not my style, sweetheart. I work hard in order to enjoy creature comforts, and I wouldn't have less for you than for myself. I always fly the best class the plane offers."

The flight attendant arrived and took orders for juice or champagne along with hors d'oeuvres, and asked about their comfort. Would they like a blanket or a pillow and would they please fasten their seat belts.

"I could get used to this kind of attention," Pamela told him. "Uh, I need to ask you something."

A frown flashed briefly across his brow. Then, he grasped her left hand, and in a gentle, encouraging and almost seductive tone, he said, "Tell me. I'm open to anything you want to discuss."

Thinking that if she wasn't careful, he would lull her into just about anything, she said, "I'm invited to an old-fashioned garden party, and the invitation says I should bring my S.O."

"What's that?"

She couldn't believe he didn't know, but she told him anyway. "It means significant other, and I don't have one. Would you go with me?" Suddenly he was holding her hand so tight that she attempted to jerk it away. "Ouch!"

"I'm sorry. I didn't mean to... Are you all right?"

She nodded. "What got into you, Drake?"

"Me? What got into *you?* What do you mean you don't have a significant other? You're telling me I'm not important in your life?"

"I don't believe in being presumptuous, and you have not asked me not to see other men."

He turned to face her as much as his fastened seat belt

would allow. "A little oversight on my part. After what's gone on between the two of us this past weekend, I didn't think you needed that assurance, but I'm too happy to give it. I don't want another man to touch you. Not a strand of your hair or the tips of your fingers. If you need an escort, and I'm out of the country, call Russ or Telford and they'll substitute for me. Do you want it any clearer than that?"

She nearly laughed at the vehemence in his voice. "Suppose Alexis or Velma objects?"

"Neither Telford nor Russ is hooked up to a stupid woman. When will this garden party take place and where? I sure hope men aren't wearing morning coats, because I don't have one."

"She said women should wear wide hats, gloves and long, wide-skirted dresses."

"Did she tell you what kind of shoes to wear? It would serve her right if you wore that slinky dress you had on at Cooper's ball."

Pamela hadn't thought too much about that. She made up her mind to wear whatever dress she chose, wide skirt or not. "You're putting wicked thoughts into my head," she said. "I'll ask her what the men are wearing."

The captain's voice came over the loudspeaker. "You are now free to walk around the cabin, but when seated, keep your seat belts fastened."

He leaned over and kissed her cheek. "I didn't even know when the plane took off. Did you?" His dark eyes seemed to grow darker, and his face revealed a vulnerability she hadn't seen in him.

She shook her head. "Until the captain spoke, I thought we were still on the ground."

His right hand eased around her shoulder. "If we were alone this minute, I wouldn't leave you until I'd locked myself inside of you and loved you until we were both exhausted."

She didn't see the point in being coy with a meaningless response, for she wanted and needed to explode with him deep inside of her. He gripped her shoulder, and when his eyes became turbulent pools of desire, she knew he'd read her thoughts. She closed her eyes lest she betray herself further, but the pressure of his lips on hers sent a fire spiraling through her nervous system and, like a nail to a magnet, she returned the pressure with open mouth to receive his tongue. His swift, short movement in and out of her brought a moan from her, and he patted her shoulder and released her. She looked up to see a smile on the stewardess's face.

"Care for a cocktail, wine, liquor? I'll be along shortly with some stone-crab legs and dipping sauce." The stewardess winked at Pamela and gave the thumbs-up sign. "Way to go."

The temptation to down a drink of straight, hard liquor to settle her nerves was difficult to shake. She settled for a Tom Collins, the lightest cocktail she could think of. Drake ordered a Scotch and soda.

"I don't have to drive until tomorrow morning," he explained.

"Where's your car?"

"It's in the garage underneath the apartment building that Russ lives in."

We're fencing again, she thought. *If he comes home with me, he's not leaving there tonight if I can help it. He knows that, so why can't we level with each other?*

She looked at the menu and chose filet mignon with puff potatoes and asparagus. "I definitely wouldn't have been eating this in economy class," she said. "In fact, I would have been eating pretzels."

"I know," he said. "*Salted* pretzels at that. When will you visit your parents again?"

At first, the question surprised her. Then it occurred to her that Drake considered his contact with her father unfinished business. Fine with her. She loved them both, and whatever happened was between them. She didn't intend to take sides unless her father persisted with his insults, and she thought that unlikely.

She finished eating, drank the remainder of the white wine she'd ordered with her meal, leaned against the back of the seat and closed her eyes. Very soon, a pillow slid between her neck and the seat back, and she smiled her thanks. When Drake's hand clasped hers, she figured that he, too, would go to sleep, and she awakened when the wheels of the big MD 80 touched the earth. She said a silent word of thanks as she always did after a successful flight, and looked over at Drake, still asleep. She let her hand brush the side of his face, and he opened his eyes.

"We're in Baltimore," she said. "I slept all the way, and that's unusual for me, so it must have been the effect of the cocktail and the wine."

"Couldn't have been the comfort of my presence, could it?" he asked her with a roguish grin on his face. "Give a guy a break. I know I don't weave a magical spell, but it wouldn't hurt you to say I do."

She stared at him, not believing what she'd heard. "Honey, you've got powers enough. You don't need magic."

They left the plane, retrieved their luggage at the baggage claim and, with the aid of a porter, found a taxi and headed into town.

"I'll take my things to Russ's apartment. You continue home in the taxi, and I'll see you at seven-thirty at your place. All right?"

She agreed, and plans for their evening began weaving themselves together in her head.

After leaving him, she went home, turned on the air conditioner, unpacked and headed for the gourmet deli, where she bought smoked sturgeon, smoked salmon, fresh salad greens, sautéed red, yellow and green peppers, Greek olives, Stilton cheese, crusty bread and assorted petit fours. Then, she stopped in a florist shop and bought flowers. At home, she put two bottles of Pinot Grigio wine in the refrigerator, set the table, added the flowers and candles, laid out the food and looked around for something to put on—something that would let him know that they were not going out. After a bubble bath, she slipped into a pair of pink bikini panties and a long, flowing, mauve-pink paisley dress that had a halter top.

After combing her hair down, she put on a pair of gold hoop earrings and stared at herself in the mirror. "I'm not beautiful, and I don't care who says so, but nobody can say I don't have sex appeal. If he doesn't hurry up and get here, I won't have a fingernail left." She told herself to be casual and nonchalant, and then her buzzer rang.

"Mr. Harrington to see you, ma'am."

"Thanks, Mike. Ask him to come up." She walked to the door, back through the foyer to the living room, turned and went into the dining room. There, she patted the tablecloth, checked the wineglasses for lint, found none and walked back to the foyer. When she realized she was ringing her hands, she locked them behind her. The doorbell rang, and she lunged toward a chair, tripped up and grabbed the edge of the door for support. With the second ring, she ran her hands over her hair, walked slowly to the door and opened it.

"Hi. Come on in." She ignored his raised eyebrow and

the brief impression of his tongue pressing his right cheek. "Thanks for these beautiful roses. I love tea roses." He walked in, and she closed the door, conscious of the fact that she'd put him off balance. Whatever he was expecting, it definitely was not what he found.

"Have a seat in there." She pointed toward the living room. "I'll be back as soon as I put these in some water."

"I don't think they need any," he said, the first sound he'd made since he rang the doorbell. "They're in a vase inside that box."

My Lord, I shouldn't be so obvious, she thought. *He looked at me half-nude in this dress and practically went into shock, and then I act as if I'm unbalanced. Get your act together, girl.* She took the vase out of the box, removed her flowers from the table and replaced them with his. How was she going to walk into that living room knowing he knew from her backless dress that she wasn't wearing a bra? She sucked air through her teeth and held her head high. *What the hell! I'm thirty years old, and I dress as I please.*

As she entered the living room, she picked up the remote from a table near the door, pressed a button and strains of "Sophisticated Lady" filled the air.

"You like Duke Ellington's music, I see."

"I do, indeed," she said, "plus Wynton Marsalis, George Harrison and Willie Nelson, and some other truly great ones."

He crossed his left knee over his right one. "Three out of four isn't bad."

"Who would you leave off?"

"Well, I guess Marsalis is okay, but I can't identify him by sound, and that means he's not unique. I love the Beatles, and George Harrison's music is identifiable as his own. The

Duke and Willie are American icons. I like music that I can sing."

"But you don't sing," she said.

A grin spread over his face. "Who told you that? Take it back, or I'll throw you down on this carpet and have my way with you."

She stared at him, but he didn't bat an eyelash. The longer she looked at him, the more amusing the idea became, until laughter rolled out of her like thunder heralding a storm.

"I'd like to know why that's so funny."

"Instead of throwing me down on the floor, say what you really want, and perhaps you can use that energy to better effect."

"What?"

Her left eyelid flexed in a fast wink, and she stood. "Let's have a bite to eat. I know we ate on the plane, but that was almost six hours ago." She held out her hand. "Come on."

"I had planned for us to go out to dinner."

"I imagined as much. I hope you didn't make reservations."

"I did, but I'm happy to cancel them." He followed her into the dining room, talking to the hostess at the restaurant on his cell phone as he walked. "It's all settled. When did you do all this?"

"I'm a well-organized woman. By the time I got home, I had everything straight in my mind. The rest was simple. Have a seat." She lit the candles.

"This is a beautiful setting. I like this, Pamela. I enjoy attractive surroundings that have a feminine touch. I don't want it in my personal sanctuary, but everywhere else in the house should feel and look like a home. That's what Alexis brought to our house. She made it into a charming home." He held her hand and said grace, surprising her, for saying grace was not a custom in her parents' home.

He savored the smoked sturgeon. "This is delightful."

"One of these days, I'll cook you a real dinner."

"Name the day. Telford and Russ got themselves good cooks, but I figured it would be my luck to get a woman who didn't know a sack of flour from a bag of cornmeal."

Did he know what he'd just said? She told herself not to hope, but she hoped anyway, saying a silent prayer that Drake would, after all, be the father of her children. She wasn't going to trick him into it, and she had no intention of trying to strike a deal with him. She loved him, and he said he loved her. If it worked, it worked. If not, she would go ahead with her plan to adopt a child.

"My father insisted that I learn how to take care of myself," she said, opting not to respond directly to his remark. "I had to learn how to clean the house properly, sew my own clothes, iron like a professional, do my own hair, cook and serve an elegant meal. He thought if I could do that, I could always get a job, take care of myself and never be beholden to a man, husband or not. And of course, he preached the virtues of education."

"Too bad more young girls don't get that advice. Hmm. This food hits the spot. What kind of work does your mother do?"

"She teaches. Would you like fruit or ice cream for dessert?"

He grinned, dazzling her with his charm and boyish innocence. "If that's the only dessert you're offering, I guess I'll take ice cream."

She'd been standing beside him, reaching for his empty plate, when she stumbled against his chair, but she gathered her composure quickly and let him know that she could give as good as she got. With a pinch of his ear, she said, "You'll get what you deserve."

In the kitchen, she poured Scotch whiskey over scoops

of rich vanilla ice cream and brought two bowls of it back to the dining room. He tasted it, and his brow knit as if he was concentrating deeply. He took in another spoonful and leaned back in his chair, savoring it. A grin around his lips spread into a smile that enveloped his face, and she couldn't help staring at him. Did she dare cast her lot with such a devastatingly handsome man?

"Don't tell me you put whiskey on this ice cream. I'm never going to eat it any other way. It's great."

"I told you you'd get what you deserved," she said, shoving the needle in and turning it.

"You mean this is all I'm worth?" he asked her with a note of resignation in his voice.

"I didn't know we were talking about your worth. I thought the issue was what you deserve. Would you like some more?"

"Thanks, but no. Let's clean up." She gaped at him—elegant in a gray business suit, light gray shirt and gray-and-red paisley tie—scraping dishes, rinsing them and putting them into the dishwasher, wrapping leftovers and turning on the dishwasher. He was so adept at it that she sat on the bar stool at her kitchen window and watched him.

"You're handy in the kitchen," she said.

"You bet, and I can cook, too. Henry taught me and my brothers how to prepare food and to cook basic things. He works for us, but he's been a father to us since our father died when I was fourteen. I was devastated, and if it hadn't been for Henry, I don't know what would have become of me. As long as I'm alive, I'll see that he has the best of everything."

She had a feeling that he'd been warning her all weekend that loving him meant loving his family and that Henry was as much a part of it as were his brothers and their wives. She handed him a bottle of white wine and two glasses, switched off the kitchen light, took his hand and went to the living room, where she sat on the sofa and patted the space beside her.

"What kind of music do you want to hear?" He said he'd leave it up to her, and she flipped the remote control to her Billie Holiday CDs. Soon Billie's world-weary soprano came forth with "Love Me or Leave Me." She had intended to play "I Cover the Waterfront," but maybe fate was telling them both something.

With an arm on the back of the sofa, he adjusted his position so as to face her. "Are you telling me something with that song? I thought we'd passed that stage."

"It was a slip of my finger."

"If it was a slip of your finger, open up to me and let me know you have confidence in me, that you feel that I love you. I don't play games with women, and I'm not playing one with you. If you can't take me for what I am, a man who loves you and needs you and who has no hidden agenda, tell me this second, and you won't have any further trouble out of me. I am not a masochist. It will hurt, but I won't let it kill me."

Chapter 8

"All the past weeks and months when I didn't know where I stood with you, each time we separated I thought I had seen you for the last time. Every time you held me and kissed me, showing me in numerous ways that I needed you and then leaving me to deal with the emptiness, knowing that if you came back I'd take those few minutes of loving only to be empty again when you left me. I hurt, Drake. I hurt something awful. And I'll tell you something else—my lectures to myself went unheeded because you would do so many things, little things that made me care. Don't think for a minute that, except to save myself, I would inflict that on anyone else."

He leaned forward, resting his forearms on his thighs. "And I'm asking for what I didn't give?"

"You gave all that you could and as much truth as you knew. I respected you for it then, and I respect you for it now. It isn't an issue."

He straightened up, and she rested her head against his shoulder. "I do have a bone to pick with you though."

"What's that?"

She looked at her watch. "An hour and eighteen minutes have elapsed since you rang that doorbell, and I'm still waiting for a kiss. I'd like a glass of wine, too."

His sheepish look surprised her. "Damned if I'm not losing panache." He poured each of them a glass of wine, took a sip and rested his glass on the table in front of them. "This isn't what I need. Come here to me," he said, his voice husky and laced with a faint tremor.

He opened his arms, and she dived into them with no thought for the nonchalance she had planned to display. The minute his fingers touched her naked back, a fire began to glow in her loins. As she parted her lips for the feel of his tongue, her one thought was that he was hers at least for the night. He brushed his lips over her parted ones, gazed down into her face—his eyes fierce and burning—and then claimed her with the thrust of his tongue. She took him in, feasting as if she were near starvation. Jolts of electricity whistled through her veins as he sampled every crevice of her mouth. His hands roamed over her naked flesh, and then his arm curved around her back and his hand squeezed her breast.

"Oh, Lord," she moaned. "Yes. Yes. Kiss me. Kiss me. You know what I want." He moved his hand and slipped it into the dress's deep V opening at her bosom and freed her left breast. Her nipple puckered beneath the air of his hot breath, and then his warm, moist mouth covered it and he sucked it, and her world spun off its axis. Her groan of passion echoed through the room.

"Drake. Oh, Drake!"

"Tell me what you want. What you need, baby. Tell me."

"I want you. *You!*"

His big hand gripped her hip and then stroked it, kneaded her belly and moved back to twirl and tease her nipple. "Honey, please. Please," she moaned.

"Please what? Tell me. I want to please you, t—"

She reached out and touched him tentatively, as if she feared doing it. Emboldened by his gasp, she gripped him, and she could feel the hot male in him breaking loose. Her fingers tightened and squeezed. Then she stroked him, and in a second, he was iron-hot, hard and bulging in her grasp. He stilled her hand and stared into her face.

Drake's senses whirled dizzily, and spirals of unbearable tension wafted through his body. The feel of her nipple in his mouth made him shudder as he thought of where that one sweet liberty could lead. Her body began an uncontrollable response to his sucking, letting him know that she was his if he wanted to press his advantage. But he had to slow down, for unless he controlled his passion he wouldn't be able to satisfy her completely, and he'd never left a woman wanting. But as if of their own volition, his lips moved back to her nipple because he loved what he found there. He didn't spare her then, but sucked vigorously, nourishing himself on her sweetness, relishing knowing that she was on the verge of losing control. Then her gentle, unschooled fingers stroked his penis, and he nearly sprang from the sofa.

"Sweetheart. My Lord, woman!" It felt so good. So good. His moans blended with hers, and he sprang into her hand, hard and ready. But because he had to be certain, he stilled her hand and gazed intently into her eyes.

"I want to make love with you. I've wanted and needed it for months," he said, hardly recognizing his voice. "Do you want me?" She nodded. "Now? Say the words, because I'm nearing the point of no return."

"I want to make love with you right now," she said. "Oh, Drake. Honey, don't you know how much I need you?"

"Where is your bedroom?" She pointed to the hallway, and he picked her up and strode through the darkened hall straight to her bed, laid her on it and looked down at the woman he loved.

He pulled the halter over her head, found the zipper at her waistline and removed her dress, leaving her body bare but for the string-bikini panties that covered the V at the apex of her thighs. Beneath his heated gaze, she folded her arms across her breasts.

"Don't. Don't hide yourself from me. Let me look at you. You're…you're so beautiful."

But she squirmed as his gaze roamed from her head to her toes. "You're still dressed. I want to take your clothes off you." He shook his head, and it seemed to her that he had a sudden and overwhelming urge to undress, for he was out of his clothes in a minute.

"Come closer," she said as he was about to take off his briefs. "I want to do that." She slipped them down his muscular thighs and let him spill into her hands. Ready for her. She opened her arms to him in a gesture as old as Eve and, with one knee braced on the bed, he leaned forward and, at last, she had him in her arms, skin to skin with not so much as air between them.

With his head at her shoulder and his lips at the curve of her neck, he whispered, "I'll never forget this moment as long as I live." Suddenly, like water rushing over a broken dam, he went at her, kissing, stroking and murmuring things she couldn't understand. She only knew he cherished her.

Her arms tightened around him as she tried to show him what words couldn't say, and as her body shifted beneath him, his penis jerked against her thigh. She tried to spread her legs, but he restrained her.

"Don't rush it, sweetheart. Let me love you the way I want to, the way I need to."

His lips trailed from the side of her face to her ear and shoulder, barely grazing her flesh. She wanted to feel his mouth on her, to have his tongue deep in her mouth… to…

"Oh, Lord," she moaned when he pulled her nipple into his mouth and sucked it so vigorously that she felt the tug at the mouth of her womb. She reached down to take him into her hands and urge him into her, but he moved aside and continued tugging at her left breast while pinching and stroking her right nipple, sending rivulets of heat through her limbs and spirals of unbearable tension to her vagina. Tremors shook her body.

"You're toying with me. I'm on fire," she moaned, as his lips tortured her belly and his hands teased her sensitive breasts.

"I want you on fire. I want to love you till you can't think of anybody or anything but me. Relax and give yourself up to me." Her thighs began to quiver in anticipation when he hooked her legs over his shoulder and began to kiss and nibble the insides of her thighs.

"Do something to me," she moaned. "I can't stand this."

His fingers parted her folds, and she stopped breathing. Her body lifted itself to him as if of its own will, and his tongue plunged into her. "Oh, Lord!" she screamed, undulating up to him, her inhibition the victim of her passion. He plunged in and out of her, licked, nipped and sucked until heat flushed the bottoms of her feet and her body went rigid.

"Get in me," she pleaded. "I want you inside of me now."

"All right," he whispered and moved up her body.

"I'm not on the Pill," she said, though she would have given anything to have all that he could pour into her.

"Thanks. I'll take care of it." He slipped on the condom that he'd placed on the night table, and she raised her knees for his entry. He looked down at her, his face enveloped in the most beautiful smile she'd ever seen and pressed his lips to hers. "Look at me now, and take me in."

She took him into her hands, led him to her portal of love and raised her hips. Her eyes widened.

"Easy, sweetheart. Let's take this slowly. I don't want to hurt you."

But she didn't want to take it slowly, and she didn't care if it hurt. She wanted him deep inside of her right then. Gripping his hips, she flung herself up to him and bit her lips at the piecing pain.

"Good grief! Is this your first time?"

She refused to brush away the tears that trickled down from her eyes. "There was one other time when I was a sophomore in college. A disaster. I don't want to think about it. I just want you to love me. It doesn't hurt anymore."

"Are you sure?"

For an answer, she brought his lips down to hers and let her kiss tell him what she needed. His fingers trailed from her breast to her belly and on to the nub of her passion where he teased, rubbed and fondled until she could feel the liquid flowing from her. He looked down at her, grinned and slowly began to move. So this was the way it was supposed to be. Within minutes he was not only deep inside her but on her, beneath her, over her and all around her. The male musk of his body filled her olfactory senses as he accelerated his thrusts and unleashed the power of his loins. A strange kind of heat rode up her legs and thighs and settled in her vagina, filling her until...

"I want to burst. I'm so full. Help me. I can't stand this... It's terrible."

"It's good. Relax and let me have you."

"I want to burst."

"You will. Just do whatever comes naturally."

She tightened her hips and tried to force relief. He had her at a precipice, suspended between earth and heaven, bringing her to it, pulling her back and dragging her to the edge again until she thought she would die. And then the squeezing and pumping began in her vagina, her thighs twitched violently and she cried out.

"Drake. Oh, my Lord, what are you doing to me?"

He increased the power of his thrusts, and she began to sink into a whirlpool of oblivion only to be tossed seconds later into the wild ecstasy of relief.

"I love you! I love you!" she screamed and went limp in his arms. Realizing that he still moved within her, she locked her ankles over his thighs, found his rhythm and rocked with him until seconds later his hold on her tightened.

"Pamela! Pamela! I love you. Love you. Only you." He moaned and splintered in her arms.

As he lay above her, still locked inside of her, one of her hands smoothed the hair on the head that rested on her breast, and the other one caressed his long back. She wanted him to know that she cherished him, that he'd given her the precious gift of true womanhood, but the words didn't come, so she continued to stroke his body.

"How do you feel?" he asked her. She had thought he was asleep.

"I haven't the words to tell you. I...I didn't know I could

be so happy. Uh...what about you?" She supposed she should ask since he asked her.

"Me? I told you, we're soul mates." He raised himself up and supported his body on his forearms. "If I had known it would be like this with you, trust me, I'm not so sure that my integrity would have won over my libido."

"What do you mean?"

"I always wanted you badly, but because I was unsure about where a relationship with you could go, I didn't let things get to the point where lovemaking was a given. Once or twice, we came close to it. But, baby, if I'd known what I was walking away from, I... Let's just say I have not attained sainthood. You played fair and never once tried to seduce me."

"You wouldn't want someone who wasn't willing, would you? Neither would I, so I didn't push you. But each time we were together, something would happen to let me know that your feelings for me continued to grow, so many little things that told me you cared. But I knew you had a will of iron, and that your mind, and not your feelings, ruled."

"Yeah." He kissed first one of her eyes and then the other, alternating several times. "All that was before my feelings—as you call it—asserted themselves and said let's have an end to this nonsense. Say, I must be too heavy for you." He attempted to raise himself and to roll off her, but she held him tighter, unwilling to release him.

"You aren't too anything for me." She slapped his buttocks and then caressed them gently. "You belong right where you are."

He raised his head, looked into her eyes and smiled, and she thought her heart would burst with all that she felt for him. He cradled her head and brushed his lips over hers. She stared into his eyes—eyes black with desire—stared until she could no longer bear the tension that had begun to build inside of her. His tongue slid over the seam of her lips, and she opened to him and sucked his tongue into her mouth. When she felt him growing within her, she lifted her body to greet his thrust, and it was all the invitation he needed. He shifted his hips and took them on a furious ride to paradise.

Drake lay beside her, his left arm holding her close to his side, lay there listening to her breathing as she slept. He hadn't kept a record, but he had known a good number of women, and after making love with Pamela, he knew that he hadn't previously realized his sexual potential. He suspected that with practice, when they really knew each other, they'd both reach heights he hadn't dreamed of. Questions darted through his mind. How could such a fireball of a woman remain celibate for almost twelve years? She'd characterized the experience as devastating, but he'd bet it was also humiliating. He would have to be careful with her.

And another thing. She wanted a child very badly, and because she loved him, she probably wanted his child. Yet she volunteered the information that she was unprotected when she could have remained silent about it and allowed him to impregnate her, knowing that if he did, he'd marry her.

She not only has integrity, he thought to himself. *She respects herself and me.* He turned on his side, facing her, raised up and balanced himself with his elbow on the bed and his hand at the side of his head. Watching her sleep, he asked himself how he ever thought he would exchange her for a career goal when nothing prevented him from having both. He slipped out of the bed and went to the kitchen to see what he could find to eat, for his belly had begun to pinch him. He made sturgeon and smoked salmon sandwiches, cut several chunks of English cheddar cheese, found some dill pickles and opened a bottle of chilled white wine. He put it all on a tray along with two glasses and went back to the bedroom. A glance at his watch told him it was ten-thirty. Sex always made him hungry. He figured that was because it took more energy than a tough day's work did. He put the tray on her night table after pushing the lamp aside to make room for it, and debated whether to awaken her then or twenty minutes later.

He looked around at the feminine setting. Lilac and soft-green satin covered the bed and adorned the windows, and a Mashad Persian carpet of the same colors lay on part of the floor. The furniture was solid walnut, and he liked that; in his opinion, furniture represented an investment and should be of the highest quality. The shade of the lamp on her night table was a graceful white swan, the only whimsical thing he'd seen in her apartment. He looked at his watch. Her twenty minutes had expired, and he was half-starved, a condition for which she was ninety-percent responsible. What the heck! He leaned over and kissed her.

"Wake up. I'm dying of hunger."

Her arms struggled to find a place above her head, and she stretched with such languor that a twinge of guilt attacked him. But guilt or not, he didn't want to eat by himself, and, besides, he wanted to share his feelings with her. He leaned over and kissed her, and as if sensitive to his touch even in her sleep, her eyes opened and she smiled, captivating him.

"Was I asleep?"

"Dead to the world. I want you to wake up so I can eat. Woman, you drained me of my energy." She sat up, holding the sheet close to her breast. Modesty had its place, he thought, but some women overdid it.

"Let me get this straight," she said, covering her mouth

while she yawned. "You want *me* to wake up so *you* can eat?" Both of her hands went up, and for the second time since he met her, giggles spilled out of her.

"Let me in on the joke," he said.

But she waved her hand, seemingly becoming more amused. "Trust me, I'm definitely not going there."

He thought for a minute or so, looking for a double entendre, and then it hit him. "You want me to wake up so you can eat," she'd said.

He looked at her as she doubled up with giggles. "You're crazy as hell," he told her as the laughter began to rumble in his throat. "The food's over here." He leaned down, picked up the tray and placed it between them on the bed. "It would serve you right if I ate it all."

"Not on your life. You sapped all of my energy and I'm starving. When did you fix this tray?"

"Half an hour ago, but you were sleeping so soundly that I didn't have the heart to awaken you, but my stomach began to protest, so… Hope you weren't saving this stuff for your dinner tomorrow."

"Nope." She savored the sturgeon. "This tastes better than it did at dinner. Maybe that's because *you* fixed it."

"If it tastes better, it's because you're hungrier."

They finished the late-night snack, he put the tray in the kitchen, came back and sat on the side of the bed. "Will it embarrass you if I leave here tomorrow morning?"

She didn't hesitate. "I'd love for you to spend the night with me. I leave at eight. Do you think you could leave at least fifteen minutes earlier? I'm not so sophisticated that I'm willing to leave along with you. If we were living together, that would be different, but we're not."

He crawled across the bed and hugged her to him. "Of course I can. I can leave at five, if you need me to. Just please do me a favor and don't put on a gown, pajamas or whatever you sleep in. I don't own a pair of pajamas, and I never expect to. Can you handle that? I did buy a robe when Alexis and Tara came to live with us."

She swallowed hard. "I guess so. But would you look in that closet and hand me that red robe on the door? I'm growing up fast, but not so fast that I'll stroll around here in the buff."

If he laughed she wouldn't like it, so he looked the other way, slid out of the bed and brought the robe to her. "Unless you want me to wrap a towel around my waist—"

She interrupted him. "Don't get modest on my account. I've enjoyed looking at you. I'll get you a toothbrush, towel and washcloth." She put on the robe, got out of bed and walked around it. He met her there, opened her robe and held her body to him, feeling her taut nipples against his chest and her nearly flat belly against his genitals.

"God knew what he was doing when he made woman," he said, kissing the tip of her nose, "and for making you, I'll be forever in His debt."

The next morning, having spent a night of loving that he would long remember, he kissed Pamela goodbye at six-thirty and headed for Russ's apartment. He rang the bell before using his key so as not to embarrass his brother or his fiancée if she happened to have spent the night there. Russ was alone. They greeted each other warmly as they always did.

"I thought you'd be staying here last night."

"That was my intention, but man, my life changed while I was down there."

Both of Russ's eyebrows shot up. "You met someone?"

Drake took a seat on the sofa and stretched out his long legs. "You could say that. Magnus Cooper and Pamela are cousins, and she was there at the family reunion. Man, this thing got to me. It was like being hit over the head with a sledgehammer. Here she comes walking arm in arm with this dude, strolling among the picnickers, and he's acting as if he's got some special rights. I wanted to put my fist straight through that empty space between his ears."

Russ flopped down on a big chair and stared at his brother. Then, he smothered a laugh. "Maybe I'd know what you're talking about if you'd start at the beginning."

He related the events of the weekend up to the time he walked into Pamela's apartment the previous evening.

"You didn't fall in love with her," Russ said. "You already loved her, but as Telford and I have been saying, you are the king of denial. Down there in Texas, you realized you could lose her and that you didn't want another man to touch her. I hope you spent the night with her."

"I did, and now I've got to give us a chance. I have to do everything I can to find out whether we're good for the long haul." He closed his eyes and leaned back. "Russ, she's... she's wonderful."

"Glad to know it. Figure out a way to spend more time with her. That won't be easy with you in Eagle Park and her here in Baltimore. I mean, you should be among other folk, and you'll know how each other behaves in different places and settings and with different kinds of people."

"Yeah, and especially with my family." A thought occurred to him and he sat up straight. "Do you think Velma would ask Pamela to be one of her bridesmaids? I know that's reserved for best friends, but—"

"I'll ask her. I think she's still working on that. She said she liked Pamela when they met at our house last Christmas Eve."

"I'd appreciate it. Don't let me make you late for work. I'm going home to put on my work clothes before I go to Frederick. I keep some things in the trailer at the housing site, but... Well, I want to touch base with Telford, so I'm heading to Eagle Park." He took his car keys from the coffee table where he'd left them the previous Thursday morning. "Just imagine. One short weekend, and it's a different world. See you when you come home." They embraced, and he took the elevator down to the underground garage where he'd parked his car. Minutes later, he was on his way home.

Pamela strolled into WRLR that Monday morning humming. She didn't know what the tune was, but she'd heard it several times during the previous weekend. She passed Rhoda's office and waved, and walked on to her own office, humming the same song as she went. She opened her office door, sat down and unlocked her desk. She expected Lawrence to saunter in and breathe on her neck when she remembered that he was still hospitalized. Slowly, the events of the preceding weeks came back to her. She telephoned Rhoda.

"I was just on my way to your office," Rhoda said. "Give me a fast minute."

Seconds later, Rhoda walked into her office, pencil and notebook in hand. "The way you were humming when you passed my door, I figured you had scored big with Mr. Right. Are you going to bring him to my garden party?"

She didn't like Rhoda's interest in how she was getting along with Drake, so she opted for an evasive answer. "You told me in minute detail what I should wear, but you said nothing about what the men should wear. Tell the men how to dress, and we women automatically know what to wear. I think that's the way it usually works."

Rhoda seemed embarrassed. "They'll know what to wear on such an occasion."

She leaned back in her chair and looked closely at Rhoda, wondering whether she was playing games. "If I'm the only woman there wearing gloves and a wide summer hat, you'll have a problem on your hands. Are men wearing morning coats, or what?"

"Well, I said men should dress according to what their date was wearing. 'Scuse me if that's not kosher. You're coming, aren't you?"

"I'll be there."

"And you're bringing…er…that guy?"

"I will be accompanied by a man, provided I can find one who doesn't mind having to guess what to wear." There were times when a little bit of Rhoda was sufficient to nearly suffocate Pamela. No one should be so transparent. *This bears watching,* she said to herself.

After getting the list of top news stories, she set about deciding which ones would receive a thorough treatment, chose four and got down to serious work.

The green button on her phone blinked twice. "Mr. Harrington on line two, Pamela," her secretary said.

Her right hand went to her chest as if to decelerate the runaway beating of her heart. "Hi," she said.

"Hi what? I expected to hear 'Hello, darling,' anything sweeter than 'hi.' You miss me?"

"Woefully."

"Good. I have a plan. Suppose you spend every other weekend with me at Eagle Park, and I'll spend every other weekend in Baltimore with you. Of course, when I have to be in Barbados, we'll get off schedule, but we can adjust it. What do you say?"

He was moving faster than she'd thought, but that was one initiative that she welcomed. "I'd like that, but what about your family? Won't they get tired of me?"

"Why should they get tired of you? Anyway, they won't. I want us to see as much of each other as possible. Say yes."

The man was a steamroller. "Yes."

"Good. I'd better get to work. I'll be in Frederick for the remainder of the working day. Call you tonight. Bye, sweetheart."

"Bye, love." Whew! She blew out a long, deep breath, tried to focus on her work and finally managed to dig out the information she needed for the two leading stories. But for the first time in memory, something vied with her work for her interest and attention.

"How about lunch?" Raynor said when she answered her intercom.

"Sure. What time?"

They agreed to meet in the staff café in twenty minutes. "What on earth did you do over the holiday?" he asked her. "You're blooming."

She grinned. "Thanks," she said, and let his question go unanswered.

Over ham-and-cheese sandwiches and coffee, he told her that Lawrence would be released from the hospital the following day, that he was on probation and had accepted the transfer to the station's Honolulu affiliate.

"I can't say I'm sorry to see him go, and I am definitely glad there's been no publicity about this. It would have been bad for WRLR," Raynor said.

She stopped eating and looked her boss in the eye. "I'm glad it doesn't reflect badly on the station. After all, I work here. But I would have testified against him with no thought for WRLR. The man is a menace, a schizophrenic capable of doing bodily harm."

"And I would have supported you. I'm only saying I'm grateful it didn't go further."

She picked up her sandwich, examined it and put it down. "How do they manage to make this stuff taste so awful?"

Raynor ran his hand over his thinning hair and allowed

himself a slight flexing of his right shoulder. "It takes talent, and the kitchen help in this building have plenty of it."

She had been back at her desk no more than five minutes when her phone rang. "Ms. Brighton on line one, Pamela." What a day for surprises! She greeted Velma warmly and then listened to the woman's request.

"I'm getting married Saturday of Labor Day weekend, and I'd be so happy if you'd be one of my bridesmaids."

She nearly gasped. Immediately, it occurred to her that Drake probably asked Velma to invite her. Well, she didn't care. If that was the case, it meant that he wanted to involve her in something that was important to his family. She'd liked Velma, so she didn't hesitate.

"I'm honored, Velma. I'll be delighted. I suppose you already have a color and style in mind for the dresses."

"Style, yes. The two colors remaining are tea rose and mauve-pink. Take your choice."

"Two good colors. Tea rose for me. I gather that rainbow colors are your bridesmaid's scheme. It's a great idea, because not all of the dozen bridesmaids will look great in the same color."

Velma gave her the name of a dressmaker in Baltimore. "I'm free Thursday night, if you'd like me to go with you. We could have dinner together and make an evening of it." She gave Pamela her home and office addresses as well as her telephone numbers.

A friend. A girlfriend, something she'd never had. Her mother had always been her best friend. In college, she'd tried to be like the other girls, but rejected that course when a man every girl wanted swore that he wanted her most of all; her experience with him proved humiliating. After that incident, she walked alone until she met Drake Harrington.

"That would be wonderful," she told Velma. "I'll be at your office around six-thirty."

She hung up and called Drake. "Did you ask Velma Brighton to include me among her bridesmaids?"

"I definitely did not. However, Russ probably mentioned it to her. Did you agree?"

"I did, and we're meeting for dinner Thursday. I liked her very much when we were together at your home, and I hope we can be good friends. I don't have a buddy...a girlfriend, I mean."

"Thanks for clarifying that. I'm glad you agreed. It's good to know you'll be a part of something that's so important to me."

"Who's best man—you or Telford?"

"I am. Russ was Telford's best man."

"That means when you marry, Telford will be your best man, doesn't it?"

"I suppose so. Can you spend this coming weekend with me in Eagle Park, or would you rather we spend it in Baltimore? At home, I can rent a horse for you, and we can go riding Saturday morning if you'd like."

"I'd love that. Eagle Park it is, then."

"Great. Love you."

"Me, too."

"What the devil does *that* mean?" he chided. "I'm a fragile person. Spell it out, will you?"

Laughter poured out of her. "You? Fragile? The thought breaks me up. Tender, maybe. Tell you what. I'll sort it out and write a report on your emotional state. Don't be surprised if I conclude that you're one tough brother."

"If that's the kind of man you like, fine with me. I'm waiting."

"I love you. Goodbye."

"Me, too," he said, his two words punctuated with laughter. "Call you tonight. Bye."

She replaced the phone in its cradle, folded her hands and rested her chin on them. "Lord," she prayed, "please don't let anything happen to take away this happiness."

On the way home, she bought a dress that she thought appropriate for a garden party that started at six in the evening: a peach-colored silk with a deep V neckline, spaghetti straps and a slit two inches above the left knee. She found a wide organdy hat the same color and considered her shopping completed. That evening, she told Drake she thought it was all right for him to wear a summer suit.

"What about a white linen one? What color is your dress?" She told him. "Good. I'll see if I can find a tie that color."

A sixth sense told her that she would destroy Rhoda's advantage, but she ignored it. What proof did she have that Rhoda had gone to all that trouble merely for a chance to make a play for Drake? But if she hadn't, why was she so interested in whether he'd be there? *If she steps out of line, I guarantee her she'll make an important discovery.*

"Some place," she said to Velma when she walked into the establishment of Brighton Caterers and Home Designers, Inc.

"Thanks. It's my dream come true. Come with me, and I'll show you around. We don't have to be at the dressmaker's before nine."

Pamela gazed, awestruck at the chrome kitchen, the food storage compartments, freezers and the big hall lined with shelves of coordinated linens and porcelains, glassware and cutlery.

"I still have to rent a lot of things, especially for large

affairs such as weddings, galas, bar mitzvahs and such, but having the basics saves me a pile of money."

"Are you going to continue the business after you marry?"

Velma whirled around, and her face creased into a deep frown. "Is there some reason why I shouldn't? My office is more than big enough to accommodate a crib and a baby carriage. I could put a partition right over there." She pointed to a corner area made interesting by a large Gothic-style window. "I even have a waterfall over there that could lull the baby to sleep. Besides, work is something I need."

She kicked off her flat shoes and put on a pair that had a heel about an inch higher. "I used to walk around in spike-heeled shoes with me feet killing me so I would look taller, but I've decided that I like me just the way I am, and Russ does, too. So I don't give a hoot who's tall, no offense intended. I also stopped piling my hair up on my head to look tall, and quit wearing caftans to hide my round figure. What you see is what you get."

Pamela laughed, not at Velma's newfound philosophy, but in relief that she liked Velma even more than when she first met her. She laughed because she suspected she had found a down-to-earth woman like herself. Testing the possibility of a friendship, she said, "I was wondering how you got shorter and slimmer at the same time. It usually works the other way."

"Honey, I got slimmer 'cause I starved myself to death and lost a few pounds. Then I decided that my genes are perfectly good ones—they keep me healthy and they let me grow up to be intelligent. If a little extra weight is the price, that's better than being sickly and stupid."

Happiness suffused Pamela, and she laughed aloud. "You're not much good at rationalizing, are you?"

Velma whooped. "Girl, I can find an excuse for anything I do." Suddenly, she sobered. "Do you mind my asking how things are with you and Drake? I had hoped for a relationship between you two."

"Until a few days ago, nothing had passed between us but a few kisses, although they'd been gathering steam, as it were. Then, this past weekend our relationship took off like a Thoroughbred out of control. It's…almost everything I've dreamed of."

Velma locked her desk and switched off the ceiling light. "Did you say almost?"

She studied the woman, wondering how much she should confide, and a rueful smile flittered across her face. "Velma, I'm almost thirty-one years old, and I want a family. I've been in love with Drake for months, and he now says he loves me. We're tight. But I want to start my family before I'm a candidate for a string of miscarriages and ill-developed babies. He hasn't said a word about the future."

"I'm thirty-two, and I'm not planning to get pregnant until I've been married two years. I'm healthy, and I'm not worried. You shouldn't be, either. And for Pete's sake don't let the man think you're only looking for a sperm machine. That kind of pressure would have sent Casanova to a Viagra clinic. I suppose you know Drake isn't what he seems to be."

"I realize that in some ways, but how do you mean it?"

Velma didn't pull punches. "Those Harrington men are very good-looking and rich, and people who don't know them wrongly assume them to be arrogant, superficial, shallow and women-chasers. That is what they think of Drake, especially, because he is exceptionally good-looking and has that smile that suggests he's a playboy. Drake hates that people take a look at him and assume he's trifling, and he drives himself to build his accomplishments, to be respected for his work."

"I learned a great deal about Drake from observing him, and he's recently told me things that led me to understand his concerns and his personality. But your summary brings it into clearer focus, and I thank you."

"No need to thank me. I'm hoping we'll be sisters-in-law."

They drove their separate cars to the restaurant, a ten-minute drive from Velma's office. Pamela saw the window sign indicating that the restaurant served soul food, and her mouth began to water for fried catfish, hush puppies and stewed collards. She gave the waiter her order without picking up the menu.

"Yes, ma'am, and would you like sweetened iced tea with that?" She nodded and waited for Velma to order.

"What kind of oil does the chef use for frying?" Velma asked the waiter.

"Pure canola oil, ma'am. For everything else, sautéing and such, he uses olive oil. We serve healthy soul food in this restaurant."

"I'll have the same." She cleared her throat, and as the man walked away she said, "If it's all that healthy, it ain't soul food. I came in here to do my weekly sinning."

"Yeah," Pamela said. "And if he cooks my collards with olive oil, I'm going make a picket sign and spend my lunch hours strolling in front of this restaurant."

Velma saw the waiter at a nearby table and called him. "I hope the chef doesn't cook collards in olive oil. Does he?"

The waiter raised his chin and looked down his nose at her. "We serve collards here, not weeds. Our collards are prepared with the finest North Carolina smoked ham hocks, water, salt and red-pepper flakes." His chin went up a bit more. "Will there be anything else?"

"No, thank you," she said, having been made to feel as if she had committed a crime. "When a brother decides to put you down, Pamela, he makes sure you know what he's doing."

After the meal, they drove across town to Jenny's Designer Fashions, owned and operated by a former homeless woman who got a second chance. "Jenny, this is Pamela, one of my bridesmaids, and she wants her dress in tea rose."

"I'm glad to meet you, Pamela. Tea rose, huh?" She took swatches of fabric and put them against Pamela's face. "That's a good color for you, but did you ever wear mauve-pink?"

"I'm not overly fond of pink."

"I don't blame you, but this is a kind of lavender pink." She put the bolt of fabric on Pamela's shoulder, wrapped several yards around her and walked with her to the mirror. "What do you think?"

"I'll take the pink. It's beautiful."

Jenny measured her. "Hmm. You've got a nice long waist. I'm going to drop both the neckline and the waistline for you. Hmm. Square shoulders. No problem there. Sewing for you will be a cinch." She gave Pamela her card. "I'd like you to come for a fitting next Thursday about this time. Can you?"

"I'll be here." She shook hands with Jenny, and they left. "How long was she homeless?"

"She lived on the street for almost two years. Slept and ate on the street. Can you believe that? I met her through a friend, Veronica Henderson, the woman who befriended her. Want to meet for dinner next Thursday?"

"You and Russ are both here in Baltimore, and you don't see each other every night?"

"Russ is drawing up plans for a shopping mall that he and his brothers are considering building in Accra, Ghana. When he's sketching plans for a kind of structure that he hasn't previously designed, he hardly leaves his desk. His mind is on that and that alone. That's why he's so good at what he does."

"And that doesn't bother you?"

"Heavens, no. I want him to be as good as he can be." She stopped walking. "If you trust your man, you'll give him the space he needs to do whatever he sets himself to do. He'll be happy, and you'll be happy. If you can't do that, stay away from strong men."

"I follow you there. What about when I need space? Am I entitled to whatever space I need whenever I need it?"

Velma leaned against the hood of her car and dangled her keys in her right hand. "We independent women lead a double life. We're capable of taking care of ourselves and managing our lives, but we are also nurturers and nesters. If we're not there for the man, he won't come home. And a man who needs you to love him is precious, Pamela. A gift from God. Does Drake need you?"

"He needs me." Tears blurred her vision as she thought of the miracle of that statement.

"You're a blessed woman."

"Thanks for talking with me, for being my friend."

Chapter 9

"Are you going to Frederick this afternoon?" Telford asked Drake. "I thought we'd sit with Russ and go over the work he's done on the Accra shopping mall."

"Can we postpone that until tonight? I've got a new man on the job, and I want to see how he's doing. If my hunch is right, he'll be an asset. See you at dinner."

He laced up his boots—he wore them on the construction site because he hated brogans—felt the back of his jeans pocket for his wallet and bounded down the stairs.

Henry stepped out of the pantry and called to Drake. "You planning to be home for supper? I'm having a nice pork roast, and I'm going to roast it out back on the grill. One of them new recipes Alexis came up with."

"You bet I'll be here. Roast the potatoes while you're at it, and put some fresh rosemary in the roasting pan."

Henry braced his hands on his hips. "I thought you was a engineer. Now you're telling me you're a cook."

Drake held up his hands palms out. "All right. All right. I stand corrected. See you at supper."

"Bring me some double-smoked bacon and a couple of ropes of country sausage. I'm out of breakfast meat for Tara and Tel."

"Okay." He looked down at Henry and patted his shoulder. "For you, anything. See you."

Thirty-five minutes later, he parked in front of the construction site. He'd been away from it for four days, but considering how his life had changed in the interim, years seemed to have passed. He got out of the car, put on his hard hat and went in search of Jack, his foreman. Instead of Jack, he met Pete's father.

"How's it going, Bond?" he asked the man. "Where's Jack?"

"Can I talk with you a few minutes, Drake?"

Drake didn't like the man's tone, and his antenna went up immediately. "Sure. Let's step over to the trailer." They went inside, closed the door and sat down. "What's the matter?"

"Well, Jack came down with some kind of fever Thursday, and he's in Frederick Memorial. With nobody in charge, a couple of the men got lazy. When I caught one loading bricks in a U-Haul truck, I called the police. After that, I stayed here day and night. I couldn't make anybody work, but I sure could see that nobody stole anything." He took two sheets of lined paper from his pocket and handed them to Drake. "Here's the notes I took."

He imagined which of the men he'd have to fire, and he didn't plan to waste time doing it. He looked at Bond's notes. "Just the three I figured you'd name. They're out as soon as I see them. How much construction work have you done?"

"That's all I've done for the last seventeen years—

ground-up plumbing, driving a crane, cementing, plastering and brickwork. What I haven't worked at, I've seen."

"I'd like you to go to Eagle Park with me tomorrow evening and meet my brothers, my partners. You've done well for me, and I won't forget it."

Bond knocked back his hat and ran his fingers over his tight curls. "I'm the one in your debt, man, and I always will be. I'll be glad to go with you tomorrow. Thanks."

Just what he needed: a problem with his workers. For the remainder of the day, he checked Bond's work carefully and as unobtrusively as possible and couldn't find one flaw. He left work at four and went to the hospital to see Jack, who, he learned, had contracted malaria while traveling in West Africa and who was experiencing his first flare-up of the disease in over two years. After telephoning Jack's wife and determining that she didn't need anything, he shopped for the meat Henry wanted and then headed home, all the while feeling a pull toward Baltimore and Pamela.

He parked in the circle in front of Harrington House, got the cooler from the trunk, strode up the walk and, as he reached for the doorbell, the door swung open.

"Surprise! Uncle Drake, did you bring the bacon for my pancakes?"

He picked Tara up, hugged her and swung her around. "Would I let my best girl down? Of course I brought it."

She giggled and kissed his cheek. "I told Mr. Henry you wouldn't forget." She cupped his right ear with her hands and whispered, "Did you notice how my mommy sleeps all the time? Is she sick, Uncle Drake?"

"Definitely not." He didn't know how much Tara had been told about her mother's pregnancy, so he didn't know what to say. While he thought of an answer, Tara put him at ease.

"I guess pregnant makes everything sleepy, so I'd better

not be pregnant till after school is over. I wouldn't be able to study."

"You nailed it right on the head," he told her. "And the longer you wait after you finish school, the better. Wait till you're thirty."

Her eyes grew large. "Is my mommy thirty?"

"Yes, indeed, she is. Where's your dad?"

"He's keeping my mommy company." She kissed his cheek again and indicated that she wanted to be released. "I gotta go study the piano a little more before supper. Bye."

From the moment he met her, that little girl had brought joy to his life. He didn't believe that all children were like Tara—she had a special way of attracting and giving love. But what he wouldn't give if his own children proved to be as joyful and happy as she. He hurried upstairs to shower and get ready for dinner.

Am I being selfish? Pamela wants a child so badly. Shouldn't I do the inevitable and make her happy? But what about me? Am I certain? He let the cool water invigorate his body, dried himself, put on his robe and had a sudden longing for the days when he walked around the house naked.

"Oh, hell," he said, "that wasn't worth a hill of beans compared to what I got in return when Alexis and Tara came here." Tara. Would he love his own daughter as much as he loved her?

He picked up the phone on his night table and dialed Pamela's number. "Hello, sweetheart," he said when she answered the phone. "Today's Monday. How'm I going to wait till Friday to see you? I have to be here tomorrow evening for a meeting with my brothers, but we could have dinner in Baltimore on Wednesday. What do you say?"

"I miss you, too. Usually my day passes so swiftly because I don't seem to have enough time to do all the things I have to do, but today just dragged. You've got a lot to answer for."

"Not one bit more than you have." He told her about the situation he faced at the building site that morning, and didn't question doing so, although he had never before discussed problems in his work with anyone other than Telford and Russ.

"If you know you did the right thing in firing those men, don't feel guilty about it. You're fortunate to have Bond."

"Yes, indeed, I am." He told her how he met first Pete and then Bond and of Bond's initial reaction to him.

"Drake, are you always so... I mean, do you always help people if you know they're in need?"

Now what was behind that question? "Of course not. I'd be a pauper. I do what I can, and if it's right in my face, I do not ignore it."

"You are a remarkable man. The more I know about you, the bigger you are. Uh...by the way, Saturday after next is my father's sixty-fifth birthday, and my mother wants me to go home. I want to, but that's supposed to be our Baltimore weekend together."

He thought for a minute. The more they were together in the company of others, the more they would learn about each other. Besides, he hadn't finished with Phelps Langford. "Well...we could make it a Texas weekend. It wouldn't be the same, but we would be together. Which day is his birthday?"

"Saturday. Are you offering to go with me? I thought you'd still be annoyed with my father."

"Never worry about such things. I can give as good as I get, and I usually do. Your father was a smartass, and I was a smartass right back at him. He won't do that again."

Her laughter floated to him through the wires, as cool and as comforting as a fresh spring breeze. "Daddy said something to that effect. I'll have to stay at home, and I'll be sleeping at one end of the house and you'll be at the other end."

He let a groan escape, though mostly for her benefit. "I've been tortured before. If it gets bad enough, I'll put my lover's sensors to work and walk in my sleep."

Her laughter—excited and joyous—suggested to him that she enjoyed flirting with danger. "Walk in your sleep? I can just see my father's face when you tell him, 'Sorry, sir. I couldn't help it. I walked in my sleep.'"

"Wouldn't you support me?"

"Who, me? You think I want my father to believe I've got a man who doesn't have the guts to go after what he wants and stand by it? Huh?"

He sat up straight, gripping the phone till the color left his knuckles. "Don't goad me, Pamela. I don't take dares, but I will happily alter that perception of me by simply going to your room and knocking on the door. Loudly. I wouldn't have anything to be ashamed of. Your father knows I want you. That's why he needled me."

"Jokes aside, I'd welcome you if I were most anywhere but in my parents' home."

To his way of thinking, a sense of propriety was to be valued. "I knew you were pulling my leg." He put his hand over the mouthpiece. "Yeah?"

"Uncle Drake, Mr. Henry said to tell you he's taking the roast off the grill and everything else is on the table. Everybody's sitting down but you and me."

"No kidding. What time is it?"

"Two minutes after seven, and Uncle Russ is hungry."

"Thanks, Tara. Be right down."

He turned his attention back to Pamela. "Look, sweetheart, I'm late for supper, and I have to dress. I left the shower and called you."

"You mean you are talking to me in the buff? Boy, do I wish I could see through this wire."

"Wouldn't do you a bit of good. I'm wearing a robe. Call you later." He hung up, dashed into his clothes, buttoned his shirt and raced down the stairs.

Pamela hung up and stared out of her bedroom window at the gathering twilight. Maybe Drake's being surrounded by a loving family accounted for his complacency about their future. Or maybe he wasn't complacent, but merely careful. No law said he had to be certain just because she'd made up her mind about him. She went into the kitchen, deviled some shrimp, warmed leftover rice, sliced a tomato and ate her dinner.

WRLR wanted a file of stories for Black History Month, and she had to figure out a way to make a story out of a group of local musicians performing at the Eubie Blake National Jazz Institute. She'd visited the institute on North Howard Street in Baltimore and interviewed musicians there, but had failed to get anything special. After fretting with ideas for more than an hour, she put her notes away and decided to go to bed. Almost immediately, the phone rang.

"I suppose you know they're sending me to Honolulu. I'm leaving tomorrow morning, but I'm only going because I didn't want to get fired. I'm not asking whether you had anything to do with my getting the ax at WRLR." She held the receiver away and stared at it, stunned by the call and what she heard.

"I suspected all the time that Raynor's had the hots for you. Well, I don't want his leavings." The caller hung up.

Poor Lawrence. She wondered if Raynor and her other superiors at WRLR understood that the man was a psychopath, a dangerous one. At once shaken by the call and curious as to how he obtained her unlisted number, she hesitated to answer the telephone when it rang almost immediately after Lawrence hung up.

"Hello," she said, holding her breath.

"Hi. You sound strange. What's the matter?"

She sat down. "Drake. Thank God it's you." She told him about Lawrence's call a few minutes earlier. "That nearly rattled me. My number isn't listed, and the station doesn't give it out."

"He probably got it when he worked there. I'm glad he's leaving tomorrow morning. What happened to your caller ID?"

"This particular phone is old and it doesn't have a window."

"I'll bring you one on Wednesday."

She heard herself telling him about her assignment to do a story on local jazz musicians and her disappointment with the results so far. "I love jazz. You know that. But I want to do something interesting and different, not just to put up some pictures of guys sitting around blowing horns."

"Right. Maybe they'll let you show the jazz scene in different cities. Kansas City, New Orleans, Chicago, New York and Washington have great jazz clubs."

Her heart leaped in her chest, and she sat forward, excited and energized. "Wow! What a story that would make." But she quickly settled down for she knew that the station manager wouldn't spend that much money on a story for Black History Month.

"Why are you planning for this now?" he asked.

"Special programs are always done months in advance. If a program is good, it will be shown repeatedly and other stations will buy it."

"What can you lose? Tell your boss what you think and see how he reacts."

"I will, and I'm going to write the proposal before I go to sleep tonight. And if you were here right now, I'd kiss you silly."

His deep, mellifluous laugh never failed to warm her and make her feel special. "Always be careful what you say to me, Pamela, even in jest. You are only forty minutes away, and in light traffic I can make it in less time than that."

"If you come here tonight I won't get this proposal written, and my boss is expecting a concrete idea at lunchtime tomorrow."

"Yeah? Well, it's a good thing we both know something about jazz. In everything I do, I think first of the big picture before I think of limiting it to what is possible. I always want to know how far I can fly."

She slouched down in the chair, comfortable and happy. "That's one of the most important clues you've given me to who you are. Too bad I have to work on this idea tonight. I would really love to see you."

His laugh held no mirth. "Temperance is a learned virtue, and I'm teaching it to myself right now." He didn't say anything for a minute, and then asked, "Do you swim?"

"Like a fish. Why?"

"We have a big swimming pool out back, so come prepared to enjoy it this weekend. Another thing. Telford is teaching Alexis to shoot pool. If you want to learn that, I'll teach you."

She realized that he was filling time, that he didn't want to hang up but didn't have anything really important to tell her, so she played along.

"I've never thought I'd like to shoot pool, but then the first time I saw you, I didn't think I'd want to...uh... Look, I think I'd better get to work on—"

"You didn't think you'd want to do what? Make love with me? Is that what you're too chicken to say?"

"Well…uh…look. I had suffered an awful humiliation at the hands of a man chased by half the women on Howard's campus. He had stunning looks, and I let myself be proud that he chose me from among girls who were beautiful and wealthy. I discovered too late that he didn't love me as he swore. His only interest was in getting bragging rights for what he called the 'initiation of the last virgin on Howard's campus.' He told so many of my male schoolmates that I considered changing schools. I stayed only because I was an honor student and wanted to graduate with top honors. If I changed schools, that might not have been possible."

"Thanks for telling me. You've answered a question that I didn't want to ask. So it took you more than a decade to trust another man that much." He didn't phrase it as a question.

"You could say that. It was your looks that put me off. After being in your company a few times, though, that stopped being a negative factor. I didn't think about your looks."

"Thank God for that. At least you tried to see me for what I am. Children could teach us something about human relations, but as soon as they understand them, they're no longer honest about them. Tara, my niece, loves me unequivocally. I know her welcome is genuine and without reservation. I—"

"Your own daughter would love you the same way."

After what seemed to her a long pause, he said, "I wonder. I'd have to discipline her. Well, I'll cross that bridge when I reach it. I'd better let you get to work. Kiss me good-night?"

She made the sound of a kiss and he returned it. "I love you, girl."

"And I love you," she said, and put the phone back into its cradle.

Had he terminated the conversation because of her reference to his own daughter? She sucked her teeth and looked toward the ceiling. He'd once gotten ticked off to the point of telling her that if she wanted a baby, he'd give her one. But she didn't want him or a baby badly enough to handcuff him. She thought about that for a minute, and laughter bubbled up in her. What fun she could have with him if she had him in a position where he couldn't defend himself! She licked her lips the way a cat licks its whiskers after a satisfying meal.

She should get to work, she knew, but encounters with Drake—whether in person or by phone—were more likely to stimulate her libido than her intellect. Needing a few minutes to climb down from the sexual hill on which he left her, she telephoned her mother.

"Hi, Mom. I'll be down for Daddy's birthday, but, unless you mind, I'm bringing Drake with me. He wants to come, and I want him to be with me."

"Does this mean you two are thinking about a future?"

"We've decided not to date other people and to see if what we feel for each other is good for the long haul."

"I'm glad about that, because he impressed me. I know your father thinks a man that good-looking can't be worth anything, but I think Drake gave him a shock. He needed it."

She took a deep breath. "Mama, if Daddy is rude to Drake again and without reason, I am not going to forgive him. He's taught me to be gracious to anyone who is in my home, and look at what he did."

"Oh, that won't happen again. How many times does a sane man stick his hand in a hornet's nest? Drake Harrington can definitely take care of himself. I liked him a lot, so you bring him with you."

"Oh, Mama, talk with him and see what kind of man he is. He's a wonderful person, and he's loving and caring, not a bit self-centered."

"So you're in love with him. I have to tell you, I like your taste. Your father just walked in here. Speak with him. Bye now."

"Bye, Mom."

"When you coming home?"

She couldn't help laughing. Whenever she called him, those were always his first words. "Hi, Daddy. Weekend after next, and Drake is coming with me."

"Has he popped the question yet?"

"No, he hasn't, and I'm not quite ready for it."

"Why not? None of these fellas you've been wasting time with around here is worth a spit. You find yourself a real man, and you have the nerve to say you're not ready for him to ask you to marry him? What's wrong with him? Maybe I should ask what's wrong with you."

She managed to close her mouth after realizing she'd been gaping. "I'm fine, Daddy. Just fine, and I'm glad you liked Drake, because he's a wonderful man."

"If he is, he's ahead of his time. *Wonderful* is too strong a word to describe a man his age."

"Oh, Daddy. I love you."

"Love you, too. I hope the fella wants a family. It's time I had some grandchildren while I can enjoy them."

Maybe it was her night for joy. She let the laughter roll out of her. "I'll tell him that's a concern of yours, Daddy." She didn't add that if she said that to Drake, he'd probably think it a genetic obsession.

Her mind at peace, she got busy and by midnight had developed some ideas that she could, with confidence, present to Raynor. With that behind her, she took a fast shower, dried off and dived into bed. If Drake slept nude, she'd have to learn to do the same, and she might as well start practicing.

The following afternoon at four, Drake saw Bond approaching him. "If you want me to go home with you, could I have half an hour to drop by my house and change?" Bond asked.

"Sure. Suppose you drive the van, and I won't have to bring you back home tonight. I'll tail you there right now. Your license up to date?"

Bond nodded, then stared at him for a minute before turning his back. He saw the man's lips quivering and realized that, for Bond, it was a very emotional moment. "Here're the keys," Drake said. "I don't doubt that you're a careful driver."

The quality of the man's driving was not the point, and Drake knew Bond was aware of that. It was a matter of trust, and by showing it, he'd overwhelmed the man. "You may drive it into work tomorrow morning," Drake said. "And if you don't mind, while you're dressing, I'll talk with Pete."

Bond turned and faced him. "Mind? You're kidding. Pete practically worships you. I'm glad you haven't forgotten about him."

They walked to the truck together. "I have a soft spot for Pete. If I ever have a son, I'll be grateful if he's as fine a boy as Pete is."

Bond put his hands on the door handle of the van and looked at Drake. "It doesn't happen automatically. Your children have to come first, and you invest all of yourself in teaching them the right way. You have to instill in them some values starting when they cry for what they want.

And they need a good, loving mother." He opened the door, hopped in and ignited the engine.

Drake got into his Jaguar, started the motor and followed Bond, although he knew the way. The man intrigued him. Whoever used poverty as an indication of lower social class may have done the poor a disservice. At the Jergenses' home, he checked Pete's arithmetic homework while waiting for Bond.

"My dad usually does this, but he's going with you, and my mom can't do it tonight because she has to make phone calls for the PTA. How'd I do?"

"Your work's fine, but you could be a little neater."

"Thanks, sir. I'll copy it over."

Bond walked into the room wearing slacks, a tweed jacket, a collared shirt and a tie.

"Ready when you are, Drake. How'd Pete do?"

"As soon as he copies it nice and neatly so his teacher can read it, it will be perfect." He patted Pete's shoulder. "Good job."

"I think you've found a good man," Telford said to Drake after Bond left them that night. "I think he's solid."

"So do I," Russ said, "and I hope that stint in the clinker taught him to control his temper."

"That doesn't bother me," Drake said. "I'll bet anything that if a man called him that name tomorrow, his reaction would be the same. He's a big guy, and only a foolish person would take him on. What do you think?"

Telford braced his hands on his knees. "I think we should groom him for foreman. He's capable and he's honest."

"Right," Russ said. "Good manner, too. We wouldn't have to worry about his behavior around our families."

Drake leaned back and studied Russ, wondering when he began to think like a married man. "Pamela will be visiting me here this weekend," he announced. "I'd better remember to tell Alexis and Henry."

"Glad to hear it," Russ said. "I'll look forward to seeing her."

Telford stepped over to the bar, opened a bottle of beer and went back to his seat. "So will I. I was getting concerned that you might have overlooked her fine qualities."

Russ laughed, and Drake still couldn't get used to the change in his brother, and especially not to his laughing. "Come off it, Telford," Russ said. "If he hadn't calculated all of her assets correctly, he wouldn't have been trying so hard to escape." He looked at Drake. "I told you to stop wasting your energy and give in to it, but you had to learn the hard way. Even so, I'm proud of you, man. I like her."

Telford slapped Drake on the back. "So do I. You two can sing duets together, and your kids will probably all wind up singing at the Metropolitan Opera House in New York City."

"You're getting too fanciful for me, brother. I'm turning in. Good night."

"Good night," Russ said. "By the way, the only reason I didn't worry about you and Pamela is because Henry kept telling me you weren't stupid enough to let her get away. And Henry is a genius at recognizing who is and who is not stupid."

"Being in love is making you slaphappy, brother. See you both in the morning." He headed up to his room. All of a sudden, he could hardly wait for the weekend.

Pamela strolled into her office and dropped herself into her desk chair, dumbfounded. Raynor had actually approved her plan for the jazz program and intended to sell it to the network. She could barely contain herself. In addition to musicians in Baltimore, she could interview jazz performers who made Washington, D.C., New York City, New Orleans and Chicago their home. He not only approved it but was enthusiastic about it. She couldn't wait to tell Drake when she saw him that evening.

Her doorbell rang that evening at a quarter of seven. When she opened the door, he spread his arms and folded her to his body, and without so much as the beginning of a smile on his face, he scooped her up and walked into her apartment.

"Hi. You ready?" he asked her.

She could feel her eyes blinking in rapid succession. "Uh…yes. But I was expecting a kiss."

He took her hand as if to leave. "We could do that, sweetheart, but the way I'm feeling right now, the chance of our getting a real dinner would be nil."

She reached up and kissed his cheek. "What happened to all that famous self-control of yours?"

His grin flashed and he held out his right hand for her door key. After locking the door, he said, "That control works when I want it to work."

"Where're we going?"

"Want to go to the Inner Harbor and check out Mo's? I've got a taste for lobster."

"Great. You know I love seafood."

"Later, we can go over to the Eubie Blake Institute and take in some jazz. You could even take notes if you want to."

How many ways could he find to endear himself to her and to let her know that he supported her? She couldn't find words to tell him how she felt, so she squeezed his fingers and stood closer to him as they waited for the elevator. When she looked up at him, the passion in his eyes stunned her, and, as shivers raced through her body, she huddled as close to him as she could. His arm went around her in a gentle squeeze as the bell rang signaling the arrival of the elevator.

"Now do you understand the meaning of the expression 'saved by the bell'?" he whispered.

She let herself smile, but the thought that the two women on the elevator might have seen them in a tight lovers' clinch didn't amuse her. Her parents had crammed her head with the importance of proper behavior. Still, she doubted she would have been ashamed because to her mind, those two women could only have envied her.

"Have you ever been caught making out?" she asked him as they headed for downtown Baltimore.

"Sure," he said. "If by making out you mean petting. But not by anybody whose opinion mattered. Anything else should be done in privacy."

At Mo's, she nibbled on fried calamari while they waited for the main course and tried to figure out how to ensure that their evening would be a happy one. She still had concerns about Lawrence's telephone call and thought she should tell Drake about her feelings.

"The strangest thing was his failure to identify himself. I have stopped trying to figure out how he got my phone number."

A silence hung over them, and she wondered if she should have mentioned it again. However, after a minute or so, he said, "You may save yourself some trouble if you get an order of restraint against him that protects you from harassment. It probably won't help much, because he's clearly a sick man."

"He's been diagnosed as a psychopath, but the station doesn't want any publicity about it, which is why he hasn't been indicted."

He leaned back in his chair and looked hard at her. "If

he ever approaches you again in any way, the station be damned. Have him arrested. Your safety is more important."

"I will. Raynor ought to know that Honolulu is only eight hours away, and Lawrence has weekends off."

"I intend to make sure that on weekends, you're with me. When that's not possible, we'll make other arrangements. All right?"

Her mother had often told her that if you want to discuss a problem, go to your girlfriends. If you tell a man about a problem, he thinks you want him to solve it, and that's what he does.

"Yes. I'll keep you posted."

The waiter brought their main course, and Drake attacked the lobster with such relish that she was glad they had already discussed her bad news and he could enjoy her good news along with his lobster.

"My boss bought your idea for my program. In fact, he is enthusiastic about it and seems sure that our national office will buy it for the network. I'm indebted to you. That's going to be the first big thing I've done for the network."

She hadn't associated an attitude of diffidence with him, but his slight shrug and half smile suggested precisely that. "I'm glad for you. You couldn't have given me better news. This makes going to Eubie's the right thing to do." He poured a glass of water and raised it to her. "I'm with you all the way. Congratulations."

She wondered at that, but she didn't doubt his sincerity. His next words confirmed her thoughts. "I think Harrington, Inc. ought to place an ad on your evening news show. We've never advertised, because we get all the work we want without it, but it wouldn't hurt us to broaden our base. I'll speak to my brothers about it."

"You'd do that? Drake, I'm... I don't know what to say."

His grin showed her a perfect set of sparkling white teeth. "I've always thought it prudent to say nothing when I don't know what to say. Let's see what we'll have for dessert."

They left Mo's and walked to his car behind a rowdy crowd of young people, all of whom sang out the virtues of cold beer. "I'm thinking of driving out Pratt Street to Howard Avenue and going north till we reach Eubie's," Drake said. "Do you know a shorter route?"

She didn't even know that one and said as much. "I live here, but I rarely drive to this part of the city." She marveled at how comfortable she was with him, how easy he was to talk with. *Lord, I hope we make it. Please don't let me lose this happiness.*

The band at the museum that night played both modern and classical jazz, and its members ranged in age from about thirty to at least seventy. When she mentioned those disparities to Drake, he agreed and added, "Jazz and blues seem to be the most binding forces in this country. Neither race, age, religion, nor gender seems to matter to jazz and blues musicians. They only care about the quality of the music. Classical musicians could take a leaf from their book."

They stayed through two sets, and at the end of the second one, Pamela went up to the leader, gave him her press card and asked for an interview at a later date.

"He's going to do it," she told Drake later. "As soon as I get the green light from my boss, I can start interviewing. They'll give me a cameraman. Oh, Drake, I'm so excited."

He opened the front passenger door for her, helped her in and fastened her seat belt. *I hope he knows I can do this,* she said to herself and immediately began to wonder how they would end their evening.

"Want some coffee?" she asked when they reached the building in which she lived.

"I'd rather have a kiss," he said, shooting straight, as usual. "Woman, I'm starved for you."

She leaned forward and stroked the side of his face. "You couldn't be that hungry. I—"

"Don't go there. I'm in the mood to be totally frank. If coffee's what you're offering, I'll take coffee."

It occurred to her that he was really adept at keeping both his thoughts and motives to himself, so she was going to make him put his cards on the table. "I didn't say coffee was all I'd offer."

He got out of the car, walked around and would have opened her door if she hadn't been standing beside it. "Next time, sit there till I open the door. It gives me pleasure to do it."

She put her right hand to her forehead in a salute. "I stand corrected."

They entered her apartment just as thunder began to roll and streaks of lightning lit up her living room. He rushed to the window, closed it and turned to face her. "I don't want any coffee, sweetheart. I need *you*."

She walked with him into the living room and sat beside him on the sofa. He slumped down and leaned his head on her shoulder. "This is new to me, Pamela. After what I experienced with you Sunday night… Well, I've always been secure in my feelings about myself as a man, but Sunday night…what we had together was as new to me as life is to a newborn babe."

He couldn't possibly know how much happiness those words gave her, words that she would tuck away in her heart. "I'm not an expert on this, as you know," she said, "but I imagine that sharing your body with the person you love and who loves you is a different experience from… well, meeting your needs."

"Tell me about it! You know, the reaction of my family when I told them you'd be visiting me next weekend surprised me. You'd have thought I'd just made it through an era of pure stupidity. They all welcomed me into the world of common sense."

"Did that annoy you?"

"Of course not. They want the best for me."

Hmm. And they think I'm it. To him she said, "I'll be happy to see them again." She let her hand smooth his hair and then stroke the side of his face. "Do you still want a kiss?"

"As badly as I want air to breathe."

She leaned over him, tipped up his chin and flicked his lips with her tongue. With lightninglike speed his arms went around her and his tongue found its home inside her mouth. The flashes of lightning and the sound of thunder excited her and gave her a sense of danger as heat roared through her body. She kicked off her shoes and straddled him, but he signaled that he needed more, lifted her from his lap and took her to her bedroom.

"Is this right for you? Do you really want me or are you—"

She put her hand over his mouth. "If you have any doubts, try walking out of here and see what happens."

She hated reminding him that she wasn't taking the Pill and hated the fact that he had to wear a condom. Why couldn't they… She pushed the thought from her mind, opened her arms and took him into her body. And then he started loving her, and she thought only of him and of the feeling she had that she was leaving this world until he brought her to a shattering climax. He followed her release with a shout of affirmation before collapsing in her arms.

Later, when he slept with his head on her breasts, she remembered Velma's question. Yes, he needed her body, but did he need her love, her warmth, companionship, approval? She thought he did. She prayed that he did. Time passed, and she woke him up.

"It's raining hard. Are you going to Eagle Park tonight?"

"I had planned to." His kiss was long, deep and drugging. "Let me get my cell phone and call Russ." He got up, found his trousers, unhooked his cell phone from the belt and called his brother. "Hi. This is Drake, and I'm in town. Do you have company tonight?" He listened for a minute. "Great. I'll be over eventually, and I have my key so go back to sleep… No? What were you doing? Great. All right. See you later."

To Pamela, he said, "He's working on that Accra shopping mall, and he's not in such a good mood. Said he'd much rather be with Velma than trying to design something for a spot he's never seen—although he has a portfolio of pictures of it." He leaned over and kissed her. "And I suspect he was a little bit jealous of me."

"Don't be naughty. Besides, you didn't tell him where you were."

"I didn't have to. My brothers and I can practically read each other's minds. Get used to it."

"I know you are very close and that you have a strong love for each other. Being with the three of you was like having a wall of love and warmth between me and the rest of the world. I've never forgotten that Christmas Eve."

She forced herself to ask him why he chose not to remain with her for the rest of the night. "I don't want to get used to it, and I am aware that you don't want us to get that cozy right now. Am I right?" She nodded. "But when I hurt, I'm gonna holler."

He grabbed his shirt from her boudoir chair and was in the process of putting his right arm in the sleeve when he stopped and knelt beside the bed. "I never dreamed I could feel for anyone what I feel for you."

She gazed into his beloved face, into eyes brilliant and revealing. She wanted to share with him the joy she felt as contentment flowed through her, but no words came. Instead, tears pooled in her eyes and soon trickled down her cheeks. He threw off the shirt, climbed into the bed and wrapped her in his arms.

He held her until she slept. He didn't know why, but what they had shared during the past hour transcended the bonding that lovemaking brings. They hadn't talked, only held each other, but he had never felt so close to her. Watching her peaceful and even breathing, he realized with a start that he wanted to take care of her, to protect her and make her happy.

But will I want that five, ten, or fifteen years from now? The rest of my life?

Suddenly, he sat up and sniffed several times. "Wake up, Pamela. Now. Get your clothes on. I smell smoke." He bounded out of the bed, threw on his clothes, found the clothes Pamela wore earlier and gave them to her. "Get dressed, baby. There's a fire somewhere." He dashed to the bathroom, put two towels in the tub and ran water on them, wrung them out, got his briefcase and Pamela's pocketbook and raced back to the bedroom. She met him at the door.

"Do you have a flashlight?" She got one from the closet in the foyer and gave it to him. "We'll have to use the stairs. If the smoke gets thick, put this wet towel over your face.

Thank God you're only on the eleventh floor. Where's your key?"

They encountered smoke in the hallway, and as they reached the stairs, a bell sounded. He tightened his grip on her hand. "Don't drop my hand no matter what," he said.

They reached street level and met a haze of smoke and half a dozen firemen who seemed headed for the stairs. "Put that towel over your face and hold on to me," he said to her as his eyes began to smart and he could barely keep them open. At last he got to the door, and when several people tried to get through it at once, he shoved a man aside and said, "Let the women get through."

When he thought he would suffocate from the smoke, he finally got outside. Realizing that Pamela still held his hand, he said, "I thought you were outside."

Her arms went around him. "I wouldn't have left you for anything."

"What do you say, buddy, we have a drink? May as well enjoy ourselves. I was watching TV, 'cause I couldn't sleep, and having a little nip. I brought my bottle and a glass."

Drake was about to say no thanks until he saw that the man held a bottle of fine, vintage wine. "Do you want some?" he asked Pamela. "A few sips might steady your nerves." She nodded, and the man handed Drake the bottle.

"I'm Mark Hopewell," the man said, "and the reason I couldn't sleep is because I'm facing the hatchet from my shareholders."

"What's the problem?" Drake asked him.

"I invested a few million dollars in a chain of condominiums, and two of them have structural damages. I can sue the builder, but that won't save my hide."

"If you're desperate," Drake said, "put together a plan to correct the problem before you have a stockholders' meeting." He took a business card from his wallet. "Give me a call, and we can discuss it."

The man looked skeptical until Pamela said, "This is Drake Harrington. He's an architectural engineer."

The man grabbed Drake's hand and pumped it. "I hope nobody got hurt in this fire, but I sure am grateful that I brought this wine down here. I'll call you tomorrow."

A few drops of rain reminded them of the storm earlier that night, but their attention was on the person who was brought out on a gurney. "Is he going to be all right?" Pamela asked a policeman who had just joined them.

"He'll be fine," the officer said, "but he was overcome by the smoke and couldn't get out of his apartment. He'll have some burns on his arm and shoulder to remind him not to smoke in bed. His bedroom is still smoldering."

Drake's arms went around Pamela almost automatically, shielding her from a nonexistent threat. "He endangered a lot of people."

"Yeah, and he may get some time for that. Hang in there." The officer walked toward the building's front door and left them to await the signal to return to their apartments.

"Would you prefer to stay in a hotel tonight? There may be smoke in your apartment."

"I'd rather stay at home if I can." Suddenly, she took a small pad from her pocketbook and began to write. "I'm a reporter, for Pete's sake, and I had forgotten that fact."

After an hour, they received permission to return to her apartment, although several people who lived on the fifth floor were less fortunate. He went with her to her apartment, closed the windows and turned on the air-conditioner exhausts.

"I think you'll be fine. I'll call you tomorrow." He fought back the urge to take her and love her until he spent every ounce of his energy. "Dream about me."

Her eyebrows shot up, and she put her arms around him and parted her lips for his kiss. Heat plowed through him, but he braced himself against it and gave her what she wanted. "You're one sweet woman," he said, kissed the tip of her nose and left.

At the elevator, he checked the time. Twenty minutes past one. It had been a long day and a revealing one. "Well," he said to himself, "every day, I learn more about myself and what I learn brings me closer to losing my bachelorhood." He shrugged, admitting that the thought didn't bother him nearly as much as it once had.

Chapter 10

Pamela walked up the steps at 10 John Brown Drive wondering what role Harrington House would play in her future. She thought it odd that Drake didn't use his door key but rang the bell instead. When the door opened, he had his arm around her waist, smiled at Henry and said, "You remember Pamela, don't you?"

Stepping away from Drake, she said, "I'm so glad to see you again, Henry," leaned forward and kissed his cheek.

"And I'm glad to see you. I'd started to think this man here was off his rocker." He lifted her overnight bag from where Drake had placed it on the floor. "You're just in time for supper, so wash your hands and we'll eat. Come with me."

She looked back at Drake, who stood in the doorway running his fingers through the hair at the right side of his head. "You coming?"

"Who, me? I'm odd man out. Henry's taken my girl."

"You can go wash your hands, too," Henry threw at Drake over his shoulder. "I'm taking Pamela to the guest room."

"We're all glad to see you," Henry told her. "And I was tickled to death when Velma told me you'd be one of her bridesmaids." He opened the door of the guest room and placed her overnight bag on the floor beside the door. "You got about twelve minutes. Alexis gets indigestion if anybody shows up late for dinner. Danged if she didn't make civilized men outta the boys, especially Russ."

"Where's the rest of the family?"

"Upstairs getting their act together. Till a few minutes ago, they were out back in the pool." He turned to leave.

"Thanks for the warm welcome, Henry. I...uh...needed it."

"That's all you'll get in this house. We'd just about given up on seeing you here. Hurry along, now."

While trying to decide what to put on, she remembered Velma's tale about her caftans and why she no longer wore them. *My burnt-orange jumpsuit will do just fine. I like it, so I'll wear it.* She opened her suitcase, took out the garment and shook it. Sleeveless with a jewel neckline and wide, almost flared legs. *Perfect,* she said to herself, refreshed her makeup, combed out her hair, and slipped into the figure-flattering jumpsuit.

"Yes?" she said in response to a knock on her door. "In a minute." She didn't want Drake in that room, at least not right then, because if he touched her, everybody in the house, including Tara, would be able to read the signs in her whole demeanor. She opened the door and her pulse rate quickly decelerated.

"Alexis! It's so good to see you."

"And you. We've done everything but hold a prayer vigil for you and Drake. Of course, we didn't speak to him directly, only through the man upstairs. I'm so happy that you've come. Are things good between you and Drake?"

She grasped Alexis's hand. "Yes. Yes. I'm afraid to wake up. We're not there yet, but we're not standing still, either."

Alexis's arms went around her. "I'm so happy for both of you."

Pamela stepped back and stared at Alexis. "You're... Are you—"

Alexis's smile was answer enough, but she said, "You guessed right."

Pamela thought her heart turned over. "Oh, how wonderful! Bless you."

They walked to the dining room arm in arm. She'd always thought it self-centered to be envious of another, and she fought it hard as they entered the dining room. A chorus of welcome greeted her.

"Hi, everybody. I'm so glad to see all of you." She looked around at Tara, Russ and Telford, who she hadn't seen since entering the house. "It's good to be here."

"If I wasn't looking at Henry, I would have thought you went off somewhere with him," Drake said. "That was a long twelve minutes." Was he complaining? He stood, looked at her and grinned, banishing that thought from her mind. "Twelve minutes, huh? It was definitely worth the wait."

"You can take care of that, later," Henry said. "I'm ready to eat. Who's going to say the grace?"

"I will," Russ said. "If I don't, my niece will treat us to a half-hour soliloquy."

After dinner, she expected to sit in the den and enjoy aperitifs and family camaraderie as they did on her previous visit, but Drake ended that idea when he said, "If you all will excuse us, we're going for a walk."

Tara jumped up from the table and ran to him. "But Uncle Drake, won't Miss Pamela be tired? I wanted her to hear me play."

He hunkered down and hugged her. "Pamela isn't tired, and you may play for her tomorrow. All right?"

Tara clapped her hands. "She's going to stay tonight, Mommy, and I can play for her tomorrow."

Pamela longed to hug the precious little girl, to hold a child in her arms. "I can't wait to hear you play," she said to Tara. "Can we make a date for right after lunch tomorrow?"

Tara ran to her and hugged her. "Okay." Then she said, "Uncle Drake says I'm his best girl."

Pamela restrained a laugh. It seemed that one learned jealousy early in life. "And I can see why. You are a darling child." Tara's kiss on her cheek was the most endearing gift the child could have given her. She looked up to see Drake's gaze fastened on her and knew instinctively that the other adults watched them. It was a moment in which she cursed her fair complexion, for she could feel the heat in her face.

With his hand holding hers, Drake said, "Come on. This is the second-best part of the day."

"And the best part?"

"Early morning at sunrise when the world is coming alive. See you all later."

As they walked along the road leading to the Harrington warehouse, the cool evening breeze brushed her hair from her face, everywhere fireflies danced and already, between the setting of the sun and moonrise, the night creatures had begun their discordant symphony. Slowly, their shadows emerged, long, El Greco–esque figures strolling ahead of them. Drake pointed to a wooded area on a slight hill half a mile from Harrington House.

"One of these days, I hope to build a home up there," he said. "It's near enough that I would be on my own and still be close to my brothers, their families and Henry. I thought of building behind Henry's cottage, but I want to be closer to the river. Everything you see around here belongs to us." He pointed to the warehouse and the wooded areas beyond it. "The next settled area is Landstown. And after that, there's Beaver Ridge, about twelve miles away, where our friends the Roundtree family live."

"It's a wonderful place for a child," she said, "but who does Tara play with?"

"She has her schoolmates, but she and Grant Roundtree are great friends, and that suits both families."

She didn't want to suggest to him that his family lived in its own world, needing only each other. But wasn't that true? "Where are Russ and Velma planning to live?"

"Russ is building farther up the hill. He and I want Telford to have the family home. He was only seventeen when our father died, but he took care of us, Pamela. Telford and Henry kept us together. Russ and I went to college because Telford worked to supplement our scholarships and to send himself to school. We've been successful because we've stuck together and because Henry has always been there for us. A woman who is a part of my life has to accept them as a part of hers."

She stopped walking and faced him. "I admire everybody in that house back there, and I marvel that three teenage orphans could make of themselves what the three of you have become." Once more he was suggesting that he wanted her to be a part of his life while avoiding saying anything that would confirm it, and every day, she was getting that much closer to a childless life.

"I never thought of us as orphans, because we had Henry."

He slipped an arm around her waist and turned back. "We've walked over a mile. I hope you aren't tired."

"Not one bit. Has it occurred to you that we seem to communicate well when we're surrounded by nature?"

A raccoon and two little ones strolled across their path, and he stopped so as not to frighten them. "Maybe it's because we both love the outdoors. I'm having my horse brought over tomorrow morning around seven and a mare for you, so I hope you brought at least a pair of jeans."

"You warned me, so I came prepared to ride and to swim." As they neared the house, she looked up at the bright moonlight and the moon shining through the trees and didn't try to control the gasp that escaped her. "No wonder you love it here. It's idyllic. So beautiful!"

"So are you." He looked down at her, smiled and his voice, dark and mellifluous, sent frissons of heat scooting down her spine.

His aura enveloped her, battling the moonlight, the scent of roses and her memories of his loving for possession of her senses. Her lips quivered and her breathing shortened, and she reached out to him.

"Baby!" With one hand beneath her buttocks and the other one at the back of her head, he lifted her to fit him. She parted her lips and he plunged into her, flicking his tongue, dueling with hers and then showing her what he needed from her. Exasperated at being denied the thrusts of his body inside of her, she sucked his tongue into her mouth and when his hand went to her breast, her hips began to undulate against him. She couldn't help it, and she didn't care if he knew it.

"Drake. Honey, please. I…"

He set her away from him. "They'll still be in the den when we get back, and they'll be looking for signs of my frustration." He laughed. "Don't look horrified. I've done the same to them. And since I'm sleeping alone tonight, I'd better not make it any worse for myself."

Laughter poured out of her. "I suppose you think I'll hop into bed like a little bunny and fall fast asleep, eh?" She joined in his laughter, but in the back of her mind, she knew that if she made herself too available, he might never want a different arrangement.

"It's really nice out," Drake said to no one in particular when they entered the den. He pointed to a big, overstuffed leather chair. "Have a seat over there. What would you like to drink?"

"Do you have any ginger ale?"

"Absolutely." He put cracked ice in a tall glass, filled the glass with ginger ale and brought it to her.

"Thanks. What are you having?"

"Since I don't have to drive, I'm going to enjoy a vodka and tonic." He got the drink, kicked the ottoman till it rested beside her chair and sat down with his shoulder against her leg.

"Pamela and I are going riding tomorrow morning." He looked at Alexis. "If I got a pony for Tara, would you let me teach her to ride? It's best she learn while she's young. I can keep the pony the same place where I board Donny Brook."

It was Telford who answered him. "She'd love it, but not unless Grant could ride with her."

"Good. Then convince Adam to buy his son a pony. My niece deserves one."

Pamela tuned out the conversation, unable to take her eyes from Alexis. The woman sat regally, leaning back in her chair with her knees crossed and her hands folded across her belly, protecting the fetus inside of her.

I am not going to cry, she said to herself. *I'm going to smile if it kills me, and Monday when I get to work, I'm going to check on that agency. Maybe Drake will make us a family, but maybe not till it's too late. Every month my chance of getting pregnant and producing a normal, healthy child diminishes. I don't hold it against him. Every person has a right to pursue his or her dream. I love him, but I'm going after my dream. He knows how I long for a child, and I am not going to mention it to him again. If he wants us to be together, he knows what to do.*

Suddenly, she felt the pressure of his head against her thigh and wondered if he knew what a possessive gesture he'd made in the presence of his family. She rested her hand on his shoulder and, to her surprise, he covered it with his own.

"Tara don't need to wait for Adam to buy Grant a pony," she heard Henry say. "If Alexis and Tel don't mind her having one, buy her the pony. She'll love it just like she loves that little dog."

"Of course, she will," Telford said. "Let her mother and me think about it."

"Think about what?" Russ asked, his tone signaling that he was about to disagree with someone or something. "She lives out here in the suburbs, practically in the country, and her closest playmate is twelve miles. Let her have the pony, for heaven's sake."

"Seems to me like you oughta build a stable. Yer paying a fortune to board yer stallion, and yer gonna pay even more to board a pony, 'cause it takes a lot of care."

"I've been thinking about that," Drake said, "though I haven't lost any sleep over it."

"I think I'll turn in," Pamela said. "We're riding early in the morning."

He stood immediately and announced, "Be back shortly," took her hand and walked with her down the hall toward the guest room.

"I'll be down for breakfast at six-thirty. Can you make it then?"

"Sure, but what about Henry? Isn't that too early for him to get breakfast?"

"No. He gets up at daylight." They reached her door. "Kiss me good-night, and please don't tempt me." When she reached up and pressed a quick kiss on his lips, he stared down at her. "I didn't mean a brotherly kiss, I meant a kiss."

She brushed the side of his face with the back of her hand. "When it comes to you, honey, there's only one kind of kiss. What'll it be?"

A grin formed around his lips, and then his face creased in a wide smile. "You know how to get what you want, don't you?" She parted her lips and took him in. "Whoa there. I'll see you at breakfast in the morning." He opened the door, pushed her inside and left.

Drake stopped by the den, told his family good-night, mostly to indicate that he was staying in his own room, and headed up the stairs. What he did was his business, but he didn't want to cause speculation about Pamela. After all, as his Seneca grandmother was supposed to have counseled, "Many suns drink from the ocean before the clouds weep and water the earth." So the less known about his relationship with Pamela, the better. Still, he'd be the first to say that each time they were together, his feelings for her grew stronger. And as the weekend progressed, it bore heavily upon him that she fitted well with his family and they would quickly and easily love her.

"How'd you enjoy your weekend in the country?" he asked her as they walked down the hallway to her apartment that Sunday evening.

"I loved it, and that surprised me, because I've always considered myself a very urban creature. I loved everything about it." Then she shocked him with the question, "Why wasn't Velma at Eagle Park this weekend? They don't seem to spend a lot of time together."

"Russ was working at Eagle Park because he needed to consult with Telford about the structure he's working on. When he's designing a structure, he stays to himself, and work is his whole life. He's fortunate in that Velma understands that and supports him."

"She is a very likable person. I am hoping that she and I will become close friends."

"Is your bridesmaid's dress ready?"

"I'm picking it up Thursday."

A rueful smile played around his lips. "Do I look like a man who doesn't want to leave you?"

She opened her arms, and he rushed into them. "There'll be other nights, darling, hopefully more than I can count."

He gazed into her eyes and asked himself what more a man could want. "I hope you're good at math," he said in a feeble effort to let her know that he empathized with her wish. "I'll call you tomorrow, and you can let me know when we can be together this week. I'll get our tickets for our flight to Texas Friday afternoon." He left her with the feel of her kiss clinging to his lips.

At seven-forty the following Friday evening, he stashed their bags in the trunk of the black Cadillac he'd rented and headed away from the San Antonio International Airport out San Pedro Avenue en route to Waverly. "I hope your father isn't planning to give me a hard time, because something tells me I'm not in the mood for it."

She didn't seem concerned. "Do you ever lose your temper?" she asked him.

He put the car in cruise control, flipped on a Duke Ellington CD and hummed a few bars of "Don't Get Around Much Anymore." "You know I am not easygoing. I keep my counsel and try not to let people and situations rile me, but I can lose it, and I definitely have done that."

She released a soft whistle. "I don't think I'd like to be there."

Remembering an encounter with a football teammate while in college, he grimaced. "No, I don't suppose you would. A classmate heckled me once too often, and I flattened him. He was out till an ambulance arrived. Scared me almost to death."

"Is that the last time?"

"It's the last time I used my fists. Watch out for the exit."

"About four miles. What time are we leaving Sunday?"

He told her and winced when an oncoming car met them with full headlights blazing. A few minutes later, he turned off the highway and into the lane leading to Pamela's home. "Here we are, and I hope I don't meet any more drivers like that one. He practically blinded me."

The brown Tudor-style house seemed eerie in the moonlight and out of place in the sleepy Southern environment. To his surprise, Phelps Langford opened the door.

"It's time you got here," Phelps said. "I'm starving." He extended his right hand to Drake. "It's good to see you again. Come on in."

Thoughts of Little Red Riding Hood and the Big Bad Wolf flickered through his mind, but he shoved them aside. "How are you, sir? I wasn't sure I ought to risk this trip."

When Phelps laughed, he saw Pamela's resemblance to him. "Oh, nonsense. I jerked your chain, and you jerked right back. Men do that sort of thing. You know that."

If that was the apology he'd get, he supposed it beat not getting one. "Happy birthday. I hope you'll have as many more."

"Thanks, but I'm not sure I want to live to be a hundred and thirty. Everybody I care about would be dead. How was your trip?" Phelps turned, looked back at his daughter and grinned. "I'm not ignoring you, it's just that—"

"I know," she said. "You're mending fences, and it's a good thing. Where's Mama?"

"She's dressing."

Drake remembered how long it took her to dress during his previous visit and figured he'd starve before he got a chance to eat. But she swept into the living room, embraced her daughter and then Drake. He could see from Phelps's expression that the man would prefer that he didn't hug his wife. He ignored the man and gave Delta the greeting that an attractive woman deserved.

If he's stupid enough to think I'd make a pass at my girlfriend's mother, let him sweat.

"I settle for three courses normally, but this is a special occasion." She raised her glass of champagne. "To my husband, the man I love and who loves me. May I stay here as long as you and leave when you go. Happy birthday, dear."

After dinner, Phelps opened his gifts, a digital camera from Pamela, a set of encyclopedias of the English and Russian languages from Delta and a gold tooled leather travel kit from Drake.

"Well, I hit the jackpot. All of you gave me something that I can keep forever." He spoke directly to Drake. "You're a gracious man. Thank you." Then he caressed the encyclopedias. "Delta knows I've wanted these for a long time. I translate…er…texts for the government as a consultant." From that, Drake gathered that the man handled secret computer-related materials.

Phelps went to the piano and ran his fingers over the keys. "Anybody willing to sing 'Happy Birthday' to me? I don't mind playing, but danged if I'll sing to myself."

Drake cleared his throat and reached for Pamela's hand. "Can you sing in the key of F?" She nodded. "Uh-huh."

When they finished singing the familiar song, Phelps opened the piano bench to look for sheet music. "You've got *some* voice, there, Drake. I won't insult you by asking why you didn't pursue voice as a career, since it's obvious that you followed your preference. Do you know 'Mariah'? 'They call the wind Maria'?"

"I haven't sung it since college, but I'll try."

He sang the song twice because Delta asked him to, and found that he enjoyed the singing, because it gave them a pleasant way to pass the evening. "I'm finished now," he said. "'O Holy Night' and Brahms's 'Lullaby' are the only things I'd ever heard Pamela sing." He looked at her and winked. "How about singing 'Villia'?" She obliged, and the evening sped away. Intent on being circumspect, he kissed Pamela's lips quickly in her parents' presence and told them all good-night.

I hope to hell I don't walk in my sleep, he said to himself, showered and went to bed.

The knock on his door shortly after six the next morning startled him. He was about to say "Come in" when he realized it could be one of Pamela's parents. He got up, put on a robe and wrapped it tightly, opened the door and looked into Phelps Langford's face.

"Good morning. Glad to see that I didn't awaken you. It's a good morning for fishing, and I thought you and I might go out and catch a few. Digger's Brook is only about a few miles down the road, and the trout's good right now. Or we could go down to the San Antonio River, but the catch isn't half as good. I've got breakfast just about ready, and Delta and Pamela will sleep till ten. We can be back by then."

Drake rubbed his fingers over the bristles on his chin and opened his eyes a little wider, aware that Phelps hadn't expected to find Pamela in his room. "Give me ten minutes and I'll meet you in the kitchen."

"Good. I like a man who doesn't waste his life in bed."

The compliment was lost on him, for he wanted nothing more than to crawl back in that bed and sleep for hours. He brushed his teeth, shaved, splashed water over his face, put on his clothes and made it to the kitchen in eleven minutes.

Phelps placed a platter of scrambled eggs, country sausage and bacon, biscuits and individual bowls of grits on the table, poured two glasses of orange juice and looked at Drake. "Coffee now or later? You Yankees are peculiar about when you get your coffee."

Drake had always thought Maryland was a Southern state. "I'm not. I want it as soon as I open my eyes."

The smile on Phelps's face lit up his eyes, and he knew he'd like the man if only because his daughter looked so much like him. "I've already had two cups." He put a wooden trivet on the table and set the coffeepot on it. "My wife uses one of those electronic coffeemakers, but I perk mine the old-fashioned way—right on top of the stove."

Drake poured himself a cup, blew it, took a sip and smiled with pleasure. "Best coffee I've had in years. I haven't done much fly-fishing, but I'd like to try."

"Well, it takes practice, so we'll go downstream and cast for mullets or catfish. How's that?"

"Suits me as long as it's relaxing. I try to keep my weekends as free of stress as possible. Enough of that when I'm on the job."

It surprised him that he found talking with Pamela's father easy. And the man could cook. "These biscuits are ready to walk. Wonderful! Who made them?"

Phelps stopped eating, rested his fork on the side of his plate and stared at Drake. "Who do you think made them? Delta can't even fry corn bread. She's great at fancy cooking, but don't ask her to cook a pot of grits. I've tried to figure out how to ruin grits, and I don't see how it's possible, but Delta manages every time."

"Hats off to you, man. I don't suppose it matters who cooks as long as there's someone in the house who does it well enough to prevent starvation."

"Right. Can you cook?"

"Sure. I'm a scientist. Give me a recipe book, and I can make anything in it. And I can cook grits."

He changed from sneakers to boots while Phelps cleaned the kitchen, and at a quarter of seven they headed for Digger's Brook in Phelps Langford's Buick LeSabre.

"Nobody around here to go fishing with," Phelps said. "I didn't have brothers or buddies growing up, my older sister treated me as if I were her toy and now I can't make close friends because of my work. Friends ask questions, and when they don't get answers, they provide their own. You know what I'm saying?"

He did, indeed. The man was saying that he'd had a lot of lonely hours. "After Pamela was born, we tried for some more, but we weren't lucky. The problem was with me, not Delta." He turned into a little dirt road and parked under a tree. "I'm hoping Pamela will give us some grandchildren before I get too old to enjoy them."

The best thing for me to do is ignore that last statement, and I hope he doesn't put it more pointedly than that. Drake directed the conversation away from himself. "Why didn't you have buddies, if you don't mind my asking?"

"We lived in the suburbs, and our house was about half a mile from the next one. The property also had a high fence and a big iron gate, thanks to my dad's paranoia about theft and privacy."

They prepared their rods for fishing and Phelps took two folding chairs from the trunk and placed them at the edge of the brook. "Might as well be comfortable," he said.

Drake dug around in his mind for references to the name Langford, found none and asked, "Was your father well-known?"

"He's still living. He was a famous Olympian in the nineteen-thirties, and he owns a company that produces a popular brand of canned fruits and bottled juices. He's also difficult to live around."

They cast their lines, and he sat back in the chair and enjoyed the cool and refreshing morning breeze. "How far are your parents from here?"

"They're up in Amarillo, thank God. I'd like to see my mother more often, but a little of my dad goes a long way with me. I'm sixty-five, and he'll immediately start telling me what's wrong with my life and how to live it. Pamela tells me you have a wonderful family."

"I have, and I am grateful for that. Russ, my second-oldest brother, is getting married in a few weeks, and we all like his fiancée. She's our older brother's sister-in-law. Telford—he's my oldest brother—has a wonderful wife, a godsend to all of us, a wonderful big sister. Our house had been a huge bachelor pad for four men—us and our cook and surrogate father—and she and her wonderful six-year-old daughter made it a real home."

He saw the red ball on his line bobbing in the water and jerked the line. "Hey, there's a fish here." He reeled in a catfish of at least three pounds, put it in the bucket and cast again.

They talked until the sun began to make them uncomfortable. Phelps opened the bucket. "Let's see what we've got in here. Hmm. Not bad. Three catfish and four mullets. Haven't done this well in a long time. I'm ready to go if you are. They must be wondering where we are."

At this point, Drake's concern was about who would scale the fish, for he didn't know how to begin. "I'll take these out back, skin the catfish and scale the mullets," Phelps said. "By the time Delta and Pamela get up, I'll have 'em iced down."

"While you're doing that, I'll heat up the coffee. You want a cup?"

"Wouldn't mind it a bit."

He warmed the coffee, filled two mugs and headed toward the back deck. It occurred to him that Phelps Langford needed a male friend, but would willingly settle for a companionable son-in-law. Well, he didn't mind filling in, but no one should think he could be lured into anything. He'd follow his own lights, though it was a relief to know that the man was likable and that he was enjoyable company. He opened the screen door and stepped out onto the deck, and his eyes widened when Phelps nailed the catfish's tail to a plank of wood, picked up a knife and pulled the skin off.

"Here's your coffee. I had no idea that those fish had skin rather than scales."

"So you're both out here. Where's the coffee, honey?" He looked up to see Delta standing in the doorway looking like a model who had a date with a photographer. He hoped Pamela didn't feel the need to look perfect every minute of the day.

"We drank it all. The pot's on the stove."

Delta went back into the house and after about ten minutes, Pamela came through the door, moving as if she had to drag herself. "Hi. Mama said you've already been fishing." She seemed to squint at him when she said, "Did my daddy get you up at five this morning?"

"No. He waited another hour. But not to worry, I enjoyed the world as it was before other humans polluted it."

Phelps stopped scaling the last mullet and looked up at him. "Heavens, I thought maybe you were already up."

He looked at the man and couldn't prevent the grin that spread over his face. "You're kidding."

Phelps returned to his task. "Well, you certainly were gracious about it."

"I enjoyed it once I got my eyes open, and I certainly enjoyed the fishing."

"Unless you have some plans, I'll fry these up for lunch, a real fish fry right over there on that grill I built."

Pamela moved closer to him, and he observed her closely to see if she was trying to tell him something. But she only wanted him to know she was glad he was beside her. He looked down at her and squeezed her hand. "Does he think we can eat those five big fish?"

"He'll bake some corn bread and stew some collards, and we will eat every tiny piece of that fish. Daddy is great at frying fish."

Her pride in her father touched him, and he was glad they had come to terms. "If he'll fry 'em, I will definitely eat my fill. Do we have time to ride over to see the Coopers before lunch?"

Her eyes seemed to beseech him. "We could, but it would be awkward. Selena wouldn't let us leave in time to get back here for lunch. Do you mind?"

He didn't mind, and he realized that making her happy and secure with him was by far the most important thing he could do at that stage of their relationship. "Of course not."

It occurred to him that Phelps, too, was putting forth a lot of effort to ensure a pleasant weekend when he said, "After lunch, we could rest a couple of hours in case you need to catch up on your sleep, and then we can go over to the club and swim. If you want to play tennis in this scorching heat, you can do that, too. Me, I just want a swim."

"Sounds good to me. What about you?" Drake asked Pamela, who hadn't moved from his side.

"I'd love to swim, but no tennis for me this afternoon." She tugged at his hand. "Come on. I'll get you another cup of coffee." He'd had three cups already, but if she wanted to be alone with him, he wouldn't look a gift horse in the mouth.

"I've had enough coffee this morning," he told her, leaning against the kitchen table, "but I'll take anything else you're offering." Her arms went around him, and she raised her face for his kiss. Looking down at her, it occurred to him that he was happy, that he felt balanced, as if he were at last centered. He lowered his head and flicked his tongue over the seam of her lips. She pulled his tongue into her waiting mouth, and as if he'd touched a live wire, electricity flashed through him. He tightened his grip on her and loved her until the feel of her hands pushing against his chest surprised him.

"Wh—?"

"I th…think Daddy just passed the door, and I didn't want him to get a shock on his way back."

He could only shake his head in wonder. "I forgot where we were. Woman, you're dangerous." He tried to make light of it, but she had stopped him in good time, because hot blood had begun to heat his loins and he would have been hard-pressed to control his reaction. "I'm not usually so careless. If I've got two free hours, I can take a nap." The feel of her lips brushing the side of his mouth didn't soothe his aroused state.

"Good idea. See you later."

He awakened an hour and a half later, refreshed. What he wouldn't give to be able to dive into a pool right then! He put on a pair of white slacks and a yellow T-shirt, followed the sound of voices to the back porch and noted with gratitude that the glass panels were closed and the place air-conditioned. He could do without the Texas heat.

Phelps came in from the garden. "You're in good time. I just put the last batch of fish in the pan, and everything else is ready. How'd you sleep?"

Drake resisted a yawn. "Like a baby."

"We'll eat right out here. I'll set up the table in a minute."

Phelps went about his tasks, and Drake decided to find Pamela and get some answers to questions that had plagued him all day. He found her in the basement watching television and knitting.

"Hi. Is your father the man I'm seeing last night and today or the one I saw when I was here before?"

She returned her knitting to its basket and flipped off the television. "I hope you slept well."

"I did. Thanks. About your father."

"He's both people. He can get as testy as anybody, and he has a temper that rarely shows itself, but...I'd say ninety-eight percent of the time he's the man you've seen on this visit. He admitted that he sized you up completely wrong and acted on that basis. Also, I wouldn't be surprised to learn that he did some research on you, because he's a thorough person."

"You mean to say that, when I was here before, he took one look at me and decided that I wasn't worth your time?"

"Right. And Mama and I read him the law. Still, he's decided that he likes you, and I'm certain of that, because there is not a phony bone in his body."

Phelps yelled down to them. "Come on up. Lunch is ready."

When Drake tasted the crispy fried fish, he had to admit that he'd never eaten better. Phelps preened when he told them so. He ate as much as he could, relaxed and waited until he could eat more. "I'd like to know how you cooked this."

"The secret is the open flame and the black-iron skillet. I mix flour, yellow corn meal, salt, pepper and some Cajun spice, rinse the fish, roll it in the mixture and fry it. I use canola oil for frying. That's all."

"Excuse me." He went to his room, got a piece of notepaper and wrote down the recipe. "We have an outdoor brick oven and grill, and if Henry can't prepare this, I will. Thanks."

Later, driving the rented Cadillac, he tailed Phelps to the club and at last was able to swim in the Olympic-size pool. He liked the atmosphere and thought it was the next best thing to having a pool in back of your house. He swam three laps, then stretched out on one of the chaise lounges and closed his eyes.

"I'm not moving until you tell me who you are and where I can find you."

His eyelids flew open and he stared at the mostly naked woman sitting on the edge of his chair and wearing the tiniest bikini he'd ever seen. His first thought was of what Phelps Langford would think if he saw that woman sitting there.

He glowered at her and could feel the anger flaring up in him. "I'd appreciate it if you would get up this second."

"Oh, don't be mean," she said, molding her face into a pout.

"Unless you want me to turn this chair over with you sitting on it, get up. I'm not one bit interested."

"Don't tell me you're gay."

He got up, resisted kicking the chair, whirled around and almost knocked Pamela down. His hand shot out in time to prevent her fall. "Am I glad to see you!" he said, holding her to his body.

"Oh, dear! Pamela, how are you? Are you and John still an item? Please tell me who this gorgeous hunk is."

He nearly laughed at the expression on Pamela's face. Irate hardly described it. "If he wanted you to know who he was, he'd have told you when you threw yourself at him." She put her arm through his. "Come with me, sweetheart. I'd like a change of scenery."

A few steps away, he saw Phelps standing with his legs wide apart, his arms folded across his chest and an unpleasant scowl on his face. Uh-oh. Just what he'd feared. Well, he was over twenty-one and paid his own bills. Phelps would have to learn not to jump the gun.

"What was that about?" Phelps asked. "I never saw such brazenness in my life."

"She did what you did, Daddy—took one look at Drake and decided he was a playboy. I got there in time to keep him from dumping her on the concrete floor."

"It would have served her right," Phelps said. "Sometimes I don't know what to make of these modern women."

Delta's response was a shrug. "Oh, the poor girl is probably lonely."

Phelps hadn't simmered down. "And well she should be. What man wants his woman to display herself that way? Nice-looking girl like that making herself cheap."

Drake laughed. He couldn't help it. Phelps had certainly catalogued that woman's assets. *Methinks you protest too much, buddy,* he said to himself in the manner of Shakespeare. The woman sauntered past them slowly as if to make sure that Drake saw her, but only his peripheral gaze captured her, for he was too busy observing Pamela. He had never seen a woman more vexed, but he kept his thoughts to himself.

"Aren't we supposed to attend a garden party next week?" he asked her, not that he welcomed the prospect; he didn't. He wanted to divert her attention from the black vixen who had waded into her space not once, but twice.

"Uh…what? Oh, yes, the garden party. That's Saturday, and wear your hard-hat outfit."

"Wear my… Hey, wait there. I didn't do anything to set you off. If you're going to react this way to every little tactless airhead who appears on the scene, I might as well take a hike. I could be a dozen other places, but I'm down here in this stifling Texas heat just to be with you. That ought to tell you something. If you don't trust me, lay it out for me right now, and I'm out of here."

"I'm sorry, Drake, but these women get on my nerves."

"You think they don't get on mine? I detest it, but I'm not going to blow a fuse over it."

"I trust you, and I am not jealous. What gets my dander up is the temerity of these women. She saw me with you when we walked in here, and she's known me since I was in kindergarten. The idea of suggesting that I have something going on with John when she knows better! How dare she! I felt like telling her to go to hell."

"Yeah. You looked as if you had a worse punishment than that in mind. Where's your father?"

She pointed over her shoulder. "Over there watching the whole thing."

"Let him watch. As long as he doesn't judge me on the basis of the way in which strangers react to me, we'll get along. And I hope he's shrewd enough to know that."

Chapter 11

The day of the garden party finally arrived. Pamela stepped out of Drake's white Jaguar wearing an ankle-length, peach-colored chiffon sheath with a split from the hem to the left knee and a matching, wide-brimmed organdy hat, elbow-length gloves, bag and shoes. She looked at Drake, resplendent in a white linen suit, violet tie and white shoes, and winked.

"Rhoda said we should dress for a formal garden party, and I had better see every woman here in a broad-brimmed hat."

As if he knew she was a little anxious about it, he grinned and winked back at her. "Why? If some of the guests don't know what's de rigueur for garden parties, I'm not going to sweat for them. You look stunning." He offered his arm. "Beautiful." And she thought he breathed rather than said the word.

"Oh, Pamela!" Rhoda exclaimed when she opened the

door. "You look… Gee whiz …" Her gaze traveled to Drake and lingered there. "Come…come on in."

The way the woman drooled over Drake, she wouldn't have been surprised to see saliva dripping from the side of her mouth. "Rhoda, this is Drake Harrington. Drake, Rhoda Hansen." She stared at Rhoda's hand as it gripped Drake's, tightened and remained there as if she was greeting a friend of long standing. Laughter bubbled up in her throat at Drake's widened eyes and perplexed expression, but she quickly stifled it. But when his obvious attempt to extricate his hand failed, Pamela could no longer contain the mirth and laughter poured out of her.

"You sure are something," Rhoda said, evidently oblivious to the drama in which she was the central character.

"He is that," Pamela said, not bothering to hide the smirk, "but I think he wants his hand back…provided you don't mind, of course."

Rhoda flinched as if she'd been struck by an unseen object, and Pamela realized that Rhoda hadn't been conscious of her behavior. *My Lord, she's actually got a crush on him.*

"Where's your hat?" she asked Rhoda. "You told me this would be a formal garden party, and that means women wear hats."

"I…uh, I know, but I couldn't find one that suited me. I rationalized that since I'm the hostess, I could get by without one. Y'all come on in and mingle." Her gaze lingered on Drake's face, and Pamela knew that if Rhoda didn't get her act together, their visit would be short.

Later, sipping punch, she asked Rhoda, "Is this the first time you've met Drake?"

"First time I met him, but I saw him with you a couple of times. The man's a knockout. Are you two serious?"

"We're serious, Rhoda. Very serious."

Rhoda seemed to shrink the way a balloon shrivels when it loses air. "You don't know how lucky you are."

She looked at the woman, almost as if seeing her for the first time. Seeing her not as a coworker and assistant, but as a woman like herself with dreams deferred and needs unfulfilled. "You're very attractive and you're only thirty-five, too young to be discouraged about life. You have a lot to offer a man, so find one who is worthy of you and who loves you."

Rhoda lifted her gaze from the floor, and understanding gleamed in her eyes. "Thanks for the compliment. You're right about the rest. I always get attracted to men I can't or shouldn't have. At least this one isn't married, which means I'm making progress."

"You mean to tell me—"

"No, I haven't had an affair with a married man, but I've had a couple of close shaves. I guess I should start going to church and maybe taking up tennis and swimming, so I'll meet some single, unattached men."

The touch of Drake's hand at her elbow alerted Pamela to his presence. He handed Rhoda a card. "You might find this group interesting. It's similar to Big Brothers and Big Sisters, but it combines the efforts of the two. The idea is that groups of three or four men and women talk with orphaned or one-parent children and offer whatever understanding and support they need, whether it's a man's touch or a woman's touch. The members of the group range in age from twenty-one to thirty-five, and most are single. If you'd like to attend, call the president. He'll be glad to hear from you."

"Thank you," Rhoda said. "I'll telephone him Monday. I really appreciate this."

Pamela could see that Rhoda was both serious and grateful and, from her demeanor, that Drake may have managed to diffuse Rhoda's passion for him. "I think that's wonderful," she told Rhoda. "If for no other reason, your garden party is a success."

Somehow, she had a sense of relief that Rhoda's interest in Drake would cool, if it hadn't already done so, for she valued the woman as an assistant and didn't want conflict with her. Furthermore, she could think of little else more devastating for a woman than to carry a torch for a man whose interest was elsewhere.

Drake made no reference to Rhoda's behavior, which he had skillfully finessed, and that pleased her. "We'll be seeing a lot of each other in the coming week," he observed. "At the wedding rehearsal on Thursday, the bridal supper on Friday and the wedding on Saturday."

"Is Russ getting nervous?"

A slight frown, like a transparent cloud, passed over his face. "Russ? I can't imagine Russ getting nervous. I'd bet that, once he made his mind, he's been counting the days impatiently. My brother knows his mind, and he would never make a commitment unless he was certain he could live up to it."

"Sounds as if you're speaking of yourself."

He gazed down at her, unsmiling. As serious as she'd ever seen him. "That is one of my credos. And let me tell you this—when I commit myself to a person or situation, I write it in stone. You know what I'm saying?"

"Yes." But her mind was focused on the commitment he hadn't made and of which she had vowed never to remind him.

He took her arm and ushered her toward a corner of the garden where daylilies grew in yellow, orange and pink profusion. "I've wanted to ask you this, and now is as good a time as any. What happened that your father was so gracious to me last weekend? That was a one-hundred-and-eighty-degree reversal, a complete about-face. I enjoyed the time I spent with him, and I appreciated his reaching out to me, but I have to tell you I was stunned."

"My father respects people who stand up to him and he admires accomplishment. He later told my mother, but not me, that the first time he met you he liked everything about you, but wasn't sure of his judgment because men who look like you are so often shallow. Plus he did some thinking, because Mama and I gave him what-for after he was rude to you."

"I'm glad to know it," he said, "though I suspected he's still a little suspicious and he's got a low boiling point."

"I'd say that sums him up fairly accurately."

"Hello, Pamela," a voice just behind her said, and she turned to see Raynor, her boss, and another man she didn't know. Raynor made the introduction and said, "Trevor is Lawrence's replacement. He'll be on from seven till midnight."

After introductions and handshakes, the two men left and she inhaled a long and cleansing breath. At last, Lawrence Parker could be relegated to her past.

"Do you think Lawrence is able to manage his life?" Drake asked her. "I mean, if he's psychotic, shouldn't he have treatment?"

She was learning that compassion, even for his adversary, was an essential element of Drake's character, and she couldn't help thinking that she wanted her children to have that—and many of his other traits. Her face must have reflected her thoughts, for when she stopped ruminating and focused on him, his eyes blazed with a look of intimacy that nearly caused her to lose her balance. It was a look that said, *I know you, I've had total possession of you and I want you right now.* She tried to shift her gaze, but as if her mind mated with his, she couldn't release herself from his snare, her breath shortened and she stopped herself just before her tongue rimmed her lips.

He stepped closer to her. "If you tell me you aren't thinking of me, remembering *us,* I won't believe you. Do you want to leave?"

She did. Oh, how she wanted the joy of exploding in his loving arms, but she looked past his shoulder and shook her head. "I could say yes to that every day, but I am not going to settle into an affair with you. I deserve more than that."

"We're already in an affair."

"Please, let's not debate this, Drake. What I've experienced with you is too important to me. Okay?"

He grasped her right forearm. "It's important to me, too, and don't you ever forget that."

She managed to force a smile. "At least we're in the same park, if not on the same park bench."

His hand went to the back of his head and she stared at him while he punished his scalp. After a while, he said, "I suppose it's natural for a woman to be impatient with a man, but trust me in this, will you? I don't think you'll be sorry that you did."

When he looked into the distance, seemingly preoccupied, she said, "Let me know when you get bored. I don't mind leaving."

Both of his eyebrows shot up, and she got the feeling that he hadn't been aware that his mind wandered. "Forgive me. I don't get bored when I'm in your company. I'm not with these people." He let his gaze sift through the crowd. "I'm with you, and that's why I'm here."

This man could be serious when she least expected it, and he could treat lightly—or so it seemed to her—incidents and things that she thought deserved serious consideration. For her articulated thoughts, he rewarded her with a frown.

"I take you seriously, even when you're joking, because everything you say and do tells me who you are, and this is something you shouldn't forget. The fact that you see my teeth in what looks to you like a smile or a grin does not mean you are looking at my heart. It also doesn't mean I'm a phony. When I can do it without sacrificing my principles, I try to put people I meet at ease with me, but I don't do that with you. With you, I am my unvarnished self."

He gazed steadily at her, and she saw the truth in his eyes. Yes, and a loneliness or a need, she couldn't figure out which. She only knew that if they had been alone at that moment, she would hold him in her arms and in her body, showering him with the love she felt for him.

"Pamela! Sweetheart!" His arm encircled her waist, and he walked with her away from that corner of the garden to the center of the crowd. "If we had remained over there," he whispered, "I'd be holding you and loving you right this minute, and the way I wanted to do it was not for the eyes of any third person. You do pick the damnedest times to open your soul to me."

She looked up at him, shaken by what she had felt, what she had exposed and by his reaction after reading her as if he could see inside of her. "Is that what I did?" She hardly recognized her voice.

He nodded. "Being among these strangers may be good for us—if nothing else, it forces us to discipline our reaction to each other."

"Is that so?" she asked him. "You speak for yourself—as far as I am concerned, your reaction to me is already disciplined enough."

He touched her nose with his right forefinger as if he didn't dare venture further. "Really? You've got a lot to learn."

Whatever he meant by that would remain obscure unless

he volunteered to explain it, for she didn't dare risk more of his candidness. If, after that rare moment of complete meeting of hearts and minds, he could tell her he had the discipline to walk away from her in spite of what he felt, she did not want to know it. She slipped her arm through his in an unspoken suggestion that they circulate among the guests. He didn't like polite banter and useless small talk, and she didn't feel comfortable with it, but a garden full of people was not the place for serious discussion of their relationship. A waiter offered them drinks from a tray that contained assorted colors of martinis, but she declined, as did he, and accepted a broiled shrimp kebab from a waitress.

"I'm not bored, but I think we should leave before you spoil your appetite. I made dinner reservations for us at The Silver Candle."

"Wonderful. But not with this hat!"

He pulled on her left ear. "The trunk of my car is scrupulously clean, the perfect place for a beautiful hat." Before she knew what she did, both of her arms went around him, and she hugged him to her body. He grinned down at her. "I want a warning before you do that again in public. Woman, you're lethal."

She had wanted to drive to Eagle Park, but he insisted that they travel together in his car, and he was glad. To his mind, Route 70 didn't offer a picturesque drive, but he cherished the minutes that they could spend together.

"Would you mind a little detour?" he asked her. "I love picnicking by the river, especially by the Patapsco. It's one of my favorites."

"I think I'd like that, too, but we don't have anything to eat, do we?"

He parked beside a grove of pine trees and opened

the trunk of his car. "I can serve you potato salad, sliced tomatoes, smoked turkey breast, whole-wheat bread and lemonade. If we sit here long enough, we'll be starving by the time we get home."

He covered the grass on a slope near the river with a white plastic tablecloth, set out the food, paper plates, forks and plastic glasses, looked at her and bowed from the waist. "At your service, ma'am."

From her facial expression, one would have thought she was seeing him for the first time. Before he could digest that, she stepped over to him, wrapped her arms around him and—with her face buried in his chest—whispered, "I could love you. Oh, I could love you."

Stunned, he tilted up her face, forcing her to look at him, until he could see her eyes. "I thought you loved me now."

She didn't look at him, but settled her gaze on objects beyond his shoulder. "Yes, but not like I could. Not the way it would be if I could let myself go."

He drew her closer. "You can't let yourself go with me? Are you saying you didn't do that when we made love? Don't you know I love you?"

She nodded. "I know, but a minute ago, when I saw one more indication of your thoughtfulness, I wanted to fling my arms wide and shout to the world what I feel for you, but I didn't because I felt as if I couldn't."

He knew that his face bore a worried expression, and he didn't try to hide it. "If you have any more to give than you've already given, I…" He'd almost said, *I want it,* but instead, he said, "I can't imagine what it is or what it would be like. You please me in bed and out, but if there's more in store for me, tell me what I have to do to help you release it."

Her gaze seemed to focus on the river and its silent

movement. "I don't think it's anything that I can communicate. I just know it's bottled up inside of me and that I won't be truly happy till I can let it out. I'm not unhappy, mind you. It's just that something in me wants to be free."

"How long have you felt this way?"

"Just a minute ago."

"And you're certain it's related to me specifically."

"As certain as I am of my name."

He loosened his tie, sat down and served their meal, and though he didn't understand why, he felt closer to her than he had in their most intimate moments. After their meal, he cleared away the remains. "Ready to go?"

"Could we stay a little longer? It's so peaceful here."

She sat with her back to one of the pine trees, and he got the plastic tablecloth, folded it several times and put it between her shoulders and the bark of the tree. Then, without giving it a second thought, he lay down beside her, put his head in her lap and closed his eyes. Her hand stroked his brow, and then her fingers twisted and mussed his hair, crawling through the strands, separating them and then smoothing them. When she began to caress the side of his face, he turned on his side, put his arms around her and kissed her belly.

Would she love and cherish him that way when he was old, potbellied and had lost his hair? The thought startled him, and he sat up.

"You keep this up," he said, "and I'll put you in that car and head back to Baltimore. You can pick the most inopportune times to make love to me."

"I was not making love to you."

"Were too." In her attempt to move away from him, she fell over on her back, and in a split second, he was on her, holding her, stroking her cheek, and when her eyes blazed with desire, he plunged into her open mouth, darting into its every crevice, dueling with her restless tongue and then plunging and withdrawing in a simulation of the act of love, promising what he longed to give her. She began to shift from side to side, and he told himself to stop, that he would never make love to her in the open where any traveler could see them, but her hand went to her breast, rubbing and fondling it until he eased up her shirt, pushed up her bra and sucked her erect nipple into his mouth.

Her moans returned his senses to him, and he straightened her clothes, stood and looked down at her. "Right now, I'd give anything for some privacy with you. Don't be shocked if I walk in my sleep tonight." He helped her to her feet.

"You wouldn't do that. We'd be the talk of Harrington House, though I suspect Henry will be disappointed if you *don't* walk in your sleep."

"*Henry?* What about *me,* woman? And are you telling me you wouldn't want me to come to you?"

She brushed his lips with her own, took his hand and started toward the car. "I have very mixed feelings about it. I would and I wouldn't."

He fastened her seat belt, turned and headed back for Route 70. She'd given him as much assurance as he needed. "Want to stop at Monocacy Battlefield?"

"Could we do it some other time?" she asked him. "Those clouds over there are threatening to open with a vengeance, and let me tell you now that the only time I am evil is when I get wet with my clothes on."

He tried to imagine it, and the picture of Pamela fending off the world like an irritated wet hen brought a guffaw from him that he didn't succeed in controlling. "All right, I don't believe in tempting fate, and I wouldn't like you to chew me out. We're going home." He looked over at her and grinned. "But don't sleep too soundly tonight."

She turned fully to face him, and he glanced at her to determine whether he had annoyed her. If he had, she wasn't revealing it. "You would do that? Knock on my bedroom door, I mean?" she asked him.

He turned onto Route 70, put the car in cruise control and shifted to the center lane. "Uh-huh. I definitely would."

When he reached Harrington House, he took out his key, but before he could use it, Henry opened the door and looked from one to the other. "I see you learned that that Jag's got room enough for two people. The idea of both of you coming here from the same place in separate cars never did make sense to me."

Drake gave Henry an affectionate pat on the shoulder, and the man's frailness didn't escape him. "I hope you haven't spent any time thinking about that. How are you?" He didn't know what prompted the question, other than his sudden realization that Henry was no longer the robust man he'd known as a child.

"I'm me same self, and I hope to stay that way."

Seeing an opportunity to say what might at another time appear threatening to Henry, he said, "We're acting as if Harrington House is a hotel. I think you need some full-time help, and I'm going to mention that to Telford."

An expression of horror spread over Henry's face. "For goodness' sake, don't say that. If you mention household help to Tel, all he can think of is Beanie, and she ain't worth spit. Ain't never done a decent day's work in her life. Spare me."

"If you say so. Where's everybody?"

"All over the place, but most of 'em's at the church practicing how to say 'I do.' As if it was a whole paragraph instead of two one-syllable words you have to say." He looked at Pamela. "Alexis said you should come on to the church as soon as you got here."

Drake took Pamela's bag to her room and put it inside the door. "I'll be ready in five minutes. It's a good thing we had our picnic, or I'd be ready to eat."

Later, as he loped up the steps, he had a persistent feeling that he was rehearsing one of his own life's chronicles, that his course had already been charted. However, he shook it off, put a look of gaiety and happiness on his face and went to his room to check his tuxedo while he waited for Pamela.

"What color is your dress?" he asked when they were on their way to the church.

"Mauve pink. I didn't think I could wear that color, but Velma's dressmaker for the wedding proved me wrong."

En route to the church, he took a shortcut through a farm region and wished he hadn't done it. A wedding was a happy event, and even the rehearsal was, for him, a time of happiness. But the sight of the run-down houses, tilted porches, barns in need of repair and useless old automobiles jacked up in neglected front yards depressed him.

"It's an ugly sight," she said, articulating his thoughts. "Sometimes I forget how much poverty there is around us." Then, as if deliberately to alter their mood, she began to sing, and "Memories" floated from her throat effortlessly.

"I like your voice," he said, and as if confirmation were needed, added, "I don't know anything about you that I don't like."

The rush of blood to her face, tinting it a soft rose, let him know that his compliment pleased her. As they walked up the steps of the First Presbyterian Church, he eased his arm around Pamela's waist, and seconds later asked himself why he'd done it. He had noted a streak of possessiveness in him, possessiveness about her, and he didn't know whether he liked it.

It doesn't matter whether I like it, it is a fact, he thought to himself, and hugged her to him just before they entered the sanctuary.

Russ came to meet him, greeted Drake with a hug and kissed Pamela's cheek. "Glad you could make it."

"How's it going?" Drake asked.

"So far, so good. Velma hasn't gotten bride's jitters yet, but I wish she would so they'll be over by Saturday."

"She may not get them," Pamela said. "She impressed me as being laid-back."

"I hope you're tight. I think she may want you up there somewhere, Pamela."

She turned to Drake and squeezed his right hand. "See you later."

Alexis stood in for the bride during the rehearsal, and Pamela tried not to envy Velma as she sat in the cradle of Russ's arms, as relaxed as if the occasion honored someone other than her. When she glanced toward Drake, she saw that he'd been watching her very intently, and though she had caught him in a moment of privacy, he didn't shift his gaze. The rehearsal continued for two hours. One bridesmaid, Mary Lou, couldn't seem to walk up the aisle without pausing between steps, and another, Dolly, had a crying jag when the usher looked down at her and smiled as they followed Alexis and the groom. When asked about it, Dolly told Velma, "As soon as the wedding is over, that usher is going back to California to his wife."

Velma rolled her eyes toward the ceiling. "Considering how much attention he's paying to *you,* be glad you aren't his wife or his anything else." That comment dried Dolly's eyes.

After the practice session, Russ took them all to Mealy's for a late supper, and it surprised her that everyone treated her as if she not only belonged with Drake but with them, as well. Maybe she did belong with him. If so, he'd better find a way of letting people know it and soon. Her patience was growing thin.

"I remember that you have a beautiful soprano voice," Telford, who sat at her right, said to her. "I had never heard 'O Holy Night' sung more beautifully. You and Drake could be famous singing together."

"I've heard him sing," she replied, "and the beauty of his voice stunned me."

Telford's long fingers stroked his chin. "He's never treated that gift as if it was special, but both his speaking and his singing voice are very arresting, at least to me."

"Me, too," she told him, surprised that she found it so easy to talk with Telford. She had been somewhat in awe of him, and she supposed it was because of his brothers' deference to him. *What a wonderful family,* she thought, as Russ stood, pulled out a chair for Alexis and assisted her in seating herself. Each brother treated the others' women as if they were blood sisters, and Tara as if she were a blessing sent from heaven. When her gaze fell on Alexis's barely mounded belly, she blinked back the tears, closed her eyes and fought to steady herself.

"Where are you?" Drake asked her. "You must have been miles away. Do I have a rival for your affection?"

All of a sudden, she wished he did have one, and that knowing it would make Drake uncomfortable. "Weddings make me sentimental."

That much was true but she didn't have a need to cry over Velma, for the woman had everything she wanted or needed. Drake's expression told her that he knew she longed to be the bride instead of a bridesmaid. He'd been leaning against the wall in the corner of the booth when he suddenly sat forward, the movement of his body communicating to her a sense of urgency.

"How about going out early tomorrow morning when the air is fresh and just walking along the river? We could ride the horses, but I…" His voice lowered several registers. "There's something special about walking when the dew's still on the ground."

She reached for his hand and would have withdrawn hers, but he caught her hand and held it across the table. "Want to?"

At that moment, she would have promised him anything. "Yes. I'd love that very much." He pressed a kiss to the hand he held, sat back and let his gaze wash over her, oblivious to those around them.

That night, she slept in a zone of twilight, her mind targeted on the moment when she would hear a knock on her bedroom door. "It's your fault," she told herself when she woke up the next morning sleepy and exhausted from turning and twisting in her restless state throughout the night. *Why don't I get that man figured out? I should have known he wouldn't risk the embarrassment of being rejected after I indicated that he shouldn't come.*

"Hi. I hope you rested well," he said when she walked into the breakfast room. "We have a busy day ahead of us."

"Miss Pamela," Tara said. "Are you going to walk with Uncle Drake? My mommy told me not to ask if I could go along. She said sometimes adults want to be alone. Do you want to be alone with Uncle Drake?"

She leaned down and kissed the precocious little girl on the cheek and stroked her shoulders. "I confess that I do, Tara." She walked around to the head of the table, where Drake leaned back in his chair gazing at her, and kissed him on the mouth. "I definitely do," she whispered and sat down before he could react.

On his face was a knowing look, an expression that

told her he knew all about her, and it unsettled her, for it reminded her of her loneliness the previous night. Then a grin began around his lips and spread over his face, developing into a smile that warmed her from her head to the bottom of her feet.

"Next time," he said, "maybe you won't be so mean."

Later, yellowing leaves dropped around them here and there as they walked hand in hand through the woods on their way to the riverbank. He couldn't count the times he walked that route alone, always deep in thought, dealing with a special kind of aloneness, something he couldn't pinpoint well enough to share with Telford—the person to whom he was closest. As he strolled contentedly with Pamela, it occurred to him for the first time that his brothers and he had always enjoyed the woods and loved walking in them, but that they had never strolled through them together. As children, they weren't allowed to play alone in the woods, and Henry accompanied them when they developed a love of fishing.

"This is the first time since Henry used to take my brothers and me fishing that I've walked in these woods with another person."

"I would think you loved walking among these trees. It's an idyllic place."

"I do, but I've always come here alone. Since we formed Harrington, Inc., I haven't had as much time to enjoy this place as I would like, but I walk here when I can. It's peaceful, de-stressing, a place where I have no difficulty coming to terms with myself. I especially enjoy it in the late autumn. Thanks for coming with me."

"I couldn't walk in the woods near our home in Waverly, because the chance of encountering a snake is so great."

"It's possible here, too, but in the summer we use the paths."

They found a rock near the river's edge and sat there arm in arm. He didn't feel the need to talk, for which he was glad. Only the singing and chirping of birds broke the silence. Several squirrels scampered by, and he reached into his jogging jacket and threw them a handful of peanuts.

Joy suffused him when a squirrel, holding a nut in his paw, gazed up at Pamela as if to ask why she didn't give him anything. "That's why we should treat animals with care," he said. "They're intelligent." He held out his hand with more peanuts, and the little animal moved toward him cautiously, took the nuts from his hand and dashed off.

"How'd you sleep last night?" He hadn't planned to mention it, but it came out, so he'd pursue it. "Don't tell me you went to sleep the minute your head hit the pillow, because I won't believe it." She inched closer to him, and he draped his left arm across her shoulder.

"I'm not in the habit of lying for no reason," she said. "Anything else you want to know?"

He drew her closer to him. "What would you have done if I'd gone to your door?"

"I would have opened the door."

He maneuvered her head to a place against his shoulder, leaned over her and ran his tongue over the seam of her lips. "I wanted you so damned bad I thought I'd go crazy." Her lips parted and he plunged into her. When she sucked his tongue deeper into her mouth, he knew he had to stop it right there. "Hold it, sweetheart. I've got a long and busy day ahead, and I don't want to spend it wrestling with my libido."

He stood, took her hand and walked with her along the riverbank until they reached a path that led to the main road. As they walked, he pointed to a hill that overlooked the river. "Remember I told you I hope to build my house there one of these days? I didn't tell you that in the winter, when the trees are bare, you can look down the river for miles."

Her silence struck him like the sound of thunder, and he didn't have to ask what she was thinking and feeling, because he knew, and he knew she wouldn't tell him if he asked. Very soon, he would have to decide either to ask her to marry him or tell her that they should go their separate ways. Yet, the idea of a choice seemed laughable, because he couldn't imagine not having her in his life. And furthermore, the thought of another man having her sickened him. *I'll give myself two months to go or stay.*

"Wha—" his foot skidded out from under him when he stepped on a patch of wet leaves. Both of her hands grabbed him, breaking his fall, deflecting what would have been a complete spill. Instead, he was able to reach for and hold on to the trunk of a young tree.

"Thanks," he said, aware that his face probably bore a startled expression. "Where did you get those kinds of reflexes?"

"They're not special. I pay attention to whatever's important to me, and you are. So I was looking at you when it happened."

He finished picking the wet leaves off his jeans and stared down at her, knowing that it was only a matter of time, a short time at that, before he capitulated.

At the dinner for the bridal party that Alexis and Telford hosted at the Francis Scott Key Hotel in Frederick that night, he didn't think he'd ever been as proud as he was with Pamela beside him. Telford and Russ had beautiful women, but neither outshone Pamela, who wore a simple lace dinner dress in a shade of red that he liked. Telford toasted the bride and groom and wished them happiness, and Velma presented gifts to her maid of honor and bridesmaids.

Henry stood, held up a glass of champagne and said, "It's been me joy to raise these boys, to see them become fine men and make a name for themselves. It didn't surprise me none when Tel showed he had good sense to marry Alexis, but I thought I was going to have to take me strap to Russ. I knowed from the first, just like Russ did, that Velma was the one for him, but I also knowed that Russ was just cussed enough to ignore what was good for him." He took a sip. "After tomorrow, I'll have me two daughters." He looked toward Drake and Pamela. "I ain't saying no more, but everybody here can guess what I'm thinking and hoping."

Why hadn't he thought that Henry would say something like that? Drake stood, saluted the bride and groom and then tipped his glass to Pamela. "By now, everybody here should know that Henry's mouth is a place without a hinge or a key, that its purpose is to release all those uncontrolled words that tumble out of him. In spite of that, I can't imagine my life without him. Russ and Velma, the two of you have found something wonderful. Take good care of it, because it can't be replaced."

Everyone at the table stared at him, but so be it. He'd spoken from his heart. *And from your own experience with loving Pamela,* a voice inside of him mocked. He knew then that he wouldn't visit Pamela in her room that night and that he would warn her to that effect. He didn't want any incident, however casual, to trivialize what he felt for her.

"You're letting it hang out there, brother," Russ said. "If I didn't know better, I'd think you just made a personal statement."

Drake raised his glass and tipped it in Russ's direction.

"You have all the answers, brother. More power to you."
He put the glass to his lips, swallowed every drop of the
champagne it contained and set it down with sufficient
precision to let them all know he didn't want to be toyed
with.

"It's a right fine party," Henry said, "but at me age,
eleven o'clock and sleep are one and the same. Drake, if you
and Pamela don't mind leaving, you can drive me home."

Henry deserved a blessing for that. He looked down at
Pamela. "Ready when you are," she said, not waiting for
him to ask her.

He reached over and squeezed her hand. "Thanks. I'm
ready. Sometimes I forget that Henry is getting older." He
stood. "Let Russ prolong his bachelor status. I'm taking
Henry home. Everybody get home safely and sleep well."

"Yeah," Telford said over his shoulder. "Do that."

He heard the snickers and knew what they implied but
didn't care. For once, he didn't feel like an outsider. Oh, he
had always had a woman with him at their social occasions,
but only for show. This time, he had the woman he loved
and who loved him, and as he assisted her in getting up from
the table he felt that streak of possessiveness returning. *I've
got to curb this. If I don't watch it, I'll become jealous, and
that would make me a bore.*

At five o'clock that Saturday afternoon, Pamela glided
down the hall from the guest room to meet Drake, who
waited for her at the bottom of the stairs that led to the
second floor.

He released a sharp whistle. "Man, have I got myself
one gorgeous woman!"

"You deserve a hug for that," she told him, "but it'll have
to wait because I can't risk getting that close to you."

"Why not, for Pete's sake? Do I have a contagious disease?"

"You may not have a disease, but you've got *something* that'll make me arrive at the church all mussed up."

He took her arm. "Your tongue is getting to be as loose as Henry's. You and I are driving Russ to the church. A couple of limousines are collecting the ushers and bridesmaids, Henry's traveling with Telford, and Adam Roundtree is bringing Tara and his son, Grant."

She looked steadily at him. "I'm feeling weepy, and it's so unlike me. Say, who's bringing Velma?"

"She and Alexis are at a hotel in Frederick. Bride and groom aren't supposed to see each other till they meet at the altar. Are you feeling teary because you're happy, or is it—"

She was glad that Russ joined them, relieving her of the need to answer Drake's question. She hadn't expected that anything would make Russ Harrington nervous until he announced, "I'll be fine if I don't have to say one word to anybody until I hear that organ begin the strains of 'Here Comes the Bride.'" She knew he was ready to fly out of his skin.

Without comment, Drake put on his favorite music, Duke Ellington's "Satin Doll." "Not to worry, brother. Just sit back and let the Duke soothe you." Russ chuckled, and Pamela had another opportunity to observe the empathy, understanding and love that the brothers shared.

At the church, Drake kissed her cheek. "See you later," he said and headed toward a side door with Russ, each elegant in identical black tuxedos, white shirts and silver accessories that matched the matron of honor's dress.

She joined the bridesmaids and marveled at the beautiful rainbow of colors. She found Jenny, the dressmaker, and congratulated her.

"It's something lovely to see, isn't it?" Jenny said. "Wait till you see the bride. Her man gon' swell up sure as shootin'."

If I ever get married, she said to herself, *I'm going to find this woman. Who would believe that three years ago she was homeless and living on the street with all her possessions in a shopping cart?* She shook her head in wonder. "Jenny, when my time comes, if it ever does, I am definitely going to look you up."

"It'll come all right. Men don't pass up women who look like you."

She let herself smile, but there had been times when she wished they had.

At six o'clock, the organ pealed strains of Mozart's "Eine Kleine Nachtmusik" ("A Little Night Music"), Velma's favorite piece of music, and the guests turned toward the door. Pamela felt the dampness on her cheeks as she walked, head high and footing sure up the long aisle that was bedecked with white lilies of the valley at the end of every pew. As she reached the altar, she glanced at Drake, who stood beside Russ, his face stricken with concern. She wiped the tears with the back of her hand and, when she did so, his frown deepened. She smiled to assure him that she was all right.

Titters among the audience alerted her to the approach of Grant—dressed as the other males in the entourage—and Tara, wearing mauve-pink from hat to shoes and dropping rose petals as she walked. At the altar, they stood beside Alexis, who had walked just behind them. Trumpets sounded and the organ began the traditional bridal song. The guests stood and Russ, eschewing convention, turned and faced the door. She knew her lips quivered, and she sucked in the bottom one to control them. A glance at Drake told her that his mind was not on the ceremony or the two lucky people about to be married, but on her. She smiled again, but he didn't smile in return.

Get it together, girl. You don't want to ruin it for him, she told herself.

Velma approached with Henry at her side, and the woman's radiance, her joy, was almost a living thing. Russ's grin had an electric quality, a message that made Pamela feel like spreading her arms out and shouting. If she had ever before seen such happiness on a man's face, she couldn't recall it. She glanced at Drake and found his gaze on her. This time he smiled as if, by mental telepathy, he knew that she was rejoicing with the bride and groom.

"Who gives this woman to be wed?" the minister asked.

"I do," Henry's voice rang out, and he took his seat beside Adam and Melissa Roundtree.

She listened intently as the couple exchanged their vows, and when the minister told Russ to kiss his bride, Pamela's gaze shifted to Drake as if she had no control over it. His eyes mirrored his heart as he looked at her and, as if to knock her completely off balance, he mouthed words that she couldn't understand and would have given anything to know. As best man, he should have escorted Alexis, but he whispered something to Telford, who stood beside him, and Telford escorted his wife.

"You had me worried for a few minutes," Drake told her as soon as he reached her. "What was the matter?"

"I was just so full. So...so many things were going on in my head. The beauty of it, the pageantry, the church, the music. Everything. When I started up the aisle, I...uh...I felt lonely for a few minutes."

"I thought it was something like that. You don't know how happy I was when I realized that you'd snapped out of it."

* * *

At the reception, Drake danced the second dance with Alexis as custom demanded, and when he looked around for Pamela to ask her to dance, he discovered that one of the ushers was dancing with her. The dance ended, and the man was requesting a second dance when Drake approached them.

He didn't hesitate. "Sorry, buddy, but this dance is mine."

"You can have the next one, pal. I was here first."

"He was here a few months before you," Pamela said to the man. "I enjoyed the dance, but Drake is my guy."

The man's eyebrows shot up. "Sorry, man. I should have known a dame like this one wasn't loose." He saluted. "Hang in there."

Drake had to toast the bride and groom, but he didn't intend to leave her to her admirer, so he took her hand and walked over to the table. No rule said she couldn't stand there with him. Besides, with the flowers, ribbons and that four-tier wedding cake, she looked better standing there than he did. When the waiters finished serving the champagne, he rapped a fork against his glass.

"Allow me to introduce Mr. and Mrs. Russell Harrington!" Following the applause, he said, "Considering the love I witness between this man and this woman, I have no doubt that they were meant for each other. Russ, Velma, my happiness for you is boundless. God bless you both." He stepped aside to make room for Telford.

With his glass high, Telford said, "You were always the wisest one of us brothers, Russ, and you showed wisdom when you chose this woman. Velma, we welcome you to our family with all our hearts. God bless you both." He beckoned Henry.

"This is one of the happiest days of me life. It's brought

tears to me eyes to see the happiness of Russ and Velma and to know me dreams for them have come true." He raised his glass. "To a long and happy life together."

"What time do you want to leave?" Drake asked Russ.

"Any minute. Velma has to change. Say, why don't you let Telford take us? The limousines can take the brides-maids and ushers to their hotels, home or wherever they're going."

Drake raised an eyebrow. As best man, it was his place to see the newlyweds to their plane. "That isn't the way it works, brother."

"This time it does," Russ said. He nodded toward the usher who was once more crowding Pamela. "You need to take care of business. See you in two weeks."

He embraced Russ and kissed Velma's cheek. "You're as beautiful a bride as I've ever seen," he told her. "Old Sourpuss here is besotted."

"Yeah." Russ grinned. "And from what I've seen lately, I'm not the only one. Take care, brother."

After telling Henry and Telford that he was taking Pamela to Baltimore, he walked over to the man who wanted to be his rival, tapped him on the shoulder and said, "Excuse me, buddy."

"You again?"

He grinned, although he wasn't amused. "Yeah, man." To Pamela, he said, "You ready to go, sweetheart?"

For an answer, she extended her hand to him. "Nice meeting you," she said to the man, mostly over her shoulder.

"I'm driving you to Baltimore. If you want to spend the night in Eagle Park, we can go back there later, but right now, I want you to myself. What do you say?"

"Fine with me. I've got plenty of clothes in Baltimore.

Won't you feel strange wearing that tux on a Sunday morning?"

So she was way ahead of him, was she? He wanted to crush her to him, but he settled for a squeeze of her fingers. "I'll stop by Russ's apartment and get a shirt and jacket."

As they entered her apartment, he found himself marveling that she could be so devoid of coyness and pretense. She knew he wanted to spend the night with her, and she wanted the same, so she didn't enter into a fencing match.

"I want to get out of this dress," she said. "It's not the most comfortable dress to sit in."

He didn't intend for her to spend a lot of time sitting, but he had sense enough not to say it. She returned quickly, wearing a green jumpsuit.

"Would you like coffee, a drink, some food? I can put a couple of frozen quiches in the microwave and defrost some frozen shrimp."

He shook his head. "I'm sure I'll take you up on that later, but right now I'm so hungry for you that I can't think of food." And he hadn't overstated it. The previous night, he had been ready to climb the wall.

She opened her arms and stepped closer to him. He steeled himself against grabbing her as he longed to do, but eased his arms around her and found her mouth. With a moan, she took him in and began to feast on his tongue. He broke the kiss and stared down at her, for her breath had already shortened to pants and he could feel her erect nipples through his shirt. He picked her up and carried her to her bedroom.

"I have to try to take it slow," he whispered to her as he settled her on her feet beside the bed. "I don't want to disappoint you."

"We have all night. If you're in a hurry, you can make up for it later. Not to worry."

With both arms around her, he brushed his lips over her forehead, her eyes and cheeks, trying to show her what she meant to him. She put her hands behind her neck, reaching for her zipper, and he eased it down. A gasp escaped him when she stepped out of the jumpsuit wearing only a red V-shaped patch that he supposed passed for panties. At the sight of her full, rounded and erect breasts, his blood roared toward his loins, and he reached for her, covered her right nipple with his mouth and began to suck it.

"Oh, Lord," she moaned, and he pushed his hand beneath the bikini, found her folds and began to tease and massage her. Her moans grew louder, and she began to undulate against his hand. She wanted him and didn't mind letting him know it. He knew he couldn't wait much longer, but he meant to fire her up until she burned for him. When her hand grasped his penis, he nearly buckled.

"Don't, baby. If you do that it will be over in seconds."

"Put me in the bed."

He turned back the cover and placed her on the pink satin sheets. Then, he undressed himself and joined her. "May I take these off?" She lifted her hips and he removed the underwear, flung it over his shoulder and locked her naked body to his. "I love everything about you, every inch of you," he whispered as he worked his way down her body, kissing and fondling, loving the insides of her thighs with his fingers and his tongue. She writhed and moaned as he lit her up.

"I'll go mad if you don't get inside of me."

Ignoring her plea, he kissed her legs, her feet and the dimple beneath her knees before spreading her legs, opening her folds, thrusting his tongue into her. She let out a keening cry, and her moans filled the room as he kissed, sucked, nibbled and twirled his rapacious tongue.

"I want to explode. Drake, honey, get in me. I need you to—"

"All right. I'll give you what you want." He reached down beside the bed, picked up the condom and handed it to her. The feel of her hands on him, the way she handled him as she quickly slipped it on him nearly sent him over the edge.

"Now," she begged. "Now."

But he meant to get her back to boiling point and teased her with his talented fingers while he sucked her nipple. He felt the fluid flow from her and lifted her hips.

"Take me in, baby. Ah, yes. Yes," he said, easing into her velvet canal. Almost at once he could feel the beginnings of her pulsations around him, and then the squeezing and pinching began, and he thought he would go out of his mind from the pleasure of it. He pumped furiously, using every skill he knew, for he wanted them to explode together, as one. And then it began in earnest as her thighs quivered, and he felt the rhythmic clutching over the length of his penis. He prayed to control it until… Suddenly a scream tore from her and her muscles gripped him with such power that he shouted aloud and gave her the essence of himself.

"I love you." The words left their lips simultaneously.

Slowly, she opened her eyes and stared up at him. "I don't believe you can share something this powerful with me and then walk away. I'll never believe it. You belong to me."

Yes. He did. But he wasn't ready to confess it. "Maybe it isn't enough for you to know that I love you and that I've never loved another woman or even imagined it. But be patient for now. Will you?" She seemed to nod her head. He'd given himself two more months, and he had to stick with it. By then, the Josh Harrington houses would be ready for occupation, as would the Josh Harrington–Fentress Sparkman Memorial Houses in Frederick. They would also have Fisherman's Village in Barbados, among other ventures, to their credit, and with his reputation assured, he wouldn't have to ever worry about making a living for himself, his family and Henry—if need be.

He wrapped his arms around her. "If you know that," he said, in response to her declaration a minute earlier, "you'll stop doubting and let yourself love me." Then, he kissed her, lay his head on her shoulder and went to sleep.

Hours later, still locked inside of her, he said, "Did you give that guy your phone number?"

"Did I... Good heavens, no. He had the dumbest lines I've heard in ages. Want something to eat?"

Lord! How he loved her! "You bet I do. I'll fix it, if you don't mind my doing it wearing nothing but a towel."

She put her hands above her head and stretched. "Whatever works for you works for me."

Heading for the bathroom, he hoped he didn't have occasion to remind her of those words.

Chapter 12

Pamela awoke early that Monday morning in her Baltimore apartment, resolute, not buoyed in spirit; far from it, but with a new resolve. Maybe Drake needed to know that she would chart her own course and go for her own dream, if not all of it, at least that part that was within her control.

If after what we experienced Saturday night he doesn't commit, I'm going to look out for myself. I'm going to call an adoption agency this very day. I know he loves me. How could he cherish me as he did Saturday night if he didn't love me? Lord knows I love him. If I lose him, it will make me ache and maybe for a long time, but it won't kill me.

She sat up, swung her feet off the bed and headed for the bathroom. An hour and twenty minutes later, she walked into her office, sat down and reached toward her in-box. Her phone light blinked.

"Raynor wants to see you right away," her secretary said.

"Thanks."

"So much for getting this office straightened out today," she said to herself. "Two days away from here, and the place is a jungle. Jeepers! And I haven't even checked my email." She unlocked her desk, got a notebook and headed for her boss's office.

"Good morning," Raynor said. "You're looking fit. I know you don't like to report on local crimes, but—"

She exhaled a long breath. "Ugh. But what?"

He leaned forward, his eyes sparkling with excitement. "This one's a real lulu. Assemblyman Hydell's been caught with his fingers in the till and with his pants down, and there's a relationship between the two, or so I suspect. What do you say?"

She stared at her boss. Was he offering her that over Timmons, his bloodthirsty crime reporter? "Crime, scandal and sex. That it?"

He nodded slowly, as if conveying something profound. "Right. And your assignment is to find out what the truth is."

She had to be sure of her ground, so she asked him, "What about Timmons?"

"Every single one of Timmy's stories reads alike. He's always positive that he's got the truth. Never allows the possibility of error in his quotes. Hydell would sue in a minute, and I can't take that chance. You don't take chances with facts, so I'm going with you on this one. You'll do a great job."

She wouldn't have thought that, on that particular morning, anything could have jacked up her enthusiasm and started her adrenaline flowing, but Raynor's words did both.

"How much time do I have?"

"As much as you want. Two weeks?"

She couldn't help laughing. To him, two weeks seemed like an eternity. "I'll do my best."

The minute she got back to her office, before she sat down, she picked up the phone, dialed the number for Children Who Need You and told the voice on the phone that she wanted a newborn baby girl of African descent. "With a health certificate," she added. The voice thanked her and blessed her for her willingness to give love and a home to an abandoned child.

"We'll have a nice healthy baby for you," she was told and assured that it wouldn't take more than two or three months. "We want you to come down here to our office in a couple of days and fill out some papers."

Pamela marveled at the ease with which she could adopt a baby outside the country, compared to the red tape she'd have to deal with to get an American child. She had taken the first step, and although she was happy for having accomplished it, her joy was overlaid with sadness that Drake would not be the father of her child. She recalled again that once, in a flash of anger when she mentioned adopting, he'd told her that if she wanted a child so badly, he'd give her one. But she didn't want his child under those conditions. Too bad! She wrapped herself in her professional cloak and got busy.

"My. Hydell, here I come."

Shortly after noon the following Thursday, she delivered the story to Raynor. "Wow," he said, after reading it. "You can deliver this on national news tonight, and you'll get a fat bonus. That was quick. I'd like to know your sources."

"Right square in the middle of Hydell's office, and not one but two, the second of whom suggested a third source that would corroborate what he said. It seems Hydell doesn't respect his promises, and members of his staff neither like nor respect him. If he ever faces a trial, he's in trouble."

"I'll say. Well done, Pamela."

"Thanks. May I have tomorrow off?"

"Sure. Jane or Timmons will cover for you."

After her broadcast that evening, she boarded a night flight to Santo Domingo, Dominican Republic, and at nine-thirty the next morning walked into the office of Children Who Need You. "I'm here to support my application for an adoptee," she told the secretary who gave her a form.

"Have a seat and complete and sign this form. That's all there is to it. We're careful about who we give our babies to, but I'm sure you'll be accepted. We'll let you know when you should come for your child."

Her heart pounded furiously. "You mean I can start preparing for it?" she asked the woman, barely able to breathe.

The receptionist smiled. "For her. Absolutely."

She left the office of Children Who Need You skating on a cloud. After the plane landed in Baltimore/Washington International Airport, her first act was to purchase a pink teddy bear in the airport commissary. During the taxi ride from the airport to her home, she became aware suddenly that her right hand pressed loving strokes on her abdomen, and she gasped aloud.

"Knock off that fantasy right this minute, girl," she told herself. "That is definitely the wrong way to go. But if it hadn't been for..." She stopped herself before finishing the thought. Drake was not the reason why she was adopting a child, and she acknowledged that he didn't have any responsibility for it. She was twenty-nine the first time she saw Drake. And if, up to that time, she hadn't responded fully and completely to a man, hadn't found love with someone who loved her, Drake was not to blame.

* * *

Two weeks after Pamela began adoption proceedings, Drake sat with Telford and Russ in the office of their warehouse in Eagle Park—half a mile up the road from Harrington House—discussing Russ's plans for the shopping mall in Accra, Ghana.

Drake scrutinized a section of the plan for the nth time. "I really like what you've done, brother, but I don't know how we can go any further with this until we examine the location and I can see what I'll have to work with. You're probably right about the bricks, but I'd like to check out the possibility of using cement."

"Right," Telford said. "We don't know how much damage to expect during their rainy season, or whether their bricks are top quality."

"I was thinking the same," Drake said.

Telford went to the little alcove that served as a kitchen, refilled his coffee cup and drank half of it while his brothers waited for the thoughts that they knew were simmering in his mind. He sat down, rested his elbows on his thighs and folded his arms. "We have to go there, all three of us together. We can't make these decisions sitting here and imagining whether we're on target. We have to know what we're doing. In fact, we need to figure out whether we want to do this project, and we can't do that sitting here. Drake, I suggest you phone Sackefyio and get a date for about two weeks from now."

Russ ran his fingers thought his hair—a habit he acquired in childhood—and frowned. "Look here! I agree we ought to go, but…man, I can't run off to Ghana and leave my wife. I've only been married two weeks and two days."

Telford snickered, but Drake cast solemn eyes toward Russ, wondering at the change in his brother. The man who charted his own course and walked alone was no more.

"She'll understand," Drake said in an attempt to appease Russ.

"Yeah, but I won't," Russ retorted.

"I feel you, brother," Telford said. "So, since this is like a return to the motherland, so to speak, let's take our wives with us this time. After we do business, we can take them on a tour of the region. What do you say?"

Russ's face beamed with enthusiasm. "Velma's adventuresome. She'd love that."

"Alexis would, too. I say we put it to them today."

Drake and his brothers had always been a team, their togetherness as tight and as seamless as if it had been sealed by a master welder. And that togetherness, he realized, had made him what he was. But now, they were not three, but two plus one, and he felt himself the odd man out. Telford and Russ were looking at him for approval.

"Works for me," he assured them with as much verve as he could muster.

For the remainder of the day, an idea played around in his mind. "Why not?" he asked himself after dinner that night. "It's not a commitment on her part or mine, and if she doesn't like the idea, she can say no." He went to his room, dialed Pamela's phone number, asked her whether she'd like to go to Ghana with him and told her why.

"If you had asked me to climb Mount Everest with you, I couldn't be more stunned. I'd love to go, provided I can get time off from work."

He didn't want to hear her say she couldn't go, and he didn't want to beg her, but he *needed* her to go with him. And needed it badly. "Promise your boss a story, and ask him to let you take along a movie camera. Telford is great with cameras, or at least he used to be."

"Great idea. I'm sure Raynor will buy that idea for the series he presents during Black History Month in February.

I'll get one of our cameramen to teach me how to use the camera. Drake, this is wonderful. I'll let you know tomorrow."

"You can't know what your going will mean to me, sweetheart."

"Do so." Her laughter, soft and seductive, sent a thrill shooting through his body. "Bye, love," she said in barely a whisper, as if she knew she could tease his libido into action as easily as the wind bends a blade of grass.

At dinner the following evening, he said to Telford, "Since you and Russ are taking your women when we go to Ghana, I'm taking Pamela. You guys are not going to put me in the shade."

"Humph. She shoulda told you no," Henry said. "You want to have your cake and eat it, too, and she oughtna let you. A fine woman like that one deserves better."

"Am I going to Ghana, Mommy?" Tara asked, saving Drake the need to answer Henry.

"No, darling. Too many mosquitoes there, and you know how you hate them. You're going to stay with Grant and his parents."

Tara clapped her hands and giggled gleefully. "Oh, goody." Then her face became solemn. "But, Mommy, what about Mr. Henry? He can't stay here by himself."

"Don't worry, darling," Alexis said. "Mr. Henry will be fishing in Fort Lauderdale."

Tara's glee seemed boundless as she laughed and danced. "And I will get some new shells." She looked at Drake, her smile brilliant. "Uncle Drake, can you eat cake and still have it? When I eat mine, I don't see it anymore."

"That's Henry's idea," he replied, allowing himself a hearty chuckle. "He'll be glad to explain it to you."

He had to check all of their building sites before they left for Ghana, and that would leave him little or no time for his private life. He phoned Pamela and gave her his schedule for the next two weeks. "It doesn't suit me, baby, but at least we'll be together all the time while we're in Ghana. I'm looking forward to it."

After a rather long pause, she said, "Something tells me you guys need a second engineer. Your work isn't done until you hand the keys to whoever's going to occupy the property."

"True, but that's the way it should be. Each of us has a job, and engineering the building of a structure is mine."

"I know that, and I know you're good at it. Don't get your dander up. Call me from wherever you happen to be. By the way, I bought two cans of spray to keep mosquitoes off. Think that's enough?"

"Probably, unless they think you're as sweet as I do. Be sure and get your shots. If you're free and don't mind, I'll see you in a couple of days."

"Be more precise."

"I'll try to make it Thursday, and don't be so fresh. Remember the kind of punishments I mete out."

"Do I ever! Uh…I'd…uh, appreciate it if whoever's making the hotel reservations would give me a separate room, Drake. I wouldn't be comfortable sharing a room with you on a trip with your brothers and their wives."

She could cool him off just as quickly as she could warm him up. "Of course you'll have your own room. It wouldn't have occurred to me to suggest otherwise. Pamela, you may trust me not to compromise you."

"Don't be offended. Wouldn't you have thought it strange if I didn't express a preference?"

He thought for a minute. "Eventually I suppose I would have. You're well within your rights, but I like to know that you trust me."

"Do you think I'd travel five or six thousand miles from home with you if I didn't?"

"Point taken. I'll see you Thursday. Blow me a kiss."

She did. "Bye, love."

On the first day of October, at Accra's Kotoka International Airport, Pamela's feet touched African soil for the first time. She didn't know what she expected, but being in the region of her roots and her mother's roots didn't give her any special sensation. Nonetheless, after passing through customs to the limousine that Sackefyio had waiting for them, she realized that she hadn't seen a white face. "Finally, something that's truly black-owned," she said under her breath.

"Amen. I heard that," Velma said. "And how sweet it is!"

Drake took her hand and walked over to a tall man who wore an elegant, royal-blue agbada. "Pamela, this is Ladd Sackefyio, one of my closest friends during undergraduate years. Ladd, this is Pamela Langford."

"Welcome, Pamela. I'm delighted to meet you," he said, extending his right hand and shaking hands with her. He then turned to Drake. "You have great taste. I wish you both blessings."

"Thank you," Drake said, and she thought he looked a little shy. Shy for him, at least.

"I'm glad to meet you, Ladd," she said. "Drake speaks highly of you."

Ladd's eyes twinkled. "I hope so. If I got into devilment, he was right there with me. Doris—that's my bride—is at home waiting for us."

Drake then introduced his brothers and their wives to Ladd, and they got into the stretch Mercedes and headed for the Sackefyio compound. Doris Sackefyio, Ladd's wife, met them at the gate. After greeting Drake, she turned to Pamela. "I'm so glad you came. Ladd and Drake have been close since their college days, and even at this distance, they've stayed in close touch. I hope you and I will be friends."

After accepting the woman's welcome, numerous questions thundered in Pamela's head. What did those people think she was to Drake? Did they consider it proper or improper for her to accompany a man to whom she wasn't married? After stewing about it, she asked Drake those questions.

His even white teeth showed in a devilish grin. "Sweetheart, you have four adults chaperoning you, and if my memory serves me correctly, only one is required."

They settled into their hotel rooms, and she was grateful for a spectacular view from her window in the M Plaza Hotel. She'd done her homework, and instead of going to sleep in order to combat her jet lag, she phoned the local television station, told the manager who she was and what she wanted, and got an offer of a translator, cameraman and chauffeured car. She thanked the station manager, but let him know that she had just arrived and needed to sleep, and that she would call him the next day. In truth, the jet lag didn't bother her, but she thought it prudent to tell Drake about her plans and to suggest that he ask Ladd for any tips he might give her. After all, she reasoned, it was Drake's business trip, and she didn't want to do anything to derail it.

"This is wonderful," Drake said when she told him after dinner that evening as they walked out on the hotel's balcony in the evening breeze that cooled the parched city. "Tomorrow and the next day, my brothers and I will be with the minister of the interior. Telford's willing to film for you, but…"

She looked around, saw no onlookers and kissed his cheek. "I'll use the local cameraman for sites around here, but when we go to the slave castles and other historic places, I want Telford to use my station's camera, because it will probably take much better pictures."

"Okay. I think Velma wants to shop for fabrics. Russ said she was trying to get Alexis to join her. Let those two artists shop for whatever, and the rest of us will take care of business. If the TV station gives you a car and a driver, we needn't worry about your safety." When she sent him a sly wink, suggestive of the wickedness that he loved in her, he said, "You know when to tease, don't you? Ladd told me that any demonstration of affection between a man and a woman is taboo with these people, so I can't even pinch your nose."

She smiled, and he stepped a bit closer to her. "Woman, your smile gives me a glow that begins with my toes and shoots up to my scalp."

"Sorry," she said, beaming at him. "You'll have to behave, and I fear for you."

"Don't be clever, sweetheart. If I knock on your door tonight, I don't doubt that you'll open it, because you wouldn't want me to wake up the entire floor."

Her shrug was slow and lazy. "Can I help it if these people are light sleepers?"

He shook his head as a feeling of joy pervaded him. Oh, how he loved that woman. "You're hopeless. Let's find the others and have a drink with them. Being here with you like this calls for more than we're allowed right now."

They found the Harringtons in one of the tearooms off the lobby. "What time tomorrow do we see the minister of the interior?" Telford asked Drake. "I want to get the business over as quickly as possible. From what I've been reading, there's a lot to see, and we'll only be here a week."

"He's sending a car for us tomorrow morning at nine," Drake told Telford, "and I asked him to invite a Ghanaian architect and engineer to join us. I figure we can learn something from them."

"Good. It's been a long day, and I don't want to tire Alexis out."

"Thanks, honey," Alexis said, "but I'm as fit as I ever was. If you'd like to turn it, though, I'm certainly willing."

Telford stood, walked over to his wife and assisted her. Drake figured that when Alexis became heavy in the late months of her pregnancy, Telford would probably refuse to leave her side. He glanced first at Russ, then at Velma, saw that they, too, were lost in each other, and the feeling that he was missing something vital stole over him. In spite of his efforts, he couldn't shake it. The two couples left him alone with Pamela and went to their beds to share themselves, to revel in their love for each other. He focused his gaze on Pamela, who avoided looking at him, and he knew why. He also knew that her thoughts dwelled on her status as a single woman traveling with her lover and not her husband. No one had to tell him that she wouldn't welcome him to her bed that night.

"What time is the car coming for you tomorrow?" he asked her, not only because the silence had become embarrassing, but because he wanted to see the two men who would accompany her.

"They'll be here at nine-thirty, and I'm supposed to be back here at the hotel at one. If I don't get all the information I need, they'll take me around again the next morning."

"I'll have our driver wait till your crew gets here. All right?"

A smile lit her face. "Thanks. At least they'll know I'm not here in Ghana by myself. I…uh…I think I'll turn in now."

She looked at him with eyes that seemed to plead with him, but he couldn't figure out what she wanted, so he asked her, "What is it? Is there something you want to say to me?"

She focused her gaze on her feet or the floor, he wasn't sure which. What a mess. He couldn't even hold her hand to reassure her and put her at ease, so he did the best that he could under the circumstances. "I love you, Pamela. Please don't be embarrassed to tell me whatever concerns you. If I can fix it, no matter what it is, I will."

She looked at him then. Steadily. Eye to eye. "I know you want us to be together tonight. I want it, too, but I don't like the implications, and I…I feel awkward."

"I realize that, and I understand why you feel that way. Come on, let's go up. Since I can't even hold your hand in public, will you at least step into my room long enough to kiss me good-night? I won't ask if I can go to your room." Suddenly she laughed. "Please tell me what's amusing you," he said.

Her laughter held a tinkle, like an Asian temple bell. "I had a picture of myself devouring you the minute we stepped off the plane in Baltimore."

"I envisioned something similar, but the thought of waiting another six days for it doesn't amuse me."

In the elevator, he held her hand, because no one could see them, and when they reached his room, he unlocked the door and looked down at her, his face a question mark. She stepped into his room, and he closed the door, but didn't lock it. He'd probably be turned on all night, but he needed her warmth and loving.

When she raised her arms to his shoulders, smiled and parted her lips, he had to fight the desire that welled up in him. "Don't pour it on too thick, sweetheart," he said, but her fingers stroked his nape, and he plunged his tongue into her. What was it about this woman? Shudders wracked him as she sucked his tongue deep into her mouth and gripped him to her body. Feeling himself near full arousal, he broke the kiss and moved away from her.

"Another two minutes of that," he said in a guttural voice he hardly recognized, "and I wouldn't let you out of this room. I'm starved for you." He kissed her quickly on her mouth and opened the door. "At least I'm not the only one knocked out," he said when he noticed that she seemed in a stupor. "Honey, you have to learn how to kiss a little bit."

"What good will *that* do me," she replied, "if you don't learn to do the same? I kiss according to the way I'm being kissed."

"I'm not going to touch that one. I'll stand here till you're inside your room." He couldn't resist a pat on her luscious hips. "Dream about me."

"Good night, love." After the lock turned on her door, he threw off his clothes and headed for a cold shower.

His room was attractive and pleasant, the mattress precisely to his taste, and the air-conditioning unit was quiet and effective. Nonetheless, at daybreak, he hadn't slept one wink. Throughout the night, as he thrashed in bed, he struggled with the knowledge that only a wall separated them, that he could almost feel her breathe, but she might as well have been in Baltimore. And for the first time in his life, he envied his brothers.

He dragged himself out of bed, showered, dressed and went down to the breakfast room, praying that the coffee would taste like coffee and that it would be strong. He drank two cups of it and, from the window beside his table, saw the swimming pool—empty and welcoming. He went back to his room, put on his swimming trunks and the terry-cloth robe he found in the closet, and headed for the pool. After swimming three laps, he felt as if he could sleep for a week. He dressed and ate breakfast alone, all the while thinking that his brothers had probably slept peacefully in the arms of their wives.

"Hell, I'm not going to let it get to me. At least she's here, and she cared enough to make this trip with me," he said aloud as he paced from one side of his room to the other and back.

"I ate a couple of hours ago," he told Russ when asked why he hadn't joined them for breakfast. "Try the pool. The water's great. If you didn't bring any decent swim trunks, you can borrow mine. That cup you wear would scandalize even the men in this place."

His attempt at jocularity was wasted on Russ, for his brother eyed him with concern. "Yeah. I'll do that."

"Here's the car," Telford said as if he didn't believe it. "Right on time."

"Can we wait a few minutes until the TV station's driver comes for Pamela?" Drake asked them.

"Sure," they said in unison.

As if by magic at the mention of her name, she walked through the door, a vision in a short-sleeved yellow-linen pantsuit. He went to meet her in order to speak with her out of earshot of his brothers.

"I hope you slept comfortably," he said, gazing into the face he adored.

Her quick shrug and the words "Not really" did not surprise him.

A car arrived bearing the TV station's logo and, damning local convention, he grasped her hand, walked with her to the big black Mercedes and opened the door for her, not waiting for the driver to do it.

"Consider yourself thoroughly kissed," he whispered.

"Consider it returned in full measure," she replied. And

when she didn't smile, he knew that her night had been like his—a battle between a tortured mind and the body's needs.

"Tonight will be different from last night," he added, without having intended to say it, surprising himself.

"Lord, I pray. I hope your day is successful. See you this afternoon."

He didn't know what she meant, but he had wanted her to be aware that he'd seduce her if he had to. He laughed at himself. Seducing Pamela was a snap if she was willing, but if she wasn't, he could forget it.

Inviting their Ghanaian counterparts to their meeting with the interior minister proved highly fruitful, for as they examined the proposed site, the two men had the answers to most of their questions. It remained, however, to determine conditions beneath the soil. The local men thought they would find clay, but Drake suspected that the water level would constitute a problem.

"Tomorrow, we'll get a drill and test it," the minister said.

When they returned to the hotel shortly after twelve, the sun had already begun to burn Drake's skin, and he remembered the adage coined by some colonial people under British rule: "Only mad dogs and Englishmen go out in the noonday sun."

"I'm going to the pool," Russ said, to no one's surprise.

"Me, too," Telford replied, "as soon as I write a note to Alexis, that is, if she's not back yet."

"I hope she isn't out in this heat," Drake said. He wanted a swim, too, but he wanted to enjoy it with Pamela, so he waited in the lobby until she arrived.

"How'd it go?" he asked her.

"Wonderful. I got a lot of good footage, and to be sure I get it right, I taped the cameraman's descriptions and explanations, although my viewers will hear my voice, not his. It's brutal out there. How about a swim?"

"I was waiting for you with that in mind. Meet you at the pool in fifteen minutes."

At the pool, he pulled back his goggles and watched as she threw off her robe and revealed a perfect, voluptuous body. "Let your mouths water, fellows, but keep your hands off," he said to no one in particular as he watched the men ogle her. He jumped up, walked over to her and took her arm in what he recognized as a show of possessiveness.

"You are one tantalizing woman."

Her face bloomed into a smile. "There're no flies on you, buddy, but you could have found something less revealing. If I keep thinking about you in that…that thing, I may drown."

"You think this is revealing? You ought to see what Russ swims in. There's more to it than these swim trunks, in case you're interested," he said, smothering a grin. "All you have to do is say the word."

"I'll bet."

They swam together, frolicking, racing and synchronizing their strokes. After half an hour, he urged her to the side of the pool. "I'm hungry. What about you?"

Her wink heated his blood. "Keep it up," he told her, "and you may expect company tonight no matter who I have to wake up."

"Yeah?" was all she said, and he intended to take that to mean *okay*.

After lunch, he told her that he needed a siesta. "I didn't sleep a minute last night. See you at about six."

* * *

On Wednesday morning, their business completed and Alexis and Velma having completed their shopping—each in possession of several bolts of fabric and varying lengths of kente cloth—the six of them got into Sackefyio's stretch Mercedes and set out for Tema, a town in Greater Accra and its port on the Gulf of Guinea.

At the Tema port, as they watched from shore, Pamela's gaze found a young couple—obviously Americans—who stood on the deck of a small sightseeing boat holding hands and gazing into each other's eyes, oblivious to local conventions. Their fellow passengers disembarked, but the couple remained in what appeared to be silent communion. When the man put both arms around the woman, Pamela couldn't bear to see more, for she could almost feel the mutual love reverberating from them. She turned to move away, and encountered Drake's hard frame. As if of their own volition, his arms enveloped her.

"There'll be a time for us," he whispered, and as she let herself revel in his embrace—though for only a second—she vowed not to let him out of her life, that he would be hers and hers alone. She wasn't going to allow him to teach her to love him and then leave her.

She moved out of his embrace to find Telford, Russ and their wives staring at them. For as long as she lived, she would remember that spot at Tema's port as the place where she swore that Drake Harrington would be her husband.

Their drive along the coast took them past eleven of Ghana's infamous slave castles, but their primary mission was to see Elmina Castle at Fort St. Jorge.

"What's so special about this one?" Velma asked their guide.

In a voice that suggested she should know, he said, "It's

the first slave castle built in the Gold Coast—which is now Ghana—the largest and the most notorious."

"Who built it?" Telford wanted to know.

"The Portuguese built it in 1482 as a trading post for gold, cocoa, ivory, sugar, pepper and human flesh, and it remained in Portuguese hands until the Dutch ran them out in 1657.

"They shoved men, women and babies in that dungeon under there," the guide told them when they reached Elmina, "and with no air and little food, they died by the thousands before any were ever put on those boats. I can get a guide to take you through there, if you want to go. I don't have the stomach for it."

Pamela stared up at the enormous white building with its windows and arches and marveled that, with all that space, the human beings that the Europeans caught and shackled were herded like cattle into a dirt-floored, windowless dungeon.

She pulled on Drake's hand. "When I see things like this, I have to try hard not to hate."

"I don't try," she heard Velma say.

"I'm going in there," Russ said. "If my ancestors came from here, I want to know what they experienced, and I'd like to see how this place was constructed."

"I knew he'd go," Drake said. "Russ has the ability to see social conditions—hurtful ones—with the eyes and mind of a scientist. That's why he's so good at what he does."

They moved on to Sekondi Castle, built by the Dutch in 1670 and currently serving as a lighthouse. But Pamela's thoughts remained with the enormous Elmina that sat on a tiny peninsula jutting out into the blue waters of the Gulf of Guinea. The sight of that dungeon, the hole through which the captors pushed their captives into slavery, would remain with her forever. From that moment, she was ready to go home.

"But you didn't go inside," Russ argued when she said how she felt.

"I saw enough from outside, and my imagination supplied the rest."

"It's well you didn't go inside," Russ told her. "I imagine I'll have nightmares tonight and for some nights to come."

"Stay with me tonight," Drake said to Pamela after dinner. "Will you?"

He thought she was about to say no, and a spasm of pain shot through his gut. But she looked at him steadily and answered, "I think it's better if you stay with me."

His heart began to thud with the rhythm of the hooves of galloping horses. He told himself to slow down. "Whatever you prefer works for me."

Inside his room, he removed his linen jacket and brushed his teeth, put his door card into his trouser pocket, waited a few minutes and then telephoned Pamela. "May I come over now?"

"Yes, but don't knock. The door will be open."

He could hardly wait to get to her. Everything in him, his body, his mind and his spirit, cried out to her. His need had never been so great, not for her or for any woman. He didn't have to have anyone—man, woman or child—to legitimate him; he was a man, and he knew it. But at that moment, he needed her with him to realize his humanity, to brush away the ugliness of slavery and the negligent massacre of innocent men, women and children whose only sin had been the color of their skin. Most of all, he needed confirmation of her love for him.

He leaned against the wall just inside his room and willed

himself to think only of her. After a minute, he locked his door, went next door and opened hers. What he saw was a beautiful woman in a long white sheath standing in a shaft of moonlight that pierced the darkness from the window beyond.

He gasped. "You take my breath away."

"Let's sit down over here," she said, motioning to the short sofa near the window.

He wanted to kiss her, to take her right then and sink into her body, but rushing a woman had never been his style. When he would have rested her head against his shoulder, she patted her lap.

"Put your head here."

Knowing the wisdom of following her lead, he did so, and gazed up at her in an attempt to gauge her mood. She stroked his hair and his cheeks, kissed his forehead and his eyes and brushed his lips with hers.

"You're so precious," she murmured against his lips and quickly moved her mouth to nibble on his ear.

His heartbeat slowed, he felt himself relaxing, calm, contented, and closed his eyes.

From a distance it seemed, he heard her mezzo-soprano softly singing "Summertime," or perhaps he dreamed it. Surely, her fingers loosened his tie, or he only sensed it. When he awoke, her arms held him, and his lips pressed against her belly. As if Providence were toying with him, his first thought was that one day his own child would grow there.

"Have I been asleep?" he asked her, sitting up and looking around the room.

Her fingers smoothed his hair. "For more than an hour."

A look at his watch told him that it was one-thirty in the morning. "I've abused your hospitality. I certainly didn't mean to sleep, but I felt so...so much peace. Do you want me to leave?"

He couldn't believe his good fortune. For an answer, she leaned toward him and pressed her parted lips to his. Excitement plowed through him, and he stood, put her in the bed and cherished her. She opened up to him as a flower unfolds its petals to the sun and gave herself to him. When he could no longer contain the awesome feeling of love that his heart held for her, he gave in to it and exploded into her pulsating warmth, certain that she was the only woman he would ever want.

"You're mine and I love you." The words tore themselves out of him as, for the first time in his life, he lost control completely and like a spent shell, collapsed, trembling, in her arms.

The next morning, he went with his brothers to the minister of the interior, pushing aside the resentment he felt for having to leave Pamela.

"What's going on with you and Pamela?" Telford asked him when they were on the way back to the hotel, a signal to him that he hadn't treated that conference with his usual critical skepticism. "You seem a bit preoccupied," Telford added.

"We're...fine. She's... I don't know, man."

"As long as she makes you happy. That's what counts."

He knew Telford was feeling him out. They were and always had been close, and he hadn't shared with his brother his feelings about Pamela. "Nothing's wrong, Telford. I'm finding my way."

Telford's grin melted into a laugh. "She's got your number, eh? Man, I remember it well!"

He didn't see the point in answering; it was useless to lie and, moreover, he didn't want to. That afternoon, he ignored his brothers and their wives and spent as much time as possible alone with Pamela. He couldn't get enough of her, and she welcomed his every gesture of affection. They played darts and various card games, and swam several laps in the pool.

"Ladd has invited all of us to dinner at his home tomorrow evening, but don't expect Ghanaian food, or at least not a full meal of it. Both he and Doris, his wife, prefer American and continental dishes. I suspect it will be a formal occasion, though, because he's probably also asked some of the local bigwigs."

Pamela dressed for dinner that evening in the long peach-colored chiffon sheath that she wore to Rhoda's garden party. She draped a matching stole around her shoulders, picked up the silver bag that matched her shoes and took the elevator down to the lobby where Drake waited for her. She breathed a sigh of relief when she saw that Velma and Alexis wore dresses similar in fashion to hers.

The dinner began with peanut soup, which she thought was delicious. Before the next course was served, however, she noticed that Selicia Dennis, the woman seated at Drake's left, occasionally put her right arm around his shoulder, patted his knee from time to time and attempted to monopolize him. When Russ's gaze moved repeatedly from Pamela to the woman, Pamela positioned herself to get a good look at her. What she saw was an average-looking, well-gowned woman of thirty to thirty-five years who couldn't keep her hands off Drake. Fuming at the attention Drake seemed to pay the woman, she waited until after dessert was served, excused herself, went to her room and locked the door.

"He will do one hell of a piece of talking before I forgive him," she said to herself. She refused to answer the telephone, and when it rang repeatedly, she placed it beneath the soft pillows. The next morning, she ordered breakfast in her room, not because she had an appetite, but because she didn't want to go to breakfast where she knew she'd find Drake. And she wasn't anywhere near ready to let go of her anger.

Around nine o'clock, Pamela saw a slip of paper that someone had shoved beneath her door. She picked it up and read a note from Alexis.

Velma and I are going shopping for an hour, and we'd love for you to come with us.

She wanted to be friends with them, especially with Velma, and temperamental behavior was not the way to begin it. She phoned Alexis and agreed to meet the women in the lobby at nine-thirty.

"That woman is Doris's best friend. You shouldn't blame Drake—he had to talk to her or seem rude," Velma said. "But, boy, is she aggressive!"

"I don't care whose best friend she is. He didn't say fifty words to me during the meal, and if he prefers me to be mad at him rather than displease that man-eater, fine. He has his wish."

"Come, now," Alexis said. "As long as you don't say anything you'll regret, let him know how you feel, but as upset as he was at your leaving him and not answering your phone, I'd say that woman didn't gain one thing."

So this was what it was like to have sisters or girlfriends her age with whom she could talk. An aura of contentment enveloped her, and she stopped worrying about Drake and enjoyed herself.

"You mean you're still mad about that?" Drake asked Pamela. "If I was interested in that woman, I wouldn't have brought you here. I met her at Ladd's wedding, and she behaved outrageously then. If you can't trust me and believe in me, we don't have anything going for us."

"I do trust you, and I believe in you. Furthermore, you know it. But if you think I'm going to sit like a wilting daisy while you let some dame crawl all over you, think again."

Russ joined them, leaned against the corner of the bar and said, "Don't let this cause a rift between you two. It's foolish. You mean too much to each other. Drake, if you were engaged to Pamela, you could have demanded that that woman back off and keep her hands off you, and she would have. But you're not engaged, and that is the crux of the problem."

Drake stared at Russ, but said nothing because he knew his brother spoke the truth.

As they flew back to the States, he couldn't bridge the chasm between Pamela and himself, no matter what he said. And when he took her home, she didn't invite him to come in. No one had to tell him that he had his work cut out for him.

"I wasn't jealous, mind you," she said. "I was hurt because you failed to acknowledge our relationship. Or maybe we don't have one."

"I won't dignify that comment with an answer. It was unfair."

He had forgotten that many people regarded him as a womanizer, a playboy. Perhaps that was what Pamela allowed herself to see at that dinner. He leaned down, kissed her cheek and left her. He was well on his way to Eagle Park before it dawned on him that her cheek had the taste of salt. Salt from her tears.

"Man, you have to let a woman know where she stands," Telford told him that night as they sat alone in the den.

"I know that, but I felt obligated to talk to Ladd's guest. If I wanted her, I'd have her. The truth is that I can't stand her, and she knows it, because I practically told her so."

Telford locked his hands behind his head and leaned back in his chair. "If Pamela understands and sympathizes with your need to be courteous to another woman, I'll buy Fort Knox." He rubbed his fingers across his chin. "I can't believe this. The two of you were besotted with each other until… Oh, hell, man. You'll find a way to repair it."

He hoped so. Oh, how he hoped so.

The next morning, shortly after breakfast, Drake headed for the Harrington-Sparkman Memorial Houses in Frederick. However, no sooner had he parked than he realized that something was amiss. Immediately, Bond Jergens greeted him with a handshake and bad news.

"We've had some pilfering here," he said, "so I've been spending the night in the trailer. Last night, I caught two fellows trying to cart off buckets of paint, and I called the police, who arrested them."

"Thanks, Bond. You'll be well rewarded for this. I'm going to the precinct, and I'll get back as soon as I can." He got into his car and drove to the nearest police station.

"Good morning, officer. I'm Drake Harrington, and my foreman tells me you're holding two men caught stealing from one of my building sites."

The officer verified the address. "You want to talk to them?"

"I'd appreciate it."

The officer stood at the door while Drake asked them what they planned to do with the paint.

"Nothing," one said. "I was just doing a job, man."

His antenna shot up. "Who paid you?" When the man

didn't respond, he said, "All right, more than paint was stolen. I'm pressing charges for grand larceny."

The man's face reddened and his eyes mirrored in fear. "A guy out in Honolulu. Name's Parker. He said you owed him plenty."

"And he paid you to wreck my property?"

"He wanted me to burn it down, but I wasn't in for that, man."

"And it's a good thing," the policeman said. He looked at Drake. "You wanna press charges?"

"I want them to stay here until I bring charges against Lawrence Parker."

At five-thirty that afternoon, he quit work, washed up, dressed in the trailer and telephoned Pamela. "I have to see you about something important. Would you rather I went to your office or to your apartment?"

After hesitating long enough to make him nervous, she said, "My apartment. I'll be there by seven-thirty."

She opened the door as soon as he rang the bell, and he stood there staring at her. So near, and yet so far away from him. After their solemn greetings with words such as strangers use, he told her of Lawrence Parker's latest antics and added, "Please beware. He seems to have long arms, and I don't want anything to happen to you."

"Thanks." After a moment of silence during which she seemed pensive, she said, "You mean he wanted someone to burn up those houses? What are you going to do?"

"Have him arrested and press charges."

"The poor dunce," she said. She got up, walked to the window, looked out and walked back to the chair she had vacated.

She didn't sit down, but stood there looking at him, and he waited for what he knew would be a bombshell.

"I think you should know that the adoption agency has located a baby girl for me."

"*What?* Are you…?" He stood and faced her. "Don't go through with it. *Please.*"

"Why not? I want a child, and this is the only way I'll get one."

Without considering his action, he grabbed her shoulders. "Like hell it is!" His hands gripped her to him, and he pressed his lips to hers. When she didn't open to him, he rubbed her nipple until she moaned and parted her lips. He plunged his tongue into her, and she grasped his buttocks and locked him to her. Then he slipped his hand into the neckline of her sweater and toyed with her breast; she cried out and undulated against him. On fire for her, he picked her up and carried her to her bed.

"If you don't want me, tell me right now," he heard himself say.

Her tongue rimmed her lips, bathing them in that seductive way she had. "I'm on fire for you, and you know it," she replied, as his lips covered her breast, and he sucked her nipple into his mouth.

She had never been so frantic for him, and he reveled in it, stripping her and then himself as fast as he could. He slipped on a condom, and when at last he sank into the sweet warmth of her body, he heard himself cry out, "You're mine. You hear me? Mine!"

"Yes," she moaned. "Yes, and you belong to me."

Minutes later, his shattering climax, following her own, drained him of all his energy, and he lay in her arms panting for breath. When he could climb down from the cloud of euphoria onto which she'd flung him, he accepted that they could not continue as they were. However, before he could voice that sentiment, she said, "I'm sorry, Drake, but as deeply as I love you, nothing has changed. I'm going through with it."

"I'm sorry, too, Pamela. You can't know how much."

"Goodbye," she said slowly and deliberately when he left, and he didn't miss the finality in her voice.

"But it's not over yet," he said to himself as he headed home. "It can't be. If she'll give me a little more time, I can pull it all together. That job in Ghana, and the consultancy I've been offered, should put me on the map, and I'll have a legacy for my children."

Shortly after Thanksgiving, he returned to Ghana to sign the contract obligating himself and his brothers to build a mall in Accra. And wherever he went there, the memory of that perfect day he'd spent with Pamela haunted him.

"Would you please turn that off?" he said to the disc jockey who provided music at cocktail hour in the hotel. Every time he heard Gershwin's "Summertime," tears spilled down his insides, for his thoughts went back to that night when she sang it to him while he lay, half-asleep, with his head in her lap.

When his plane landed in Baltimore, he called home. "Yer girlfriend called here twice for ya," Henry told him. "She seemed upset. Better see what she wants."

He telephoned Pamela. "Henry said you called me."

"I did. I...I've been so upset. That adoption agency isn't reputable. They want me to pay for the baby. A lot of money, too. But that's...that's illegal. I can't do it."

"I'm sorry. I—"

She interrupted him. "I don't need sympathy. I...I need a family of my own."

His efforts to console her failed, and he had no choice but to go on home. But when he got there, Telford, Alexis and Tara were ecstatic because Alexis's unborn baby had moved in her womb, and their hands were pressed to her in the hope of feeling the movement again. He slipped, unnoticed, into his room and, for a second time, he felt like an outsider in his own home.

When he arrived at work the next morning, Bond greeted him jubilantly with the news that his wife was pregnant. He stared at his foreman. "Uh…that makes six, doesn't it? Sounds to me as if…" He didn't finish it, for he saw the delight on the man's face, the face of a poor man who struggled to make ends meet.

"I see you think I'm crazy," Bond said. He looked into the distance as if counting memories. "A woman carries a baby for nine months, losing her pretty shape, sick half the time and then she has those awful pains. You and I couldn't do that. My wife knows what to expect, but she's still as happy as she can be. I'd do anything for her. Having children together creates an unbreakable bond between a man and a woman. You think you love her, and then she gives you a child, and she's a hundred percent more precious to you."

For over a week, Bond's words dominated Drake's thoughts, and he could concentrate on little else. "Am I selfish to want my life to be perfect before I marry and settle down?" he asked himself. "I love her, and I want what she wants—a home, family and children. My children and hers. I don't have to be the greatest architectural engineer in the country. I only have to do my best. She needs me, and I need her."

After supper, he told Telford that he wanted the plot of land up the road from where Russ was building a house for himself and Velma.

"Does this mean you're getting married?"

"It means I don't want to live without her, and I'm going to ask her to marry me."

His brother's face beamed with happiness. "When?"

"Tonight, if she's home."

"You have my blessings and my prayers, brother," Telford said, opening his arms and embracing him.

Pamela answered the telephone after the first ring. "Hello."

"This is Drake, Pamela. I'm in Eagle Park, and I'd like to see you tonight as soon as I can get to your place." She remained silent.

"I need to get my life in order, and that means I have to begin with you."

"I'll be here when you get here."

"Thanks," he said. That was all. Nothing but thanks. Well, at least he was in a mood to finalize something, though she didn't know what or how. She called her mother because she needed moral support. Not that she intended to tell Delta details of her relationship with Drake—she didn't. She needed the sweet, calming influence of her mother's voice.

"How's Drake?" Delta asked after they spoke for some minutes.

"He's on his way over here now."

"Then, for goodness' sake, why are you talking to me? Pamper yourself so you'll be fresh and lovely when he gets there. Good night, darling." She hung up.

Pamela stared at the telephone, and then laughed. Her mother was a femme fatale and a genuine romantic. Her mother also knew how to hold a man. She showered, applied Opium bath oil over her body, put on the long white sheath that she wore for Drake in Accra, combed out her hair and slipped her feet into a pair of flat white sandals. When the doorbell rang after what seemed like years, she rushed to the door and flung it open.

"Hi. You look…wonderful," he said and handed her a bunch of pink calla lilies.

"You're a sight for sore eyes," she said, hoping to make him feel welcome. "Come on in."

He took her hand, walked into the living room and sat with her on the sofa; she was sure he could hear the thumping of her heart.

"I told myself that I wouldn't marry and start a family until my accomplishments as an engineer made me nationally known. That was an easy vow to keep until I fell in love with you." Chills raced through her body. Was he calling it off? "I've been selfish, thinking only of myself. I want what you want.

"I know you want children, my children, and I want you to be the mother of my sons and daughters. These last weeks have been terrible ones for me, as I know they have been for you."

He released her hand and knelt on one knee. "Will you forgive my stubbornness and be my wife? I love you, and I will cherish you and our children for as long as I live."

She slipped to her knees and cupped his face with her hands as tears streamed down her cheeks. "Yes. Oh, yes. I want to be your wife, and I want you to be my husband. I have never loved any man but you."

Tears glistened unshed in his eyes. "Will you spend Christmas at Harrington House with me and my family?" She nodded, unable to speak, for the joy she felt overwhelmed her. "How soon can we get married?" he asked.

She threw her arms around him and hugged him. "Depends on what I can negotiate with my mother. If I get Velma to plan the wedding, we can probably marry on Valentine's Day."

He frowned. "That's years away, but our house won't be ready till late spring or early summer." He gazed into her eyes, a smile glowing on his face. "You're really going to marry me?"

"It's what I've wanted for months."

"How're you going to work in Baltimore if we live in Eagle Park?" he wanted to know.

"Not to worry. I'll get my job description changed."

"You wouldn't believe how much I love you. Kiss me, woman."

Hours later, he pulled her sated body to his, and with one hand cupping her breast and the other on her belly, he kissed the back of her neck, and they dozed off to sleep.

* * * * *